S0-AYE-517

FRANKLIN COUNTY LIBRARY SYSTEM
101 RAGGED EDGE ROAD SOUTH
CHAMBERSBURG, PA 17202

GROVE FAMILY LIBRARY
101 RAGGED EDGE ROAD SOUTH
CHAMBERSBURG, PA 17202

SHADOW OF POWER

ALSO BY STEVE MARTINI

Double Tap
The Arraignment
The Jury
The Attorney
Critical Mass
The List
The Judge
Undue Influence
Prime Witness
Compelling Evidence
The Simeon Chamber

STEVE MARTINI

SHADOW OF POWER

A PAUL MADRIANI NOVEL

**Doubleday Large Print
Home Library Edition**

𝓌𝓶

WILLIAM MORROW

An Imprint of HarperCollins*Publishers*

This Large Print Edition, prepared especially for Doubleday Large Print Home Library, contains the complete, unabridged text of the original Publisher's Edition.

This book is a work of fiction. References to real people, events, establishments, organizations, or locales are intended only to provide a sense of authenticity, and are used fictitiously. All other characters, and all incidents and dialogue, are drawn from the author's imagination and are not to be construed as real.

SHADOW OF POWER. Copyright © 2008 by Paul Madriani, Inc. All rights reserved. Printed in the United States of America. No part of this book may be used or reproduced in any manner whatsoever without written permission except in the case of brief quotations embodied in critical articles and reviews. For information address Harper-Collins Publishers, 10 East 53rd Street, New York, NY 10022.

ISBN 978-0-7394-9637-4

This Large Print Book carries the Seal of Approval of N.A.V.H.

To my cousin Al Parmisano, to my assistant, Marianne Dargitz, and to my daughter, Megan, without whose constant encouragement and support this work would not have been possible

SHADOW OF POWER

PROLOGUE

May
Curaçao, the Dutch Antilles

The sugar-white powder was so hot on their feet that they skipped and took long strides across the distance to the darker sand cooled by the surf. Here incoming waves piled up small pieces of sharp, broken coral and created a steep shelf in the shallow water.

Arthur Ginnis had trouble hobbling through the ankle-deep waves and nearly fell as his feet slid down the coral shelf into deeper water. To someone still recovering from hip surgery, the warm, clear salt water of the Caribbean was like therapy. He moved out until it was up to his chest, at which point he slipped his mask and snorkel on top of his head and started to pull the swim fins onto his feet.

The sun glinted off the aquamarine surface of the sea. Behind them a large four-masted schooner was tied up to the dock at the end of the jetty, full of tourists on a trip to one of the other islands. Another, larger vessel, a research ship, was moored farther back in the lagoon. The island was dotted with deep lagoons and coves cut into the coral rock by eons of erosion. It was a smuggler's paradise.

But Ginnis and his young friend had another mission in mind. Locals had told them about a small tugboat sunk on the reef several hundred yards out. Hip or no hip, Ginnis was determined to dive on it. The doctors wouldn't allow him to use tanks any longer. They told him he was too old. So he was relegated to free diving with a mask and snorkel. The tug was said to be in shallow water, not more than twenty feet down. It was perfect, even though his wife had protested, raised hell as only she could, and told him she wasn't happy, that he was being foolish. Ginnis was tired of being housebound, after months of recovery from the surgery. If this was a vacation, he was going to enjoy it.

The hot sun and tropical images triggered all the senses of the imagination, of adventure and romance. At seventy, Ginnis was an irrepressible romantic. Whenever he had time to read for pleasure, which wasn't often, *Treasure Island* remained from his youth as one of his favorite books. It was for this reason that he always returned to the islands at least once each year. The vacation house they owned on St. Croix had been damaged the previous year in a hurricane. So this year they'd rented a house in Curaçao. It was perfect, since nobody on the island knew who he was. Even the local paper was published in Dutch. It was something from a pirate fantasy. It kept him close to the dreams of his childhood—the adventure of tropical seas and the lure of finding something of history buried in the sand. As foolish as it might appear for a grown man, particularly someone of Ginnis's stature, these surroundings gripped his imagination and held him captive.

He considered it a major coup that he'd managed to ditch the U.S. Marshals

Service, his usual companions. He had accomplished this with the help of Alberto Aranda.

Aranda was in his early thirties, old for a court clerk. But then he had gone to law school late, after serving a stint with the Peace Corps in Africa, in, of all places, the Sudan. He was as tough as a marine, and an expert diver. Ginnis didn't tell anyone, but it was one of the reasons he'd hired Aranda, that and the fact that he liked him.

As always, Ginnis was thinking ahead, in this case planning for the summer. After all, he was on light duty from the Court. They didn't expect to see him back full-time for at least six months. Time to have some fun.

"You can count this as one of the better perks of clerking." Ginnis puffed a bit. He was out of shape, the result of his long recovery. With the new hip, he now had as much metal in his body as your average robot.

Aranda, six feet and slender, looked at him, smiled, the kind of expression Ginnis might have expected from the son he never had. His only regret was that Aranda had not been on staff in the same year as

Trisha Scott, the surrogate daughter he'd had as a clerk the year before. Aranda was the kind of man Trisha needed, not that fraud Scarborough, a counterfeit intellectual addicted to self-promotion. Ginnis spit into his dive mask and worked it around. The whisper of a smile lingered on his lips as he considered what was about to happen.

"You sure you're up to this?" Aranda interrupted the reverie. "First time in open water since the surgery, you should take it easy. That's what the doctor said. Go slow."

"I'm fine. And the doctor isn't here. Just try to keep up." Ginnis pulled the strap behind his head and dropped the mask over his face. He mouthed the snorkel, took a few deep breaths, then launched himself headfirst into deeper water.

He was stiff as a board. The muscles in his legs ached from lack of exercise. He had tried to stay fit all his life. With hardly an ounce of fat, he was as sinuous and wiry as in his youth. It was true that many of his generation, given the advances in medicine, genetics, and the new drugs, might well live past one hundred. And given the political knife's edge, what passed for balance on the Court these days, there were members of Congress who prayed daily for judicial immortality.

Visibility in the clear water made it seem as if he were looking through air—infinite. Large oval masses of brain coral loomed up from the bottom as Ginnis glided over them, flicking the fins on his feet, his arms trailing along at his sides, like flying in a liquid sky. A small camera in a sealed plastic case hung from a cord around his right wrist. He snapped pictures as he went, stopping to catch coral growths, some angelfish, and at one point the smiling face and large eyes of Alberto Aranda peering out through his dive mask.

A hundred yards out, three massive mooring platforms anchored to the bottom marked their path of travel. They had gotten detailed directions to the sunken tug from the dive shop on the jetty. As they swam between the first two mooring platforms, the bottom dropped away.

Ginnis floated through a mass of bubbles rising to the surface, then saw two divers beneath him, their tanks emitting

used air from the regulators. It was difficult to tell how deep the divers were. The
magnification caused by the clear water
played funny tricks with depth perception.
It looked as if Ginnis could reach out and
touch them, but the two figures appeared
to be in miniature. Ginnis knew they were
farther down than they looked from the
surface, perhaps thirty feet, maybe more.

As he passed the third mooring platform,
the surface began to take on the undula-
tions of the sea. They were now approaching the point of land where the inlet to the
lagoon poured into the open sea. Here the
water was rougher. Curling white ribbons
of froth capped some of the waves. The
afternoon trade winds were kicking up.
Ginnis struggled against the current as the
neglected long muscles of his legs burned.
Still he pushed himself. It was the only way
to full recovery, and Ginnis was determined
to recover all his former strength and agil-
ity. At his age he knew that anything conceded was gone forever.

He lifted his head from the water,
dropped his feet, and did a slow pirouette
looking for Aranda. He didn't see him. He
put his face back into the sea, scanning

beneath the surface. As he did, seawater entered the open end of his snorkel. Ginnis panicked. He struggled to keep it from entering his mask as he coughed up salt water.

For an instant the cold, irrational hand of dread gripped him. Ever since he first started diving, he had learned that fear, particularly the blind fear of quick panic, was the deadliest killer in deep water, far more lethal than sharks or any other natural predator. And the only antidote was self-control. If you wanted to stay alive, you had to fight it, master it, as he did now.

He cleared the water in the snorkel's tube and looked around again. There was still no sign of Aranda, but no reason for concern. Aranda was a strong swimmer. He knew what he was doing in the water. They had become separated, that was all, a common enough occurrence in open water.

Ginnis regrouped. Rather than remove his mask in the chop of the sea, he cleared it by blowing air out through his nose, holding the top of the mask to his forehead.

He placed his face back in the water to

test the seal and to see if Aranda might have dived down to look at something on the bottom. It was then he saw it: a bleak gray form resting on the bottom, an occasional glint, the orange flake of rusted metal. It was the stern of a small boat beneath him and perhaps thirty feet farther out to sea.

As it had been with the divers, it was hard to tell how deep the wreck was. It looked as if it lay on a shelf. Ginnis guessed that it might have hit the shallow reef as it cut too close to the point coming out of the harbor, since its bow was facing toward the sea.

The vessel was small, maybe twenty feet in length, and old, one of the little working tugs that might have been used years earlier for close work in the many small inlets that served as harbors around the island. From its state of decay, it appeared that the boat had been on the bottom for a while.

As Ginnis floated listlessly, facedown on the surface, a small school of French angelfish, their bulging yellow eyes blackdotted by the pupils, flashed in front of him, then just as quickly returned, stopped, and seemed to stare at him. Ginnis groped for the camera on his wrist, brought it up to his eye, and snapped another picture. He lifted his head from the water and scanned the surface one more time for Aranda. The clerk must have turned back or taken the wrong route between the large mooring platforms. Sooner or later he would turn up.

Ginnis returned his attention to the sunken tug, sucked in a lungful of air, then flipped head over ass and pulled for the rusting metal hulk on the bottom.

*   *   *

June
San Diego, California

"I'm going to tell you something I haven't told anyone else. Can you keep a secret?" the man at the mirror said.

"You have to ask?"

Scarborough was busy shaving in the palatial master bath in the top-floor suite at the Presidential Regis Hotel in San Diego. The room overlooked the bay and the arching Coronado Bridge off in the distance.

Dick Bonguard, leaning against the

frame in the open doorway behind him, was a talent and literary agent, a man with media connections and top-notch PR skills. He had picked up Terry Scarborough as a client on the rebound from a New York literary agency a year earlier. Scarborough had wanted edgier representation, an agent who, like the second stage on a rocket, could boost his self-made celebrity beyond the grip of gravity.

Bonguard had this in spades. In his thirties, tall, blond, blue-eyed, and ruddy-faced, he had become part of the young power set in New York media circles. Even though Scarborough was ten years older, if you stood the two of them together dressed alike, they would look like a matching pair of salt and pepper shakers, Bonguard light and fair, Scarborough darker.

The relationship paid off in a smash-hit book for both men. *Perpetual Slaves: The Branding of America's Black Race,* authored by Scarborough, was on its way to becoming one of those "must-reads of a generation," as one review said. The book was cemented at the top of the bestseller list and showed no sign of budging anytime soon. Scarborough was earning his bones as the hottest fire-belching political dragon on the national scene. Colleges and universities couldn't get enough of him. That the roots of slavery were deeply embedded in the United States Constitution and still showing was his message.

"I'm thinking about using the opportunity tonight to leak the letter," said Scarborough.

"What? Why would you do that?" Bonguard stood in the doorway, stunned.

"I know what you're going to say. Just listen to me for a second. I mean revealed with skill, in an offhand manner. What better venue for something like this than Leno? Scarborough looked up to make sure that Bonguard was following him.

The two men had been using code words to talk about this in front of others for months. They called it the "J letter." It was the second and burning secret of slavery, the glowing embers of which Scarborough had stirred with his book.

"I thought the plan was to hold the letter for the sequel?" said Bonguard.

"Plans change," said Scarborough.

The author was already sitting on $22 million in book royalties. Every week *Perpetual Slaves* stayed at the top of the list, the royalties grew. They hadn't even started counting foreign sales, and with anti-American fervor peaking in Europe, Latin America, and the Near East, the prospects loomed large.

"Listen to me," said Bonguard, "you don't want to do that. Outing the letter now would be a huge mistake."

"You think so?"

"Yes. There's a rhythm to all this—it's called timing, and if you screw with it, you're going to pluck the golden goose." The agent was flummoxed. As far as he was concerned, this had been nailed down months ago.

"You forget, I *am* the golden goose," said the author.

"Of course you are. I know that. But we've been all over this," he said. "You ride the first book to the bank as many times as it will go."

Naturally, this meant that Bonguard was hanging on the back, riding the animal with him.

"In the meantime you take the letter,

you write the second book, nobody knows anything about it, we just tease the mobs every once in a while to keep them awake, 'blockbuster revelation on the way—same topic—plumbing the true depths of white bigotry at the founding of our nation.'

"Then, when the fury over *Perpetual Slaves* is just starting to ebb, we unpack the boxes and load the hardcover sequel onto the shelves. That's when we leak it—discovery of the parchment of national shame." Bonguard stood there looking into the mirror, making sure his client got it.

"Trust me, between the millions of zealots on the right who don't believe it and the millions on the left who say I told you so, the fallout will send the second book into orbit."

Scarborough continued to drag the razor across his face. "I don't think so."

"Are you getting cold feet?" said Bonguard. "I know you're taking a lot of heat out on the circuit, a lot of criticism from the press about the flamethrowing speeches. . . ."

"Screw the press." Scarborough laughed, and a halo of fog covered the mirror. "What used to pass for the fourth estate is now a duplex," said the author. "Where have you been? Online bloggers are eating their circulation, and cable news has their advertisers. And the day I can't jack up the print press, light a fire under their ass, and enjoy the warmth, you can retire me."

"Then what's the problem?" said Bonguard.

"No problem. It's just time to begin outing the letter."

"What's in the damn thing?" said Bonguard. "If you're going to tell Leno, why don't you at least let *me* in on the secret? Why don't you just show it to me?"

This was a sore point with Scarborough. Since he'd acquired the copy from the source, who had the original, he'd never allowed anyone to see it. It was part of the deal. He could write the book, but the original letter stayed with the party who possessed it, and no one else could see the copy. Of course, that was before the beginning of the time of reckoning.

"I didn't say I was going to tell Leno what was in the letter," said Scarborough. "I'm just going to tell him *about* it."

"Okay, fine, I don't have to see it," said

Bonguard. "I've heard enough of the details from you to know. If even half of what you say is there, this thing's going nuclear. I'm telling you, cable news, the networks, a banner headline in the *Times* big enough to make people think World War II has ended again. How could it not? Discovery of a secret letter—Footnotes to the Declaration?"

"All of that is true," said Scarborough. "But there's something else."

"What's that?"

"I'm not at liberty to say right now."

"Either you trust me or you don't," said the agent.

Scarborough's silence answered the question for him.

"In time you'll know everything," he said eventually.

"Yes, come death, we'll all know the riddles of life," said Bonguard. He hated the Zen-like conundrums of this guy. Terry Scarborough was like the kid in the clubhouse who always had the biggest secret and wanted everybody to pound the crap out of him to get it because it made him feel important.

As he looked at his client in the mirror,

the thought crossed Bonguard's mind that maybe Scarborough was talking to another agent. In his business, especially in the stratosphere where they were playing now, you always had to look for poachers dangling the prospect of a better deal. It was the reason Bonguard was glued to him on this book tour. You never want to let a $22 million prick walk around alone.

"After the show we can talk about a few details. We won't have to worry about chasing the media. They'll be coming to us," said Scarborough.

"Yeah. A year early," said Bonguard. "In this business, timing is everything."

"I'm getting tired listening to the same song. The J letter is national poison, and there's no expiration date on the bottle," said Scarborough.

People in the White House were already pulling their hair out over the first book, and there was nothing they could do. It could only get worse when the J letter was revealed.

Strangely enough, the controversy that Scarborough had ignited with the current book swirled around arcane language in the Constitution. Like original sin, the words had been there since the beginning, since 1787, the year the Constitution was first adopted. They had been overridden by a civil war and later amendments, but they were still there.

The words may have been dead-letter law, but to a generation sensitized to racial slight they were offensive. And because of the peculiar manner in which the Constitution is published, they were still visible in public print, right there in the organic law of the nation. They were the original words of slavery.

To a broad public unschooled in the stylistic nuances of codebooks and statutes, the vast majority of Americans, the fact that these shame-filled words and their hidden meanings still graced their Constitution was news the minute Scarborough published his book and took to the trail on his publicity tour. Suddenly people who had been outraged that some states could even consider flying the Confederate flag were confronted with words that confirmed African American bondage and defined black people as "three-fifths" of a human being, and then only for purposes of voting by their white slave masters. The public outrage, in black communities, in colleges and universities across the country, exploded.

Slavery may have ended, but the stigma and the sudden reminder that it was embedded in the Constitution brought back history with a vengeance. The words were there for all time, for their children and grandchildren, for all of posterity to read.

The problem was that government was powerless to remove the offending words. Republicans and Democrats all stumbled over themselves trying to placate the African American community. There were resolutions of comfort in Congress. The president had done everything but go on national television to offer a public apology. He had been quoted, while heading to Marine One on the White House lawn, as saying, "We're all looking very hard at this, in a bipartisan way." He talked as if words engraved in the Constitution more than two hundred years ago had suddenly uncoiled themselves, slipped up behind the entire country, and strangled us all in our beds.

Without realizing it, the founders had

created a literary monster in the way they'd amended the Constitution. Unlike federal statutes where laws once repealed were removed from the codebooks and disappeared from view, provisions of the Constitution repealed by later amendments remained in the document. They may have been dead-letter law, but they were still there for everyone to read. And this wasn't like the repeal of Prohibition, with alcoholics stumbling through the streets demanding the removal of language foisted on them by Carry Nation.

Supported by sociological studies, statistics on prison population by race, disparities in income since the Civil War, and psychological data showing long-term damage rooted in race, Scarborough's book punctuated it all with the words of slavery still visible in the Constitution.

The book was peddled to a mass market that had never put all the pieces together before. Many of them now saw the old words of slavery staring at them from the nation's most fundamental, organic law as a national insult. They were carrying placards in the streets bearing the preamble to the Constitution superimposed over the Confederate flag.

Scarborough couldn't believe that someone else hadn't exposed it decades earlier, during the Civil Rights movement of the 1960s. It had been left there for him to pluck, like some ripe fruit.

Still leaning against the frame of the bathroom door, Bonguard was getting nervous. He had never seen the letter. Now he wanted to see it.

"Do you mind telling me where the letter is?"

Scarborough turned and looked at him. "In a safe place."

"I just thought I'd ask. What I'm afraid of is you're gonna go on Leno tonight and blow it."

"You don't have to worry. I'm not going to tell them everything tonight," said Scarborough. "I mean, if they came unglued over the words of slavery, I'd need to peel the contents of Jefferson's letter for them like an onion so that they can get the true flavor before I add the special seasonings"—he stared at Bonguard as if there were some hidden meaning in his face—"drop it all in the pot, and cook it with a book."

Another brain teaser, thought Bonguard. "But why not save the details?"

"Oh, I'll have all the details in the book, all right." He ran a comb through his hair and headed for the bedroom with Bonguard following.

"This revelation. What exactly . . . ?"

"Wait and learn," said Scarborough. "Feelings of racial discord in this country run deep. Roll out the letter with all the details, the real in-depth story, and if everything goes well, we may have a new American Revolution."

Scarborough pulled a shirt off a hanger in the closet, still talking as if to himself. "I wonder how many of them were involved. It had to be more than one," he said.

"One what?" Bonguard looked as if he'd stepped into the Twilight Zone.

"Stay tuned," said Scarborough. "Besides, if I did it on a hard-news show, they'd nail me. A million follow-up questions. Where did I find the letter? How long did I have it? Who does it belong to? Why hadn't I revealed it earlier? How could I? I didn't know all the facts. I was in the middle of an ongoing investigation. But why get into all that when I can do it on Leno? I was disarmed by humor, caught up in the comedy of the moment. I let my guard down. Next thing I know, there it is, history's biggest national turd on America's living-room floor. More news later." Scarborough smiles at the thought.

"Well, if you're going to pop the letter tonight there are probably a few other things we should talk about first."

"Yes?" Scarborough looked at him.

"Like what's happening outside." Bonguard reached over and picked up a copy of the *L.A. Times* that was lying on the nightstand. There were stories of racial violence in three major cities, one of them Los Angeles, where police acting quickly had barely quelled a riot the night before, all based on the rising furor over Scarborough's book. The author had fed the flames in local news interviews with the media the day before.

On the national scene, it was like watching a torchlight parade. Inner cities had lit up across the country on a swath that corresponded precisely with Scarborough's book tour. People marching through the streets demanding that the language be removed from the Constitution found themselves met by police.

Scarborough was a lawyer first, a writer second. He had thought about this. Not the riots and violence, but the manner in which the Constitution was amended. This was time-honored and hallowed. It had been followed for two hundred years and would require a constitutional amendment itself to be changed. It was perfect. The book gave light to a problem that politicians couldn't fix by waving their legislative wand and merely passing a law. It could take years to remove the slavery language from the Constitution.

The more Scarborough flogged the issue on television, the louder was the outcry from people who'd never realized that the words were there to begin with. It was like an accelerator on a car—the harder he pressed, the more anger it produced. The racial heat generated controversy, which in turn produced sales. All the while, Scarborough, his hair flying in the breeze, was enjoying the ride.

Bonguard picked up the newspaper and looked at the pictures and the story. "Of course, if L.A. or other cities burn, it wouldn't do to be caught carrying gasoline," he said. "What I mean is—"

"I understand what you're saying. I have done nothing to provoke violence. I have said nothing to encourage people to take to the streets."

"Still, unless Osama nukes us," said Bonguard, "it looks like we'll be displacing terrorism on the front pages for a while. The Black Congressional Caucus is already engaged. When they hear about the letter tonight, they'll ransack all the old dusty volumes in the Library of Congress looking for the original."

Nice try, thought Scarborough. "Well, they won't find it there. Look at it this way: All we're doing is exposing history to the light of day. We didn't put the words in the Constitution or decide how it should be amended. And I certainly didn't write the words in that letter. No, we're just messengers delivering the message."

Scarborough smiled at him. It was the kind of roguish grin that usually kept even his enemies from disliking him entirely.

"Of course, your publisher's gonna be a little nervous," said Bonguard. "No doubt they'd have convulsions if they knew what you were going to do tonight."

"Let's not bother them with it."

"It is their book tour." Bonguard caught his client's eye. The author's expression answered his question, the reason all this was so secret.

There was a knock at the door.

"Speak of the devil. That would be Aubrey," said Scarborough. James Aubrey was Scarborough's editor. "Not a word about tonight."

"Your call." Bonguard knew that if the publisher found out, Scarborough would fire him in a heartbeat, since he was the only possible source. He headed for the door.

Scarborough could hear their idle chatter.

"Dick."

"Jim. How'd you sleep last night?"

"Good. And you?"

"Fine. Went out, had a drink. Hit the sack early."

"How's our man?"

"He's in the bedroom. Come on in."

A couple of seconds later, the two of them appeared in the door to the bedroom.

Jim Aubrey was in his late twenties, looking harried and a little frazzled. He wore
thick-rimmed glasses, a sport coat, and a
tie that looked as if it had been inherited
from an earlier generation.

"Morning," said Aubrey. "You up for tonight?"

"Ready as ever," said Scarborough.

"I guess you guys saw the protesters
down in the lobby."

"How many?" Bonguard wanted numbers.

"I don't know. I didn't count 'em. Probably twenty-five or thirty."

"It'll grow toward the afternoon," said
Scarborough. By now he was used to
the throng of demonstrators and support-
ers. Like Cicero on his way to the Senate,
Scarborough seemed to have his own
throng of backers in every city, self-
appointed lictors who pushed their way
through crowds and yelled insults at their
opposite number, those who thought
Scarborough was an agitator seeking to
stir up racial trouble. Bonguard had
started to wonder whether hired security
might be necessary. He had weighed in
on the issue with the publishers the day

before, but for some reason they had put him off.

"I think most of them downstairs are in support of the book." Aubrey looked nervous, as if he might be chewing his nails to the quick. "You saw this morning's *Times*?"

"Yeah."

"Twenty-four cars torched in Central L.A. last night, before they got it under control," said Aubrey.

"Gives the city an upscale appeal. Starting to feel like Paris." Scarborough laughed, trying to take the edge off.

It didn't work. "New York is very nervous," said Aubrey. "They're worried about tonight. A large national audience. That something you might say could set it off."

"Not to worry," said Scarborough.

"You'll keep it light?" said Aubrey.

"Absolutely."

"I want you to understand that no one is more committed to this book than I am."

Scarborough turned to look at him. "Jim, I know that."

"I put my job on the line several times when others wanted to kill the project."

"And I appreciate it. I thank you for it," said Scarborough.

"There's talk of a federal grand jury probe because of the riots," said the editor.

Scarborough was busy getting his clothes together, rummaging through his suitcase, which never seemed to get unpacked, a new hotel every night.

"I know. I saw the article in the paper. I wouldn't call them riots, exactly. But I'm not surprised. People in the White House have to do something to look as if they're on top of it," said the author. "But I suspect that congressional hearings will probably come first." Scarborough didn't seem to be concerned in the least about any of this.

"What congressional hearings?" said Aubrey.

"Oh, there are certain to be congressional hearings. And those are sure to be public and televised."

Aubrey knew that Scarborough was connected politically in D.C., in the same way an L.A. hood might be connected with Chicago or New York. He could detect political rumbling before anyone else heard the drums. The thought of the author sitting at a green-felt-covered table in the Capitol in front of blinding television lights with a national audience was not something that the publisher had considered.

"I hate to tell you this, but there's already some noise in New York about pulling the plug on the tour," said Aubrey.

This stopped Scarborough in his tracks. He turned and looked at the editor.

"It's . . . it's not my decision," said Aubrey. "Just until things cool down. They called me this morning and wanted to know what I thought about it."

"And what did you say?"

"I told them I'd have to talk to you and get back to them."

"That's fine. So now you can go to the phone, call them up, and tell them that both you and I disagree. That the book's on a roll. That it may be the biggest bestseller they've had in years. That they need to grow some balls. That if they pull the plug now, they'll never be able to bring it back. And if that doesn't convince them," said Scarborough, "you can tell them for me that if they do, I will sue them seven ways from Sunday."

Aubrey was left speechless in the doorway.

Scarborough thought for a second. "No, on second thought, tell them that I'll go public. I will accuse them of being in lockstep with the White House and involved in a racial cover-up. That's much faster, and it doesn't involve all those nasty little pieces of paper that seem to fly around courtrooms."

The thought of the publisher's Manhattan office illuminated by burned-out cars and flaming trash cans flashed through Aubrey's brain like a strike of lightning.

Scarborough turned back to his suitcase looking for a pair of socks. "They have a number-one *New York Times* bestseller, rocketed there out of the box, and they want to end the publicity tour." He found the socks and tossed them on the bed.

"Not end. They didn't say end," said Aubrey.

"They don't have to. I can read between the lines. Go away. Don't call us, we'll call you. The check's in the mail." Scarborough was working up a head of steam. "Listen," he said, "I want you to give them a message. Tell 'em it's from me. Tell them that they didn't put this book on the list. The media put it there. Twenty million angry African Americans put it there. So if they think they're gonna plant their tail between their legs, drop the book, and run, they're wrong. Why? Because black people finally woke up and realized that the words that kept them in chains for two hundred years are still in black and white, right there in the Constitution for the world to read. Well, it isn't gonna happen. Your people are not going to cap the book. Not this book."

"Nobody is talking about capping the book," said Aubrey.

"Good. Then we can move on with the tour and pretend that this conversation never took place."

"I . . . I don't know," said Aubrey. "I'll have to call them."

"You do that. And you give them my message. Word for word. You understand?" Scarborough turned and fixed him with a glare. "Now I need to get some rest. Dick can show you to the door. Unless you want to use the phone out in the living room to make the call?"

"No. No. I'll call them on my cell." Aubrey wanted to do it from outside the room, as far away from Scarborough as he could get, so that the author couldn't hear the screaming from the other end in New York. Aubrey felt very much like what he was at this point, the man in the middle.

"Dick. I need you to go, too," said Scarborough. "I need to be alone for a while, to get some rest, have a light meal in the room, and then I need to relax and pull my thoughts together for tonight."

The agent took the hint, put his arm around Aubrey's shoulder, and headed for the door. A few seconds later, Scarborough heard it close behind them. Between the hall and the lobby, in the elevator, Bonguard would be busy pumping concrete up the editor's spine and giving him advice on how to deal with his boss, the CEO and publisher back in New York.

Scarborough finished up in the bathroom, picked up the newspaper, and went out into the living room. He called room service and ordered breakfast—two eggs scrambled, toast unbuttered, a small cup of mixed fruit, and black coffee. He could never wake up entirely until he'd had his coffee.

Then he unzipped a large leather portfolio that he always carried with him wherever he went. It contained background materials for Leno and another document of several pages folded in thirds. He took this out and looked at it, made a few mental notes to follow up on later, and placed the portfolio and the folded pages on a small table near the television. The limo taking Scarborough to L.A. for the late-afternoon taping would arrive shortly after noon.

He took the other papers and settled into one of the large club chairs opposite the big television screen and started reading about the details from last night's mini-riot. When he finished, he turned to his notes.

He had briefing notes from two talent agents in New York and L.A., people with celebrity clients who'd made recent appearances on Leno, filled with information on everything from what to expect in the greenroom to how to sit, and where, on the couch. Ten minutes passed, and there was a knock at the door. Breakfast was here. He was in the middle of a back-grounder on Leno. First rule in any game: Know who you're playing.

Still reading, paper in one hand, he got out of the chair and headed for the door. Without taking his eyes off the words on the page, in one smooth movement he reached for the knob, pulled the door open, turned back toward his chair, and said, "Come on in. Put it on the table. Leave the check, and I'll sign it later." In less than four seconds, he was back in the deep slouch, surrounded by the crushed-leather pillows of the club chair. His eyes continued to devour the words on the page.

A slight breeze from out in the hall fanned the small hairs at the back of his neck from the open door behind him. There was an instant glimpse, a reflection of movement in the dark screen of the television. Before he could turn his head, a bright flash pulsed through his brain, jagged and vivid as fireworks. The roiling pain from his torn scalp and punctured skull registered but for a brief instant as he bridged the gulf between consciousness and the lightless pit of eternity.

ONE

I open the envelope and start to paw through the photographs, the stuff sent to me in response to our discovery motion two weeks earlier. There are color glossies of the murder weapon, a common claw hammer with a fiberglass handle covered by a molded-rubber hand grip. In the photo it is lying on a tiled surface in a pool of blood. A small ruler lies on the tile next to the hammer for scale.

The next picture is a close-up of the claws themselves. A patch of bloody skin trailing several wisps of dark hair clings to the edge of one of the claws. The police photographer must have shot with a macro lens to get all the detail. No doubt they will want to use this one in front of the jury.

The next photo shows an elongated skid mark, apparently made by a shoe that slid in the blood and left a red comma coming to an end at the wall. The skid mark arcs out of the picture, making clear that its owner must have gone down when he hit the blood.

The fourth photo is a particular problem for us. I show it to Harry, who is seated next to me at the small metal table in the jail.

Harry Hinds and I have been law partners, "Madriani & Hinds," since our days back in Capital City years ago. We handle many kinds of cases, but predominantly we do criminal defense. Harry is more than a partner. For years he has been like an uncle to my daughter, Sarah, who is now away at college. I am widowed. My wife, Nikki, has been dead for almost fifteen years. To look at him, Harry hasn't seemed to have aged a day in the twenty years I've known him. He takes the evidence photo in his hand and looks at it closely.

It shows a palm print in blood and three very distinct fingerprints: the first, second, and third fingers of the right hand superimposed in rusted red on the clear white tile of the entry hall's floor.

"And they're a match?" he asks.

"According to the cops," I tell him.

"How did this happen?" says Harry. "How did you get your fingerprints not only in the blood on the floor but on the murder weapon itself?" This, Harry puts to the young man sitting on the other side of the table across from us.

Carl Arnsberg is twenty-three. He has a light criminal record—one conviction for assault and battery, another for refusing to comply with the lawful orders of a police officer and obstruction of justice during a demonstration in L.A. two years ago.

He looks at Harry from under straight locks of dark hair parted on the left. The way it is combed and cut, long, it covers one eye. He snaps his head back and flips the hair out of his face, revealing high cheekbones and a kind of permanent pout. Then he rests his chin on the palm of his left hand, elbow on the table holding it up.

The pose is enough to piss Harry off.

There is a small swastika planted on the inside of Arnsberg's forearm, discreet and neat. It has all the sharp lines of something recent, none of the blurring that comes as flesh sags and stretches with age. His other arm is a piece of art. The words OUR RACE IS OUR NATION wrap his right forearm. This is followed by a number of pagan symbols in ink.

Arnsberg's pale blue eyes project contempt for the system that placed him here. It is an expression sufficiently broad to embrace Harry and me. I'm sure Arnsberg sees both of us as part of the process that keeps him here, in the lockup of the county jail.

"I asked you a question," says Harry.

"I told you what happened. How many times do I have to tell you?"

"Until I'm satisfied that I've heard the truth," says Harry.

"You think I'm lying."

"Trust me, son, you don't want to know what I'm thinking right now."

"Fine! I brought him his lunch to the room," says Arnsberg.

"Thought you said it was breakfast?" says Harry.

"Maybe it was. Maybe he slept late. I don't know. What difference does it make?"

"Go on." Harry has his notebook open and is jotting a few items now and then.

"I knocked on the door. Like I told you before, and like I told the cops, the door opened when I hit it with my hand. Not all the way, just a crack. I didn't use a passkey. I guess whoever closed it last, it didn't catch. That would probably be your killer," he says. "That's who you should be looking for."

"You didn't see anybody pass you in the hall, between the elevator and the door?" I ask.

"No. Not that I remember."

"Go on."

"So when the door opened, I just leaned toward the crack a little and hollered 'Hello?'—like that. Nobody answered, so I pushed the door open a little more. I didn't look in, I just yelled again. Nothing. I knew I had the right room, the big Presidential Suite on the top floor. I'd been there plenty of times, delivering meals and picking up trays. So I sorta backed in, pushing the door with my back and shoulder. I yelled again. Nobody answered. At the same time, I started to undo the tablecloth with one hand, let it sorta drop down in front of me."

"Why did you do that?" I ask.

"You learn to do it so you can fling it out on the table and put the tray down on top. But I did it for another reason, too. To give myself some cover," he says. "You hear stories—waiters who barged into a room and found the guest, maybe a woman who didn't hear 'em knock, coming out of the shower in the buff. It's happened."

"So you thought whoever was inside was probably in the shower?"

"There or maybe in the bedroom. It's a big suite."

"So you're standing there inside the door with your back to the room, tablecloth in front of your face. How did you find your way around the room?" says Harry.

"Like I say, I've been in that room enough times to know the layout. It never changes. I knew where the table was, the chairs, and I could see enough light and shadow through the cloth. So I just moved in the right direction with the tray up on my shoulder. Listen, I tol' all this to the cops."

"We want to hear it from you," says Harry. "Humor us."

"Fine. I couldn't see exactly where I was going. Just enough to know I wasn't gonna walk into any furniture. It wasn't until I got to the carpet off the tile in the living room, when I noticed something was wrong. I felt the squishing, you know, under my feet. I thought somebody musta spilled water. My first thought was the bathtub overflowed." With this his face comes up off his propped-up hand. From the look in his eyes, he's starting to relive the moment.

"I had to put the tray down before I could look. So I found the table."

"You didn't look down to see what it was, the dampness in the carpet?" asks Harry.

Arnsberg shakes his head. "I was juggling the tray. All I needed was to drop coffee and orange juice, on whatever else was there on the floor. And all the time I kept yelling, 'Hello? Anybody here?'"

"How far away was it, the distance to the table from where you were then, when you first felt the wetness in the carpet?" I ask.

"I don't know. It was just a small table. It

was off to the right as you entered the living room, a few feet. Maybe a couple of steps."

"Go on."

"I could sort of see the shadow of the table through the tablecloth."

"Do you remember whether the carpet was wet all the way to the table as you walked?"

"I don't remember," he says. "No. No, it musta been, because of what I saw later."

"Go on," I tell him.

"So I spread the tablecloth, put the tray down, and turned around. That's when I saw him, on the floor. His head was down. His butt was sorta crunched up against the chair. All that blood. I remember I looked down, and I was standing in it. And his head, I panicked. I started to run for the door. Musta got maybe two steps onto the tile when I went down. That's what I remember. That's how I got the blood on my pants. I figure that's probably when I musta done it," he says. "Touched the hammer, I mean."

The cops had found a single partial print on the murder weapon, one finger that seems to match the little finger, the pinkie, of Arnsberg's right hand.

"That's the only way it could have happened," says Arnsberg.

"Not according to the cops," says Harry.

"Well, they're wrong. All I remember is I got the hell outta there fast as I could. You would, too, you walked in on somethin' like that."

"Have you ever seen this item?" Harry slides a photograph across the table. It's a picture of one of those cheap clear-plastic raincoats, the kind you can fold up and slip into a pocket or a purse. Some of them come with their own tiny little bag for storage. This one doesn't, but it is covered in the rust hue of dried blood.

Arnsberg shakes his head. "No. Never seen it before."

"The police found it in a Dumpster behind the hotel, near one of the parking lots. But you've never seen it before?"

"No."

The cops have confirmed that the blood on the raincoat belonged to Scarborough. They have scoured it inside out and subjected it in a chamber to the vapor of hot

superglue, looking for any sign of fingerprints. They've found none.

"After you found the body, why didn't
you tell somebody?" asks Harry.

This was the clincher as far as the police
were concerned, the fact that Arnsberg ran
rather than reporting what he'd found.
Though he didn't run far. It took them just
one day to track him down at his apartment
before they could question him. By then
they had enough to book him.

"I don't know. I panicked. You'd panic, too,
if you had some dead guy's blood on your
pants, all over the bottom of your shoes."

"And that's the only reason you ran?
The blood on your clothes?" Harry pushes
him.

"Yeah. No. I don't know. I guess I knew
what people would think."

"And what was that?" says Harry.

"Just what you're thinking now. That I did
it. That I might have a reason to kill him."

"Because of the artwork there on your
arm?" Harry points with his pen at the tat-
too.

"Yeah, I suppose."

"Or was it because of some of the friends
you're keeping these days?"

He looks at Harry, the devil with all the questions. "That, too."

"Let's talk about some of your friends," I say. "Did any of them discuss with you the fact that Terry Scarborough was staying at the hotel where you worked? That you might actually see him, have access to him?"

"I . . . don't remember."

"Come on," says Harry. "It's a simple question. Did you talk to any of your buddies about Scarborough being in the hotel?"

"I might have."

This is an angle the cops are working overtime trying to nail down, the question of whether there was a conspiracy to kill Scarborough.

"You knew that some of your friends were seen protesting out in front of the hotel?" I ask. "The cops have them on videotape."

"Yeah. I knew they were there. I didn't know about no videotape."

"Did you talk with them about Scarborough before he was killed?"

"We might have."

"Did you or didn't you?" I ask.

"Sure. Why shouldn't we? No law against talking."

"What did you talk about? What did you say?" Harry now bores in.

"We . . . we talked about the fact he was an agitator, causin' problems, stirrin' up trouble."

"Scarborough?"

"Yeah. We got enough problems," he says. "Mexicans crossin' the border by the millions. Politicians sayin' we can't get 'em out. Illegals marchin' in the streets, carryin' Mexican flags, tellin' us they own the country. Then this guy comes outta nowhere, with this book, trying to get the blacks all riled up so he can start the Civil War over again. Only this time he wants to put *us* in chains."

"And who is 'us'?" says Harry.

"The white people," says Arnsberg.

"And this is what you talked about with your friends?" I ask.

"Yeah. He was a troublemaker. You asked me, so I told ya. If you wanna know the truth, as far as I'm concerned, he got what he deserved."

One thing is certain. Come trial, Arnsberg is not likely to be his own best witness.

"So you talked about this with your

friends when? How long before Scarborough was killed?" I ask.

"I can't remember exactly."

"How many times did you talk with other people about Scarborough?"

"I don't know. I can't remember. Maybe a couple," he says.

"Twice?" says Harry.

"I don't know. Do you always know how many times you talked to somebody about something?"

Harry wants a list of names, the people Arnsberg may have talked to in the days leading up to the murder, the places where they met, whether it was on the phone or in person, and how many witnesses were present.

"So we talked about him. Doesn't make me a killer."

"Ah, yes," says Harry, "but there's the rub. You don't get to decide who the killer is. The jury does that. And I can guarantee you that they will be positively riveted by any information concerning things you might have said about Mr. Scarborough to others, especially in the period right before he was killed. They're funny about that. Juries, I mean."

GROVE FAMILY LIBRARY
101 RAGGED EDGE ROAD SOUTH
CHAMBERSBURG, PA 17202

The kid doesn't seem to like Harry's sense of humor. I suppose it too much resembles lectures he's gotten at school and in other places of authority.

He turns to me. "The guy was stirring up crowds everywhere he went. You saw the news," says Arnsberg. "Way he was going, sooner or later somebody was gonna nail him."

"There again you have a problem," says Harry. "He wasn't, as you say, 'nailed' somewhere else. This particular hammering took place in the hotel where you happened to work, and according to the cops all the evidence points to you being the last person in that room with him."

This from his own lawyer. The look on the kid's face is a mix of anger and fear. "I thought you were here to help me," he says.

"We're tryin', son. But you have to give us the tools," says Harry.

"You got a cigarette?" Arnsberg looks at me.

"I don't smoke."

"Me neither," Harry lies.

People v. Arnsberg is the kind of case that is made up of hard circumstance, assorted pieces of physical evidence, and the fact that the defendant fits the expected profile of the killer like a fat man in stretch pants. Whether he did it or not, he can be seen to possess the kind of insane motive that is easy to peddle to an inner-city jury—blind hatred based on race. In fact, the evidence came at them so fast that the cops fell over themselves in a blind rush to arrest the defendant.

To listen to the media, Arnsberg didn't kill a person of color. He did something worse. He killed their self-appointed messenger, in this case a lawyer, author, and celebrity, all the ingredients to whip up a hot story, except for sex, and they're relying on innuendo for that one. The media mavens are now calling the case the "San Diego Slavery Slaying," and they're camped all over it, 24/7.

"I talked to my dad. He says you can get me off." This the kid directs at me.

"We'll do whatever we can. But there are no guarantees. We can't do anything unless we know everything. That means everything *you* know. If you withhold information from us, even something you might not think is important . . . then you're just wasting our time. You can bet the cops will find out about it—that is, if they don't already know—and when they start dropping surprises on us in court, there will be nothing I or anyone else can do to help you. Understand?"

He swallows, then nods, not something hip or cool, but vigorous, like someone who suddenly realizes that the threads of security, whatever it is that tethers him to this life, are far thinner than he ever realized. "Yeah. I told you everything I know. Really," he says. "I didn't do it. I swear."

"All right." We lecture him on jailhouse etiquette, not to talk to anyone—guards, cellmates, even family—about events in the case. Anything told to them can be repeated in testimony on the stand. Even family members can be forced to testify against him. "You talk only to us, Harry or myself, that's it."

"Somebody in the jail wants to talk about the weather, fine. Sports, feel free. But anything having to do with your case, with Scarborough, with race relations in general, you're a mute," says Harry. "If you have to, swallow your tongue. If we're in trial and somebody asks how it went in court, you don't know."

"I understand," he says. "I talk to no-body. Only the two of you."

"And your buddies, the ones you may have talked to before the event, don't talk to them at all," says Harry. "As far as you're concerned, they don't exist. If they come visiting during hours, you don't want to see them, and you don't want to be seen talk-ing to them."

"What do I tell them?"

"You don't tell them anything. If they call the jail and want to talk to you, you don't take the call. If they show up in the visit-ing room and you see them, you don't sit down. You turn and you walk. Anything you tell them can be used against you. It can be twisted for whatever reason and end up being your word against theirs as to what was said. Worse than that," says Harry, "the cops may be listening in. Friends have been known to wear wires. Just figure that if any of these old friends show up to give you moral support, and you talk to them, you may as well have a heart-to-heart with the D.A., because you probably are."

He nods nervously, in the stark realiza-tion that he is alone, a dying man in a desert, with only me and Harry to toss him the occasional drop of water.

Harry and I start collecting our papers and notes, the photos go back into my briefcase.

"I need to know one thing," says Arnsberg.

"What's that?" I ask.

"They aren't serious? They don't really wanna . . . well, you know . . ."

I stop with the briefcase and look at him. "No, I don't."

"I mean, they're not gonna really execute me?" he says. "They're sayin' that just to put pressure. Right? They're thinking squeeze hard enough and I'll do a deal. That's it, isn't it? Sure. That's gotta be it. Scare me and they figure I'll confess, tell 'em I did something I didn't do. I can understand that. I mean, I won't do it. I mean, confess to something I didn't do. But I understand it. It makes sense." In half a second, his eyes flash from me to Harry and back again.

At this moment I wish his father were not my friend, that instead I was dealing with the child of a stranger, where my only psychic connection to the outcome would be just the blood that ordinarily oozes from my pores whenever I stand with a client to hear a verdict.

"Carl. I can call you Carl?"

He nods.

"Carl, I want you to understand this because you'll save yourself a lot of pain if you get it into your head and come to grips with it now. The police, the D.A., the State of California are not testing the water here. They're not playing *Let's Make a Deal*. Given the case, the media hype, and racial politics, unless something major breaks our way, I can't see that they would ever accept a deal, though if things get bad, we may have to go there before we're finished. They're doing this because they believe they have the evidence to convict you, send you to the death house at San Quentin, and inject enough lethal drugs into your body to kill you. I wish I could tell you it wasn't true, but if they have their way, that is exactly what they intend to do."

It's hard to tell whether he even hears all this. His face looking up at me is that flushed. A second later the breath seems to leave his body as his shoulders slump and he sags in the chair. His head is down.

The nightmare is real. He begins to tear up, then sucks it all back in a boyish effort to keep his nose from running. He wipes his eyes with the back of his forearm, the one decorated with the swastika. Carl Arnsberg may be twenty-three and halfway to becoming a hard-baked race case, but at this moment I would gauge his social age to be no more than ten, with the hardness quotient of his heart somewhere in the neighborhood of hot Jell-O.

* * *

"I don't know what happened. I guess it's my fault. Somehow I lost touch with him. You know how hard it is to raise kids."

Sam Arnsberg is a friend of long standing. We went to college together, belonged to the same fraternity, dated some of the same girls.

Today, seated in one of the client chairs across from my desk, Sam doesn't even look like the same person I once knew. But for certain aspects of terminal cancer, there is nothing I can think of in life that will destroy a person faster than the perils of dealing with the American judicial system. Even mired in the middle of it as I am, I cannot imagine what Sam is going through, a child facing a possible death sentence.

"Maybe you should find someone else to do this," I tell him.

"No! I trust you. I have faith in you." He says it as if he were reaching out to grasp one of those life rings they toss from a passing ship to a man who is drowning.

"Maybe a little too much faith," I tell him. "I never knew your son as a child. And you and I may be a little too close. Sometimes it can cloud judgment," I tell him.

Over the years since college, Sam and I stayed in contact, first by phone and letters and later with e-mail. We exchanged stories of family life. When Nikki died, Sam came out to California and spent almost a week helping me to pick up the pieces of my life. During later years he became an important voice on the phone, one of the few people with whom I could share intimate thoughts.

"I know it's bad," he says.

"I would be lying if I told you it wasn't. There's a lot of evidence. Almost none of it, as far as I can see, is going to be good for Carl."

"Let me guess what's bothering you.

You're afraid that if you lose, if Carl dies, I'll blame you, that we won't be able to look each other in the eye again. Won't happen," he says.

"What? I won't lose?"

"No. If Carl dies, there is only one person to blame, and that's my boy. Will you do it? Will you take the case?"

Sam has been to two other lawyers already, both of them major criminal-defense hotshots, people to whom I referred him when he first came to me. Whether it was the evidence in the case or the racial hot wires attached to it, neither of them would touch it.

Sam could step away. His son is an indigent, eligible for the services of the public defender. But he doesn't want to do that.

"All right. Let me talk to my partner, but I'm sure he'll go along." I know Harry well enough to know that he will, though he will chew my ass raw and reserve the right to do so again the first minute the case goes sour.

Sam smiles as a tear runs down his face from out of the corner of his eye. Like father, like son.

"Why did he run?" asks Sam. "Did he tell you?"

"I suppose because he was afraid."

"Did he say—"

"Stop!"

He looks at me.

"You're his dad. You and I are friends. It's going to be hard, but there are going to be things that I will not be able to share with you. Most of the things that Carl tells me, lawyer-client, I cannot tell anyone else, including you."

"I understand. But I have to know. One thing."

"What's that?"

"From what you know, did he do it? Did he kill that man?"

"If you mean did he confess, did he make any admission, the answer is no. He maintains his innocence."

"Thank God," he says, heaving a long sigh as he looks up at the ceiling. "You know, I don't know what got into him. All this stuff. The tattoos, his friends. Where did he get all that? We didn't raise him to be that way."

I shake my head.

"We used to play baseball together. I

coached his Little League team. Babe Ruth when he was older. We played catch. He used to pitch to me." He looks down at the desk, his eyes tearing up again as he thinks back. "When he was small, he thought he might play in the big leagues someday. The dreams kids have," says Sam. "Then I looked up, and he was gone. Now this."

At seventeen, after an argument with his father, Carl dropped out of school, moved out of the house, and began to drift. It was the last real contact his family had with him.

Sandra is Sam's wife of nearly thirty years. They have two older children, a daughter, Susan, who is in grad school and a son, James, who is married with children and works with his dad in the family business, a small insurance agency.

"Susan's talking about dropping out of school," he says. "She's enrolled at Columbia. It's gonna be tough. Tough." I know he's talking about finances. "She's a smart kid."

"Yes."

"It's hard. It's on the news, twenty-four hours a day. Her brother's name, his picture, lawyers and judges—they call them experts—all speculating on things they don't know. Susie has friends at school, but she's having a hard time. She says she'll just drop out for a while and go back later. But I don't want her to. It's enough that it destroys Sandy and me. I don't want it to affect the other kids. They have their own lives. Besides, it's not like she can hide at home. These people are camped outside our house," he says, "trucks with satellite dishes, people with cameras, microphones, lights. The middle of the night, they light up your bedroom. They chased Sandy down the driveway of her own home. Her own home," he says.

"I saw it on TV," I tell him, half a minute of tape showing his wife rolling out the trash, fending off questions and dodging boom mikes. Film of this from different angles tumbled through the news cycle on each of the cable networks every fifteen minutes for two days. "Breaking news" is now anything on videotape that can be used to punctuate the ever-rising flood of ads. Every story, no matter what or where, is now national in scope. Johnny has a fight with Jimmy in the third grade, and the whole country is told about it by breathless "reporters" hanging from news choppers hovering over the school. Park a police car by a building and call in a rumor, and whatever you say will be broadcast around the world twice before you can hang up. Unless you knew better, you might swear that Chicken Little has taken over the newsroom and bolted the door. Hyping hysteria and peddling panic around the clock is now an enterprise listed on the Dow Jones ticker. And everybody watches, anxiety junkies cruising for another hit, just in case there's some real news. After all, another 9/11 could happen, and we might miss it.

"Anything else you need from me?" Sam asks, then slaps his head. "Of course there is. Let me write you a check."

"Listen, we'll talk about it later," I tell him. "I've got another meeting, and I'm running late."

"Sorry. I shouldn't be taking up so much of your time."

"If not you, then who?" I walk him to the door.

He turns, squeezes my arm at the shoulder. "Thanks."

"Try not to worry."

He nods and is out the door. Gone.

I close the door behind him. I have no appointment. But I couldn't think of any graceful way to stop Sam from talking about money. The fees and costs in a case like this will bankrupt even an upper-income family. Welcome to the justice system.

TWO

It is an axiom of criminal defense that a good lawyer must know his victim at least as well as he knows his own client. To that end, Harry and I are huddled this morning in the conference room at our law office on Coronado Island near San Diego.

Even before the picture appears on the screen, I can visualize his image and facial expressions. Terrance Scarborough is sufficiently familiar to anyone who has ever heard the word "law" that you could say he has the kind of recognition that Washington has on the dollar bill. Scarborough has been the ultimate media monger for more than a decade, on constant call as a legal expert for any network or cable channel that would have him. Set up a camera with a red light and Scarborough would cut a swath through humanity to get to it.

It is rumored that instead of legal briefs he carried only a clean shirt, a tie, and some Pan-Cake makeup in his briefcase. He had racked enough frequent-flier miles on trips between the networks in New York and CNN in Atlanta that he could fly to the moon for free.

Although he was an adjunct professor of law at Georgetown, I have yet to find anyone who took a class from Scarborough. While technically on faculty, he spent his time writing treatises on radical social theories. Like Mao, he seemed to be working on his own Little Red Book, anything to inspire discontent and class strife.

He garnered enough traction to generate a fair amount of social heat, and along the way he made himself a staple of television's cable age. Without question, Scarborough had a messianic need to be the constant center of attention. According to Harry, he has now achieved that ultimate goal, posthumously, and, if I am reading

my partner correctly, deservedly. So mea-
ger is Harry's sympathy for Scarborough
that I have been left to wonder a few times
whether Harry's hammer is missing from
his own toolbox.

Scarborough's motives, like most things
in life, are a question of perception. It was
Benjamin Franklin who is reputed to have
said that "revolution in the first person is
never illegal, as in 'our revolution.' It is only
in the second person, 'their revolution,'
that it becomes illegal." Perspective, being
a fine line, involves walking in the shoes of
another. Yesterday's demagogue is tomorrow's committed leader when his message
begins to resonate with the public—and
so becomes elevated to today's political
martyr when he is murdered.

We have gathered a number of recent
news video clips from an online clipping
service and had them burned onto a
DVD.

As Scarborough's image flickers on the
screen, it is impossible to deny that he
possessed a certain charisma. Six-one
and slender, so that dark power suits hung
well from his body. Everything about him
lent an edge of authority to his argument,

from his emerald eyes and sculpted cheekbones to the dapper cleft in his chin. If you
turned down the sound and just looked,
you might see vestiges of Cary Grant, until you listened to the words.

"What is so insidious, so sinister, is the
way in which the nation's Founding Fathers, people like Madison, Franklin, and
Adams, concealed the words of slavery
from the public and from history. They
slipped the offending language into the
Constitution, where it slithered like a hidden serpent through their grand experiment in Democracy," says Scarborough.
"And to this day no one has seen fit to remove those words.

"You can complain about the Bolshevik
Revolution and its failure to deliver," he
says. "But there is no deal in history dirtier
and more deceptive than the inclusion of
slavery in the United States Constitution.
What is worse, these offending words are
still there, for all to see, there in the organic
law of this nation. They may be dead-letter
law, no longer enforceable, but they are
still visible, AND THEY ARE STILL OF-
FENSIVE!"

This is the point of Scarborough's thesis:

the manner in which the Constitution is amended. The video we are watching is from a speech he gave in the weeks before he was killed. It was delivered at a university near Chicago while he was on tour for his book *Perpetual Slaves.* The audience is mostly young, many of them black.

"If you don't believe that the old Rebel flag of the defeated Confederacy should be hanging outside in front of state capitols in this nation, just beneath the Stars and Stripes, then how is it that the language of slavery should remain visible in the United States Constitution? Is there a different standard for the federal government?" he asks.

"What is so intellectually dishonest is that these 'great men,' the minds of the American enlightenment—Adams, Franklin, Madison, and others—dodged the use of plain language when it came to concealing slavery. And nothing has changed. The leaders of this nation continue to dodge it today.

"Look, search, and you will not find the words 'slave' or 'slavery' anywhere in the Constitution. No, they insult the descendants of slaves, and the national government has seen fit to continue to allow these to exist in print to this very day.

"Look at the infamous fugitive-slave clause, Article Four, Section Two, of the Constitution. This was the cardinal law of slavery crafted at the birth of the nation, the provision that crushed even the shadow of a dream of freedom for African slaves. And did it use the words 'slave' or 'slavery'? No, of course not.

"It uses the euphemism 'No person held to service or labor' who escaped to a free state was to be freed. Why? Because the Constitution at its inception says that they should be dragged back and delivered up not to their 'masters' or 'owners' but to 'the party to whom service or labor may be due.'

"And have these words been removed from the Constitution?" Scarborough puts a hand up to his ear and listens.

Some in the audience shout, "NO!"

"That's right. The language is still there, a monument to the guile and craftiness of the slave owners who crafted our Constitution.

"Read Article One, Section Two, the

insidious three-fifths clause, and tell me what it means or, more important, WHY IT IS STILL THERE. The continued appearance of these words is a national offense, an insult to every African American walking on this continent.

"Historians know what it means, because they study it. Lawyers know what it means. The federal courts know what it means, because they enforced it. Congress knows what it means, because they passed the enabling statutes that allowed the institution of slavery to function. And Congress has done nothing in more than a hundred and fifty years, since the Civil War and the repeal of slavery by the Thirteenth Amendment, to remove the offending words from the Constitution. Members of Congress sit there and complain about the Dixie flag, and the states that fly it, while they have this *stink* on their own hands," says Scarborough. He allows the fiery oratory to settle on the audience.

"In simple terms the three-fifths clause identifies all the classes of people in the United States at the time of its founding. They needed this for purposes of taxation and apportionment, the formula to determine the number of representatives each state would get in the new Congress.

"The clause identifies 'free persons.'"

"It identifies 'Indians.'"

"It identifies 'those bound to service for a term of years,' indentured servants and debtors working off their debts.

"And then, last *and certainly least,* the clause identifies 'three-fifths of all other persons' then remaining in the new United States of America."

Scarborough allows this to settle for a moment.

"Now, who do you think these 'other persons' were? Who could they so conveniently and easily carve up into three-fifths of a human being, like a turkey on a platter?

"Who could it possibly be that these enlightened men of the founding generation were talking about?"

"African slaves!" The words are shouted by someone out in the audience.

"That's right, African slaves. 'Other people' who weren't treated as people at all, because they were owned by white Americans as property, traded and sold like animals. They were being counted as three-fifths of a human being not so that they could vote for members of Congress but so that their owners, their white masters, could have the power of this franchise added to their own. White slave owners could increase the power of their own vote by buying more slaves. This was the incentive, the inducement carved into the cornerstone of the Constitution at the nation's founding—AND THESE WORDS ARE STILL THERE!" Scarborough pounds on the podium with this, his theme. "Read the book," he says.

The chant of "Take it out . . . Take it out . . . Take it out" starts to rumble through the audience.

He may be a writer, but Scarborough knows how to work an audience. He is a firebrand. Whether you like him or not, I would be willing to take bets that at this moment he is not pretending. This is an issue in which he clearly believes. He allows the chant to continue for twenty or thirty seconds before he cuts it off with his hands in the air.

"Read Article One, Section Nine, of the Constitution, where it says, 'The migration or importation of SUCH PERSONS'"—he holds up his hand and shakes his finger to emphasize the words—"would not be prohibited by Congress but by the various states then existing. Were they talking about people who wanted to migrate here from Norway or France? NO! So who *were* they talking about?"

"African slaves!" Now it comes back automatically from the audience, more voices and much louder.

"Yes! They were talking about African slaves, using nice words like 'imported,' as if they were fine wine or cheese—human beings dragged here in chains, all at the will of the various states.

"Do you believe that these words should be removed from the Constitution and thrown into the dustbin of history?"

"YES!" A crushing chorus from the audience.

"WHEN?"

"NOW!" This is even louder. The speakers from the set we are watching vibrate under the strain.

"Everywhere you look, they concealed the dirty deal by avoiding the words. They wanted to traffic in SLAVES, all right, but they certainly didn't want to say it, not so that the whole world and posterity would see it in print. And if the avoidance of language is not evidence of their guilt, then I will produce it," he says.

"The founders will tell you that they tried to end slavery but they were not able. STICK AROUND," bellows Scarborough, "because I will tell you the truth. The sequel to this book"—he holds up *Perpetual Slaves*—"Volume Two, will end the myth of American history once and for all. I will tell you what really happened, why they avoided the words. What propelled their fear, their trepidation? You won't find it in any history book," he says. "So don't bother looking.

"We are talking about a continuing national insult to more than twelve percent of the nation's population, more than thirty-five million people, and about the absolute stone silence of the country's leaders on this point. They run for office. They're out there now on the stump, but ask them about this and they will dodge and weave and avoid the question. They will tell you that the Constitution is the province of the Supreme Court. They will tell you anything that avoids a commitment to take the

words out—to remove the offending language."

The chorus of "Take it out" starts again.

"Some of them will tell you, 'NO, leave it
there as a historic relic, as a reminder of
what white masters did to their black
slaves.' But the permanent and enduring
stigma of these words, the offense that
they carry, is deep!" says Scarborough.

"Ask yourselves . . . ask yourselves
why these ploys on language, these aging, offensive euphemisms, have not been
removed? They will pull down the Confederate flag, but they won't remove this from
your own Constitution? It says 'We the
People,' but the words remain offensive,"
he says.

The chant starts up again, but Scarborough shouts over the top of it.

"Can they sweep it under the table as
the founders did?"

"NO!" The entire audience is on its feet
now, hands cupped to mouths, clenched
fists pumping on the ends of raised arms.

"Because I will tell you something more.
I will give you another document, a document that the world has never seen, a
secret letter written in the hand not of *one*

of the founders but *the* founder, confirming the darkest deal in American history. If you want to see the original sin of slavery unmasked at its inception, evidenced in the handwritten words of God himself, then wait for the sequel," says Scarborough.

Tumultuous cheers, diagonal blue lines across the screen, as the video ends.

* * *

Less than twenty-four hours after Scarborough's speech, a rally in downtown Chicago, demanding action to remove the words of slavery from the Constitution, turned violent when police moved in and clashed with demonstrators.

The next day the national media picked up snippets of Scarborough's speech, and like a trail of gunpowder, flashes of violent confrontation followed his book tour across the country as sales of the book exploded.

"My question is, how did the guy live so long?" says Harry. "If I talked like that, I'd have blown a fuse years ago. And how did he get so close to the Supreme Court?"

"Did he?"

"That's certainly the image he projected," says Harry. "The ultimate in-the-know Court watcher."

"Maybe it was just that, an image," I tell him.

Scarborough had argued a single case before the Supreme Court almost ten years ago now and won, not a landmark decision by any stretch. He had coupled this with an uncanny ability to hang on the social fringes of the Court and get his picture taken.

It was rumored in his earlier career that he coveted a spot on the Court for himself. However, given the passion of his politics and its public airing, he had little chance of being nominated and none whatever of being confirmed in the Senate. Some might argue that bitterness over this only drove him to further excess.

Harry and I look through a number of film clips, mostly interviews of Scarborough on his most recent book tour. The screen flickers between clips, and another face appears, a different venue this time.

"This is what I was telling you about," says Harry. "This is Scarborough's literary agent." Harry looks at his notes. "Guy named Richard Bonguard."

The other image on the screen is familiar to anyone who has ever turned on a television set, Jay Leno.

"This was two days after the murder," says Harry. "Scarborough was supposed to appear with Leno that night, the night he was killed. From what I was told, the agent filled in."

The interview is somber, not the usual fare for Leno. There is a text bar under the picture, AUTHOR MURDERED.

Leno: "So you two guys knew each other a long time? Not just an agent, you were his friend, right?"

Bonguard: "That's right."

Leno: "You have our sympathy. We really appreciate you taking the time to come in here and talk with us. It can't be easy. It's absolutely shocking. I can't even imagine. We were expecting to see Mr. Scarborough as a guest here on the air that day, the day he was killed. You can imagine the surprise when we heard the news. Do the police have any idea who might have done it?"

Bonguard: "Right now, as you can imagine, everything is a bit sketchy. From what I understand the cops are still in the hotel room as we speak, looking for evidence. They're being very careful. I don't think anybody knows exactly what happened or why, at least not yet."

Leno: "Except for the murderer."

Bonguard: "Well, yes."

Leno: "It's just crazy. Do you have any idea why he might have been killed? Do you think it had to do with the book?"

The host props up a copy of Scarborough's book on the desk as the camera focuses in. *Perpetual Slaves: The Branding of America's Black Race.* The camera cuts to the author's photograph from the book's dust cover.

Bonguard: "Certainly I think the police have got to be looking at that possibility. There had been a great deal of controversy over the work. I know that Terry had received death threats in the mail."

Leno: "Really?"

Bonguard: "Oh, yes. Anytime you write a book that involves politics or social controversy, you're bound to get some hate mail. But in this case it was more than usual, mostly anonymous."

Leno: "Those would have been turned over to the police, right?"

Bonguard: "Oh, I'm sure. Most of them were in the hands of the publisher. But they would be turned over, if they haven't already been."

Leno: "It's certainly a very important book. I read it last week before all this happened, and it's stunning. I mean, I'm not a lawyer, but I never realized that the language of slavery was still right there in the Constitution. I'm sure most Americans don't know that. I'm surprised that somebody hadn't brought this to public attention before this."

Bonguard: "Terry thought the same thing. He was surprised that it had never been exposed in this way. Of course, that's only part of it. . . ."

"This is the good part," says Harry. "Listen to this."

Bonguard: "There was more. He was going to do another book based on a historic document that went right to the core of the controversy over slavery. He didn't write about it in this book because he was planning a follow-up, a sequel. He was preparing to expose some kind of deal that was cut at the time the Constitution was first written. According to what Terry told me, it involved slavery and a number of prominent historic figures, men who were involved in crafting the Constitution."

Leno: "A deal? What kind of deal?"

Bonguard: "That, I don't know. That's why this letter was so important."

Leno: "Do we know who wrote this letter?"

Bonguard: "Well, I don't know that I can say too much more at this time—other than to say that the letter was important to an understanding of the history of slavery in America."

Leno: "Well, that would be pretty important. How did your client, Mr. Scarborough, get this letter?"

Bonguard: "Again, I can't say."

Leno: "Do you have this letter?"

Bonguard: "No. In fact, I've not seen it. Terry referred to it several times in conversations that we had. According to what I understand, he had it in his possession, or at least a copy."

Leno: "He had it with him when he was killed?"

Bonguard: "I don't know."

Leno: "So I assume the police must have it now?"

Bonguard: "I don't know."

"Wow." Leno turns away from his guest to look directly at the camera. "Well, you heard it here first, folks. A real bona fide murder mystery. You will keep us informed?"

"Absolutely," says Bonguard.

Leno rises from his chair and shakes Bonguard's hand. "We'll have to have you back." There are a few muddled words exchanged between the two of them. The audience begins to applaud as the screen flickers and then goes dark.

"That's everything," says Harry.

"What about the letter?" I ask. "It sounds like the same thing Scarborough was talking about in his speech—the promise to deliver in the next book, the fiery rhetoric of some big secret."

"The cops don't have it," says Harry. "No record of it listed in any of the materials seized from the hotel room or from Scarborough's apartment in D.C."

"Have the cops questioned this guy Mr. Bonguard?"

"More than that," says Harry. He flips me two pages stapled together, what appear to be photocopies of some handwritten notes. "San Diego homicide sent a detective back to interview him, and the detective took notes. They never even typed them up, just ran copies out of his notebook and threw them in the pile with the other items from our first discovery request. Obviously they must have thought that it wasn't very important. Otherwise they would have never taken notes, or sanitized them so we wouldn't see them."

Interview: Date: 7-26
(V)ictim: T. Scarborough
(S)ubject: R. Bonguard

"Second page," says Harry. He reaches across the table and points with his pen. "Right here."

S. told detective has no idea who might have killed V. Much hate mail following book. Racial orientation. Some death threats. Most are anonymous. Talk to publisher. Check to see if suspect is on record writing. See if any e-mails.

S. mentioned letter . . . (J letter).
Unclear. S. says J letter impetus for
entire book 'Perpetual Slaves.' S.
says J letter what prompted V. to
write book in first place. S. asked if
we had letter. S. no idea of location
of letter, never saw it.

"Am I understanding this? Bonguard is
telling them that without this letter, the J
letter, Scarborough would never have written *Perpetual Slaves*?"

"That's what the cop's notes seem to
say," says Harry.

"I don't get it. The book made a fortune.
There's nothing about any letter in it, and
yet according to Bonguard the letter is
what drove the book?" I look at Harry.

"And Scarborough threatens to unveil
the letter in the next book. The one he'll
never write," says Harry. "And if the cops
didn't find this letter, could be that whoever
killed Scarborough took it."

"Why didn't we see more in the press
on this following the Leno show? Bonguard talked about the letter there."

"Because by then the cops had already arrested our man, that afternoon, as

Bonguard was sitting in the studio taping the show. The arrest took the edge off of everything else. The media wasn't interested in any sideshow. The cops had their man. That's probably why the police never followed up on any of this. Since they didn't find the letter on Arnsberg or in his apartment, to them it's irrelevant," says Harry.

Certainly it didn't fit the theory of the state's case. "Get everything you can on this letter, who wrote it, when, its contents. Get a copy if you can. And find out if Scarborough made any notes referencing it. We'll need to lay a foundation if we want to get it into evidence."

"You're thinking what I am," says Harry. "Historic letter, probably a collector's item. If so, it might have been worth a bundle."

Like every good defense lawyer, Harry is centering on plausible alternative theories for murder.

"One thing is for sure. Our guy wasn't found with any letter when they arrested him. Fact is, I doubt if he can read," says Harry. "We might want to talk to an expert, find out what something like that might be worth if it were sold. The letter, I mean."

Right behind passion, money is always the easiest motive to peddle before a jury when it comes to murder.

"It's possible. It's also possible somebody didn't want the letter to see the light of day, if, as they both claim, this letter is a smoking gun giving rise to slavery in the land of the free."

"You think somebody would kill to keep from tarnishing a burnished image?" asks Harry.

"I don't know, but I'm not closing off any avenues at the moment."

Harry is jotting notes, a small pad on the table in front of him.

"You'd have to think that if this letter exists and if it's that significant, there would be some reference to it in other documents," I say.

There are voluminous treatises covering the correspondence between the framers. These include hundreds of thousands, if not millions, of footnotes, the Federalist Papers, followed by entire libraries of books written on the subject.

"Someone would have had to have mentioned it somewhere." I am talking about the mystery letter. "Check it out. Get somebody to do some research. If not here, in D.C. Try the Library of Congress."

"We can hire a research service, but it's gonna cost," says Harry. "We don't have much to go on. No date. No author for the letter. All we know is that it dealt with slavery and cut some kind of deal. Research could take a while."

So far we have lined up a few experts to go over the lab reports on physical evidence found at the scene. We have investigators out talking to some of Arnsberg's friends. Except for the letter mentioned by Bonguard and the fact that Scarborough seemed to fall back more than once on the same item in his speech, there is nothing else to go on.

"I tried to call Bonguard to talk to him," says Harry. "Left messages."

"And?"

"He never called back."

"In your message did you tell him what it was about?"

Harry nods. "Uh-huh. Which has me wondering if he's willing to talk to us at all."

With Scarborough dead, the only one who can tell us about the mystery letter is

Bonguard. This suddenly pushes him to the top of the curiosity list.

"Do you want to try to call him?" says Harry.

"What good would that do? If he's not going to talk to you, why would he talk to me?"

"Maybe you have better phone karma," says Harry.

Harry and I talk for a while. Over all of this, the mystery letter seems to hang there like a thread, daring us to pull on it.

"You know what troubles me more than anything else?" says Harry.

"What's that?"

"Scarborough. For all the fiery rhetoric—call it manipulation," he says, "still, what he said about the language and slavery, the Constitution, it was accurate, all of it. I mean, he fudged around the edges a little."

"He did a bit more than fudge at the edges," I say. "From my reading, slavery was the third rail of politics during the Constitutional Convention. Nobody wanted to touch it, neither pro-slave nor anti-slave. They all knew that any attempt to recognize it or abolish it would result in the new nation being stillborn. Move in either direction and half of the states would refuse to play, take their ball and go home."

"That may account for the covert language," says Harry. "But there's no denying that they recognized slavery. Like it or not, Scarborough had it right. It may have been the only deal possible, but that doesn't dry-clean it or make it any less grimy. And the fact that the words are still there, visible to the entire world, is indisputable."

"Your point is?"

"Since none of this is new—that language has been out there for what, going on two and a half centuries?—why now? What caused Scarborough to pounce on it at this moment and in this way, unless he was spurred on by someone or some *thing.*"

"You're thinking what I'm thinking —whatever it is, is in that letter."

He nods. "If Scarborough knew what was in it, and we have to assume that he did. If he's not going to stretch the language of the Constitution to fit his convenient yen for a second American Revolution, why would he exaggerate the contents of this letter?"

"So if that's the case, whatever is in that letter must be pretty bad," I say.

"That's what I was thinking," says Harry. "And if this is true, the letter could be sitting in the middle of our case. The reason Scarborough wrote the book, the reason he was so far out on the limb of rhetoric, and just possibly the reason he was killed."

For several minutes we massage the question of what to do. But no matter how we come at the issue of the missing letter, we seem to arrive at the same conclusion.

With Scarborough dead, the only one who may be able to tell us what is in the letter, and where it is, is Mr. Bonguard. Since he's not returning phone calls and since, for the moment at least, we can't make him come to us, all subpoenas being kept dry like gunpowder for the trial, we are left with only one alternative, and it is not one that we can put off.

*   *   *

"Why do you have to represent him? Why can't somebody else do it?"

"Because his father asked me to, and his father is an old friend. You don't always get to pick and choose your clients."

"There must be somebody else who can represent him? Why not the public defender? He can't have much money. Not from what I've read and heard."

"Sarah, I told you, I've already taken the case."

"But it's embarrassing, Dad. People at school are saying after what he did, he doesn't deserve a trial."

"Then those people are living in the wrong country."

My daughter is home from college, doing a summer internship on break. She is indignant that I'm involved in representing Carl Arnsberg and wants me to withdraw.

"Somebody who does something like that doesn't deserve a trial."

"Sarah! How long have you watched me try cases? What has it been, fifteen, sixteen years?"

"Dad, don't lecture me."

"Why? Only your professors at school can do that? Lecturing you is one of the privileges of fatherhood," I tell her.

"Don't start," she says. When we have these bouts, which is not often, Sarah sounds so much like her mother that at times I can hear Nikki's voice. Though Nikki has been dead now for nearly fifteen years, I can often see her eyes staring out at me from my daughter's face when Sarah is angry. Sarah's mother died of cancer when our daughter was small, and so my memories of the two of them together seem limited.

"You're assuming that he did it." I'm standing in my bedroom over my open suitcase, which is laid out on my bed, half filled with the items I need for my trip to the East Coast. This is a large part of the reason that Sarah is upset. She was hoping that I might take some time off while she was home on break. She is standing in the open doorway to my room, one hand on her hip, looking angry and hurt.

"Sarah, listen. The whole purpose of the trial is to determine whether he did it. And I don't think he did. What if someone accused you of doing something like this? Wouldn't you want me to defend you?"

"Dad, that's not fair. Everybody knows he did," she says.

"I'm not concerned with what everybody knows. I'm concerned with what a jury says, and then only after they've seen, heard, and studied all the evidence."

"For God's sake, Dad, he's a neo-Nazi. Even my political science prof says so."

"Then your political science professor can convict him of that, and on that charge I promise I won't represent him."

"Dad!"

"But on the charge of murdering Terry Scarborough, I am his lawyer, and on that charge he is entitled to a fair trial, just as you would be."

I return to packing, laying out shirts and underwear on the bed before loading them into my luggage.

"My prof says that Professor Scarborough was the victim of a hate crime. He says that it was a political crime and should be punished that way."

I'm going to have to make a note to keep my daughter away from the prosecutors. She may give them ideas.

She stands there for a moment collecting her thoughts, trying to come up with a different twist on her argument. I can smell mental rubber burning.

"Fine! How long will you be away? Can you tell me that?" The edge goes out of Sarah's voice. She realizes that she has lost this bout, though, knowing my daughter, I realize she is not giving up.

"Three days, four at most. I have business in New York. I won't be sure until I get there. I'll call you every day and let you know when I'll be home. And I'll get back as soon as I can."

"It's just that I thought we could spend some time together," says Sarah. "I was hoping that maybe we could go down to Mexico for a while, maybe Puerto Vallarta, one of the beach resorts."

"I will make it up to you. I promise. You'll be home again in a few months, and we can go somewhere. You can pick the spot."

"You'll be in trial," she says. "Don't promise what you can't deliver." She turns and walks away down the hall.

I stop my packing, one of my folded shirts still hanging in the air. "Tell you what!" I holler after her down the empty hall.

"What?" She is already halfway down the stairs.

"How would you like to do some shopping in New York?"

There is a nanosecond of silence, and she appears like magic back in the doorway. "You mean it?"

"Call the office, tell them to get another ticket on the flight, and book one more room at the hotel—adjoining, if they can manage it. Then get in gear and pack. We don't have much time."

"Sure! Won't take me a minute."

THREE

Seven hours in the air allow me to make up for lost time with my daughter. We talk about life on Coronado Island, how the city has changed in the time we've lived there. We talk about Harry. Sarah spends a good bit of the flight laughing as only young girls can. Her memories of Harry are of an aging and somewhat hapless uncle, even though she and my partner are not related by blood, marriage, or anything else. They have always been close.

We dredge up old memories, some of them painful: the early years when she was a small child in Capital City, when

Nikki was alive and we were a family. To my surprise, Sarah has more vivid recollections of this period than I might have credited. It is one of those imponderables, the snippets of life that engrave themselves on the mind of a small child.

Somewhere high over the flatlands of the Midwest, above the constant drone of jet engines, our conversation turns from distant memories to what she is doing at school, and finally to my practice. Sarah has always had a knack for getting me to talk, so much so that I may have to put her on the law office's payroll when I return home in order to maintain attorney-client confidence with Arnsberg. Sarah picks my brain on aspects of the case I should not discuss.

Strangely, the question that seems to perplex my daughter the most is how, after its repeal following the Civil War, it is possible that the old language of slavery can still be visible in the Constitution today. It is this very fact that Scarborough pounced on and exploited in his book.

Sarah is reading from a *Newsweek* article, a story on the author's murder and the impending trial.

"It says here that according to Scarborough this language in the Constitution represents 'an ongoing and perpetual stigmatizing of the African soul.' That's a quote from his book," she says. Then she reads on. "'While slavery was repealed in 1865 by the Thirteenth Amendment, the offending words that legalized the so-called peculiar institution at the origin of the nation remain in black and white as a visible legacy of America's principal document of state to this very day.'

"I don't understand. How can that be?" she says. "If they were repealed, why are they still there?"

I try to explain it to her. "What Scarborough discovered was a seam in the way in which the Constitution is published. Its system of publication is unique to that document."

Fortunately for Scarborough and unfortunately for the country, removing the language of slavery from the Constitution is not something that can easily be done.

I explain to her that "this is likely to require a separate constitutional amendment altering the style of the amending process. Scarborough knew this. So he knew he wasn't wasting his time publishing *Perpetual Slaves.* The book would have a long shelf life, because Congress couldn't wave its magic wand and pass a bill to fix the problem and the president couldn't do it by executive order.

"There is no simple procedural mechanism for this," I tell Sarah. "The process and style for amending language in the Constitution have remained the same for more than two hundred years. It's not like a statute or bill passed by Congress. There, the language that is repealed or amended is stricken from the codebooks and no longer appears in print after a short time following its amendment. On the other hand, words repealed from the Constitution will always remain in print as part of the document, even though they may no longer be enforced and are dead-letter law."

Sarah thinks about this for a moment, then starts to read again.

"According to the story, it says here, 'Now, with a spotlight cast on them for all to see, the offending words of slavery fester like some open wound, threatening to give rise to race riots unseen in the nation since the 1960s.'"

She looks at me. "Do you really think that could happen?"

"I hope not, but there's already been violence. Mr. Scarborough and his book stirred up a hornet's nest."

"But wasn't that the purpose of his book? Social justice?" she says. "According to political theory, what I'm reading now, violence is sometimes the price that has to be paid. Jefferson said—"

"I know. 'The tree of liberty must be refreshed from time to time, with the blood of patriots and tyrants.'"

"You read that?" she says.

"Many years ago."

* * *

As it turns out, her interest is sufficiently piqued that when I set forth the following morning headed for Richard Bonguard's office, Sarah is with me. She says she will not utter a word. She will sit in the corner like a mouse.

Sarah and I are in the back of a taxi stopped dead in traffic, the remnants of rush hour and the parking lot that is midtown Manhattan.

I warn her that Bonguard may not be friendly. He is, potentially at least, a hostile witness.

"Gee, you think, Dad?" Sarah looks at me, one eyebrow arched. "Your client did kill his cash cow."

"Is accused of killing," I correct her.

She ignores me. "Besides, I've never seen a literary agent before, so this is a first. Who knows, I may want to write a book someday. What was he like on the phone?"

"Businesslike and guarded," I tell her. Bonguard agreed to talk with me as much out of curiosity as anything else. From our brief conversation on the phone, it was clear. He is seeking a mutual exchange of information. "I suspect he wants to know whatever it is that I know."

"Like what?" asks Sarah.

"Mostly he wanted to know about Arnsberg—what he's like, his background. And of course the big enchilada—why he might want to kill Scarborough."

"Maybe *he's* planning on writing a book," says Sarah.

"Nothing would surprise me. Let's hope that's all it is."

"You worry too much," she says.

"I get paid to worry."

What has me worried in this case is that Bonguard, a close acquaintance of the victim, would normally be high on the list of possible prosecution witnesses. The cops would be all over him, urging him not to talk to the defense and, if he does, to pump us for as much information as possible. Talking with him could be tantamount to a conference call with the cops.

"He's probably just curious," says Sarah.

"Let's hope so."

"So what are you going to tell him?"

"As little as possible."

"What about this letter?" As it has with Harry's and mine, the mystery letter mentioned by Bonguard on Leno has captured Sarah's interest.

"All I know is what he said on television."

"But the police must have checked it out?" she says. "They must know something."

"If they do, they aren't sharing it with us. Besides, there's a certain dynamic to a case like this, once the cops start to focus on a suspect. And they arrested ours—"

"Yours," she says.

"Mine." I smile at her. "They arrested Arnsberg very early on. In that kind of a situation, where they focus early on one suspect, unless there's an alibi—the suspect was somewhere else at the time of the killing and can prove it—or some other hard evidence that points away from their suspect, the cops can be very myopic. Shortsighted," I say.

"Dad, I know what 'myopic' means."

"Sorry. I keep forgetting you're not a kid anymore."

The taxi takes a right, and we head down one of the less-congested cross streets toward the East River. Here we are surrounded on both sides by well-manicured multistoried brownstones. The cab pulls up in front of one of these and stops. We step out, and I pay the driver.

I check the address against the note I'd taken during my telephone conversation with Bonguard. "This is it." I had been expecting a commercial high-rise.

There are baskets of colorful hanging flowers adorning the wrought-iron trellis that arches over the doorway at the top of the stairs. The small-paned windows are framed by neatly painted green wooden shutters, the paint glossy and fresh. Sarah and I head up the steps. On the door a small brass plate announces:

BONGUARD & ASSOCIATES
Talent and Literary Agents

I ring the bell, and an instant later a buzzer unlocks the door, so I push it open, and we enter. Inside is a large vestibule, polished hardwood floors, and solid millwork, a heavy beamed ceiling. Dark mahogany banisters flank a curved stairway leading to the upper floors in what was once an impressive private home.

Set back and off to one side is a small Louis XV desk, dark enamel and gold leaf. Seated behind it, a pretty young woman is talking on the phone.

"I'll give him the message. I'm sure he will get back to you as soon as he can." She hangs up, makes a quick note, and then looks up at us. "Can I help you?"

"We have an appointment with Mr. Bonguard. Paul Madriani." I hand her a business card. She takes the card and glances down at a calendar in front of her.

"Just a moment." She picks up the telephone receiver and pushes two buttons on the desk set, waits a couple of seconds, and then, to a voice on the other end, says, "A Mr. Madriani here to see you. Your ten o'clock. Yes." She hangs up. "Someone will be right with you. Please have a seat." She points toward a Louis XV sofa that is fitted into the curving wall supporting the staircase. The couch is one of those antiques with fluffed-up pillows the air from which will dissipate the moment you look at it.

Between planes and taxis over the last two days, we have been sitting for a long time, so we elect to mill around studying the artwork.

"Can I get you some coffee, a soft drink?" the receptionist asks.

I look at Sarah. She shakes her head. "I'm fine."

"We're fine," I tell her.

We spend five minutes checking out the prints on the walls, copies of early Manhattan landscapes, sailing ships in the harbor, and Wall Street when the stone wall it was named for was still in place. I am beginning to wonder whether Sarah is regretting that she didn't go shopping.

Finally I hear footsteps on the landing overhead. They move quickly down the stairs. When I turn to look up, I see the face I saw on Leno, a little thinner than I remember on the tube.

"Mr. Madriani." He holds out his hand as he reaches the bottom step. "Richard Bonguard." He is younger and a little taller than he appeared on television, and his smile is broad. If he retains any reticence regarding our meeting, he covers it well.

I take his hand, and we shake. "Good to meet you." We pass a few pleasantries until he realizes that there is someone behind him, standing in his shadow. "This is my daughter, Sarah." He turns to look, takes her hand, and shakes it as well.

"So do you practice with your father?"

"No. No. Just on vacation," she says.

"Oh, good, then it's not all business." He smiles, large and buoyant, an affable soul. We talk about the trip, the endless hassle that is now American air travel. Finally he motions us toward a set of double doors off the entry hall. "We can talk in here. Janice, maybe you can bring us some coffee. What would you like?"

"Just some water," I tell him.

"Bottled water, Janice."

He asks Sarah, and she begs off again.

He leads us through some double doors, what used to be the front parlor, now a sizable conference room with a large oval table in the center ringed by comfortable executive leather chairs. "Have a seat, wherever you want."

Bonguard settles into the chair at the small curve of the oval, the head of the table to my left. Sarah and I take the two closest chairs, our backs to the door, Bonguard to my left and Sarah on my right.

"Is this the first time you've been to New York?" Bonguard asks her.

"No. I've been here twice before. But I was pretty young."

"Then you have to stick around for a while and enjoy the city. Tell your dad to hold over for a few days, and I'll get you some Broadway tickets," he says.

"That would be great." Sarah's ready to put the arm on me.

"I wish we could. Unfortunately, business calls." I am the ogre.

"I regret that we have to meet under these circumstances," he says.

"I agree. I do appreciate your willingness to talk with me."

"Oh. No problem," he says. "Why not? After all, you're just doing your job. I can't imagine how I can possibly help you, but ask away."

I know that the cops have already talked to him. This was reflected in the investigator's notes immediately following the murder. They caught up with Bonguard before he could leave San Diego. I mention this.

"Yes, I talked to them," he says. "Not that I wouldn't have cooperated, but they didn't give me much choice. They threatened—" He stops, thinks for a moment. "'Threatened' may be too strong a word. They intimated that they might be compelled to name me as 'a person of interest' with the press if I didn't tell them everything I knew."

A fact that of course was not in the investigator's notes.

This, according to Bonguard, was because he was the last person to see Scarborough alive, except for the killer.

"You can imagine what that would have done to my business," he says. "Half my clients would have bailed on me before morning."

I am packing a subpoena for Bonguard to appear at trial. It is in my coat pocket. Depending on what he says here, it may or may not stay there.

"It was fortunate for you that the police landed on Carl Arnsberg so quickly," I say.

"One person's misery is another's relief," he says. "But so that there's no misunderstanding, I have no problem talking with you. I talked to the police, I'll talk to you. Fair is fair," he says. "So how can I help you?"

"I suppose you knew Mr. Scarborough as well as anyone. Do you know anyone who might have wanted to kill him?"

"Besides your client, you mean?"

"My client had no reason to kill Mr. Scarborough."

"Of course." He smiles at me. "Well, as to the issue of potential suspects, you might say that you have an embarrassment of riches. As you may have guessed by now, Terry was a man who went out of his way to collect enemies, most of them anonymous.

I'm told that more than a little of his fan mail included death threats, though I suspect that most of these were from cranks who had no intention of carrying them out. Still, it may be grist for your mill," he says. "As for me, the long and short of it is, I don't have a clue as to who killed Terry or why. If you don't mind my asking, why are the police saying your man did it?"

"Based purely on circumstantial evidence that places him in the hotel room at the wrong time," I tell him.

"That's it?"

"As far as I know."

"I have to assume they have something to go on. Of course, I make no judgments," he adds.

"Good. Do you mind if I take a few notes?"

"Not at all. Let me ask you," he says. "Have you talked to your client about the possibility of a book?"

I take out a small notebook and pen from the inside pocket of my coat. "No."

"You might want to think about getting the rights," he says. "Depending on what happens, the level of publicity." He's looking at me from across the table over the top of his coffee cup. "From what I see in the papers, he doesn't have a lot of money. It could help in defraying your fees."

"I'll think about it."

"You should," he says. "And feel free to call me if you need any help."

"You said that except for the killer you were the last person to see Mr. Scarborough alive?"

"As far as I know."

"Do you recall arriving at Scarborough's hotel room that morning?"

He nods.

"Did you let yourself into the room, or did Mr. Scarborough let you in?"

"I didn't have a key. He had to let me in."

"The door wasn't open?"

"No."

"Did you try it?"

"Why would I do that? It was a hotel room. They're always locked."

"But you didn't push on it to find out, or turn the doorknob?"

"No. I told you."

"And when you left the room, after your meeting with Mr. Scarborough, do you recall, did he accompany you to the door, or did you let yourself out?"

On this he ponders for a moment. "As I recall, he had finished up shaving, in the bathroom. We talked. He was tired, said he wanted to get some rest. You know, I can't remember, but I think I let myself out."

"Can you recall when you left, did you hear the door close behind you?"

"I don't know. How do you remember something like that? You realize that the cops asked me the same question. Why is it important?"

"I'm sure they did." I don't answer his question.

"Are you sure that it latched all the way closed?"

"I didn't check it, if that's what you mean."

"Did you hear it close?"

"I can't remember. I wasn't paying that much attention. Sometimes I check my own door when I'm staying in a hotel, but I don't usually check anybody else's."

"Can you tell me what the two of you talked about, you and Scarborough in your last meeting?"

"What do authors and agents always

talk about? Book sales, how his tour was going. The usual," he says.

"As I recall, Scarborough's book was doing pretty well at that time."

"'Well' is an understatement," says Bonguard. "It was flying off the shelves. It's high on the bestseller list even now. I believe Terry would be astounded that the book is doing so well even after his death."

"Perhaps *because* of the death and the controversy surrounding it?" I say.

"It's possible. When it comes to books, controversy usually sells."

"Was there any talk of a follow-up book?"

He smiles at me. "You saw the tape of Leno. Yes, he was preparing to write another book."

"Based on the historic letter you mentioned during your interview with Leno?"

"That's what he told me. You have to understand that at the time of the Leno appearance I was still trying to flog the current book. I was standing in for Terry. He was supposed to have appeared on the show the night he was killed. You can't believe everything you hear on television," he says.

"So you're saying there was no letter?"

"No, I'm not saying that. It's just that it was the last chance we were going to have to push sales. You know how it is?"

"And the letter?"

Before he can answer, the door behind me opens. It's the secretary with a tray bearing a carafe of coffee, three cups, and accoutrements—sugar, cream, teaspoons —and two bottles of water.

He pours himself a cup of coffee—black, no sugar. I take one of the bottled waters and look at Sarah. She declines. "I'm waiting to hear about the letter," she says.

"So you're a history buff?" Bonguard turns the question on her.

"I like history. Better yet, I like a good mystery."

"Well, there was a letter, at least that's what Terry told me. He led me to believe he was holding it for a sequel. With books as with most things in life, when you're successful, it's always good to have a second act."

"So he had this letter in his possession?" I make a note.

"What he said was that he had a copy.

Mind you, I never saw it. Whatever he had, he was keeping it close to the vest. Now, let me ask you a question," he says. "Did the police find such a letter when they searched Terry's apartment? Or in the hotel room?"

I shake my head. "Not according to their notes and the list of items they seized."

"I'm not a lawyer," he says, "but I assume that if they found it, a letter like this, it is something they would have to disclose to you?"

"Assuming they knew its significance, yes."

"And by now they would know its significance?" he asks.

Bonguard may not be a lawyer, but he knows the rules of the road when it comes to discovery. I nod. "By now they would know."

Harry and I have nailed the state's feet to the floor over the issue of any missing letters. If they are holding back, it would have dire consequences for their case at trial, creating prosecutorial misconduct that even if they can get a conviction could bury them on appeal.

It is now clear why Bonguard has agreed to talk to me. He wants to know where the letter is.

"And I suppose they didn't find it on your client when they arrested him?" he asks.

"No."

"One point for your side." He settles back in his chair again and runs one hand through his blond hair while he thinks.

"If all he had was a copy, wouldn't that be problematic, assuming he tried to publish based on it?" I ask.

"You mean authentication?" says Bonguard.

I nod.

"That's true. A publisher could be taking a real chance going forward with a book unless the letter could be established as authentic."

"And without the original there's no way to analyze the paper and ink."

"Right. And as you know, handwriting can be copied, and it's hard to be sure sometimes, experts all disagreeing," he says. "Before you know it, people are crying fraud and the author is looking at jail time."

A few years earlier, it was all over the

media and in the press. An antiquarian dealer claimed that he had discovered multiple volumes of Hitler's handwritten diaries, all of which were scrupulously maintained, a veritable storehouse of the dictator's most intimate thoughts during the war. It was a treasure trove, except for one little thing: The entire collection was a modern forgery.

"So a copy would be useless for purposes of publication?"

"In point of fact," he says. "But political wacko though he may have been, Terry was nobody's fool, especially when it came to money. He may have been an avowed socialist at heart, but when it came to book sales, he was a capitalist through and through. What he said was that he knew where the original letter was. What's more, he knew someone who could get it for him."

"Did he say who?"

Bonguard shakes his head. "I asked him, but he wasn't talking."

"Do you have any idea who it might be?"

"Only guesses."

"Would you like to share them?"

Bonguard gives me a face, a little shrug

of the shoulder. Now that he knows neither I nor the cops have the letter, he is becoming more reticent. I move on.

"Scarborough makes no reference to the letter in *Perpetual Slaves*?" Both Harry and I have scoured Scarborough's book from cover to cover and found no reference to any secret letter.

"No. It was a conscious decision not to include it in this book," says Bonguard. What is more interesting here is what Bonguard doesn't say. He doesn't tell me what he told the cops, that the so-called J letter was the impetus, the driving force that caused Scarborough to write *Perpetual Slaves* in the first place. Why? For the moment I leave it alone. I don't ask him.

"Could it be that whoever had the original of the letter didn't want to release it to him?" I ask.

"Could be," says Bonguard. "Or it could be, knowing Terry, that he wanted to fan the flames of discontent with *Perpetual Slaves* and throw more fuel onto the fire later with the letter. That would be his style. And the letter wasn't necessary to the sales of *Perpetual Slaves*. He had roused the masses with the revelation that the language of slavery remained in the Constitution. For Terry that was the first blow. I got the sense the letter was the clincher. According to Terry, the letter would have blown the top off of things."

"Do you know who wrote the letter, the original author?"

"Not with certainty. As I say, I never saw it."

"Do you know when it was supposed to have been written?"

"Terry never said, though he referred to it cryptically on a few occasions."

"Cryptically?"

"Alphabetically," says Bonguard. "He called it the 'J letter.'"

"J?"

"You can form your own conclusions. If you work from a list of the politically prominent at the time that the framers crafted the Constitution, your list becomes very short fairly quickly."

"Jefferson?" I ask.

"Or John Jay. There are a couple of others. But Jefferson would get my vote," says Bonguard. "At the time the Constitution was being written, Jefferson was in Paris serving as American ambassador. This would account for the fact that he would be compelled to reduce any thoughts to writing. We know there was considerable correspondence between Jefferson and others back in the States at the time. We also know his position on slavery, at least his public position. He is on record as favoring abolition. Yet at the time he was one of the biggest slave owners in Virginia. You might call him ambivalent on the subject, since his words and his actions were a bit at odds. He vowed to free his slaves during his lifetime but never did. Economics, it seems, always got in the way."

"My American history is a little rusty," I tell him.

"He's right, Dad," Sarah chimes in.

"I'm not a history buff either," says Bonguard. "But when you have a client bringing in the kind of money Terry was and he mentions a letter as a basis for another book, you tend to do a little research."

"Any idea as to who this letter was directed to?" I ask.

"Your guess would be as good as mine. Terry never said."

"Do you have any idea as to the monetary value of this letter?" I ask.

"Umm . . ." He looks at me with a dull gaze as if suddenly I've jumped the tracks on him. He thinks for a moment. "Assuming it's authentic, that it's never seen the light of day, publicly at least, I have to assume that it would be worth a good deal to collectors."

"And how do we define 'a good deal' in the literary antiquities market?" I ask.

Bonguard smiles at me. "I'm certainly no expert on the value of historic correspondence. But assuming all your assumptions are correct, it would go at auction, one of a kind. And if it's as explosive as Terry suggested, my guess is it would be worth multiple millions, perhaps. I don't know. Given a good airing with a bestselling book as Terry was intending, that would drive the price very high."

"So that would make whoever possessed this letter quite wealthy," I say.

"Umm . . ." He sips his coffee, studying me over the brim of the cup. "I know what you're thinking," he says. "People have killed for less. Except for one thing. If Terry was to be believed, he only had a copy of the letter. That in itself was worthless un-less it could be authenticated."

"Maybe the killer didn't know that," I say.

He mulls this for a moment. "That's pos-sible. If you can sell it to a jury." He smiles again.

"You have no idea how Mr. Scarborough may have gotten his copy of the letter?"

He looks at his watch. "Your dozen questions are about up," he says. "I have a meeting in a couple of minutes. I don't know how he got his copy of the letter. He didn't tell me."

"Do you have any guesses?"

"It's only conjecture," he says. "And don't say that it came from here, but Terry had a girlfriend. An on-again, off-again thing. I believe it was off when he was killed, since they hadn't seen each other in a while. The woman's name is Trisha Scott. She's a high-powered lawyer with one of the big firms in D.C. Terry met her when she was clerking for the Supreme Court. She was just out of law school, quite a bit younger than he was. If I had to guess as to a source for the letter, I would start there."

"Why is that?"

"Because this whole thing, the idea of writing *Perpetual Slaves,* seems to have had its genesis about the time that Terry picked up with Scott. That and other things," he says.

"What other things?"

"His interest in Arthur Ginnis, the justice that Scott clerked for. Do you know him?"

"I know *of* him, naturally. Never met him. Supreme Court justices and lowly trial lawyers live and operate in different legal universes," I tell him.

"Well, Ginnis isn't exactly the sort that I would expect to take up with Terry. I know Ginnis only slightly. I've met him twice. No"—he thinks for a moment—"actually, it was three times. Anyway, I was introduced to him by his wife, Margaret. She's a lovely woman. For a while she was a client. I met her in New York at a political function. She was publishing a fascinating cookbook. The woman has a positive flair for finding an unusual niche and marketing it. *The Favored Dishes of the High Court*—that was the name of her book. She did a sequel and went historical on the next one, *Meals from Marshall to Warren.* That one didn't do as well.

"She actually got Justice Scalia to pose for the cover on the first one, smiling with a toothpick in the corner of his mouth. Do you know Scalia?"

I shake my head again.

"Actually, I don't know him either, only by reputation. But I'm told that even if you don't agree with him politically— And I don't," he says. "I'm hoping for better things following the election. Still there's one thing that everyone agrees on. Scalia, like his politics or not, is the wit on the Court. Man has an incredible sense of humor. And sharp as a knife, if you know what I mean. Margaret's book wasn't *The South Beach Diet,* but in its market it did very well."

And it never hurts to do business, even at the fringes, with the influential, names you can drop if you're sniffing on the trail of a lawyer for a book deal following a hot trial, for example.

"You were talking about Justice Ginnis?"

"Oh, yes. Affable man," he says, "engaging, politically to the left of center. But his chief claim to fame is that he can swing from the middle. I'm no Court watcher, but lawyers here in town tell me that at the moment he holds the balance of power on the Court. The word is that if you want five votes on anything controversial that's before the Court, you will have to get Mr. Justice Ginnis."

"Maybe Scarborough was trying to woo him politically," I say.

Bonguard shakes his head and rises from his chair. "Terry had given up on the Court long ago. He was as far out on the left wing as you can get without falling off. There were those who knew him who would say he'd already tumbled. He was living in a fantasy world of rebellion and revolution, dreaming of impeachments that would never happen. Terry was not someone that Ginnis would take to—or for that matter would want to be seen talking with."

"But you're saying that they did talk."

"Do yourself a favor and talk to Trisha Scott. I have a feeling she knows more than I do."

The meeting is over. He ushers us toward

the door, chatting sociably with Sarah, about her major in college, what she wants to do when she graduates. As we pass through the door, he shakes my hand one last time and turns to head toward the stairs. Then, as if lightning has struck him in the brain, he suddenly turns back toward me.

"Could you do me one favor?" he says. "If you find the letter, the copy or the original, could you give me a call and let me know?"

"Why is that?"

"I'm curious as to what it says. Terry would never let me look at it. I might also be interested in getting a publishing deal for the contents, perhaps in book form, maybe around the context of the trial and Terry's death. It could be a good story. Who knows, it might even help your client."

"If I find it, I'll give you a call."

The code words of slavery in the Constitution may have fired Scarborough's rhetoric and made him rich, but his book, his smoke-belching antics on the stump, and the violence that ensued had their genesis in some other, more startling and subterranean force. And unless I miss my bet, that hidden volcano is somewhere in the pages of what Bonguard is now referring to as the Jefferson Letter.

FOUR

At the airport, my trip from JFK in New York to Reagan International in D.C., I do the TSA drill to get through security. Partially disrobing, I take off my shoes and pull my belt from my pants as everyone in line does calisthenics with luggage in plastic boxes.

Harry has talked about forming a new airline and calling it Amistad Air. Harry's idea is to cut through the marketing hype and achieve the ultimate goal of every American carrier: to stack human cargo on planes like cordwood, using historic schematics of old slave ships. According to Harry, if fuel prices continue to climb, they'll be putting out oars and telling us all to pull.

In the midst of this chaos, Sarah and I part company, she on a flight home to San Diego while I head to D.C. I am chasing the grail, Bonguard's musings that Scarborough's mystery letter or at least some thread leading to it might be found in Washington.

I have placed three calls to the law offices of Barrett, Coal & Johnston on K Street in an effort to arrange a meeting with Trisha Scott, Scarborough's former girlfriend. She has failed to return my calls, so I'm taking a shot that I can track her down before heading home, that maybe she will talk to me.

Time is running out on us. Next week Harry and I are in court on pretrial motions trying to keep evidence linking Carl Arnsberg to Scarborough's murder away from the jury. Most of this is a long shot. Still, it is necessary, both for trial as well as for any appeal should he be convicted.

At trial it is the nature of the game to dot every i and cross every t. Anything omitted is conceded to the prosecution, lost to us forever. We are now less than a month from trial, and our theories of defense are thin. What is worse, they're shifting, an ominous sign this late.

With physical evidence connecting Arnsberg to the scene, with no alibi, and with an apparent motive, I have been forced to consider the defenses of last resort, diminished capacity or possible insanity. These are inevitably a hard sell to any jury. Besides, I have had my client examined by experts, shrinks who know their stuff, and the tea leaves are not good. While Arnsberg claims to possess blanks in his memory immediately following the trauma of the murder scene, his story is always the same, that Scarborough's dead body and the blood were already there when he arrived in the room. His lapses of memory all come afterward. He cannot recall touching the hammer, according to the police the murder weapon. He can't account for how his palm print became superimposed in the victim's blood on the floor. He does remember entering the room, for which he did not have a passkey. According to Arnsberg, the door was ajar, so that when he pushed, it opened.

According to the theory advanced by the cops, Scarborough let him in, since it is established that he ordered breakfast, only to turn his back, take a seat, and be murdered.

Without evidence of another person at the scene and some overriding motive for this phantom to have murdered Scarborough, the classic SODDI defense—"some other dude did it"—is a long shot. For this reason the lure of the missing letter and its potential value has opened the possibility, fleeting as it may be. So I pursue it.

* * *

My flight lands in D.C. midmorning. Early September, eleven-thirty, and the day is beginning to heat up. I make my way to what is known by locals as Gucci Gulch, the concrete canyon that is K Street in the nation's capital. Here high-rise offices house some of the most powerful lawyers and deal makers on earth. Twenty years ago they reveled in publicity. Books celebrated them as the "superlawyers," until politicians, always anxious to keep the spotlight on themselves, painted the bull's-eye of reform on their ass. Ever since, the goal has been to remain invisible, like the mob.

Law firms with two and three hundred partners are not unusual here, sometimes with offices in Singapore, London, Beijing, and Paris. These give new meaning to the term "global economy," peddling power and influence around the world. Every politician running for office runs from these firms, except at milking time, when lobbyists jerking on the udders of the industries they represent fill pails with campaign dollars that are quietly shuttled down K Street by bucket brigades of congressional staff and hired consultants.

I have read that the Jefferson Monument is slowly sinking, settling into the ancient swamp that is now dubbed the Tidal Basin. This may be symbolic of the visionary who dreamed of America as an agricultural utopia and whom history has shown to have been so badly beaten by his nemesis, Hamilton, who favored a commercial and industrial nation run by money managers and corporate markets.

A major chunk of the business done from K Street is lobbying, hustling the 535 members of the Congress, the Senate with its legions of staff, and the hundreds of administrative agencies that crank out regulations governing everything from milk price supports to Social Security. It has long been known that if you want to talk, you go to Congress. If you want something done, you go to K Street.

The men who crafted the Constitution must be doing wheelies in their graves. To the eighteenth-century mind in the Age of Reason, an American government obsessed with controlling every aspect of individual existence, with its hands in every pocket up to its national armpits, would be a greater source of terror than the atom bomb. Had they known, the Bill of Rights would not have ended with ten amendments. It would be a perpetual work in progress with periodic political lynchings made part of the fabric of government.

The cab drops me in front of a smoked-glass high-rise. I pay the cabbie, and a minute later I'm in the air-conditioned lobby, leaving the oppressive humidity of Washington outside. I check the building's directory. Barrett, Coal & Johnston takes up the top three floors of the twelve-story office building. Those entering have to clear security at a desk in order to access the elevators.

As I edge across the lobby toward the main desk, I feel the vibration at my belt. I take out my cell phone. It's Harry. I flip it open.

"Hello."

"Where are you?" says Harry.

"In D.C. The law office," I tell him. From our telephone conversation last night, Harry already knows where I'm headed and why.

"Then I caught you before you found this Scott woman?"

"Yes. Why?"

"If you catch up with her, press her on Ginnis," says Harry.

"Any particular reason?"

"I'm still digging for all the details," says Harry, "but it's starting to look like Ginnis could be the lead to the letter."

"Can you give me specifics?"

"Not right now," says Harry. "Trust me. Just see if you can find some way to get to him. But call me before you talk to him. By then I should have more information."

"You got it," I tell him.

"Talk to you later." Harry hangs up.

Juggling my briefcase in one hand, I pocket my phone and hand the guard at the desk one of my business cards. I tell him I have an appointment with Trisha Scott at B, C & J. This lie gets me a phone call to reception upstairs. Four minutes later I am treated to the officious click of heels on the hard terrazzo. A woman, blond, blue-eyed, in her late twenties, dressed in a dark business suit. She collects my card from the guard and approaches.

"Mr. Madre . . ."

"Madriani," I help her out.

"I understand you have an appointment with Ms. Scott?" The lilt in her voice leads me to think that she has already searched Scott's calendar and not found my name on it.

"I called twice and left messages. I was in New York on my way back to my office in California and wanted to stop in and see her. It would only take a moment and would save us both an immense amount of time."

"Does she know what it regards?"

"It's a personal matter. I'm sure that if she knew the details, she would want to see me."

This stumps her. She looks at my card

again: "attorney-at-law." If it said "sales-
man," I'd be out on the street looking back
through the glass by now.

"If you'll follow me," she says. "I'm not
sure whether Ms. Scott is in."

We head to the elevator. A minute and a
half later, I've made it to the next level, the
reception area upstairs. Here there are
deep plush carpets and floor-to-ceiling
windows of smoked glass with shaded
views out over the city. Across the street
lies Farragut Square. One block beyond
lies the squat Roman temple that is the
U.S. Chamber of Commerce building. Over
the top and beyond is Lafayette Square,
and in the distance behind the park is the
White House. Toward the southeast the
Capitol dome sprouts like a half-hatched
Easter egg in the noonday sun. The executive offices of Barrett, Coal & Johnston
possess an eagle's-nest view of all the
power spots in town.

"If you'll take a seat," she says, "I will
check with Ms. Scott's assistant."

As the phalanx of gatekeepers grows,
the mesh of their screen becomes finer. I
may be wasting my time. By now Scott
would surely be following the news reports

of Arnsberg's trial. If so, she will have seen my name. What I am banking on is her curiosity. A lawyer, she would know that I could subpoena her to the trial, put her on a witness list, and let her cool her heels. What is more difficult would be to get her to talk to me. If she refuses, there is little I can do, and to put her on the stand at trial and ask questions to which I do not already know the answers would be its own form of Russian roulette.

The receptionist disappears to the back behind the large ebony reception counter and the mirrored glass wall separating me from the firm's engine room, where power is spun into gold.

Barrett, Coal & Johnston is sufficiently large that to dispense separate business cards for the many partners and associates out on the counter would require a vending machine. Instead there's a glossy brochure that outlines the firm's services and specialties. I pull one of these and take a look. To no one's surprise, the firm is heavily invested in regulatory law, with a sideline in patents and appellate practice, all keyed toward business and commerce.

The firm sports two former United

States senators as "of counsel," a kind of emeritus status in which work is often not required, only the name engraved on a brass plaque on a door. The firm claims association with three former Harvard fellows, professors of law. One of these is nationally known and appears with sufficient regularity before the Supreme Court that I have heard legal pundits sometimes refer to him as "the tenth member of the Court."

The last three pages of the brochure are taken up with fine print, the names of partners and associates. Many of these are followed by asterisks and other symbols, all keyed to honors and awards. I find Scott's name and after it a symbol in the form of a small dagger. I check the code: "former U.S. Supreme Court clerk." I do a quick count of these. I am beyond two dozen and counting when I'm interrupted.

"Mr. Madriani." I turn to see a different woman. Clear hazel eyes. She holds my card in her left hand as she extends her right toward me. "Trisha Scott," she says. "I'm told you have some personal business to discuss?"

She is blond, her hair cropped in a kind

of pixie cut that gives her tall, slender body a fairy-tale elegance. Her face is angular, bearing a becoming smile. She reminds me of a taller version of Meg Ryan, a kind of bewitching look that asks questions even in silence.

"How do you do?" I take her hand, just the fingertips, and give it a gentle shake as she continues to study my card. "I'm sorry to bother you. I suspect you're busy, but I wanted to talk with you before I headed back to the Coast."

"Will it take long? I only have a few minutes," she says.

"That'll be fine." Anything to get my foot in the door.

"How can I help you?" She wants to do it here, standing at the reception desk.

I glance over my shoulder toward the receptionist. "Is there somewhere we can talk in private?"

"My office," she says.

I follow her past reception and down a long corridor with offices on each side. Here the paneled mahogany walls are adorned with colonial lithographs elegantly framed and set off by small brass-covered museum lights. This is the "holy of holies," province of former senators and senior partners, where most of the offices are double-doored with occasional cubicles carved into the elegance for minions, the obligatory personal assistant or executive secretary.

She leads me to another elevator, this one small and private. We descend one floor and exit into a rabbit warren of cubicles, clerical and other assistants in the center. Around these are arranged offices on the outside walls, where windows with views and natural light are the perks of junior partners and associates on the move, either up or out.

From the exterior appearance, these offices are not nearly as elegant as those on the level above. Still, they are large, judging by the distance between doors. Enough room to accommodate a good-size desk, filing cabinets, probably a credenza against the windows, and a view.

Halfway down the corridor, she turns to the right and enters an open office door. I follow her.

We are no sooner inside than she closes the door behind me. "San Diego," she says, still looking at my card. "I recognize your name. You're the lawyer representing the man who killed Terry." Her countenance is less pleasant now.

"Carl Arnsberg. He stands accused," I say.

"Of course. I don't see how I can help you, but have a seat." She offers me one of the client chairs across from her desk. The office is neat, not large, but there's that view, what must be toward the west, as I can see a plane descending into what I assume is Dulles International in the distance.

She settles into the chair behind the desk, crosses one leg over the other, her hands set securely on the arms of the chair as if she were about to take a ride. "I figured sooner or later someone would show up. I pictured an investigator, not the lead defense counsel," she says.

"I was in New York. I looked at our list of possible witnesses as well as those the state might call, and your name popped up," I tell her.

"Why would you want to call me—as a witness, I mean?"

"I don't know that I do."

"I see. The police did talk to me. An

investigator from San Diego. That was about . . ." She thinks for a moment, then riffles some pages on her desk calendar. "About two months ago now. What took you so long?" she asks.

I could say it was the absence of a good defense theory, but I don't. "Can you tell me what they wanted to talk about?"

"Hmm?"

"The cops."

"Oh." She smiles. "Three guesses, and the first two don't count," she tells me.

"Your relationship with Scarborough."

She nods. "Were we lovers?" she says. "I told them what I'm telling you, that the bloom was already off that particular rose. At one time we were what you might call an item, but that ended more than a year ago. I've been seeing other men, and I assume that Terry had someone else. We were still friends. I saw him occasionally at social events. We ran in the same circles. But that was all."

"So you weren't seeing each other at the time he was killed?"

"No."

"Do you mind telling me how the two of you met?"

She has to think about this. "I believe it was at a dinner. A judicial affair, the circuit court if I remember right. That must have been three or four years ago now. Someone introduced us. One thing led to another, Terry called me up, and we started seeing each other."

"You dated? How long?"

"What is this, a sequel to the Kinsey Report?"

"I have to think the cops would have asked," I tell her.

"We lived together for a while. We had an apartment in Georgetown. It wasn't much. Given Terry's traveling schedule, he was never there. You have to understand that with Terry there was only one person who mattered in life, and that was Terry. The live-in thing lasted about seven months. In the end I decided that living alone in Terry's apartment wasn't what I had in mind. I found other people, another life. So I moved out and got my own place. That's the long and short of it."

"No angry words? No late-night disagreements?"

She shakes her head. "I can give you the address, and you can check with the neighbors if you like," she says. "The parting was quite amicable. I left. When Terry got back from his latest fling on Court TV or CNN or whatever it was, I was gone. Simple as that. Sorry to disappoint," she says. "No big blowup, if that's what you're thinking. I sometimes wondered when he returned whether Terry even noticed that I was gone. That was Terry." She smiles. "You had to love him. I guess you could say the relationship just sort of ran its course. In the end we simply went our separate ways. There's a lot of that in this town, politics and human ambition being what they are."

"And when was this parting of the ways?"

"About a year ago. We still talked every once in a while."

"When was the last time?"

"That we talked?"

I nod.

"I'd have to think." She does. "It must have been last Christmas." She toys with the fingers of one hand at the arm of the chair. "Yes, it was Christmas. We had some mutual friends who'd invited us to a Christmas party. I don't think they'd gotten the word that we weren't living together any longer. Terry got the invitation and wanted to know what to do with it. He called me, and we talked for a while."

"Mind if I ask what you talked about?"

"What do two former live-ins talk about? The weather, our health, mutual friends we've seen . . ."

"Did you happen to discuss Justice Ginnis?"

With the mention of his name, she looks up directly at me. "No. Not that I recall."

"You did clerk for him?"

"Yes."

"I'd been told that Mr. Scarborough and he were friends."

She laughs at this. "I don't know who you've been talking to or what you've been reading, but they weren't friends. I mean, they knew each other. They were acquainted, but they operated in different orbits. Terry was a hanger-on around the Court. Arthur Ginnis is the genuine article, a member of the Court."

"That's funny."

"Why?"

"I'd gotten the sense that they were quite close, that in fact Justice Ginnis may have been the impetus for Mr. Scarborough's book."

"You mean *Perpetual Slaves*?"

I nod.

"That's ridiculous."

"That's what I heard."

She sits upright in her chair, hands gripping the arms until her knuckles turn white. "I don't know who told you that," she says. "But I can say with certainty that Arthur—Justice Ginnis—had nothing to do with that book, and in fact he believed that the entire concept of dredging up dead-letter law from the Constitution and using it in that way was, in a word, despicable. It would have been an embarrassment for him. A sitting Supreme Court justice. No. It was part of the reason he distanced himself from Terry. He was concerned about Terry's lust for publicity. The fact that Terry was constantly on television, flogging his books and trying to pretend that he was some kind of a Court insider, when he wasn't."

As I listen to Scott, she confirms one of Harry's witticisms: that there are two classes of people who wield immense power and who shun the public light—

mobsters if they have a brain and members of the Supreme Court.

"Do you know how the two of them met, Scarborough and Ginnis?" I ask.

"As a matter of fact, I do. I introduced them. I don't know if they'd ever actually spoken before that. It was at a reception when I was clerking. At the time I didn't fully understand why Justice Ginnis was so reticent. But he was gracious. Arthur is always the gentleman. Terry was my date. They shook hands and talked. Briefly," she says. "Why is all of this so important?"

"I'm looking for information regarding a letter that belonged to Mr. Scarborough. Actually, I don't know if it was his or if he was just borrowing it."

"A letter. What letter?"

"It could be an important historical piece, correspondence dating back to the time of the Constitution, late eighteenth century. I'm told that Scarborough had this letter in his possession when he was killed."

"Go on." There's a look in her eyes. Perhaps it's the way they're darting at the moment, taking in everything in the room except me.

"It's possible that the police found it.

Except for one thing: It hasn't shown up on any of the lists of evidence that they've produced. You wouldn't know anything about it? This letter, I mean?"

"No."

"Well, you lived with Scarborough for a while. I thought maybe you might have seen it?"

"Oh, I understand. No. I don't know anything about a letter."

"Then I guess you wouldn't know whether Scarborough might have obtained it from Justice Ginnis?"

"What? What makes you think that?" she says.

"Some people think he might have gotten the letter from the justice."

"Who?"

"Some people," I tell her. "But since you don't know anything about the letter, perhaps you would know how I might get ahold of Justice Ginnis? While I'm here in Washington, that is."

"Why would you want to talk to him?"

"To see if he knows anything about the letter."

"Why is this letter so important? I mean,

what does it have to do with Terry's murder?"

"I'm not sure. But that's what I'd like to
find out."

"No!" This seems to light a spark, a point
of ignition deep inside her. "I'm sure there's
nothing he could possibly tell you—Justice
Ginnis. He wouldn't know anything about
any letter. He barely knew Terry. I think
they met only once or twice. At social functions. They hardly knew each other."

"Still. Is there any chance I could talk to
him? I figured you being a former clerk,
you might be able to open some doors for
me. Just a brief conversation is all I'm looking for. Five minutes of his time. I could
truck on over to the Supreme Court building alone. But getting through the phalanx
of marshals downstairs is another matter."

She laughs. "You're right. You wouldn't
get in."

"I suppose I could call over there, talk to
one of his clerks, mention the letter . . ."

"You'd be wasting your time," she says.
"I'll tell you what I will do. I can make a
phone call. But he's a very busy man. I really don't think he's going to appreciate

being bothered by all this. In fact, I'm not even sure he's in town. The Court's in recess, and Justice Ginnis is recuperating from hip surgery."

"I understand. But if you could check, make a phone call. Perhaps he'd agree to see me. Just a very brief conversation. I really would appreciate it."

She looks at the phone on her desk, then at me. "Where are you staying?" she asks.

"The Mayflower." I give her my cell-phone number in case I'm out when she calls.

"It'll take me a few minutes. I *am* busy this afternoon. But let me make a few phone calls. I'll get ahold of you either at your hotel or by cell. I wouldn't hold out much hope, though. Justice Ginnis is almost always out of town when the Court's in recess."

I thank her. She shows me back to the elevator, and five minutes later I'm standing on the hot concrete of the sidewalk waiting for a taxi.

FIVE

I had barely entered my hotel lobby when I felt the tickle from the vibrator on my cell phone at my belt.

"Hello."

"Mr. Madriani." The melodious tone of her voice was still in my brain from our meeting. "Trisha Scott here. I did as you asked. I called Justice Ginnis's chambers. As I suspected, he's out of town, on vacation. They didn't tell me precisely where. They never do. Just somewhere in the Caribbean."

"Did they say when he would be back?"

"No. But it will probably be a while. The Court doesn't reconvene until October, and as I told you, Arthur is recovering from some surgery, so he's on light duty. He may not be back immediately at the start of the session when they reconvene."

"You mean a member of the Court can be absent?"

"Sure, it happens. They just have to go with eight justices until the absent member returns."

"They can't have someone from the circuit court sit in?"

"No. Not on the Supreme Court. It's constitutional. No one can sit on the Supreme Court until nominated by the president and confirmed by the Senate. Arthur would have to step down, retire before that could happen. And if you knew Arthur, you'd know that isn't going to happen anytime soon, particularly in the current political climate."

Scott's talking about the current partisan division among members of the Court. Anyone who thinks that judges aren't political should buy a bridge or two. At the rarefied level of the Supreme Court, this doubles down in spades. There are justices who are thought to call the White House for direction on one side and powerful members of the Senate on the other before rendering an opinion on hot issues before the Court. Some would say that the situation has worsened in the last twenty years. Many of these are suffering from a lack of perspective when it comes to history. They forget that FDR threatened to amend the Constitution in order to pack the Court with more members to get his way on New Deal legislation back in the thirties.

"So what you're saying is that if I want to talk to him, I'm going to have to either wait or trek down to the Caribbean and try to find him?"

"That's about the size of it," she says. "But I'd like to suggest another alternative. That is, if you're in town overnight?"

"Currently I have a flight out tomorrow afternoon. I was going to extend it, if needed, in the event you could reach the Justice."

"Listen. How about dinner tonight?" she says. "I can show you some of the sights of the city. Also, there's something I need to tell you."

"What?"

"Over dinner," she says.

"All right."

"Then dinner at seven. I'll pick you up at your hotel. In the lobby, at six-thirty."

Before I can say anything more, she hangs up.

* * *

"I was a little abrupt this afternoon," she apologizes.

I'm looking at Trisha Scott through dim lamplight over a white linen tablecloth in a Georgetown restaurant called 1789, her pick since she's driving.

The unlit fireplace, partially covered by a summer-front, and the beamed ceiling give the décor a distinctive Colonial feel, though I'm told that the building is a nineteenth-century renovation, a town house with rooms carved into intimate dining areas accented by Early American antiques. Equestrian prints cover the walls. In the background there is the light hum of chatter at nearby tables.

"I'm sorry, but you caught me by surprise. I guess I've been too busy lately, under a lot of pressure," she says. "I hope you can understand?"

"Sure."

"Of course, *I'm* sitting here telling *you* about pressure. I can't imagine the responsibility of trying a capital case."

"You don't do any criminal law?"

She shakes her head. "No. I get the jitters when large sums of money are involved, and then I only see it after all the fast trial guns have fired, the smoke has cleared, and everything's up on appeal. I'm what you would call the law's Monday-morning quarterback," she says. "I can't imagine what it would be like if someone's life were on the line, doing it in front of a jury. The thing with Terry was enough for me. His death," she says. "No doubt he wasn't the best of people. In the end he was just someone I'd known. But the fact was, I *had* known him, shared meals, slept with him. I helped his family with the funeral arrangements when they came east with the body. There was only his mother and a sister, but they seemed lost. I'd met them a few times when we were dating, so I did what I could."

"That was good of you."

"What else could I do? I'm sorry I took it out on you."

"Hmm?"

"This afternoon," she says.

"Not at all. You were very polite."

"But not very helpful." She smiles at me.

"Well . . ." I offer her an expression of concession.

"That's why I wanted to talk to you. I didn't tell you everything. In fact, I didn't tell you the truth."

"About what?"

"About the letter. There *was* a letter," she says. "Mind you, I never actually saw it. But there were references to it."

"References?"

"In an early version of the manuscript for *Perpetual Slaves.* He wanted me to proof it for him. We were still living together. He was the wordsmith writing books, I was the wordsmith writing briefs. I really didn't have the time. I told him so. Terry never took no for an answer. It wasn't in his lexicon. I think what he really wanted was to see if I would be shocked by the content of what he'd written."

"And were you?"

She looks at me and nods. "He had strewn the thing with references to this letter. I only got a glance," she says. "Because I didn't actually proof it—the book, I mean. We got into a disagreement. It ultimately led to a rupture in the relationship. That's what ended it."

"Disagreement over what?"

"Whether he should use that kind of material in the book."

"What kind of material?"

"I'm assuming it came from the letter you're talking about. According to Terry, it was an indictment of everything American, hypocrisy piled on hypocrisy, all documented at the inception of the country's founding. As I recall, Terry referred to it, in the manuscript, as 'the infamous Jefferson Letter.'"

"Do you mind if I take notes?" I ask.

She looks at me. "You have to promise me one thing."

"What's that?"

"That you won't call me as a witness."

"I can't promise that."

Her face is suddenly a mask of exasperation.

"How can I promise that? With Scarborough dead, you may be the only one who knows anything about the letter."

"As I said, I never actually saw it. Whatever he told me, whatever he wrote that I might have seen, is now hearsay. I'm not a trial lawyer, but without the letter itself and some way to verify its contents it would be inadmissible. Am I wrong?"

"No. You're right. Perhaps now you can understand why it's so important that I find Justice Ginnis."

Our drinks arrive. Scott picks up her tumbler, scotch and soda, and takes a sip as she looks at me over the glass. I can tell by the expression in her eyes that she's weighing whether to say anything more. I'm worried that she may get up and walk. At the moment it's her word against mine that she knows anything at all.

"I can't say anything more unless I have assurances that you won't call me as a witness," she says.

"I won't call you unless I absolutely have to. If I can find another source for the letter," I tell her, "I won't have to."

She thinks about this.

"If you stop now, you're my only source. I will have nowhere else to turn. If you tell me what you know, you may give me other leads, in which case there's a good chance I may not need you."

I'm making a sales pitch. She knows it. She considers this for a moment, the canny lawyer behind the icy tumbler. She puts the glass down. "You have to promise that you will do everything possible to keep me out of it."

"Agreed."

"All right." She takes a deep breath. "As I said, I just saw references to the letter in the early manuscript. And then I only got fleeting glimpses. I never actually had a chance to look at the manuscript in detail. We never got that far."

"But there was no reference to any Jefferson letter in *Perpetual Slaves*," I say.

"No. Terry removed it all before it was published."

"Why?"

"We'll get to that," she says.

"Do you know where the earlier manuscript is?" I ask.

"It was destroyed."

"You're sure?"

"I was there when he shredded it. Terry always shredded the earlier versions of what he wrote. He said it was because of liability if he ever got sued. He didn't want other lawyers rummaging through his files looking for early rewrites and trying to infer what was really going through his mind when he published the final book. He said it was safer that way. Terry was more than a little paranoid, especially about his work. He saw conspiracies under every rock and behind every bush. No pun intended," she says.

"He couldn't have been afraid of libel or slander," I say. "If Jefferson wrote the letter, he's long dead. Unless they changed the law when I wasn't looking, you can't libel the dead."

"It wasn't libel or slander he was worried about."

"What then?"

"Violence," she says. "Terry was convinced that what he was writing had the potential to incite a race war. Mind you, I'm not sure Terry would have objected. I rather think he would have applauded the actual violence. From what I understand, when the riots erupted on his tour for the current book, he was tickled that there were people who actually sat up and took notice of what he'd written and were motivated enough to burn vehicles and break windows."

"Riots being the highest form of flattery," I say.

"In Terry's mind, probably true. But the letter was another matter. According to Terry, if readers had seen the actual text of the Jefferson letter, they would have torched Washington, every monument and stick in the place. There wouldn't have been much left anywhere in the inner city. At least that's what he said."

"So he didn't want to be the cause of this?"

"Not exactly. The problem was, he couldn't authenticate the letter. What he told me was that he possessed a photocopy, but he was certain that at some point within a few months he'd be able to get his hands on the original. Then he could authenticate it using state-of-the-art forensics. Once he did that, what he'd be publishing would be history, and you can't blame the author for that."

"At least he thought it through," I say. "The consequences, I mean."

"Actually, he didn't. I did. It's what we

argued about," she says. "For all his supposed legal expertise, the truth of the matter was that Terry wasn't much of a lawyer. He allowed his passions to run away with his head. He wanted to use the material, the letter, even though all he had was a copy. When I asked him if he knew whether it was authentic, he said he didn't care. Even if it wasn't authentic, it accurately reflected what had occurred regarding slavery and the hypocrites who founded the country. That's what he told me. Almost his exact words."

"And what did you say?"

"I told him he was sticking his head in the lion's mouth. What if it spawned violence and people were killed? Terry told me that that was always the price to be paid for social progress and past injustice.

"I told him he wasn't thinking clearly. That if he published it, the letter was likely to gain a lot of traction in the press—in newspapers and on television. I told him that people who don't read books were likely to see the contents of the letter in the media because of its controversial nature and the fact that it had never been publicly revealed before. I told him that if it wasn't authentic and if violence erupted, he could be responsible for anything that happened, legally responsible for inciting riots."

"I'll bet that put the chill into him."

"He didn't say much, not at first. There was a lot of silence. He hadn't considered it. You should have seen the look on his face. He was like a child whose toy had been taken away. It was like, 'I asked you to look and listen to what was in my book. I didn't expect you to actually tell me there was something wrong with it.' He kept me up all night talking, trying to figure some way to get around this. I asked him where he got the letter, that he might be able to authenticate it if he could get his hands on the original. He wouldn't tell me where he got it, only that the source was unimpeachable and that if I knew where he'd gotten it, I wouldn't be questioning it either. But he still wouldn't tell me. By morning I don't know if he was just exhausted or if reason had finally set in, but he realized he couldn't use it—the letter, I mean—not without authentication.

"He shredded the manuscript, the only printed copy," she continued. "I told him not to, that he might wait until he had a chance to get the original letter, but he wouldn't listen. He was angry with me. It wasn't the message he wanted to hear, so he wanted to shoot the messenger. He had to call the publisher and tell them he would be late delivering the book. It set him back several months. He had to do a heavy rewrite, building up the slavery language in the Constitution, using that as a stepping-off place. But I know that he was intent on using the letter for a later book."

"He told you this?"

"More than once. It was as if he blamed me for forcing him to do the extra work. I just told him the facts. But Terry didn't like facts when they got in the way of something he wanted to do or say. It was the beginning of the end for us, though I didn't realize it at the time. I had come between him and his mistress."

"His work?" I say.

"Publicity," says Scott. "Terry needed the celebrity for validation. He had a big emotional hole inside him."

"About the letter," I say. "Assuming it's authentic, you're sure Jefferson wrote it?"

"All I know is that Terry referred to it as

'the Jefferson letter' or 'the infamous Jefferson letter.' As I said, I never saw it, and even the references in the manuscript I only got to glance at. As soon as he told me what he was doing and I told him there would be problems, Terry pulled the manuscript away from me. I never got another look at it."

"So you don't know the date, when the letter was written?"

She shakes her head.

"Or whom it was written to?"

"No."

"Not much to go on," I tell her.

"No, it isn't."

"Still, it's more than I had this afternoon." I smile at her from across the table, close up my notebook, and slip it back into the inside pocket of my coat along with the pen. "Did you mention any of this to the cops, when they talked to you?"

"They didn't ask. I had no reason to think it might be important until you mentioned it." She takes another sip of her drink. "There is one other thing," she says. "It's about Justice Ginnis. I'm certain that Terry would not have gotten the letter from Arthur."

"How can you be so sure?"

"Because Arthur despised Terry. He had no use for him. He saw Terry as an opportunist, somebody who would use anybody to get ahead and dump them as soon as he got what he wanted. He warned me not to get emotionally involved. He wouldn't have crossed the street to help Terry with anything, especially anything as controversial as Terry's book. Believe me, as a former Supreme Court clerk—there wasn't a member of the Court who wouldn't lift their robes and run shrieking to put distance between themselves and anything Terry wrote."

"You say Ginnis despised Scarborough?"

"Oh, here we go," she says.

"Sorry. I can't help picking up on little words."

"Forget I ever said it." She reaches for her purse under the table, ready to walk out.

"Don't get angry. I'm just looking for background. I need to know who Scarborough was, the kind of man I'm dealing with as a victim."

She wears a stern expression. Then she softens, puts her purse back down.

"I'll tell you," she says. "You will have no difficulty finding enemies of Terry Scarborough in this town. Just turn over any rock," she says. "I didn't know it when I first met him. I was young, naïve, impressionable, straight out of law school. Terry was a well-known published author, on television almost daily. I was dazzled.

"It wasn't until later, months later, that I found out that Terry had savaged Justice Ginnis in one of his earlier books. It was the case of the century," she said, the presidential election almost twelve years ago now, the squeaker decided by the Supreme Court.

"Terry published a book that kicked the insides out of the Court. He claimed to have sources, people privy to private conversations between the justices and those on the outside, the parties and their lawyers. The decision by the Court came down five to four; it ended the election and effectively anointed the new president. Arthur was the swing vote, and Terry excoriated him for it in public print. He called

Arthur a party hack and claimed that he'd been in direct contact with lawyers for the new president before he voted on the case. It wasn't true. It hurt Arthur, and it hurt him deeply.

"But that's the thing about the Court—you just had to sit there and take it. They all knew that. It was the price the nine of them, and all their predecessors, paid for a lifetime appointment to an institution that's not supposed to be political. When somebody takes a shot, they can't go to the media and fight back. You just have to live with it, and Arthur did. It's the reason I laughed when you said someone had told you that Terry and Arthur were friends. Justice Ginnis would have put an ocean between himself and Terry Scarborough if he could have. When I introduced Terry to him at the reception, I thought Arthur would choke. The next day Arthur took me into his office and warned me that Scarborough would try to use me to find out what was going on in chambers, to dig up dirt on cases. I told him I would never reveal anything like that."

"Did he? Scarborough, I mean?"

She nods. "More than once. I told him I

couldn't discuss any part of my work at the Court, and I wouldn't. I did two years clerking for Arthur. I was getting ready to leave the Court—this was about the time that Terry was finishing up the early draft of *Perpetual Slaves,* the one that included the stuff from the letter. By then we weren't living together any longer. I think Arthur was relieved, for me, if not for himself."

"It sounds like you and Justice Ginnis are very close."

"Friends," she says. "No, it's more than that. Arthur has a father complex. Almost all the clerks who've ever worked for him have felt this. He means well." She pauses, smiles, and looks down at the table for a moment. "And I owe him a lot. He could have fired me. I mean, he knew that Terry was a threat to the confidentiality inside the Court. I was living with him. Other members of the Court would have either fired me or found some less-important duties for me outside their chambers. Arthur didn't do that. He warned me. I gave him assurances, and he trusted me. I can't explain it," she says, "but there's a kind of almost nuclear bond that forms from all of that."

"And Terry Scarborough?" I ask. "How did he fit into all this?"

"In the beginning I suspect he gravitated to me because I could mingle with people Terry wanted to be seen with."

"I think you underrate yourself," I tell her.

"Thank you. But you have to live in this political hothouse to understand it," she says. "It may be the power center of the world, but it's actually a very small town. Everybody knows everybody. They attend the same receptions, do the same parties, and the press hangs out. The media make mental notes of who's talking to whom. It was important for Terry to be seen at functions socializing with members of the Court and Court staff. You see, Terry sold himself to the national media as one of the prime legal insiders, on call twenty-four hours a day to go on the air, to be quoted in the *Washington Post* or the *New York Times*. He lived to be seen and heard."

"And of course only a fool would fail to grasp the symbiotic relationship between face time on the tube and book sales," I tell her.

"With Terry it was more than that."

"What do you mean?"

"He liked being recognized at airports, in crowds. He craved it. Someone would come up to him and tell him that he looked familiar, and Terry would casually flip the celebrity over his shoulder like some people discard a cigarette butt. He would say, 'You probably saw me on *Larry King* last night,' and walk away. He loved it. They say that celebrity is its own narcotic. For Terry it was the drug of choice. I remember at one point he told me about the night he did his first appearance on cable news. All his friends called to tell him how they'd seen him on the tube. For Terry it was like doing lines of cocaine. He couldn't get on the next show fast enough. He hired a PR firm with media connections. He told me he was paying them seven thousand dollars a month on his teaching salary, dipping into savings while he was writing his first book on spec. That was part of the problem with the relationship," she says.

"In what way?"

She looks at me, suddenly realizing that maybe she's already said too much. "Nothing. But you get the picture," she says.

"So Ginnis was relieved when you broke it off?"

"Hmm?" I catch her musing, lost in thought.

"Your relationship with Scarborough."

"Oh, absolutely. He told me I'd get over it, move on, find someone else. He was right. It was better for me, much healthier."

"So where do you think I could find him?"

"Find who?"

"Ginnis."

"You haven't heard a word I've been saying. You're dogged. You're awful." She laughs. "Do you have any idea how difficult it is to contact a sitting justice of the Supreme Court? I mean, unless you're a personal friend or a family member, it's probably easier to get through to the Oval Office. I told you, he doesn't know a thing about Terry's book or the letter. You're chasing rainbows—give it up," she says.

"I wish I could, but there's a man sitting in a jail cell back in San Diego, and unless I can figure out who else may have had a reason to kill Scarborough, Carl Arnsberg is looking at a possible death sentence."

SIX

If you think politics is the occupational calling of the Antichrist today, you should have
been around in Jefferson's time." Harry
gestures toward the pile of paper in front
of him. "This stuff gives me a whole new
insight into the founding generation."

Harry has been doing research while I
was gone. Spread out on the table in our
conference room are notes, stacks of
photocopied pages, and computer printouts. "If they didn't invent partisan bicker-
ing," says Harry, "they sure as hell took it
to the level of a whole new art form.

"The current crop in D.C. would have

nothing on these guys," says Harry. "Jefferson kept his own muckraker-in-chief on payroll. A guy named James Callender. Callender was a kind of one-man Defamation Incorporated. And he didn't need a word processor. For a fee he would do a journalistic gut job on anybody you wanted. Lies passed through his quill at a rate that would make the turkey feathers wilt. What's more troubling," says Harry, "is that Jefferson didn't seem to be too bothered by any of this. When it came to political enemies, he wasn't interested in sweating the details. Paint 'em with a broad brush," says Harry. According to my partner, the author of the Declaration of Independence followed his own creed of political warfare: defame 'em first and let posterity sort out the facts.

"What we didn't learn in high-school history," I tell him.

"Along with Sally Hemings, the slave bride," says Harry. "But we'll get to that later. The problem for us is the volume of documents."

According to Harry, when it came to letter writing, Jefferson didn't know when to quit. "You get different numbers when you go to different sources, but everybody seems to agree that the total is somewhere north of twenty thousand," says Harry.

"Separate letters?" I ask.

Harry nods. "No Internet and no computer, and the man wrote letters on everything from Eskimos to enchiladas. He did have a machine to make copies so he could file them away." Harry paws through his notes. "Ironically, it was called a polygraph." He flips me a page across the table from one of the stacks in front of him. There's a small picture of the device and some brief script. A machine Jefferson acquired in 1804, which was patented a year earlier. According to the article, Jefferson called it "the finest invention of the current age."

"What's more," says Harry, "the authorities seem pretty certain that not all of his letters have been found or documented to date."

"So there's a chance there might be some authentic correspondence still floating around out there?"

"A good chance, though documenting it could prove difficult, depending on where it's found and under what circumstances."

"Fortunately for us, all we have to show is that the killer believed it was authentic," I say.

"But according to what Bonguard told you, Scarborough only had a copy," says Harry.

"True."

Harry shakes his head. There is no seeming answer to this riddle. According to Harry, Jefferson's papers are spread around, scattered in several different places. Most of them are in the Library of Congress. But a wild piece of correspondence that has eluded scholars all this time could be anywhere.

"Let's start with the Library of Congress," I tell him. "That *is* why you called me when I was back in D.C., right?"

"Right," says Harry. "According to everything I can find, Jefferson's papers with the Jefferson Library—that's the Library of Congress—" says Harry, "include twenty-seven thousand documents. That's correspondence, commonplace books in Jefferson's own hand, financial accounts. The man was a fanatic about keeping financial records. There are also manuscript volumes written by Jefferson. In addition to this, there are rare book manuscripts, part of Jefferson's original library that was sold to Congress in 1814 after the Brits burned the capital in the War of 1812. A lot of controversy over that," says Harry.

"What controversy?"

"Jefferson was getting on in years and teetering on the personal financial precipice when Congress paid him a lot of money for his library. People squawked. They thought it was too much, twenty-some-odd-thousand dollars. It doesn't seem like much now, but back then it was a bundle. More than that," says Harry, "the library was what you might call eclectic. It contained everything from philosophy to cookbooks. There were those in Congress who thought it included items that weren't appropriate for a government library. According to Jefferson, if it was printed on paper and bound between two covers, it was a book, and that's what libraries were made of. The man read everything."

"So where do we start?"

"That's why I called you in D.C.," says Harry. "Congress formed a commission about eight years ago to digitize private presidential papers held in the Library of Congress, to put them on computers for access by the public. The group is called CEPP, short for Commission on Electronic Presidential Papers."

"So?"

"So guess who the chairperson is."

I shake my head.

"Arthur Ginnis. It seems history is one of his passions. They must have figured the commission could use somebody with his bona fides—a member of the Supreme Court."

"Could have been just a ceremonial role," I tell him.

"That's a possibility, except for one thing," says Harry. "Scarborough's notes. The ones the cops seized from his Georgetown apartment."

"What about them?"

"There are at least four references in Scarborough's own hand to CEPP."

"Yes."

"And a note in one of the margins." Harry hands me a photocopied page.

I study it. Double-spaced typed notes, some underlined in pen with interlineated handwritten notations I assume are Scarborough's. Toward the bottom of the page, in the margin in ink, the words "get the letter from CEPP." I read the typed notes in the body of the text. Scarborough is talking about the economics of slavery in Colonial America, where the most valuable import was Africans in bondage.

"Think about it," says Harry. "If you're Ginnis, you have an army of staff combing through piles of historic documents that no one has looked at in a long time. There's no telling what you might find. What did she tell you?" Harry is talking about Trisha Scott.

"She knew about the letter," I tell him. "She says Scarborough made reference to it in earlier drafts of the manuscript, before the book was published, but that this was all deleted because she says Scarborough couldn't authenticate the letter. She claimed Ginnis wouldn't know anything about it. That he wasn't the source."

"Did she tell you about his participation in this little venture?" Harry means CEPP.

"No."

"You have to figure she clerked for him. A close friend, she must have known what he was involved in. So what do we have?" says Harry.

"A tiger by the tail," I tell him. "A Supreme Court justice who probably won't talk to us. Unless we can subpoena him."

"That'll be a neat trick," says Harry, "getting through the phalanx of federal marshals that guard the Supreme Court building. And we don't know what he's gonna say."

Harry is right.

"Let's face it," he says. "The letter is problematic. We don't know what it's worth on the open market. We don't know whether someone might kill to get it, only that it's a possibility. According to everything Bonguard and Scott told you, Scarborough only had a copy of the letter."

"And that he may have had access to the original through someone else," I add.

"Ginnis?"

"Maybe."

"Still, we can't prove that he had the original in his possession when he was killed," says Harry. "Without that, you can't prove motive for murder."

"There is another possibility."

"What's that?" says Harry.

"That whoever killed Scarborough didn't do it to get the letter."

"Then why?"

"To keep its contents from being published."

Harry gives me a quizzical look.

"Scarborough's book, the language of slavery, the fact that this was still in the Constitution—these were known facts," I tell him, "though not generally items of controversy until Scarborough mainlined them, put them up on a marquee, at which time they stirred up riots around the country."

"So?"

"So people often don't pay much attention to government until it hits them in the head like a two-by-four. Scarborough spelled it out in big letters, the continuing stigma, the national insult. If the letter is as explosive as he believed, there's no telling what kind of fires it might ignite if it were published, especially in the kind of flammable prose used by Terry Scarborough. Not some dry scholarly work but a racial call to arms."

"In which case it wouldn't matter whether he had the original of the letter or a copy," says Harry.

"Exactly."

"But who would kill him for that?"

"Not our client," I tell him.

"No," says Harry. "Probably not."

* * *

Harry and I have had our share of high-profile cases, but this one, tinged as it is by the issue of race, possesses an explosive quality all its own. To the extent possible, I have avoided the media, for there are obvious pitfalls here, questions the answers to which can be twisted to fit a dozen different political agendas.

This morning one of these has exploded on us like a roadside bomb during our trek to trial. In an effort to extinguish the flames from this, Harry and I meet with Carl Arnsberg at the jail. It is nearly seven in the evening, the first chance we've had to talk to him. Harry and I have been locked up in court all day with jury selection and pretrial motions.

Inside the closed cubicle, the little concrete conference room, Harry is first to erupt.

"Why the hell didn't you tell us about these people? Surprises like this can lead to the death house. Who are they?" Harry's face is flushed. He is angry.

Arnsberg avoids eye contact. "Friends," he says.

"Why didn't you tell us about them?"

"Didn't think it was important," says Arnsberg. He is sitting at a small stainless-steel table that is bolted to the floor, his head resting in his hands as he gazes down at its scratched surface.

"Not important?" Harry's voice rises a full octave. "Lemme ask you. Do you know what they're saying?" Harry looks at him.

"No."

"They're saying that you talked openly about kidnapping Scarborough, that you tried to talk the two of them into helping you. And that this all took place just two days before Scarborough was killed."

"It's not true." For the first time, Arnsberg's gaze comes up from the table. He looks at Harry straight on. "That's a lie. I never asked anybody to help me. I was only talking."

"We have their statement," says Harry.

"I don't care what you have. It's a lie."

It is a game played by prosecutors: Bury the needle in a stack of other needles. In reply to our request for discovery, the district attorney, in addition to reports and photographs of the physical evidence, has sent us a list of more than three hundred potential witnesses—people who worked at the hotel, acquaintances of the defendant, some of whom have known him but not talked to him since grade school, others who might be eyewitnesses who may have seen Arnsberg in the hall outside Scarborough's room that morning. Harry, with investigators for our side in tow, has been forced to waste valuable time checking all these out. Most of them are chaff, people the D.A. will never call, because they have nothing of value to offer in his case. They are put on the list to distract us, to waste our time and limited resources. Most of all they are there to provide camouflage, to hide the handful of razor-sharp pieces of real evidence lying just beneath the surface over which they hope to drag us and tear us to pieces. Unfortunately for us, Walter Henoch and Charles "Charlie" Gross threaten to do just that.

"You say you were only talking to these friends," I chime in. "Talking about what?"

"Passin' the time o' day. Shootin' the shit. You know. Just talkin'."

"About what?" If he could, Harry would waterboard Arnsberg at this point. To my partner, torturing a client who lies to his own lawyer should be part of the attorney-client privilege. Misdirection from a client is one of the things that sets off Harry's naturally short fuse.

"All right, sure we talked about the man."

"Scarborough?" says Harry.

Arnsberg nods, then puts his head back in his hands, elbows propped up on the table.

"Look at me," says Harry. "What did you tell them? Specifically. Details."

"I told 'em it would be a piece of cake." Arnsberg still won't look at him. "So what?"

"What would be a piece of cake?"

"Kidnapping him. I maya mentioned it, that's all. But it was only talk. We weren't gonna do anything. I never talked about killin' him." To Arnsberg this seems to make everything all right.

"Still, the man's dead," says Harry. "Somebody did something."

"Wasn't me."

"How long did you know these two guys?" I ask.

"I dunno. Charlie I known for a year, maybe a little more. The other guy—"

"Walter Henoch."

"Yeah. I didn't know him hardly at all."

"I see," says Harry. "Just well enough to discuss a kidnapping with the man."

"You make it sound bad." Arnsberg finally looks up at him.

"Not half as bad as the prosecutor will make it sound. Believe me," says Harry.

Arnsberg's eyes are bloodshot, as if he is missing a lot of sleep in the jailhouse maelstrom at night.

"Wheredidyoumeettheseguys—Charlie and Walter?"

"Like I said, we just had a few drinks. Met at a bar."

"Does the bar have a name?" says Harry.

"Del Rio Tavern. Place out offa I-8, near El Centro."

"Why way out there?" says Harry.

"We were meetin' some other people."

"The Aryan Posse?" I ask.

The kid looks at me, kind of cross-eyed. "Some of 'em might have been members."

I have been alerted to this by Carl's father, who warned me that his son had gotten involved in something called the Aryan Posse, a neofascist group with connections out in the desert halfway to Arizona, at some kind of meeting place. Mail used to come to the house when Carl was living there with his mother and father. His father saw it and raised hell. But it didn't do any good. This has been the other shoe waiting to drop. There have been a few items in the newspaper, references to Arnsberg as a neo-Nazi, but to date nothing definitive. This makes me wonder what the cops have that they will drop on our heads come trial.

"We'd just had a few drinks together, after work. You know. We'd shoot the shit." This according to Carl.

"And you drove all the way out into the desert for that?" says Harry. "What's the matter? No bars in town that suit your taste?"

Arnsberg looks up at him through one eye but doesn't answer.

"Carl, you may as well tell us. It's going

to come out during trial. Were you a member of the Aryan Posse?"

"No. You keep askin' me, and I keep tellin' ya. No, I never joined. Just went to a couple of their meetings out there. That's all."

"You were on their telephone list. They called you for events," I tell him.

"Lot of people got called to go to events. Doesn't mean they're members. You go to a meeting, they get your cell number."

"Did you talk to anybody at any of these meetings about Scarborough?" I ask.

"No. Not me. Never. I mean, there was a lot of talk about him. They had pictures of him."

"Of Scarborough?"

"Yeah."

"Where did they get these pictures?"

"I don't know. Maybe off his book."

"You mean off the book jacket?" says Harry.

"I don't know. But they shot it all up."

"His picture?"

"Yeah. They made it into, like, a target. His face in the bull's-eye. Put it out on the range and shot it all to hell." He laughs.

Carl thinks this is cool. He won't be

nearly so cavalier if the prosecutor gets wind and paints the image for the jury.

"Did you shoot at it?" I ask. This would have devastating consequences if prosecutors can get testimony of Arnsberg shooting at images of the victim days before he was killed.

"No. I shot a few rounds. But not at the target. Some empty beer cans. At their range. Somebody handed me a gun. It looked like fun, so I shot a few. But I don't remember shootin' at anything that looked like Scarborough."

"You don't remember," says Harry.

"No."

"Wonderful. Now we have a good mental image to go along with the words, verbal musings over how easy it might be to abduct the man. D.A.'s gonna have a field day," says Harry.

"Hell, it was all over the papers, on the news," says Arnsberg. "Guy was stirring up trouble. He was a shit disturber. Fucking agitator. You want to know the truth, he got what he deserved."

It is becoming increasingly clear that we may not be able to put our client on the stand. One statement like this before the jury and they will erect a scaffold in the jury box and hang him there on the spot out of sheer principle.

"Tell us exactly how the issue of kidnapping came up," I say. "When you were talking to your friends? By the way, was anybody else present, besides the three of you?"

"No." He thinks for a second. "No. Just us three."

"Go on. How did it start?"

"Lemme think," he says. This time it takes him a couple of seconds. "I'm pretty sure it was the other guy, that guy Walt. He said there was a lot of talk out on the reserve. That's what they called the place the Posse met. He said there was people talking about gettin' this guy."

"Scarborough?"

"Right. He said something like 'their blood was up.'"

"Walt said this?" says Harry. "What did he mean by that?"

"They was mad. You know. Then he said I was lucky, cuz I was workin' in the hotel, and according to the newspapers he was gonna be staying right there where

I worked. So at least I could see him up close, like that."

"Walt said this?" I ask.

"Walt, or it mighta been Charlie. I'm not sure. One of 'em said it. That's how it got started."

Harry's following all this as he pages through the witness statement.

"Who suggested kidnapping?" I ask.

"I don't know. I mighta said something. That it would be easy to do. Ya know, it was cool. Just talking with guys. I had a few beers. I was never gonna do it," he says. "Just talk."

"What did they say then? Walt and Charlie?" I ask.

"They said, 'Yeah. Cool, man. Right on.'"

"Yeah, they wanted to do it, or yeah, it would be easy?"

"I think they meant it would be easy. I'm not sure," he says.

"Well, let me read to you," says Harry. "Maybe it'll refresh your memory." He flips a couple of pages. These are stapled together at the top left-hand corner. He finds his place, then lowers the spectacles a little on the bridge of his nose so that he can look over the top of them at Arnsberg.

" 'Walter Henoch: You'd do that?

" 'Carl Arnsberg: Yeah.

" 'Walter Henoch: Kidnap him?

" 'Carl Arnsberg: Yeah. I'd do it. I might need some help, but I'd do it.

" 'The three of us did high fives at the table. I ordered another round of beers.' This is Henoch speaking," says Harry.

Harry flips a page, scans down it, then another. "Here," he says.

" 'Carl Arnsberg: It would be easy. Rap him up the side of the head, throw his ass in a laundry cart, and take him down the service elevator. Hell, we could have his ass out in the desert tied to a post in front of a firing squad before he knew what hit him. Skin his ass before we shoot him.'

"Did you say that?" Harry looks at him.

"No. No, no. I don't think so. Like I say, it was a while ago. But I don't remember anything like that."

"Maybe all those beers, you forgot?" says Harry.

"No. No. I never said that."

"You're sure?"

"Yeah. Yeah I'm sure." His words are emphatic. The look in his eyes is anything but. Like a kid caught pissing against the side of the schoolhouse by the principal.

"You're sure?" Harry asks him again.

This time all he gets is a shrug from Arnsberg. "I think so. If I said it, I didn't mean it."

"So you might have said it?"

"Hey, I don't think so. I know I didn't talk about killing him." The gravity of all this is beginning to settle on Carl Arnsberg, like stone weights used to crush a man. Up to this point, the case has been circumstantial, physical evidence at the scene that tied Arnsberg to the location of the crime and the time it was committed. Apart from his associations and his potential motive of hate, he also had a business reason for being in the room that morning. He was delivering breakfast, by all rights an innocent act. This, however, is something else: witnesses who can put words in Arnsberg's mouth in the period immediately prior to the murder, especially when those words cut close to the events of the actual crime. This could give the state a case with legs. It is not something complex and hard to comprehend, like DNA with its infinite mathematical probabilities, something the defense could flip on its head and play with. If the jury believes the witness statements, they become a pipeline to the defendant's innermost thoughts, a statement of intentions.

Worse is the part that Harry and I are not telling him. These particular witness statements are not in the usual form, a loose narrative of paraphrased remembrances jotted down from recall days or weeks after the event.

These witness statements are in the form of a transcript, chapter and verse, with quotation marks at the beginning and end of each passage, direct quotations. There is only one way that such a transcript is normally made—that is, if one of the participants to the conversation is wearing a wire.

Our best guess is that this particular gathering of neo-Nazis popped up on some law-enforcement radar screen. If the cops rolled one of the members, perhaps nailing him on drugs or some other charge, and then cut a deal, getting him to wear a wire whenever he talked to his friends, this would explain how Carl was caught on tape. He may not have attended many meetings, but he was at the wrong place at the wrong time, shooting off his mouth.

Sit down at a street-side café with an intimate friend to have a confidential conversation and your words along with pictures may show up on YouTube and the World Wide Web. If Harry had to guess, his candidate for wearer of the wire would be Walter Henoch, the newest man on the scene, the one Arnsberg didn't know that well, the man who got him talking.

SEVEN

Upstairs, the walls of the main courthouse are decorated with pictures of the local worthies, mostly judges, some of them dating back to just this side of the California gold rush. Here the noise and commotion, the jostling of bodies, is different from in the lobby downstairs. Most of the lawyers, clerks, and courthouse staff seem to have some goal and direction, even if the cases they're working do not.

There are two separate courthouses in this town, one civil and the other criminal, connected by a bridge that spans the street between them. And for all intents and purposes, it is the *only* thing that connects them.

It is just my view, but on the civil side it would require a peculiar wit to call it a justice system. Buried in mud over the axles twenty years ago, lawmakers threw up their hands and pushed everything on the civil side out of the courthouse door and into arbitration. This became the toll-booth you had to pass through to get back into the courthouse.

Once there, however, any claim, no matter how frivolous, often results in the defendant's ponying up money rather than being bankrupted by years of litigation or facing the prospect of death by old age in a courtroom full of busy lawyers flinging pieces of paper around.

On any matter that even hints of the complex, it can take years to get through trial, followed by decades on appeal. On anything that is in fact complex, a lawyer can spend his entire career on that single case, and many have done so.

Businesses and corporations that make up the economic backbone of the state long ago opted out of the state's civil court system, using instead mediation, binding arbitration, and in many cases private judges working for local firms to preside over the case and render a judgment—the businessman's express toll highway to a quick and final decision. Just as with health care and medicine, no one can afford the high cost of government-administered justice any longer.

That is, except for the scions of the criminal courts. A private judge cannot send your client off to prison for a few lifetimes or direct others to stick a needle in his arm, transporting him out of this world. When they figure that one out, we'll all be in trouble.

A female clerk sashays down the corridor past me, clicking heels on the hard floor, all to the accompaniment of the plastic badges she flashes on her chest. Living in the age of security as we do, badges are everywhere. Ubiquitous clip-ons for temporary visitors behind the scenes, a requirement if they wish to enter the inner sanctum of a judge's chambers. There are more permanent hard laminated ones hanging from chains around the neck for seasoned staff. Some of these are worn two and three together or from multiple chains, emblems of status, an outward display of who can enter the sanctum sanctorum. If you can't get a bump in salary, you can at least have another badge and, if you're real good, a shiny new chain to go with it, something to dazzle friends and impress the public on cafeteria coffee breaks.

With plenty of time, I saunter down the hall past Departments 11 and 12. Off to the right, I see the sign over my destination's door, DEPARTMENT 13, and wonder whether our assignment to this court portends something ominous.

The purpose of this morning's gathering is an off-the-record meeting, under the guise of a pretrial conference, this so that the judge can lay down the law. Not the statutes printed in the codebooks or the case law handed down by the appellate courts, but the law from on high, the holy writ according to the Honorable Plato Quinn, whom we have drawn as trial judge in *People v. Carl Arnsberg.*

Of course, all of this is off calendar, away from the prying eyes of the press or notice to the public. If a trial is theater, you can consider these to be notes on stage direction: where you will stand and how you will comport yourself, how the judge's word is final on everything, from what evidence will come before the jury to when you can empty your bladder and by how much.

The last two weeks, I have wheeled and dealed and burned a few bridges. In periodic gatherings with the presiding judge of the superior court and the county's public defender, what gentlemen might call meetings to those of us present became a desperate game of financial chicken.

I have known from the beginning that Sam Arnsberg's savings, plus what he earns selling insurance, would never come close to covering the fees, let alone the monstrous costs, in this case.

His son, Carl, qualifies as an indigent, public-defender bait. The problem was to convince the public defender that he didn't want the case and that there were at least arguable legal grounds for him and his office to bug out. The bigger problem was to convince the court to go along with this, to officially declare Arnsberg an indigent and to appoint me to represent him at public expense.

The public defender already had enough cases stacked up against the walls in his office to make convincing him he didn't need this particular circus twirling on top of his desk not all that hard.

It is a rule carved in granite that for reasons of conflict of interest, lawyers in the same law firm cannot represent more than one criminal defendant charged in the same case. The catch here was that there was only one defendant charged in this case, our client, Carl Arnsberg. But there was at least the glimmer of other miscreants looming just over the horizon, the other branded bozos that Carl ran with, the people he talked to, the state's star witnesses. True, they weren't charged, but they could be, they might be, and since nobody knew exactly what they might say at some point in the future if pressed, the case could end up in a conspiracy involving the entire Third Reich.

At first the judge wasn't buying. As far as he was concerned, multiple defendants meant just that, real people actually charged. But as time went by, as the trial loomed closer, as the public defender and I slipped his head into a vise and turned the handle, he began to see the light. Gentle hints that if forced to the wall I might

have to withdraw, along with estimates by
the public defender that he would need at
least two more full-time lawyers and six
months to come up to speed on the
case—these finally turned the tide.

This morning I called Sam Arnsberg and
gave him the news. The county will be
funding not only the prosecution but the
defense, including our experts and investigators. What I didn't tell him is that my fee
will be a fraction of my usual hourly rate.
No doubt my statement of hours along with
Harry's will be chiseled down further by
the presiding judge, who will review, ap-
proving or modifying, our billings for each
month, part of the deal. But it gets us over
the hump.

I pull open one of the heavy wooden
doors at Department 13, pass through the
darkened airlock between the two sets of
double doors and into the courtroom. The
place is empty except for a lone figure sitting in the front row. I could have anticipated
this. Bent and a little stooped, wearing a
tweed suit with the look and cut of something from another decade, is a withered
form. His hands are pocked by age marks,
and his arthritic fingers claw a sharpened

pencil in one hand, a reporter's notepad in the other.

Harvey Smidt must be seventy if he's a day, the oldest salt in the courthouse press corps. Harv shuns pack journalism. He works alone, often in silence like a Trappist monk, and rejects technology. He won't use a computer. Smidt still knocks out daily copy on an old Underwood manual typewriter, not even electric. It is the perennial courthouse mystery where he acquires his store of typewriter ribbons. He has an assistant who keys his stories in for him online when he is done and sends them to the pressroom, which in Harvey's case is up in Los Angeles. His paper tolerates this because Harv does his work the old-fashioned way. He uses shoe leather. Two years ago he won a Pulitzer Prize for a series on the trial of the Santee Seven, a Mexican gang implicated in killings that ranged across four southwestern states and involved trafficking in enough drugs to swamp a Colombian cartel.

Nothing happens in the courthouse that Harvey isn't aware of. He is the one person who doesn't need a badge. His face is known to every bailiff, sheriff's deputy, and clerk. It is rumored that he has his own set of keys to most of the out-of-bounds areas where courthouse files are kept. Smidt has been around since before the cornerstone was laid for the building. I'm not surprised that today he is sitting here alone. When it comes to a story, Harvey keeps his own counsel.

He is tall and slender, bent in the upper back from years of leaning into filing cabinets pilfering legal dirt, his neck calcified by decades of journalistic warfare, so that when he turns to look at me, he moves his whole body on the hard wooden bench.

"Mr. Madriani." As he says this, his eyes have not quite caught up with me, as if he's detected me by his keen sense of smell, like an animal of prey.

"Harv. How are you?"

"Good. Good. Do you have a minute?" He stands up. His smile is sly and personable, and he shows me his notebook, already open and ready. "What's happening here today? This wasn't on the calendar," he says.

I might ask him how he found out about it, but he would never tell me.

"I'll know when you know," I say. "I'll read about it in the morning paper."

He smiles only a little. "What does the judge want to see you about? Hmm? Come on, off the record," he says.

I keep walking.

"I saw Mr. Tuchio go in a few minutes ago."

"Did you ask him?"

"I did."

"And what did he say?"

"Said he didn't know. Wasn't sure."

"There you go," I tell him.

"Can we talk when you come out?" he asks.

"Harvey." I shake my head. "There's a gag order."

He smiles. "Not for me."

I try to get past him. For a man as frail as he is, he manages to block my way with practiced ease. "Something's happening. What's going on?"

"You've been around long enough, Harv. Probably just ground rules," I tell him.

"You sure that's all? Come on. You help me out and I'll make sure they give you the luxury cell if the judge puts you in for contempt." He gives me his most comely smile.

We both laugh.

I finally get past him through the railing at the bar, headed for the little hallway and the judge's chambers in back.

"Any truth," he says, "to the rumor that the prosecution's got witnesses who will testify that your man only wanted to kidnap Scarborough?"

"Where'd you hear that?"

"I'm under a gag order there," he says.

I don't answer. To Harvey this is a yes.

"If so, it could be manslaughter," he says.

"Maybe my client should have hired you," I tell him. Arnsberg could do worse. Harvey is a graduate of the University of Hard Knocks Law School. He has sat through enough trials that he could do a credible job defending a multiple ax murderer.

I keep walking, though now there is a steady drip of adrenaline on my heart. Harvey has been talking to the prosecutors or the cops. You can build a gag order, but you can never fill all the little crevices that leak. Trying to undo the damage later is like bailing a flood from a broken levy with a bucket. If Harvey reports the kidnap rumor and the fact that the state has witnesses, it will be all over the media by tomorrow morning. Talking heads will be using it as a teaser to keep viewers tuned in between the commercials. Even with the jury impaneled and the judge having instructed them not to read or watch news concerning the case, this information, blaring from every cable network and sliding past on the electronic ticker tape running under the pictures, is a virtual certainty to reach them. If they believe that Arnsberg had any plan for Scarborough, whether kidnapping or killing, they'll be leaning so far toward conviction that they'll topple like dominoes the first time they climb into the jury box.

"See you on the way out," says Harvey.

Smidt can be relentless. I will ask the judge to let me out through the back corridor and hope the prosecutor takes the same route. I turn past the bench and down the hall. In the distance, ten feet away, I can see the judge's clerk, Rudalgo Ruiz, sitting at his desk just inside the door to the judge's anteroom.

Ruiz is known to courthouse staff as R2.

Not because of the two *R*'s in his name. Instead this is short for R2-D2. Ruiz is short, built like a barrel, and bald. The only things missing are the wheels and the discordant bleeping tones for communication. Though in some sense it would be preferable to what he has to say to me this morning. It is blunt and to the point. "They're waiting for you," he says. This from under black, furrowed brows, the only wisps of hair he has on his head. "I called you three times. Dun you have a secretary?"

I look at my watch—9:48. "My calendar said ten o'clock."

"Judge bumped it up this morning." Ruiz says this with adamancy. "Nine-thirty." He taps the crystal on his wristwatch like maybe the judge can issue an order to make time go in reverse.

"On the second day, God shortened the hour," I tell him.

He shakes his head at this blasphemy, then smiles, but only a little. "You better get your ass in there." He nods toward chambers, where the door is open just a crack. I can hear voices inside, some muffled laughter.

I tap on the door.

"Come on in." A booming voice.

I swing the door open and am greeted by the raised eyebrows of his eminence Judge Plato Quinn. Quinn has been on the superior court for more than two decades. A graduate of the D.A.'s office, he spent the first ten years of his legal career prosecuting major felonies and is not particularly beloved among the defense bar, though this is not all bad. Quinn is a man highly sensitive of his reputation. At times he will bend over backward to dispel any hint that he might carry water for the prosecution.

"I take it you don't have a clock?" he says.

"Your clerk says I need a new secretary," I tell him.

"Anything to bring you into the modern age." The judge glances under the edge of my suit coat, looking for the telltale pouch on my belt.

I lift my coat a little, making it easier for him to visually frisk me.

"Only lawyer I know doesn't own a cell phone," he says.

At the moment my cell phone is in my briefcase.

"My having lost three of them going through security downstairs, the phone company wants my daughter as collateral to get another," I tell him. "They tell me the last one I lost is still making phone calls long-distance from Beirut."

As I close the door, I see the D.A., Bob Tuchio, seated on the couch, as if he were playing hide-and-seek behind the swinging door. "Your cell carrier should cut off services," he says.

"It's a two-year plan. They don't like to lose the business," I tell him.

He smiles, a dark eminence. Tuchio has eyes like two black olives, and a five o'clock shadow an hour after he shaves. His complexion is something from the heel of the boot in Italy. He is intense in court, but not emotional, at least not so that the unschooled eye would notice.

"Okay, so we wasted twenty minutes," says Quinn. "I'll take it out of your opening statement." He looks at me and winks. "I gather that the two of you know each other?"

"We've never been formally introduced," says Tuchio, "but I know Mr. Madriani by reputation."

"Then it looks like you're in trouble." The judge regards me and smiles.

Tuchio rises from the couch and in a single smooth gesture closes the center button on his suit coat and offers me his hand. We shake.

Tuchio is a shade under six feet, slender, a cipher by way of demeanor. Power suits, this morning a dark blue worsted, flatter his lean frame. The chief deputy district attorney of this county for more than a decade, it is rumored that he is "D.A.-in-waiting," until his boss retires, which is supposed to be next year. Tuchio's only weakness may be what he can't see. He is known unaffectionately behind his back by much of the defense bar as "Bob the Tush," not so much because of the size of his behind as for its motion when the man gets wound up in court. He has acquired a kind of circular gyration as he speaks, this to offset the movement of his hands. If you cuffed his wrists, it would transform him to a mute. It is said, though I have not seen this, that when he gets up to speed, he can rattle his ass like a washing machine on spin cycle with the load out of balance. Unfortunately for many who have witnessed this, there may be a kind of mesmerizing effect to it, for it usually comes on closing argument just before the opposing counsel's client goes down for the count. Tuchio has a conviction rate of better than 96 percent. He hasn't lost a case in more than five years, though as chief deputy he can pick and choose his shots.

That he has selected Arnsberg to prosecute is not a good sign for our side. Tuchio will be heavily invested in the case, particularly on the eve of his rise to power. The last thing he needs is a loss under the glare of television lights as a prelude to his coronation.

"I thought it would be good if we all sat and talked. Sit down." Quinn gestures with his hands toward the two client chairs across from his tufted throne on the other side of his massive mahogany desk. This is littered with files, one of which is ours. The judge slides this toward him, opens the cover, and begins to look at notes that he has apparently made for this meeting.

We sit, Tuchio to the right, me to the left.

"I don't want any misunderstandings

when we get to court," says the judge. What Quinn means when he says *we* should talk is that *he* will do the talking and we will do the listening.

"First order of business," he says. "I don't want any gamesmanship. I know that the stakes are high here. A lot of the media is watching. That doesn't mean a goddamn thing as far as I'm concerned. They already asked for cameras in the courtroom. I already said no."

Quinn looks at me as if this were a major concession for which he is now free to plant land mines in the courtroom with some roadside bomb for the defense.

"Gag order is in effect, as you both know," he tells us.

"That's good, Your Honor, because someone has already violated it," I tell him.

"What are you talking about?"

I tell him about Smidt outside in his courtroom asking questions about witnesses and theories of the case to which only those who are trying it and their agents are privy.

The judge's gaze has not even fallen on him, and Tuchio is already in denial mode. "Didn't come from my office. I issued a memo last week. Anyone violating your order will be fired and prosecuted. And I mean it."

This is the boilerplate that is issued in every case where the media operatives are digging for dirt. It may as well be printed on little squares of toilet tissue for all the good it does.

"So you can tell us sitting here today that it didn't come from one of the cops working the case?" I ask.

"You tell me which one," says Tuchio, "and I'll nail his ass."

Now, there's the rub.

"Do you have a name?" asks the judge.

I look at him and smile. A good lawyer, he knows the answer before he asks the question.

"Maybe we should invite Mr. Smidt to join us," I tell him. "You could put him under oath and ask him."

This sets a little crease in the judge's forehead at the thought of going to war with the media, holding Harvey in contempt for refusing to reveal a source.

"Why? Make him media martyr of the month?" says Quinn. "For what?"

"It's your gag order," I tell him.

The judge swallows some pride. "I'll talk to him later. Privately," he says.

"Is that off the record?" I ask.

He shoots me a glance to kill.

"Next item," he says. "Friday morning I want everybody to be up and running, ready to go. Understood?" He glances quickly at Tuchio, then spends a good long time looking at me. "No continuances. The jury is ready to go. Is that understood? Are *you* ready?" He directs this at me.

"One question, Your Honor. Why are we starting on Friday?"

"You have something better to do?"

"Why not Monday?" I say.

"Because my court is available on Friday," says Quinn.

"Friday's fine with me," says Tuchio.

I'm sure it would be. The fact is, I begin to wonder if there isn't some design in this. Any lawyer I know, given a choice, would deliver his opening statement to the jury as the last order of business before a weekend, leaving them to ponder his every word for two days before confusing them with the evidence.

"So I take it you'll be ready to go on Friday with the rest of us?" Quinn is once again looking at me.

"Barring any more surprises," I tell him. "But the fact is, the prosecution goes first." I deflect the question to Tuchio.

"Oh, we'll be ready, Your Honor."

"Good. That's good. This then leaves the question of the jury," says Quinn.

Our jury has already been picked and primed, seven women, five men, with six alternates. As in any case of this kind, it is probable that the most I can hope for are a few strong-willed individuals for whom the seed of doubt is always germinating in their minds, or at least easily planted— people who will fight for their convictions or, better yet, who might be easily insulted, digging in their heels if others try to push them. My jury consultant, after shaking her psychic bag of bones over the juror questionnaires and after my having questioned them in the selection process, believes that we may have two who could fit this bill. On the other hand, African Americans are potential anathema for us. We have three on the panel, one retired military, another a janitor from a local school, and last a female investment adviser from one of the big firms downtown. There is no way to keep them off the jury on racial grounds, even though it is a given that Tuchio is likely to play the race card, even if from the sidelines.

"Is there a problem with the jury?" I ask.

"Whether they should be sequestered," says Quinn.

I had been halfway expecting this. It is clear that Tuchio and the judge have talked about this before my arrival, as the D.A. is already looking over at me for arguments.

"Not as far as I'm concerned, Your Honor. Not at this point at least."

"I'm not so sure," says Tuchio. "Letting the jurors go home at night with the paparazzi salivating, following them to their front doors," he says. "We could easily end up with a costly mistrial. Besides," he says, "if we're not going to sequester, we're likely to need more than six alternates on the panel."

"Hmm . . ." This sets the judge to thinking.

"If the court wants more alternates, we should get them," I say. "But I would strongly oppose any motion to sequester without some showing of cause, a reason in this particular case."

The argument here may seem strange to the untutored, but it is holy writ that locking a jury up for the duration in hotel rooms with bailiffs to tuck them in at night has devastating consequences for the defense, particularly in a lengthy trial. Jurors come to resent the isolation from family and friends. They begin to see themselves as incarcerated, which in fact they are. They place the blame invariably on the defendant, who should be the one in jail, even though in this case he is. Tuchio may have a legitimate reason for wanting to avoid a mistrial, but he also has an underlying agenda: to subtly poison jurors against the defendant.

"It's too late for more alternates," says Quinn. "I've already released the jury pool. If we proceed unsequestered, I want it to be understood that we will be running on a very thin thread." It becomes clear that this is the purpose for this discussion, to put me on notice that the court can pull the trigger at any time. "The first hint of anything inappropriate," says Quinn, "any untoward communication with a juror, and they're off to the Hilton. Is that understood?" He looks at me yet again.

I nod.

"Good. Next item," he says. "Witness lists. I want them finalized and submitted before close of business on Friday." He looks at both of us for a change.

"Your Honor, until we see all of the People's experts, we won't know who we'll need to counter them."

"We'll work that out," he tells me. "In the meantime I want to see witness lists in pretty much final form by Friday."

"With some exceptions?" I ask.

"With a few reasonable exceptions," he says. "And I emphasize the word 'reasonable.'" He looks down at the sheet in front of him in the open file. "That's everything on my list," he says.

"There is one issue," I say.

He looks up at me as he hadn't planned on either of us having an agenda.

"There is the matter of the victim's computer files," I say. "To date we've received only partial material from these. We have reason to believe that there are voluminous materials that the state has not turned over pursuant to our discovery motion."

Quinn looks at Tuchio. "What about this? I don't want any delays," he says.

"Your Honor, we're doing the best we can. Counsel is right—the requested materials are massive. It appears that only a part of the requested items are in the actual computers. According to my experts, my IT guys, Mr. Scarborough made a habit of moving data from the hard drive of his computers into storage on external hard drives. Thus far we have identified only some of these. We know that there are probably more. Here's the problem," he says. "We took out six, eight boxes of materials from his place in Washington, the town house. We have yet to process all of these."

"Well, get on it," says Quinn. "You have more people. Put them on it."

"We have other cases going, Your Honor."

"Then hire outside help," says Quinn. "I want these materials in the hands of the defense by next week, understood? No ifs, ands, or buts."

"We'll do the best we can," says Tuchio.

"No, you'll get it done," says Quinn.

EIGHT

The framers of the Constitution may have been brilliant, but they weren't perfect.

They lived in another age—lawyers, merchants, and gentlemen farmers— amateur politicians all. For their time the concepts they introduced were radical, but they were not unrestrained. The preamble may have been orchestrated for "We the People," but the fine print kept the common fingers off the piano keys.

The founders were men of property, in an age when only men who owned property could vote. The concept of common suffrage, to say nothing of women voting, was alien to them, something they would have rebelled against as vigorously as they fought the British Empire.

Campaigning for election to office was an act of personal dishonor.

They could not conceive of their experiment falling into the hands of full-time politicians steered by armies of consultants, forming committees to suck millions in "donations" from those seeking favor from government; permanent officeholders who would wield the levers of power with the partisan ruthlessness of warlords.

A Congress routinely hijacking essential national legislation just to load it with amendments like tumors, hauling pork back to their districts to solidify their death grip on power—this would have been as alien to them as E.T.

When Lincoln sat in Congress for his single term, beginning in 1847, he considered himself lucky to have a desk with a drawer for his private papers and the privilege to borrow a book from time to time from the Library of Congress.

Only the insane of the eighteenth century could foresee that a bleak two lines added to the Constitution a century after its creation, authorizing the collection of a federal income tax, could result in a seventy-year rampage by government to mentally rape its own citizens with millions of pages of totally unintelligible tax laws, rules, regulations, and forms.

Today we have special federal tax courts because the law is so convoluted that ordinary federal judges are presumed too ignorant and unschooled to understand the complexities of laws and forms that every citizen down to the village janitor is required to understand, to obey, and to sign under penalty of perjury and threat of imprisonment.

Nor could it be possible in the Age of Reason to foresee a Social Security system that if run by a private business would result in their arrest, prosecution, and conviction for operating a Ponzi scheme. In the real world, taking invested funds in the form of Social Security taxes, paying current claims, and skimming the rest for other purposes is called embezzlement. When government does it, it is simply called politics. In either case the arithmetic is always the same. When the scheme goes belly-up, its operators, if they're smart, will be in Brazil, or, in the case of Congress, retired, which is the political equivalent of being in Brazil.

With all of this, the people in what is touted as the greatest democracy on the planet have no effective recourse. They cannot act directly to fix any of the obvious open sores or seeping wounds in their own government, because the founders didn't trust them with the only effective medicine, the power to amend their own Constitution. That is reserved for the serpent its creators never saw.

Short of revolution, something Jefferson urged take place at least every twenty years, the average citizen is left to pound sand by casting a largely empty vote to replace the devil-in-office with the devil-in-waiting and hope that the caustic nature of power to corrupt can somehow be neutralized.

Praying for the devil to grow a halo, we all plod on, one foot in front of the other, trusting that somehow we will not follow the Soviet Union over the national cliff.

It is little wonder, then, that the founders

failed to envision the minuscule procedural crack that allowed the language of slavery to remain visible as a festering sore in the Constitution more than a century after the institution had a stake driven through its heart in the Civil War.

It would have taken a soothsaying of monumental capacity to foresee that Scarborough 150 years later could pick at this scab, the language of slavery, and open it to the point of inducing race riots and the civil unrest that now looms like a battle scene on Broadway out in front of the county courthouse downtown.

Early February, Friday morning, opening day of trial, and I'm being escorted by four burly sheriff's deputies through the throng of people, a horde I would estimate at more than a thousand as it jams the sidewalks. There are groups of angry protesters hurling insults like mortar rounds from one side of the street across the four broad lanes of traffic to the other side in front of the main entrance to the courthouse.

A huge banner, letters three feet high in black paint, has been unfurled and is now being displayed on the sidewalk in front of the courthouse:

END BLACK SLAVERY

Separate lines of deputies have been deployed along the whole block, all dressed in riot regalia, holding ballistic shields to keep the two warring armies from charging each other and doing battle around the cars and buses that are now stalled in traffic. A few crazies have managed to infiltrate the enemy camp on this side of the street, one of them trying to rip at the banner. Three uniformed cops are busy trying to keep them from being killed, struggling to pull them through the mob back to the ideological safe zone on the other side, where their own band of crazies is located.

I am reminded of the politically sensitive phrase that the city prints on many of its forms in big bold type:

DIVERSITY BRINGS US ALL TOGETHER

They'd better hope not, at least not today, or there's going to be one hell of a mess in the middle of Broadway.

Deputies at the fringes are confiscating any sign attached to a stick. Verbal insults are one thing, war clubs another. The sheriff has prepared buses normally used for jail transport so that if things get out of control, these can be rolled into place like a barricade to block the street directly in front of the courthouse. Thus far they've avoided using these.

So wild is the melee that Court TV, which wanted to film the trial but failed to get approval from the judge, has abandoned its outdoor perch, a covered enclosure set up on a scaffold near the corner at the intersection. Some in the crowd have now taken hold of the green metal pipes that support the scaffold. They are pushing and pulling them so that the entire structure, cameras included, is shimmying as if in an earthquake.

Many of the demonstrators in front of the courthouse are African American, some of them singing, others shouting. One woman, the veins on her neck protruding like electric wires under the skin, has blown her vocal cords. So hoarse is her voice that despite all the energy coiled in her body I can barely hear or make out her rasping words as I pass her with my escort, barely ten feet away.

As yet no one has taken particular notice of us. There are so many cops on the street that four more with a guy in a suit don't even register. Lucky for me. If this continues, once my picture gets around and they realize I'm defending Arnsberg, I may need an armored car just to get to court.

The other side of the street looks like Halloween, people in costume, some of them wearing hard hats and white T-shirts with the sleeves rolled to the armpits. They might pass for construction workers on break, except that their clothes look like they just came out of the washer. A small group, maybe six or eight nutcases in starched brown uniforms, all sporting swastikas on their arms, give the cops indignant looks and prance at the curb as if they're waiting for the second coming of the Führer.

One of them ventures into the street and gives a stiff-armed Nazi salute to the cop in front of him. The deputy returns the greeting by nudging the guy with his shield, pushing him back up onto the sidewalk, where he lands on his ass. A few feet away, Oberführer Number Two tries to get

a bullhorn past security. A tug-of-war en-
sues. The cops end up with the bullhorn,
and the field marshal ends up on the
ground, his hands behind his back, being
prepared for nylon handcuffs.

Surrounded by the escort, I hoof it
quickly to the steps at the main entrance
when something flies past my head. It hits
one of the cops in the back. A partially
crushed and fizzing can of soda shoots
bubbles and jets of tarry liquid as it spins
like a bottle rocket on the sidewalk at his
feet. The officer is angry. Even with the
armored vest he's wearing under his shirt,
he'll have a fair-size bruise on his back by
tonight. We stop momentarily while they
scan the crowd, trying to identify who threw
it. A few seconds and they give up. Even if
they could identify the pitcher, pulling him
out of an angry mob could turn what is a
budding riot into a rampage. We make it to
the front door.

Inside, the decibel level drops a hundred points. My escort takes a few seconds to regroup. One of them wipes some
of the Coke off of his colleague's back with
a handkerchief, and they head back out.

On the ground floor of the courthouse,

security is tight. Nobody gets in without going through the metal detector. Every briefcase and purse is scanned on the conveyor belt. Today there are uniformed officers questioning people as to their business, their purpose in the courthouse. If they're loitering to see the action, they're sent outside. By now every chair in the courtroom upstairs will be filled.

Anything, even a loud voice inside the lobby, will draw uniforms before you can move. I've sent boxes with all our trial documents and other materials ahead of me. Two young staffers hired part-time were assigned by Harry to deliver them to the courtroom early in the morning, before the storm troopers and the rest of the mob outside got out of bed.

It takes a couple of minutes to get my briefcase with the notebook computer through security. Before I can retrieve everything at the other side of the scanner, two reporters, one of them with a camera crew, jump me. The camera's lights catch me in their glow.

"Does your client know what's going on outside?"

"I don't know. I haven't seen my client

this morning." I'm walking, a good pace to get to the elevator, dodging people milling in the lobby.

Somehow the reporter with the camera is keeping up.

"What is he feeling?"

"Is he feeling any remorse?"

"Remorse for what?"

"He is charged with murder, isn't he?" The one reporter has his microphone in my face, camera aimed at me from over his shoulder as they sidle along, three of us like a human crab.

"Mr. Arnsberg has pleaded not guilty and is therefore presumed innocent. Why should an innocent man have feelings of remorse?"

"What about the evidence, his prints at the scene?" The guy with the camera is goading, pushing for some flare, a show of anger—cum—sound bite.

I finally get past him.

"The public doesn't buy his plea." He says this to my back as I head to the elevator.

"Then the public has a serious problem with our system of justice. Maybe you should go and talk to them about that."

"Does your client know any of the people in Nazi uniforms across the street?"

I ignore them and keep walking.

"Does he have a Nazi uniform?"

If he does, I'm hoping that Harry got to it before the cops and had the foresight to burn it. So far we haven't seen any pictures produced by the prosecution or otherwise showing Arnsberg in any uniform. But I don't tell the reporters this. There's always room for surprises. I keep moving toward the elevator, taking long, fast strides.

The cameraman, his lights blazing, trails me, capturing shots from behind. I can feel the heat of the lights on my back all the way to the elevator doors. *See the defense lawyer running away. Details at eleven.* I step inside and push the button—sanctuary. Upstairs is off-limits to cameras. The worst they can do now is sketch me.

* * *

Inside the courtroom the scene is enough to make the owner of the local cineplex green with envy. The center aisle is jammed, people trying to find empty seats. Uniformed deputies are everywhere, against the walls, mixed in with the mob.

One of the bailiffs is confiscating black baseball caps with white stitching above the bill reading END SLAVERY. These are being worn by a group of people who want to sit together. The First Amendment may still be in effect, but not in Plato Quinn's courtroom. If you want to send a message to the jury, you're going to have to use invisible ink.

A muscle of a deputy, beef on the hoof, is posted at the gate to the bar railing, making sure nobody gets up near the bench or back behind the scenes. Rudalgo Ruiz, Quinn's clerk, keeps a nervous eye on the crowd as he shuffles papers at his table in front of the judge's bench.

Tuchio is already here, seated at the counsel table to the right nearest the jury box, privilege of the prosecution. Next to him is one of the homicide detectives, Brant Detrick, the man who worked up the case against Arnsberg. Tall and blond, Detrick is a veteran of homicide. With almost twenty years on the force, he's the kind of witness that defense lawyers hate. You could turn him upside down and shake him, and Detrick would show not the slightest bias or personal stake in the outcome of the trial. "Just doing my job," while he quietly hangs your client. If anything, he has gotten more difficult over the years. Now that he's getting closer to retirement, the touch of gray at the temple and the wrinkles where his glasses crimp the bridge of his nose give him a kind of professorial look. At the far end of Tuchio's table is a woman I have not seen before, one of his assistants, a female prosecutor, African American. Only the blind would not be aware of the racial elements in this case. It's more difficult for jurors to ignore this issue with a minority sitting at the counsel table.

At the far end of the defense table, I see the large, hulking form of Herman Diggs, his bald black head glowing like a beacon under the courtroom's canister lights. Herman is our investigator. A human mountain originally from Detroit, Herman backed into his current vocation after a promising football career ended with a blown knee. We found each other in Mexico, on a case that grew ugly with violence. Herman and I came up realizing that we were the only two in sight who could trust each other. With Herman at my table, Tuchio would no doubt accuse me of playing the same card.

Herman is busy checking the boxes, seven of them stacked against the wall near his end of the defense table. These transfer cases with lids on them contain the materials delivered early this morning, documents and other evidence we may need during trial.

I lay my briefcase on the table. Herman lifts his head out of one of the boxes and turns to look.

"You come in through that mess outside?" he asks.

I nod.

"People got nothin' better to do," Herman mumbles to himself, his head going back halfway into one of the boxes. "You see all that crap back at the office? Damn truckload. That stuff have to come over here, too?"

"I won't know until Harry goes through it all."

"Yeah, Harry's up to his ass," he says.

Harry is back at the office pawing through boxes of printed data from Scarborough's computers. Tuchio dumped all of it on us this morning at eight o'clock, when a small van backed up to the sidewalk out in front of our office and unloaded boxes of documents. How long the D.A. has had these is uncertain, but Tuchio can prove that it was all printed within the last forty-eight hours. Of that he made sure.

It's all part of the game of modern litigation. Try your case while your opponent pushes a mountain of paper over on top of you.

"Excuse me, Counselor."

I turn. Tuchio is behind me, smiling, his radiance. He approaches from across the divide, the space that separates the two counsel tables. This morning he is decked out in his best power suit, blue pinstripes and a club tie, starched cuffs with gold links. Marching behind him as if in lockstep is his female deputy and the detective Brant Detrick.

Detrick I know. Tuchio makes a short introduction, and we shake hands. Herman comes over. I introduce him.

Then Tuchio presents his assistant. "I'd like you to meet Deputy District Attorney Janice Harmen."

"District attorney?" I say. "Have I missed

something? We aren't on appeal yet, are we?"

Tuchio laughs just a little. "Ms. Harmen is on loan. She'll be with my office for the duration."

She shakes my hand with a firm grip, no limp fingertips. Brown eyes, smooth coffee-colored complexion, her hair long to the shoulders with a slight wave. As she lets go of my hand, she looks me dead in the eye. The message is clear: woman on the rise. She intends to make her bones on my client.

"So how are you doing?" Tuchio stays and talks. His assistants return to their table. There's something almost longing in the way Tuchio approaches you, as if he were actually earnest about making a new friend.

"Frankly, I'd be doing a lot better if my partner wasn't back at the office picking through piles of paper we should have had two weeks ago," I tell him.

"Oh, that. Yes, I know. I do apologize for the lateness. But there was nothing I could do. I got the stuff myself only late yesterday afternoon."

"Is that right?"

"Absolutely," he says. He looks almost hurt that I should question this, then glances over his shoulder. "Janice." In the hum of the courtroom, a reporter is leaning over the railing talking to the deputy DA. "Janice." This time he says it louder. He gets her attention. "Can you get me a copy of that certificate? You know, the one from IT."

She nods and breaks away from the reporter, turns around and goes fishing in one of the sample cases under their table. These cases are commonly used by lawyers to carry heavy legal volumes and books.

"We got the materials to you as soon as we could," says Tuchio. "Our IT guys tell me there was hell to pay lifting the documents from Scarborough's hard disks. To begin with, there was a ton of material. I suppose you could figure that, the man being a writer. But some of it was old, archived on his computers but using software that's been off the market for ages. I'm no computer buff, but—"

Before he can finish, Janice is at his shoulder with a piece of paper. He takes it, looks at it briefly, then hands it to me.

It is an affidavit prepared by the police

department's forensics lab and signed by one of their techs, showing the date they started working on Scarborough's computer hard drives. According to the affidavit, they started more than a month ago, only to run into endless problems.

Tuchio tells me that Scarborough used three different word-processing programs over the years. Something called Word-Star, WordPerfect, and finally Word.

"That made it hard enough," says Tuchio. "Some of the older versions of these programs aren't supported any longer. Nobody sells them. I assume nobody uses them anymore either." He leans over and looks at the affidavit with me. "See, right here." He points to the paragraph where his technicians verify this.

"I assume your people have heard of ASCII?" I ask him. That's the thing about trying cases—you tend to learn a little bit about a lot of things, sometimes just enough to get you in trouble. ASCII is a common machine language usually readable from PC computers. Most documents, if they're the product of an obsolete program, can still be converted into ASCII and from this printed into text.

"I don't know what that is," says Tuchio. "You obviously know more about this than I do. But whatever it is, that wasn't the biggest problem."

"So what was?"

"Scarborough must have been at least a little paranoid," he says.

"Why do you say that?"

"Because everything in his computers was hidden behind a zillion passwords, and according to our technicians, he knew how to make them, the passwords, letters and numbers," says Tuchio, "nothing simple. Our IT people had to run software day and night for almost two weeks trying to crack 'em. They'd unlock one, only to run into another. Well, there it is," he says. "Now you have everything that we have." He smiles and then starts to turn to leave.

"Are you sure your people got everything that was on the hard drives?" I ask.

"Um . . ." He turns back, thinks for a moment, then offers a slight shrug. "Why do you ask?"

"I just want to be certain."

"Can any of us ever be sure of anything? They tell me that they were very thorough. But if you think we may have missed something, you're free to have your experts examine the drives. We can make arrangements. Do you want them?"

"Let me look at the materials first, and then I'll let you know. In the meantime you will preserve the drives?"

"Of course." He shakes my hand one more time. "Good luck," he says. "You can keep that." He smiles and taps the affidavit in my hand, then turns and heads back to his counsel table. Tuchio knows that at this moment he has knocked me off balance. I make a mental note to send him a letter confirming our conversation regarding the computer drives, with a copy to the court.

With the affidavit showing that the prosecutor did everything in his power to produce the materials from Scarborough's computers, any complaint by our side to the court asking for time to review the documents would be fruitless. With the jury impaneled and mobs in the street, the judge will tell me to read this mountain of paper while the state puts on its own case.

The prosecutor has done one better. He's gone out of his way to plant a small seed of confusion in our case, hoping, no doubt, that we will be distracted, waste time, perhaps chase this thing down some dead-ended rabbit hole. He has posed a question with no answer: Why would Scarborough, who wrote books to be published so that the whole world could read them, bother to conceal everything he wrote behind an infinite array of passwords?

NINE

Every seat is now filled. The overflow is sent back outside the courtroom to stand in line and wait for those with weak kidneys to start giving up their seats.

"Keep it down," comes a booming voice from a sheriff's sergeant at the back of the room, and a quiet chill settles over the audience.

Up front, a door at our side of the room opens just a crack. Through the small mesh-wired window in the door, I can see part of the head and shoulder of a uniformed deputy. He looks out at the crowd, checking everything one last time. Finally the door opens all the way. Out come two big deputies, more beef from the guard detail at the jail. Behind them, almost lost in their shadow, walks Carl Arnsberg, his head down, arms at his sides. He is wearing a new suit, his dark hair clipped short and parted on the left, slick and clean. He looks as if he's been polished using a high-speed buffer. Even his perennial five o'clock shadow is gone.

There are some hushed, muffled whispers in the audience as people point at Carl.

Herman, who delivered Carl's suit to the jail, whispers out of the side of his mouth, "Think ah used too much makeup."

I get a glimpse between the deputies. Arnsberg's face has a kind of white, bloodless look about it, like maybe a mortician got hold of him.

As they frog-march him toward our counsel table, suddenly the silence in the room is punctured by a loud shout: "Fucking fascist!" I turn my head to see a guy standing in the third row behind Tuchio's table, looking wild-eyed at Carl. The guy scrambles over the row of seats in front of him, stepping on people as he goes. He hurdles the next two rows. Before any of the cops can reach him, he runs over the bailiff standing at the gate and through the railing.

He is two strides from Arnsberg when I lash out with one hand. I catch just a piece of his blue T-shirt as he blasts by me. Everything after that is lost in a blur of motion. Somehow this is launched off the top of our table like a rocket out of a silo. It nails the guy in the side just above the diaphragm. You can hear the breath go out of him like a crushed bellows as he is driven into the floor by something that looks like an SUV wearing a suit. Herman bounces on him once, then comes up straddling the guy like a cowboy on a steer.

Two of the guards from Carl's contingent pile on. They cuff the man. He's lying facedown on the floor, dazed, probably wondering who put him in the Super Bowl without a jersey or a number. The cops don't even bother to pick him up. They just slide him, belly down, across the floor like a hockey puck and through the door to the lockup.

The other two guards, the ones who were chaperoning Arnsberg, are busy dusting off Herman, checking to see if he's okay.

A phalanx of deputies has now formed, strung out along the bar railing so that no one else in the audience has a chance of going upstage.

Out in the gallery, the crowd is milling. Up out of their seats like jack out of his box, their voices elevated, gestures animated. Give them a few glasses to hold and it could be a party. "Did you see that?" This is followed by the occasional instant mental playback, all with hand gestures for color. "Who is that guy?" "Must be a cop."

If I told them that Herman was Superman's African brother, half of them would believe me. How else could a mountain move that fast? Mixed in with the free radicals, some wearing black T-shirts as a show of solidarity, there are a good number of regular courthouse-goers here, retired folk who spend their days watching trials because it's better than the three hundred channels on cable. Where else can you see real bullet holes in the wall? Live theater, the best ticket in town, it's free, and getting better now that they've brought contact sports inside.

From the corner of my eye, I see Sandra Arnsberg, Carl's mother, standing on her tiptoes trying to see her son through the forest of uniforms in front of her.

I motion to her that I will get him.

In the rush of adrenaline, everybody but her has forgotten about Arnsberg. He is left standing by himself off to one side like some abandoned urchin. The guards talking to Herman cast an occasional glance his way just to make sure he doesn't walk off. Where would he go with a wall of guards at the railing?

I walk over to him. "Are you all right?"

"Yeah," he says. "What was that all about?" Evidently Carl hasn't seen the action out on the street.

"Just some crazy," I tell him.

"Yeah. Guy's nuts." Carl looks over his shoulder at the door to the lockup where they dragged the guy, probably wondering if he has to go out that way when we're done.

"I thought you were supposed to come to the jail this morning?"

"I was." I tell him about the D.A. dropping a ton of paper on us at the last minute.

This seems to unnerve him.

"Anything bad?" he says. "What? What did they send? Why so much at the last minute?" Carl doesn't understand a lot of this. Any little wrinkle tends to send him into panic.

"It's okay. It's material we've been trying to get for some time. Printouts from Scarborough's computers."

"Oh."

I take him by the arm, walk him to the counsel table, where we sit.

He smiles, then waves at his mom through a crack between the cops.

"They told me I can't have any exercise time in the dayroom anymore. Something about not enough staff," he says.

Carl has been doing twenty-three hours a day in solitary since they arrested him. Now he'll be doing twenty-four. The sheriff has had to segregate him at the jail because they know they can't protect him. With the media hype, Carl has become the ultimate symbol in the great cause of every jail and prison in the country, the war of the races. The Aryan Nation would claim him as their own, force him to join whether he wanted to or not, and kill him if he refused. To the Black Brotherhood, he's a dead man walking, top priority to be shanked in the shower or have his throat cut in the yard at the first opportunity. If they could do this in the middle of the trial, it would send a message—the only one that counts when you're behind bars: "Don't fuck with us."

"Quiet!!!" Suddenly the booming voice of the sergeant at the back door again. "Everybody sit down." The festivities out in the audience are over. As if somebody had pulled the plug in a game of musical chairs, there is a dash for seats. Within seconds the noise level drops.

Herman comes back to the table. On the way by, he slaps out a quick if low rendition of the brothers' handshake with Carl—crossed palms, cupped fingers, and a light slap.

"Hey, man, you're gettin' better," he says. Herman has been doing this ever since Carl's first week in jail, after they broke the ice on information from the kid, leads that

Herman had to run down with the leather of his shoes.

As Diggs sits, Carl leans over. "I owe ya, man."

Herman shakes it off. "You owe me nothing."

"No. No. I mean it. You nailed that guy," says Carl.

"If I didn't, the cops would have."

"Yeah, but you did it."

"Now let's see if I can get outta bed in the morning, and after that I'll have to see if I can move." He laughs it off.

I know that Herman is taking heat. He has received some ugly phone calls, wrong numbers to "Uncle Tom." Some hip artist did graffiti on his car. I've told him that there is no dishonor in begging off on this case. It's one thing for a lawyer to take on a controversial cause. If John Adams was right, even the devil deserves a defense. I've told him that there are other investigators who can step in. Herman would be busy full-time just doing the other cases in our office.

To all of this Herman has said no. Part of this is the man's nature. No one is going to tell him what case he can or cannot work. He is not a joiner of clubs—social, political, or otherwise. He is not afraid of anything that walks on two legs and could probably thrash most that walk on four. If you're counting on group dynamics to change his mind, be advised that organized intimidation, whether racial or political, is much more likely to fuse his backbone into titanium than turn it to jelly.

And there is one thing that I know about Herman, because he has told me. Herman Diggs is the progeny of slaves. If the laws of genetics hold true, they must have been proud people, because if they are any kin to Herman, their masters never broke them.

I see a shadowed figure approach from the hallway leading to chambers. It's Ruiz, the judge's clerk. The show is about to begin.

Ruiz comes out and stands near the foot of the bench, his shoulders back, his chest puffed out, and in almost a squeaky tone, what passes for the voice of authority from R2-D2, announces, "All rise. Superior Court for the State of California, County of San Diego, is now in session, the Honorable Plato Quinn presiding."

There is the hushed friction of cloth as it leaves every seat in the room, all on their feet. Quinn strides out, black robes flashing. He climbs the few steps to the bench and takes his seat. The high-backed leather throne swivels a little. He tries the gavel, and there is the shotlike clap of hard wood. "You may be seated."

Everybody in the room drops as if legs just gave out.

The judge sits for a moment looking out at the courtroom, a death stare, his eye scanning the crowd, his expression one of paternal irritation. "Before we start," he says, "I want to make a few things clear. Those of you in the audience, no matter what you might think or how strongly you might feel, *you* are not participants in this trial. You are here to watch and observe, and that is all. There will be no demonstrations or disturbances allowed in my courtroom. Any talking, clapping, booing, hand signals, written signs, or other gestures, any demonstration of emotion of any kind, and you will be removed. I don't want to see any newspapers, books, magazines, or anything else being read in this courtroom while the trial is going on. If I do, you will be removed. If you want to read, go to the library. There will be no food or beverages anywhere in the courtroom, no candy or gum. If you want to stick gum under a chair, do it at home at your kitchen table, not here under my benches."

He goes through the routine about cell phones, cameras, and recorders not being allowed inside the courtroom. "If you have any one of these, give it up now or lose it." He pauses a second. Nobody holds up a hand or steps forward. "If I hear a cell phone ring, you may as well hand it to the bailiff to answer, because that phone now belongs to the county.

"Cause a problem in my courtroom and you will go to jail." He gestures with his gavel toward the door at the lockup, which is now closed. "You will not pass go, and no one from the press will be allowed to talk to you so as to immortalize your message to the world. Do I make myself clear?"

Some in the audience are probably wondering whether this includes having Herman pulverize them in the form of a human blocking sled before they get to go to jail.

"If it becomes necessary, I will clear the courtroom. If this happens, no one will be allowed back into the audience. You can watch the trial on closed circuit downstairs. I will tell you right now that that room is tiny, the chairs are uncomfortable, and the bailiffs are just as uncompromising."

He continues directing his death gaze out at them for what seems an uncomfortable eternity, then settles back in his chair.

"The clerk will call the case."

Ruiz reads from a single typed sheet in his hand. "People of the State of California versus Carl Everett Arnsberg. Case number . . ."

We waive a formal reading of the charges, and then Quinn looks over at one of the bailiffs. "Bring in the jury."

From a door just off to the right and next to the jury box, they come out, two men, one of them middle-aged, wearing a suit and a stern expression, followed by a younger man in blue jeans and a slip-over shirt. Then three women file out, two of them African American, one dressed neatly in a pantsuit, the other in jeans and a brightly colored top. The third woman is older, wearing a black wool skirt and a matching top with a Chinese red cashmere scarf around her neck, one end tossed over her shoulder. She is sporting bright jewelry—large rings on three fingers of one hand and a gold bracelet on the wrist of the other. When she leaves at the end of the day, you'll be able to find her by following the parade of felons attached to her jewelry after she passes the probation office downstairs.

The procession into the jury box continues.

We have dossiers on all of them, information down to whether they have nicknames and if so what they are, their jobs, income levels, the churches they attend if any, the number and names of their children and grandchildren. If it is possible to psychoanalyze them without shooting them up on drugs, we have done it, both sides, Tuchio with his state-paid consultant-cum-shrink and we with ours.

Like any jury, this one is a microcosmic social cauldron, an economic, racial, and political melting pot with the burner turned off. Other than being voters or having a driver's license—which is how they got pulled into the jury pool to begin with—and besides the fact that they breathe air and will bleed if cut, there is almost nothing that any of them have in common. They're here for two reasons: because the witch doctors of jury consulting believe they possess some hoped-for bias that will help either one side or the other or because one of us, Tuchio or I, ran out of bullets in the form of peremptory challenges to blast them off the jury.

They file into the jury box until it is full. The last six take chairs that have been set up just outside the railing to the box, directly in front of it. These are the alternates. For the time being, all of them are sleeping at home, comfortable in the thought that at least at night they can return to the real world and their families.

As soon as the last one takes his seat, Quinn starts in.

"Good morning!" He beams down at them from the bench—Mr. Happiness. Those in the audience have to be wondering if they've drawn Jekyll and Hyde as a judge and, if so, where he keeps his syringe.

Plato Quinn may play God in his own

court, but he has presided over enough trials to know that in a case like this there is one group he has to cater to, come hell or high water. He's looking at them now, flashing more teeth than the average alligator. He will feed them, worry about their bladders, give them regular breaks along with a steady diet of entertaining homilies from the bench, and if possible get them home early whenever he can.

This is an expensive, high-stakes case. Quinn knows that if he ends up with an unhappy or rebellious jury, he can find himself staving off a mutiny as he bails to avoid a mistrial. When taxpayers fork over millions on a case that will be constantly on the airwaves, with updates every minute or so, the last thing anybody wants is a story with no ending. The political powers aren't likely to forget who was at the helm if the trip has to be taken again and the case tried over.

"I hope you all slept well last night." He gets a few nodding heads, some half grins, and a broad smile from the woman decked out in her best going-to-court outfit, complete with rings and jangling jewelry.

"We have a little work to do today, but it

shouldn't take too long. I'm hoping for a light day. I know it's Friday, so I hope to get you out of here and on your way home before the rush hour."

This brings a lot of vigorous, happy nodding from the direction of the box.

The judge shoots a look at Tuchio, whose opening statement is the principal order of business for the day, a little gentle stage direction from on high not to be too long-winded.

"We'll also get to know each other a bit better. I hope you're all comfortable with the court staff." Quinn introduces his clerk and the bailiff, whom they already know. What they don't know is that if they are sequestered, he will become their personal jailer.

"These people are here to make sure that your time on jury duty is as pleasant and comfortable as we can make it." Quinn makes it sound like a party, cookies and milk over photographs of Scarborough, his head all bloodied by the claws of a hammer.

Some of the jurors are looking around, taking their first gander out at the bleachers, where there is standing room only and a sea of serious faces, some of them still flushed by the threats from the judge. The jurors are probably realizing for the first time how important they are, the random hand of government having given them the power, like the emperor with his arm outstretched, closed fist with thumb protruding, suspended over the question of life and death.

Quinn does a few more introductions. He starts on us.

"You already know Mr. Tuchio, the district attorney."

The Tush gives them a big smile and waves from his chair.

"And Ms. Harmen, who will be assisting him."

She nods and favors them with the pearly whites.

"And of course counsel for the defense, Mr. Madriani." The judge nods pleasantly toward me. "I see Mr. Hinds is not with us today."

"He couldn't make it, Your Honor." I could tell him that Harry has become the recycling king, buried under a pile of last-minute paper by Tuchio, but why bother?

Quinn skips right over my client, the

eight-hundred-pound gorilla, the reason we're all here, and instead finds himself looking at Herman, whom he doesn't know.

I get up out of my chair, fingering the middle button on my suit coat, and give the jury my best college smile.

I introduce Herman, who stands and half bows toward the jury. "And last but not least my client, Carl Arnsberg. Carl." I gesture for him to stand.

This catches Carl completely off guard. Nobody told him he was going to have to stand up and meet people. He becomes what he is, a kid stumbling over his feet trying to get up. When he finally makes it, he looks over at the jury and offers a kind of sheepish grin that slowly blossoms into a full smile. This becomes infectious when a few of the jurors begin to smile back.

Tuchio is halfway out of his chair, worried, I suspect, that Arnsberg might try to say something, like, *Please don't kill me. I didn't do it.* This is matched by Quinn's stark expression up on the bench, judge in the headlights.

It is one of those moments when dumb luck plays a hand, surprise aided by awkward innocence and the ill-fitting suit that

Herman picked off the rack giving Carl the image of a prairie schoolboy. All that's missing is a stalk of hay dangling from his teeth.

It's a good thing none of the jurors have X-ray vision, or they'd be looking at the edgy artwork, swastikas, and other social commentary tattooed on his arms and upper body.

Carl stands there grinning, casting an occasional shy downward glance. The judge finally pushes his heart back down into his chest and says, "Thank you, Mr. Madriani."

Under the glare from the bench, I put a hand on Carl's shoulder, and we both quietly sit.

Quinn is not happy having his dog and pony show with the jury hijacked. But on the scale of things at the moment it is not worth his wrath.

When you're defending, the one thing you don't want sitting in the chair next to you at a murder trial is the invisible man, a silent, emotionless cipher of a client charged with crimes so vile that normal people have trouble imagining them.

When I look over, Tuchio is hunched at

his table, working over the notes for his opening statement, his pen whittling away. He has a kind of benign no-crime, no-foul grin on his face, though you can bet he is seething inside. If he wants to put Carl to death, he will have to burn out of their brains the image of the defendant standing in front of the jury, smiling at them with the homespun geniality of Will Rogers.

"I'm going to give the jury a brief break. Ten-minute recess," says Quinn. "I will see counsel in chambers."

TEN

Ten minutes turns into an hour, a good part of which is spent with Quinn giving me more than a small slice of his mind. "If you want me to introduce your client to the jury, I'll be more than happy to do so," he tells me. "But under proper guidelines and with clear instructions to the defendant that under no circumstances is he to make any statement or say anything."

"He didn't, Your Honor."

"Damn lucky for you," he says. "And what's this business with your investigator? Where the hell is Hinds?" He reminds me that Harry is assigned the penalty

phase of the trial in the event that Arnsberg is convicted and the jury has to decide whether he gets life or death. "He's
supposed to be here."

"When the evidence comes in," I tell
him. "When the first witness is sworn, he'll
be here."

"I asked you where he was."

"You want to know where he is, ask Mr.
Tuchio."

Quinn looks over at the prosecutor, who
is lounging on the judge's couch against
the wall in the corner. "I don't know where
he is, Your Honor."

"He's back at the office checking for
roadside bombs tucked into the truckload
of materials from the victim's computers
that your office delivered to us at eight
o'clock this morning."

"Oh, that," says Tuchio.

At this, Quinn looks up from his desk,
flustered. "Those were supposed to be delivered a week ago."

Tuchio's turn to wiggle.

"What about it?" says the judge.

The Tush fishes the affidavit from his IT
people out of his briefcase. "We sent the

court a copy as soon as we got it," he says.

"What the hell is this?" Quinn gets his glasses on and starts reading. "Why wasn't I told?"

"We didn't know ourselves until the last minute," says Tuchio.

The judge tries to throw the paper. It seems to add to his frustration when it lands with all the force of a fallen leaf on the blotter in the middle of his desk.

"Get Hinds over here," he says.

"When do we get to look at the materials?" I ask. "I know it's a small point, but they may be central to our case."

"You think maybe Scarborough left a suicide note in his computer?" says Tuchio. "'I'm angry with the world. I'm depressed. P.S.—I'm gonna beat my brains out with a hammer.'"

"I want it on record"—I ignore him—"that this stuff came late. That the cops didn't even see it before they charged."

"You can look at it over the weekend," says Quinn.

The fact that the cops haven't even had the time, let alone the inclination, to look at these leaves open the question whether there are e-mails with death threats strewn all over Scarborough's hard drives. And God knows what else.

"It's a safe bet, given the subject matter of his writings, that there were probably regional chapters of 'Hate Scarborough' committees," I tell them.

"Yes, but did they all have their finger-prints on the hammer?" says Tuchio.

"For all you know, there could have been a line forming outside that hotel room door with people paying quarters to take a whack at the back of his head," I tell him.

"Yes, and they all wiped their finger-prints off the hammer except your client."

"Enough," says the judge. "You." He points at me. "Call your partner. Get him on the phone and tell him to get over here now."

*   *   *

It takes Harry almost an hour in midmorn-ing traffic to cross the bridge, drive down-town, park his car, and hoof it to the courthouse.

Quinn is angry at my antics with Carl in front of the jury, so he takes it out on Harry. He lets us cool our heels while he sits in chambers as the clock edges toward the lunch hour, then sends Ruiz out to announce that his lordship has released the jury and gone to lunch. Court will reconvene at one-thirty.

* * *

"Did you find anything?" I ask.

Harry and I eat stale sandwiches out of wrappers from a deli around the corner. We are standing up at a counter listening to the strains of "We Shall Overcome" over the backdrop of the percussion section of the Nazi National Orchestra beating their hard hats against garbage-can covers they've turned into shields.

"There's a lot of stuff there," says Harry. "And there's no way to be sure we got it all." He tells me that he has left two paralegals separating the materials by date and subject. The most important—the stuff pregnant with possibilities, according to Harry—are Scarborough's e-mails, though he did a quick toss, turning as much of the stack as he could upside down looking for early drafts of Scarborough's book. It is here, according to Trisha Scott, that Scarborough left references to the letter supposedly written by Jefferson, the would-be dynamite for Scarborough's next book.

"Nothing," says Harry. "Maybe she's right. If he shredded the printout copies of all his old work, maybe he erased everything from the computers as well."

The state's theory is that Carl killed Scarborough for reasons of racial animus, not because the author was black, since he wasn't, but because his words both written and verbal threatened the Aryan sense of racial superiority—that, and to impress others with similar views.

Over all of this, the missing Jefferson Letter now looms large. There is the question of its intrinsic value as a motive for murder, assuming that the original letter was available and Scarborough could get his hands on it. It is also possible, though there is no evidence at the moment, that perhaps the author had the original at the time of his death. If so, the fact that it is missing and that the police did not find it on Carl or at his apartment in the hours following the murder may be the stuff of which a credible defense is made.

Beyond this is the information from Trisha Scott, how Scarborough tried to use the letter in *Perpetual Slaves* and how she convinced him not to, for reasons of questioned authenticity. We have the detective's note, following his interview with Bonguard, that the letter was the inspiration for all—the book, the tour, and what is now approaching $30 million in earned royalties. It is possible that whoever possessed the original of the letter, and who presumably gave Scarborough his copy, might be jealous. Maybe he wanted a cut of the book's earnings and Scarborough refused to give it up? All of these are possible motives for murder, and from everything we know, none of them apply to Carl Arnsberg.

The Jefferson Letter is the seething force that inspired Scarborough's historic venom. It is there, throbbing, at the heart of our case. We cannot see it, but its effect and its force are palpable.

*   *   *

It's one forty-five when the wizard finally comes out from behind the curtain and takes the bench. Quinn shuffles a few papers as he looks down to make sure that Harry is really there and that it's not somebody in a Harry mask.

Finally satisfied, he looks down at Tuchio. "Is the prosecution ready to proceed?"

Tuchio stands. "We are, Your Honor."

"Then you may present your opening statement."

The prosecutor circles the front of the counsel table until he is standing before the jury, no more than six feet from the alternates seated directly in front of him. His arms are folded, feet slightly apart, the power suit draped on his body. He looks at them for a few long seconds in silence, studying the twelve in the box from one end to the other before he finally speaks.

"Why are we here?"

He allows the question to linger in the air just long enough. Tuchio has a sense of timing.

"I'll tell you," he says.

Somehow I thought he would.

"We are here so that the People of the State of California can present evidence to you"—the volume of his voice rises now—"evidence of a heinous, cold-blooded crime, the most serious crime possible, the intentional taking of another human life, the capital crime of murder.

"I am going to tell you a story, ladies and gentlemen. It is a true story—"

I was hoping for Hansel and Gretel.

"—with evidence to support it and witnesses who, under oath, swearing to tell the truth, will sit right there." Tuchio points with an outstretched arm toward the now-empty witness box. "Witnesses who will tell you in their own words what they saw and what they heard. You will see the murder weapon. You will see photographs of the crime scene in all its horror. You will hear experts, scientists and others, explain to you their professional opinions concerning aspects of the evidence and how they came to arrive at their conclusions.

"After you have seen all the evidence and heard all the testimony, you will be instructed by the judge on how to evaluate what you have seen and heard here in this courtroom. And then you will be asked to render a verdict.

"Your Honor, I would ask the defendant to rise."

The judge wasn't ready for this. Neither was I. Quinn looks befuddled, but he complies with Tuchio's request. "The defendant will stand."

Carl looks at me like, *What's going on?*

I tell him to stand, to look straight at the jury. Don't look away.

We both get up. Carl faces the jury once more. But this time he isn't smiling. He looks scared.

Tuchio turns back to the jury box. "You will be asked to decide whether that man"—he turns, again with an outstretched arm, his finger pointed like a cocked pistol at Carl—"whether on July eighth of this year, the defendant, Carl Everett Arnsberg, in cold blood and with malice aforethought, murdered Terrance Scarborough."

Tuchio drops his arm and stands there in front of them in silence. Carl is still standing, looking at the jury like a stone statue. No one is smiling at him from out of the jury box this time. I tug gently on his coat sleeve, and we both sit.

Tuchio turns and looks at us, wrings his hands a little, then starts again.

"On the morning of June fourteenth, a warm, sunny day here in San Diego, Terry Scarborough, a man of letters, an author of some considerable note, who was to appear on national television that night, was busy in his hotel room preparing to appear on Jay Leno's show."

Tuchio doesn't mention that Scarborough was also a lawyer. Why risk tweaking a broad public bias?

"Mr. Scarborough had everything to live for. He had just published a new book, a book that had become a number-one national bestseller." He nods his head, strokes his chin with one hand, and begins to move in front of the jury, pacing. "Oh, it was a controversial book to be sure. It was a book that dealt with serious issues." He ends up at the prosecution table right on beat, and from a cardboard box on top he plucks a copy of Scarborough's book. Then he heads back toward the jury, studying the book's cover, opening it, fanning a few pages until he gets back to the closed cover. I have now seen this enough times that the image on the book's jacket is burned into my brain.

The Tush and I have argued behind closed doors with the judge about whether the jury should be allowed to read the book. For the moment the answer is no, though Quinn has left himself enough room to change his mind if he chooses to. The question is whether the book is relevant. Tuchio says that it is, his argument being that it was the content of the book that formed the motive for the murder, or rather Arnsberg's resentment of that content. The judge is not satisfied that the state has established this. He wants to see more evidence.

"Perpetual Slaves: The Branding of America's Black Race," Tuchio reads the title to the jury. Then he holds the book up so that they can all see the front cover.

Even from a few feet away, they can't miss the large, rust-hued photograph, probably a daguerreotype dating to the Civil War. It is a picture of a black slave, his hands chained as he stands withered and dazed, his head lifted, looking straight ahead. Around his neck a heavy iron ring has been bolted closed. Sprouting outward from this ring, like rays from the sun, are footlong sharpened spikes, so that the man cannot even lay his head on the ground to rest. If you look closely, you can see scars on his shoulder where the lash of a whip has opened the skin like a plow turning furrows in the earth.

"This is a book about the evils of slavery." Tuchio looks over at me as he says this, almost begging for an objection.

He knows Quinn would slap me down. As long as Tuchio doesn't veer into argument or dally too long at the fringes, the judge will give him leeway in his opening, enough to make his case if he has the proof.

"It is a book about the burdens and brutality of an institution that many believe has left painful social stigmas. Stigmas that still divide this country, even today."

"Amen." A single loud male voice from the audience.

Quinn grabs his gavel and slaps it once as he looks out from behind an angry stare.

He could have the deputies start searching the aisles for the miscreant, but Tuchio doesn't give him time.

"Among other things this book recites portions of the United States Constitution, provisions written more than two hundred years ago, provisions that allowed human beings, African Americans, to be held in bondage, owned by other Americans as slaves. Of course, most of us are aware of this, the history of slavery, the Civil War, all of that. But what's more, this book informed the public of what many people, people who are not lawyers, did not know— that this language, the odious language of slavery written so many years ago, that this language remains to this day a part of our Constitution." A few eyes in the jury box open up wide at the revelation.

"Oh, slavery was abolished sure enough, repealed by amendments after the Civil War. But the language of slavery was never actually removed from the text of the Constitution. Most people don't know that," he says. "And many are offended by it. It remains there in the Constitution as a visible stigma of what it is to be black in America."

"Your Honor, I'm going to object." I'm on my feet.

The judge is nodding. "I agree. Mr. Tuchio, what does this have to do—"

"I've made the point, Your Honor, if you'll allow me to move on."

"Please do."

Tuchio thinks for a moment, regroups. "This book, and the message that it contained, was the reason Mr. Scarborough was in San Diego that day, the day he was killed. He was on a book tour, doing readings at local bookshops and sitting for news interviews on television and radio."

He turns the book over in his hand so that when he holds it up again for the jury to see, they are no longer looking at the front cover, but the back, the full-size color photograph of Scarborough taken somewhere in a studio, his blue eyes peering out at them, his dark hair neatly combed, his tanned face smiling in the full flush of life.

The Tush has more pictures of Scarborough. The jury will see those later. I've seen them already, crime-scene shots from the hotel and others from the morgue. The contrast between the one in his hand and those will not be good for our side.

"What Terry Scarborough could not know that morning, what he didn't know that day, was that it would be his last. Because as he sat there in that hotel room savoring his success after a long, hard effort of research and writing, Terry Scarborough was brutally and savagely beaten to death, by a killer using of all things the sharp, naked claws of a carpenter's hammer."

A couple of the women on the jury wince. Tuchio now has their undivided attention.

"So ask yourself, what led to this crime? Was it the result of some dispute, an act of passion or rage following an argument? We don't know what was going through Mr. Scarborough's mind at the moment of his death, other than the claws of that hammer. But what we do know, based on evidence that we will produce here in this courtroom, is that the killer did not confront his victim face-to-face. We will produce evidence showing that the person who killed Mr. Scarborough did not give him even the slightest chance to defend himself. No. No. The state will present evidence that Terry Scarborough"—he points again to the picture on the book jacket—"never saw his killer, because the person who struck him with that hammer came at him unseen from out of the shadows, from behind, as Terry Scarborough sat in his hotel room, in a chair, making notes."

He finally drops the hand holding the book.

"This is not a long and tortured story, a

tale of intrigue, of some dark deed in the heat of passion between people who knew each other. In fact, if we were able to bring Terry Scarborough back to life and bring him here into this courtroom today and point to his killer, Mr. Scarborough wouldn't recognize him, because he never knew him. He never met him, except in that brief instant of violence at opposite ends of a bloody hammer.

"Ladies and gentlemen, the state will present evidence that the defendant"—he points at Carl—"Carl Everett Arnsberg, was an employee at the hotel where Terry Scarborough stayed, the hotel where he was killed. We will show that the defendant, Carl Arnsberg, had access to master keys that would allow him to enter the rooms of hotel guests, including the room of the victim, Terry Scarborough."

Tuchio takes a few steps.

"The state will present evidence that the murder weapon, the hammer used to kill Terry Scarborough, belonged to that same hotel where the victim, Terry Scarborough, was staying and where he was murdered. We will present evidence that this hammer was normally kept with other tools, locked inside a maintenance closet located on the same floor as the victim's room, and that the defendant"—he points again— "Carl Everett Arnsberg, possessed a key to that maintenance locker."

Tuchio starts with the little stuff and works up. Always leave them on a high note.

"The state will present evidence of shoe impressions, impressions left in the blood of the victim on the floor of the hotel room where Terry Scarborough was murdered, impressions that match shoes"—his finger is like a pistol now—"owned by, and found by police in the residence of, the defendant, Carl Everett Arnsberg."

Tuchio's tush is beginning to rock and roll.

"The state will present evidence from witnesses who will testify that fingerprints found on the bloody handle of the murder weapon, the hammer used to kill Terry Scarborough, match the fingerprints of the defendant, Carl Everett Arnsberg." He points again, now getting into high gear the rapid staccato of his case. From behind he's starting to move like Buddy Holly.

"The state will present evidence that when he was arrested, the defendant, Carl Everett Arnsberg, had in his possession, both on his person and in his apartment, items showing the schedule and locations where the victim, Terry Scarborough, was slated to speak and to sign books."

It is this that forms one of the bases for the death penalty, the theory that Arnsberg was stalking his victim.

"Finally we will produce witnesses who will testify here before you in open court that in the days just before Terry Scarborough was murdered, this defendant, Carl Everett Arnsberg, met with others and made statements indicating a clear and open hostility toward the victim, Terry Scarborough. We will show that that hostility was based on the defendant's objections and his outright hatred for the ideas and thoughts espoused by Terry Scarborough and published in this book." Tuchio now holds it up high. "We will show that the defendant, Carl Everett Arnsberg, in the presence of others, stated a clear willingness and intention to commit serious acts of violence upon the victim, Terry Scarborough."

It's Tuchio doing Elvis on Steriods.

Movement or not, he is slick. He avoids overstating the evidence, though the inference is clear. He would have the jury believe that Carl threatened to kill Scarborough and did so in front of witnesses. It's a fine point, but from what we know from the state's witnesses, the only conversation was about kidnapping Scarborough. Nor is it entirely clear who first suggested the idea.

If you aren't careful, you can fall into this pit and end up jerking the jury around at the worst possible time, in your closing argument. It is a favored game of defense lawyers. What did the state promise, and what did it prove? Like everything else, you have to measure the words. If you aren't listening or, worse, fail to get the transcript and read it, you end up arguing that the prosecutor promised but failed to prove that your client threatened the victim's life. Then, while you're choking on the transcript of Tuchio's actual words from his opening statement, he will be pointing out to the jury that kidnapping is in fact a crime of violence, which is all he ever said.

By then lawyers' hour will be over, with the jury in no mood to split more hairs. Kidnapping, killing, it won't matter. Carl will be kissing his mom good-bye and packing his toothbrush for a trip to the death house.

"Ladies and gentlemen, there may be many reasons a person will kill other human beings. But to do it because of what they think or because of what they write surely must be among the worst."

"Mr. Tuchio."

Before I can object, Quinn is on him, looking down from his perch. This is argument, pure and simple. Tuchio knows it.

"The jury will disregard that last statement," says the judge.

Sure they will.

"We will show," Tuchio goes on as if nothing has happened, "that it was this book and the thoughts and statements contained in it that are at the heart of this case, the reason Terry Scarborough was murdered." He hammers the point home.

Tuchio turns and aims the cover of Scarborough's book toward our table like Moses brandishing the tablets.

I have coached Carl that in moments

like this he is not to look down or to allow the prosecutor to force him to avert his eyes.

"Ladies and gentlemen, we will prove beyond any reasonable doubt that that man, the defendant, Carl Everett Arnsberg, murdered Terry Scarborough and that he did so in cold blood and with malice aforethought. Thank you."

There is a sprinkling of applause from the audience. It is quickly graveled down by the judge.

If Tuchio is grandstanding, he's doing a bang-up job. As for the race card, there was never any question. It had to be played. From the beginning the state had a problem. They needed a motive for the crime. Thanks to Scarborough, they picked the only one seemingly available, the one that screamed out at them from everything Scarborough said and wrote, the motive that would fire the fury of any reasonable juror to believe that Terry Scarborough died at the hands of a crazed bigot.

Let them chew on that one for the weekend.

ELEVEN

Saturday morning, and the small Craftsman bungalow on Coronado, the place I call home, seems cold and empty. My daughter, Sarah, is gone, off to college in Colorado. It's been almost two years now. Still I miss her, the quiet talks we once had, the animated chatter of her friends when they came to visit, the late-night runs for pizza, teenagers sprawled on the sofa and chairs of my living room talking and laughing. They would take over the house, and I would head upstairs, listening to the muffled music of their voices down below. I miss it all.

This morning there is no clatter of dishes, no smell of pancakes on the griddle. These days breakfast alone is a little fruit, maybe a piece of toast if I'm in the mood, and call it good. My doctor may be happier. I'm not sure I am. I can't remember the last time I made a full pot of coffee or cooked anything outside the microwave. Now my coffee comes either from the little single-cup French press on the counter or from one of the kiosks that seem to sprout like poppies all over town.

Once in a while, I will run into one of Sarah's old high-school friends at the village grocery or window-shopping the boutiques on Orange Avenue. When asked how she's doing, I will say fine, and she is, blossoming, becoming her own person, spreading her wings, new friends and horizons. I talk with Sarah on the phone every few days, more often if I can get her to answer her cell. She comes home every summer, at least for now. I see her at Christmas and Thanksgiving and whenever I can tear myself away for a weekend in the Rockies. The rest of the time I spend learning the emotional dimensions of the empty-nest syndrome, what it is to be alone. Friends tell me I will get used to this.

This morning I pad around the cold confines of my house in slippers and a robe, carrying the morning paper in one hand, a cup of coffee in the other. I plop down in one of the chairs facing the television and click the set on with the remote. This has become my Saturday-morning ritual, one hour of all the bad news I can handle.

The screen flickers on, goes silent for an instant, and then the sound comes on: "You know, I think Paul Madriani is probably a very good local criminal defense attorney. I certainly have nothing against him." It's lawyers' hour, as if that ever ends on one of the cable news channels. A gal wearing some red lace frock outfit—all that's missing is a peacock feather in her hair. I've seen her before. She's one of the regular electronic legal mouthpieces. "What this case needs is someone with national credentials, somebody who can put together a kind of racial political dream team."

"I agree entirely with Gladys." Some guy claws his way onto the screen, bow tie and preppy sport coat. "Otherwise his client is going to get steamrolled. I can tell you right now that in this case the state is gunning for bear. They know what happened in O.J. It was a career killer for those who prosecuted. They're not going to make that mistake again."

I turn to the front page of the newspaper, another bombing in Baghdad, trouble with Iran—who could have guessed? The kicker at the top of the paper tells me the dollar is sliding again. Pretty soon we'll have to use pesos to stay ahead of inflation.

I open the paper hoping maybe things will get better inside. Page two, there's a three-column picture of the melee in front of the courthouse yesterday morning. The reporting seems to cover the brawl outside more than the events inside, which for us is just fine. The story spends only four 'graphs recapping Tuchio's opening statement, though they hit the high points, a summary of all the damaging evidence the state promises to present and of course the erroneous interpretation that the state has witnesses who will testify that Arnsberg threatened Scarborough's life.

I continue reading. Next page a head-

line at the top: DEMOCRATS AT WAR WITH THE
WHITE HOUSE.

Republicans are accusing Democrats
in the Senate of holding up two nominations to the federal circuit court of appeals
in Washington, D.C. They claim the Democrats are playing politics with the courts,
hoping for better tidings following the next
presidential election, now less than nine
months away.

Democratic leaders in the Senate vowed
to work with the president. But from all appearances, members of the Senate Judiciary Committee have their feet planted
solidly in cement.

As one Republican critic put it, "Given
the Mexican standoff in the Senate, nobody is going on the D.C. circuit unless
Democrats are allowed to take the nomi-
nee into the Senate cloakroom and per-
form a lobotomy."

I read on. The District of Columbia circuit court is seen as the incubator and
launching pad for future appointments to
the Supreme Court. The story explains that
the high court has been evenly split along

party lines for more than a decade. It talks about some of the hot-button issues, abortion and the death penalty. Whether the Court should be urged by Congress to more clearly define the war powers of the president. Whether government should be allowed to intercept private e-mails without a warrant. Whether citizens should continue to be allowed to own and possess firearms. The list goes on.

According to one Court observer, "Decisions involving important social, legal, and political issues now teeter on the edge of a knife; judicial edicts that can dictate the rules of society for a hundred years increasingly are being decided by a single swing vote on the Court."

Members of Congress realize that the current political equilibrium between the Court's liberal and conservative members cannot last. According to one source, there are at least three members of the Court who would like to retire but who feel they cannot until there is a changing of the guard at the White House.

The piece goes on to discuss some of the senior members of the Court, three of them in their seventies and one who is eighty-seven. Two of them have had recent illnesses. Should any of them retire or die, it would be considered a coup by the current White House, since the power to name their replacement would significantly alter the balance on the Court.

"One of these justices, Arthur Ginnis"— my eyes perk up as they run over the type with his name—"who is 67 and underwent hip surgery last winter, has been on and off of medical leave from the Court for several months due to complications. Ginnis was expected to return to the Court full-time in the fall, but that didn't happen. According to reports, he is making progress but still recovering at an undisclosed location outside Washington. Political pressure is building for Ginnis to either return to the Court or retire. There is no law that requires him to do so, and there is some historic precedent based on other long-term absences for illness.

For the moment the high court is hobbled, unable to take up a number of controversial cases in its current term. This is because, according to Court watchers, it is Ginnis who is seen as the pivotal swing vote in many of these cases. According to these observers, decisions as to whether to take up these cases will simply have to wait for his return.

I have a letter out to Ginnis's chambers at the Supreme Court and have left a telephone message. I've asked him to contact me and introduced myself as defense counsel in the Scarborough murder case. I have not mentioned the Jefferson Letter or asked any specific questions, only made a request that we speak. So far I have received no reply. I turn back to the article.

Politicians on both sides of the aisle seem to comprehend the significance of the moment, that a change of epic proportions in the ideological makeup of the high court may be just over the horizon, a change that could dictate social and legal policy in the country for much of this century.

As for the question of who will control the Court, leaders in both political parties see the current skirmish over nominations to the D.C. circuit court as the opening salvo in a looming war.

To quote one lawyer who has argued cases before the Supreme Court, "Given the number of imponderables, the fact that it is impossible to anticipate what momentous issues will be presented to the Court in the future, stocking the Supréme Court with your believers is now the biggest political endgame in America."

I close up the paper and put it to the side. There is no rocket science in this. The federal courts are untouchable. The framers of the Constitution made them that way. Where else could a beverage company take your house for a new bottling plant and have the elevated minds of the high court define this as a public purpose under the eminent-domain powers of the Constitution?

One federal appellate circuit occasionally goes off on a wobble so erratic and out of conformity, not only with precedent but with strictures of ordinary reason, that at times it has been referred to quietly by some who practice before it as the "Ninth Circus."

TWELVE

Monday morning, and Quinn's courtroom is like a pool filled with gasoline. Now that there is no longer any doubt that the state's case will be racially charged, we're all swimming in it, and the air is electric.

First up into the witness box are two patrol officers, the first to arrive on the scene immediately after the crime was called in. They each testify that they took one look and concluded that the victim was dead. They did a quick search of the entire suite to determine there was no one else inside and then sealed the area, making sure that no one else entered. One of them took a statement from the hotel maid who'd opened the door and found the body slumped on the floor in front of a chair in the living room.

This is all preliminary and sets the stage for Brant Detrick, the lead homicide detective. If you're looking to settle a jury down and get them into the rhythm of your case, Detrick is a good opening witness.

According to his testimony and based on notes he made at the time, Detrick was on the scene within forty minutes of the initial call to 911.

The D.A. then takes a few minutes to qualify the witness not only as an experienced homicide detective but as an expert in crime-scene reconstruction, for which Detrick has taken courses both locally and with the FBI.

Tuchio then has him lead us on a verbal and visual tour of what the cops found at the scene. He has Detrick stand in front of an easel with a mockup of the floor plan of Scarborough's hotel room. This shows furniture drawn to scale and situated where it was on that day.

In the process, the detective offers testimony, a partial re-creation of the events at the scene and how according to the police they unfolded. He identifies the chair, the one the cops believe Scarborough was seated in when he was murdered.

"There was a considerable amount of blood on the headrest at the upper back of this chair, leading us to conclude that the victim was seated in this chair when he was struck from behind," says Detrick.

He moves on to the area where the body came to rest, on the floor, in front of the chair, and off to the right as you look into the room.

"We believe that the victim either toppled or slid from the chair, as a result of one or more of the impacts from the murder weapon as it struck him or because lividity caused the body to slide out of the chair and onto the floor at some point after he died."

Tuchio and the witness get into a discussion explaining to the jury the hydraulics of lividity, the movement of blood in the body after death by the force of gravity, and that this can sometimes move a body, especially if it's propped in a chair or leaning toward the edge of a bed.

"When you arrived that morning, what else did you see?" asks Tuchio.

"There was a lot of blood and spatter evidence," says Detrick. "The floor around the chair in the living room near where the body was found was pretty much covered in blood, as was the tile floor in the entry."

"What do you mean by 'spatter evidence'?" asks Tuchio.

"I'm talking about droplets and spray that are usually flung out in an arc of some kind when a weapon, a blunt instrument, or a knife has become covered with blood and is repeatedly swung. This tends to throw out a spray of blood, sometimes tissue, that ends up on other surfaces—a wall or the ceiling, for example."

"And you saw evidence of such blood spatter in this case in the victim's hotel room?"

"I did."

"Where?"

"There were patterns on the ceiling, directly above and to the front, and behind the chair near where the body was found."

Tuchio has him draw a dotted line on the room diagram in the direction and location where the spatter evidence was found. "There was also some evidence of spatter on the television screen, here." He marks the location of the television directly in front and several feet away from the chair. "And on a small table, here, and a light briefcase, a leather portfolio that was on that table. And farther off to the right, we found some traces on the surface of a small table, underneath a tablecloth and tray with food on it."

"But not on top of the tablecloth or tray?" Tuchio makes this very clear.

"No."

Harry and I have been wondering how they're going to deal with this. Blood under the cloth and tray but not on top means Arnsberg would have had to kill Scarborough while juggling a tray full of food and a tablecloth in one hand while he hit him with the hammer in the other.

"Did you find anything else?"

"We found a carpenter's framing hammer."

"When you say framing hammer, can you describe the hammer for the jury?"

"It was a typical hammer, the kind you might find in any hardware store. A metal hammer with claws for pulling nails or prying wood apart."

"Was there anything peculiar about this hammer that brought it to your attention?"

"Yes. It had a considerable amount of blood on it, along with traces of tissue and hair stuck to the hammer in the area of the claws."

"Okay. In relation to the other items in the room—the area where the victim lay, the chair, the television—where did you find this hammer?"

"It was on the tile floor a few feet off the carpet in the entry."

Tuchio has him mark the diagram with the location where the hammer was found.

"When you saw this hammer, did you form any conclusions based on its location and the fact that it bore signs of blood and tissue?"

"The obvious one," says Detrick.

"And what was that?"

"That there was a good chance that this was the murder weapon."

Tuchio then walks over to the metal

evidence cart that has been rolled out in front of the clerk's desk. He picks through several paper bags, each of them sealed closed with a labeled tape from the police crime lab. He checks the tag on each bag until he finds the one he wants. Without opening it he carries the bag to Detrick, who is now back in the witness chair, and hands it to him.

"Would you open it, please, and remove the item inside?"

Everybody in the courtroom already knows what's there, but the little drama keeps us all looking.

Detrick, who is wearing a pair of white cotton gloves, tears open the top of the bag, reaches inside, and removes the hammer. He holds it gently in both his gloved hands so the jury can see it. What appears to be rust but in fact is dried blood can be seen on the claws and head of the hammer.

"Detective Detrick, do you recognize that hammer?"

There is an evidence tag hanging from a string tied around the handle near the head. Detrick looks at the tag. "I do. It's the hammer that was found on the floor in the entry hall not far from the body of the victim, Terry Scarborough."

"Can you tell us anything else about that particular hammer? Its size, shape . . . ?"

"According to our investigation, it's a thirteen-ounce, smooth, octagon-face, straight-claw fiberglass hammer with a rubber grip and a twelve-and-a-half-inch-long handle."

"When you say fiberglass, what part of it is fiberglass?"

"The handle, which is covered by rubber at the grip."

He has Detrick point to the hammer's claws. "And straight claw," says Tuchio. "As opposed to what?"

"Rounded or curved claw," says Detrick.

"It sounds like you've become an expert on hammers," says Tuchio.

"No, we made inquiries, mostly telephone calls, based on the manufacturer's information stamped into the metal regarding model numbers, and that's the information we got back."

"Can you tell us who owns that particular hammer?"

"Based on a mark painted on the handle

and a number stamped on the head of the hammer, it's part of the tool inventory belonging to the Presidential Regis Hotel in San Diego."

"Is that the hotel where the victim, Terry Scarborough, was staying on the morning he was killed?"

"It is."

Tuchio has the witness put the hammer back in the bag, then has it marked for identification and returns it to the evidence cart. He won't move it into evidence, not yet, not until other witnesses from the crime lab and the coroner's office identify trace evidence that was found on it, hair and tissue along with blood, tying it directly to the victim. Instead he reaches underneath to the second shelf on the cart and finds the next item. This is in a manila file.

"Before we move on, let me ask you," says Tuchio. "Besides the hammer you've just identified and the blood and spatter evidence that you've testified to earlier, did you find anything else unusual in the immediate area around the victim?"

There is some confusion here. Detrick is not precisely sure where Tuchio is trying to take him.

"In the tiled area of the entry hall," prompts the prosecutor.

"You're talking about the shoe impressions?"

Tuchio doesn't say it but nods.

"Yes. We found shoe prints, impressions from the soles of two shoes, as well as what appeared to be a partial human palm print and three separate fingerprints."

"Where did you find these?"

"They were quite obvious. They were on the surface of the tile floor in the entry. They were imposed in the partially dried blood on the tile."

Detrick comes off the stand long enough to locate on the room diagram the general area where these were found. He has trouble marking the area of finger- and palm prints, as it is almost on top of where he placed the hammer.

Detrick is back on the stand.

"Let me ask you, Detective, as the lead investigator on the scene, did you have occasion to have photographs taken of the crime scene and the area around it that morning?"

"I did."

Tuchio now hands him the file from the

evidence cart that he has been holding and asks him to look at the photographs inside. "We have provided copies of all these items to the court and to the defense," says Tuchio.

The judge nods and opens a file in front of him on the bench.

Tuchio and I argued over these for the better part of two days in front of the judge in chambers, during and just after jury selection. There were nearly two hundred photographs of the scene taken that day by police from various angles and distances. We have culled them down to twenty-eight photographs, close-ups and distance shots showing the layout of the room, the scene from different angles. There are close-ups of the television set and a leather briefcase, a kind of thin zippered port-folio on a table next to it, both showing signs of a light film, which we know to be the fine spray of blood flung out by the centrifugal force of the hammer as it was swung to strike Scarborough's head. There are a few distance shots showing the body on the floor, a few papers scattered under and around him, shots of the hammer and the location where it lay on the floor in the entry, pictures of the shoe impressions with rulers for scale and two of the palm and fingerprints, again with a ruler for scale. There is one showing what we believe to be the elongated skid mark in the blood, the comma that comes to an end at the wall.

There are only four shots that show close-ups of the victim, close enough to see the gaping wounds with clotted blood and brain tissue at the back of his head. One of these, a shot from above showing not only the wounds but Scarborough's left eye wide open, pupil dilated like a fired camera lens, is the most startling. Tuchio fought for this photograph to come in as if it were the Holy Grail. I argued that the graphic nature was so shocking as to be prejudicial in the extreme. It was the end of a long day, and the prosecutor's tactic of holding this for last worked. Quinn was tired, worn down by too many arguments. He swept mine away with the comment that "after all, there *was* a murder."

Detrick looks at the photos, identifies each of them as having been taken at the scene. Under questioning he identifies photographs of the hammer, the shoe prints, and the single palm print and fingerprints.

Tuchio has each of the photographs marked for identification and immediately moves them into evidence.

"Any objection?" says Quinn.

We both know he will swat down anything I say, since we have argued this already, but for the record, possible appeal, it is necessary. "As to People's Thirteen, the one photograph we object to based on Evidence Code section 352. That the prejudicial content so clearly outweighs any probative value."

"Overruled," says Quinn. "The items are admitted into evidence."

Tuchio immediately moves that the jury be allowed to see them.

"So ordered," says the judge.

The photos begin to circulate through the box. While this is happening, Tuchio poses a number of bland questions to Detrick—whether he or any of his officers searched other rooms in the suite, whether they found anything in those rooms, if he or any of his officers collected witness statements from any of the hotel employees—this without getting into any real details, nothing that might cause any juror to listen or take notes. He would read the phone book to them if he could. Tuchio wants nothing here that might distract from the photographs circulating through the jury box at this moment. Some of the jurors are looking at them wide-eyed and slack-jawed, the thought never having entered their minds that a hammer, a tool so common that most of them have at least one in their own homes, could do this to a human head. They will be looking at their toolboxes in the future with the same cautious glance they now aim over the top of the eight-by-ten glossies toward Carl, sitting next to me.

Finally, when he can't dawdle any longer, Tuchio starts another line of questioning.

"Detective Detrick, have you ever had occasion to meet or personally talk to the defendant, Carl Arnsberg?"

"I have."

"When was the first time you met him, if you can remember?"

"It was the day after the murder. The following morning, I believe."

"Can you tell the jury why you met with the defendant?"

"In order to interview him."

"Why?"

"We were in the process of questioning all the employees who were on duty at the Presidential Regis Hotel on the day of the murder, and information came to us that the defendant, Mr. Arnsberg—"

"Objection, Your Honor. Hearsay."

Quinn looks up.

"We don't even know what the witness is going to say, Your Honor." Tuchio tries to edge in.

"May we approach the bench?" I want to get it away from the jury.

The judge waves us forward. He pushes the little button on the bench. This creates a tone barely audible to the human ear, but if we were to shout, people in the jury box as well as those in the audience would never hear a word.

"We know what the witness is going to say, Your Honor." I talk before Tuchio can get a word in. "He's going to tell the jury that Arnsberg ran, that he fled the scene, when in fact there's no evidence of that at all."

"He left work unannounced," says Tuchio. "He didn't tell his supervisor or anyone else why he was leaving or where he was going. And that's why the police bumped him up on the list of employees to be interviewed. Pure and simple," says Tuchio.

"That's not why the prosecutor wants it in, Your Honor. He's wants it to infer flight from the scene."

"It is what it is," says Quinn. "The jury will have to decide."

"It's also hearsay, Your Honor. The witness is testifying to information given to him by others—the hotel supervisor, for one—and he's not on the stand."

"Oh, he will be," says Tuchio, "to testify that your man disappeared, didn't say a word to any of the other employees, and that the last time anybody saw him was before the victim's body was found by the maid and reported."

"Overruled," says Quinn.

Just like that we're back out, the dead button switched off. The prosecutor puts the question to Detrick again.

"As I was saying, we were in the process of interviewing all the hotel employees who were on duty that day—"

"The day of the murder?" says Tuchio.

"Yes. And information came to our attention that the defendant, Mr. Arnsberg, had left work early that day, unannounced. He hadn't told his supervisor or anyone else that he was leaving. So we wanted to interview him at the first opportunity."

"And that opportunity was the following day?"

"Correct."

"When you interviewed him the next day, where did that interview take place?"

"At the defendant's apartment in downtown San Diego."

"And did you ask him why he'd left work early the previous day?"

"I did."

"And what did he say?"

"He said he wasn't feeling well, so he went home."

"But he didn't tell his supervisor?"

"No."

"Or anyone else he worked with?"

"Not that we've been able to locate."

"Did you ask him why he didn't tell his supervisor?"

"I never had the chance."

"Why was that?"

"Because I received a phone call on my

cell phone from headquarters that fingerprint evidence from the crime scene had
been analyzed and that that evidence appeared to link the defendant, Mr. Arnsberg,
to the crime."

"What did you do then?"

"We took Mr. Arnsberg into custody."

"You arrested him?"

"That's right."

Now Tuchio starts making repeated trips
to the evidence cart and back to the witness on the stand. First comes a paper
bag containing the plastic raincoat. Detrick
identifies it, along with a bloodied towel
from the hotel that the raincoat was wrapped
in when police found it in the Dumpster
near the hotel parking area.

Another trip, another paper bag, this
one larger than the bag containing the
hammer.

"After you arrested Mr. Arnsberg, did you
at any time obtain a warrant to search the
premises of his apartment, the location
where you first questioned him?"

"One of my officers did."

"And did you conduct a search pursuant
to that warrant?"

"We did."

"When did you conduct that search?"

"The same day. The day we arrested the defendant."

"And did you find anything during the course of that search?"

"We found a pair of dark slacks that appeared to have a few small stains of what looked like dried blood. These appeared to be ground into the fabric near the knee and hip areas."

"Can you tell the jury where you found these slacks?"

"In a clothes dryer in the basement of the apartment building where the defendant, Carl Arnsberg, lived."

"So these slacks were being dried after being washed?"

"Objection. Calls for speculation."

"Sustained," says the judge.

Still, the point is made. Unless he was removing wrinkles, why would Arnsberg be drying a pair of slacks if he hadn't washed them?

"But they were being dried?" Tuchio comes right back.

"They were already dry," says Detrick. The machine was off, but it was still warm when we found the slacks inside."

"Did you find anything else during your search?"

"We found a pair of dark Nike running shoes with rippled soles that appeared to have traces of blood in some of the grooves. There were also stains that looked like they could be blood on the outside of the upper part of the right shoe."

"And where did you find these shoes?"

"They were on the kitchen counter near the sink."

"Did you find anything else during the course of this search?"

"A small, hard-bristled brush and a can of cleanser," says Detrick.

"Where did you find these?"

"On the sink right next to the shoes."

This time Tuchio comes back from the evidence cart with an array of bags. One at a time, he hands them up to the witness, and they do the drill.

Detrick, still wearing the white gloves, identifies the dark slacks found in the dryer, then the shoes, along with the brush and the can of cleanser that was found on the sink next to them.

The jury is taking it all in, most of them busily making notes.

Like pixels on a screen, the pieces of evidence in Tuchio's case start to flicker and glow with the early outline of a picture. At the moment there's nothing I can do to dim it, the image of a killer diligently doing his laundry, busy scrubbing the blood of his victim from his slacks and shoes.

Finally he has Detrick recap the evidence presented so far by putting it all together. He asks the witness, as an expert in crime-scene reconstruction and based on his investigation and observations at the scene, to give the jury his studied opinion as to the sequence of events surrounding the commission of the crime.

According to Detrick, the killer entered Scarborough's hotel room probably by using a master key, as there was no evidence of a forced entry. The killer probably already had the murder weapon, having secured it from a maintenance closet on that floor by using the same master key used to enter the victim's room. The electronic key employed in a lock by someone who is experienced in its use would be virtually silent. According to the witness, the killer was already wearing the clear plastic raincoat that the police found in the Dumpster near the hotel parking area, this to prevent blood from splattering all over his clothes. The perpetrator approached the victim, who was seated in the chair facing away from the door and was probably engrossed in studying or reading documents that were later found near the body by police. According to Detrick the killer could have covered the eleven feet from the door to the back of the victim's chair in less than two seconds, striking the victim with the murder weapon from the right side and making contact in the area near the base of the skull, thus immediately rendering Scarborough unconscious.

"This was followed," says the witness, "by a savage attack involving multiple blows with the murder weapon to the top or crown of the victim's head, the rear at the base of the skull, as well as the lower right side of the victim's head around the right ear and just behind it." The medical examiner will give chapter and verse, the details of all this. "For this reason," says Detrick, "we conclude that the assailant was right-handed."

This of course includes 90 percent of the world, including our client.

"In addition," says Detrick, "we believe, based on the patterns of blood-spatter evidence and the various locations where this was found, that at some point in the attack—and most probably from its very inception, including the initial blow to the victim's head—that the perpetrator used both hands to wield and swing the murder weapon, the hammer."

I look over, and Harry is staring back at me. Unless Carl has a secret life that includes juggling in a circus act, the cops have just abandoned any notion that he was holding the tray while swinging the hammer. So how did the tablecloth and tray get on top of the blood they found on the table? While I can dream, it is not possible that they could have missed this.

"Based on the evidence at the scene, blood spatter on a small table testified to earlier, we believe—it is my opinion—that the perpetrator then proceeded to put into place what he thought was a carefully contrived cover story by retrieving a tray of food and a tablecloth which we suspect he may have left outside the hotel room's door, probably on the floor in the hallway."

This is neat, since every hallway in ev-

ery hotel has a few trays on the floor outside rooms, and therefore no one walking
by would notice.

"Based on the evidence, it is my opinion
that these items—the tablecloth, tray, and
food—were brought inside the room and
carefully laid on a table a few feet from the
body of the victim after the crime was committed."

This is how they explain away the presence of the food, the tray, the tablecloth,
and Carl's explanation of how he came to
be in the room. The cops have always had
two problems here. Explaining away the
blood on top of the table and the absence
of blood on top of the tray and tablecloth
was only part of it. Even if they could somehow sweep away the blood evidence, how
could they possibly explain to the jury how
Carl could enter the room, waltz behind
Scarborough sitting in the chair, set the
table that was off to the side, and then
walk back and nail Scarborough from behind with the hammer? Harry and I have
scratched our heads over this one for
months. We thought it was possible they
might argue that Arnsberg did just that—
set the table, got behind, and somehow

distracted the victim, perhaps with the meal check to be signed. In the chair, while he was writing and looking down, Scarborough would have been a perfect target. But the meal check was still on the tray when the cops found it, unsigned and pristine, with no blood on it. Detrick's explanation, a story that in one fell swoop takes care of all this, is the kind of result-oriented theory that causes your average cynical and jaded defense lawyer to wonder if just maybe his client isn't telling the truth after all.

"Based on the evidence," says Detrick, "at some point we believe that the perpetrator became startled, panicked, and ran, and that during this flight his shoes picked up substantial quantities of blood from the carpet in the area surrounding the chair and the victim. This blood was then transferred to the tile floor in the entry as he exited the carpeted area, resulting in two shoe impressions." The witness points at the location on the diagram.

"This, coupled with a quantity of blood already accumulating on the tile floor in the entry area, caused the perpetrator to slip and fall, resulting in what appears to be the skid mark here"—Detrick points at the chart—"as well as the finger- and palm prints left on the tile." He points again to the diagram. "Based on the evidence from the scene, it is my opinion that the raincoat worn by the perpetrator at the time of the crime failed to cover or shield his entire body, so that portions of his clothing made contact with the victim's blood when he fell."

This is the final stroke. Tuchio's witness has tied it all up in one neat package. They will argue that the reason Arnsberg left work and ran home without telling anyone is that he had blood on his clothes, something he hadn't planned for in the original scheme. Tuchio will tell the jury that Carl simply didn't think fast enough to come up with the story that he ultimately told the cops, the one he related to Harry and me during our meeting at the jail when he admitted to the slip and fall.

This brings the prosecutor to the final order of business with this witness, Carl's statement to the police the day they arrested him.

Detrick establishes that they Mirandized the defendant, told him that he was entitled to legal counsel, that a lawyer would be appointed if he couldn't afford one, that he had the right to remain silent, but that anything he said could be used against him. Then they asked him if he wanted to talk.

Of course, by that time Carl was a veritable motormouth, his jaw jacking with every little detail of what he saw and what he did, right down to the slip and slide in the entry hall, everything out on the table so that the police could understand and give him a lift home as soon as possible.

For their part, the cops were measuring the size of the swastika on the inside of his forearm and wondering how hard it would be to get photos of this, or better yet the real thing stretched out and nailed to the top of the jury railing, where the twelve good citizens could study it, a picture being worth a thousand words and all.

The statement in the form of a transcript, questions and answers, is in essence chapter and verse what Carl told Harry and me at the jail—the tray up on his shoulder as he backed into Scarborough's room, tented under the tablecloth. This along with vigorous denials each time the interrogators, Detrick and his partner, accused him of killing Scarborough. During their questioning they also got into the issue of the bloody pants and shoes. At one point Detrick asked Arnsberg why he simply didn't burn them, drop them off a pier into the ocean, or toss them into a Dumpster somewhere, where they could not be found. Carl gave him a simple answer, one so hapless and unvarnished that it might just pass for the truth. Carl told the cops that he couldn't destroy his clothes, because he couldn't afford to buy new ones and he needed them for work.

It's one of those ironic situations that can crop up in a trial. As a rule you never want a client to say squat to the cops anytime, anyplace, about anything. But in this case I'm not at all certain that Tuchio would introduce this statement, as there is virtually nothing in it that is incriminating, unless they can punch holes in it with their later witnesses. It also provides us with the argument that, armed with advanced knowledge of the defendant's explanation for his conduct, the state then reverse-engineered the theory of its case to account for every detail of Carl's story. Detrick's reconstruction is just a little too neat.

The reason Tuchio brings the statement in is that he knows if he doesn't, he can be sure that I'll ask Detrick about it on cross-examination, in which case Carl's words would take on much more credence, the inference being that the prosecution was trying to hide them.

While neither Tuchio nor I can be certain how this will play out in front of the jury, one thing is sure: The D.A. cannot cross-examine the printed statement as he could with Carl if I were to put him on the stand. All in all, it may not be such a bad way for Carl to get his story in front of the jury.

Tuchio tries to have Detrick testify as to particulars, the actual content of what was said during the interrogation.

In a snap I'm on my feet objecting. "The document speaks for itself, Your Honor."

"So it does," says Quinn. "Sustained."

The state moves it into evidence, and we spend the next twelve and a half minutes listening as Ruiz, Quinn's clerk, reads the statement aloud to the jury. This avoids all the inflections, comments, and inferences that you can bet would slip in with Detrick's color commentary.

When R2-D2 finishes reading, Tuchio turns and looks at me. "Your witness."

THIRTEEN

By the time the prosecutor finishes with Detrick, the morning has already crawled past noon and is edging toward one-thirty. Quinn adjourns for lunch. Harry and I scramble to find quick sandwiches and a quiet place where we can closet ourselves. We compare notes, trying to find loose threads from Detrick's testimony, anything to tug on in cross.

So intense is our focus that, as it does for a patient under anesthesia, the dimension of time seems to disappear. In what seems like seconds, the lunch break is over and we're back in court.

"Detective Detrick." I start my question standing behind the counsel table and slowly move around it toward the witness stand. "Do you recall whether—when you entered the hotel room that morning, the scene where the body was found—whether the television was on or off?"

He gives me a kind of quizzical look, raised eyebrows that the jury can clearly see, as if perhaps next I might ask him if the evidence techs were busy channel surfing, looking for reruns of *CSI* with the remote as they mulled over the body.

He shakes his head, smiling. "No, I think the set was off," he says. "You can see it in several of the photographs."

"And when your officers arrived on the scene, the first responders, was it on or off then?"

"They're trained not to touch anything in a situation like that. Unless it's something that threatens to disturb the scene or destroy evidence, they wouldn't touch it."

"So we can be fairly confident, then, that the set was off when they arrived?"

"I'd say so, yes."

"How big is that set, would you say, Detective? Just the size of the screen?"

"I'm no expert on televisions. I'd have to put a tape on it and measure it," he says.

"I'm sure you watch television once in a while—football games, baseball?"

"Sure."

"So you have a television at home?"

"Yes."

"I'll bet you have one of those big-screen sets?"

"I guess you could call it that."

"How big is the screen on your set?"

"I get the feeling I've stumbled onto the Home Shopping Network," he says.

Lots of laughter in the jury box.

"I hate to tell you this," he goes on, "but I don't know how big the screen on my set is. My wife bought it."

The jury laughs again. By now we're all smiling.

"You've got a good wife," I tell him.

"Yes I do," he says.

"She probably won't mind, then, when we all come over on Sunday to watch the game?"

More laughter.

"She might draw the line at that," says Detrick.

We smile and laugh, jocularity all around.

Then I drag him back to the point: the size of the screen on the television in the living area of Scarborough's hotel room.

He finally concedes that it's a good-size screen.

"And when it's turned off, as you testified it was on the morning that you arrived at the scene, the screen surface on that set would appear as a dark, glossy glass. Is that a fair description?"

"Yes. I suppose." I can tell by the look in his eye he's starting to see it now, where I'm going.

"If you were to stand or sit in front of that big, dark, glass screen when the set was turned off, as it was when your men arrived, is it possible that you could see your own reflection in that screen?"

"Sure. It's possible."

"In fact, when that set is turned off, for all intents and purposes the screen acts like a mirror, doesn't it?"

He looks at me but doesn't answer. He wants to think about this.

"Yes or no?"

I turn back to my counsel table and pick up a copy of three of the photographs now in evidence.

"I don't know if I'd go that far," says Detrick, "but you could probably pick up reflections."

"May I approach the witness, Your Honor?"

Quinn waves me on.

"Like the reflection in this photograph?" I hand it to the witness as I identify it so the prosecutor and the court can look at their own copies.

He looks at it quickly. "I suppose. Yes."

I retrieve it from him and hold it up for the jury to see.

"Am I correct that this is a photograph taken by one of your crime-scene technicians?"

"That's right."

"And can you tell the jury what you see on the television screen in that photograph?" I show it to him again.

"I'd say that's the reflection of the photographer and some flash from the strobe on his camera as he shot the picture."

"And this one?" I hand him another photograph and identify it. "Tell us what you see on the dark television screen in that photograph."

He puts on a pair of reading glasses

now and holds the photo up to the light. "It looks like the reflection of one of my technicians."

"And where is that technician standing, in relation to the chair that you marked in the diagram? The chair you believe the victim was sitting in when he was struck from behind?" I point to the chair in the scaled mock-up.

"Looks like he's behind it," says Detrick.

"Based on what you can see in that photograph, the reflection captured off the television screen shows one of your technicians standing behind the chair where the victim was murdered, is that right?"

"That's what I said."

"Detective Detrick, based on what you've seen in these two photographs, if you were sitting in that chair, looking at that dark television screen, and someone approached you from behind, wouldn't you see his reflection in the screen?"

"I suppose if I was looking directly at the screen at the time."

"Even if you were doing something else—say, reading, looking at some information on paper while seated in that chair—and someone approached you from behind, isn't it likely that the reflection of the person's motion on that screen would draw your attention?"

"I don't know. Can't say. Too many variables," he hedges.

"Like what?"

"Well, like how focused his concentration was on whatever he was doing. Whether he was looking down at the time, maybe reading something in his lap. Maybe the victim's peripheral vision wasn't that keen," he says. "Maybe he was snoozing at the time." Detrick smiles just a little.

"Let's suppose that he wasn't snoozing. Let's suppose that instead the victim was reading, looking through some papers. By the way, while we're on the point, besides blood, did you or your officers collect anything else from the area directly around and under the victim's body?"

"Yes. Some typed pages," he says.

"Do you remember whether you or your officers examined any of those pages as to their content?"

"We did."

"And what did you determine with regard to those pages?"

"The victim appeared to be going over notes, apparently in preparation for a television appearance that was scheduled for later that day."

"Ah, so let's assume that the victim wasn't sleeping, that instead he was reading these papers at the time he was killed. Don't you think if he was doing that and someone approached him from behind, the victim might see that movement in the television screen?"

"As I said earlier, I really can't say. The answer would depend on too many things that I don't know."

"You mean, like the intensity of the victim's concentration, his peripheral vision . . . ?"

"That and whether he was actually in a position to glimpse the screen at the particular moment, whether the set was on or off . . ."

"But you said earlier that the set *was* turned off when you arrived and that it was off when the first officers arrived on the scene, did you not?"

"That's correct. But that doesn't necessarily mean that it was off at the time the victim was killed."

"I see. So you're assuming that after the murder someone turned the television off?"

"I'm not assuming anything," he says. "I'm just saying it's a possibility."

"Well, let's see. Who could have turned the set off? Certainly not the victim."

"No."

"Perhaps the maid who found the body? Did you or any of your officers ask her if perhaps she tiptoed around all that blood, found the remote, and turned the television off before she reported the body?"

"No."

"Well, maybe she came back after reporting the body and turned the set off then. Did you ask her that?"

"No." Eyes that had laugh lines at the outer edges a few seconds ago are now two little slits projecting death rays from the witness stand.

"Ah, I see. You think the murderer, whoever killed Professor Scarborough, beat him to death, spraying blood all over the ceiling and walls, carried a tray with food into the room from out in the hall, laid it all out on a table, and then, before he panicked and ran from the scene, the perpetrator took the time to find the remote and turn off the television set?"

Two of the jurors are now laughing.

"Anything's possible," says Detrick. "What I'm saying is that I simply don't know."

"Well, maybe we should just stick with what we do know, that the television set was turned off when the first officers arrived at the scene. That much we know, right?"

"Right," he says.

"By the way, Detective, do you know where the remote device for the television was located that morning as your officers and technicians processed the scene?"

"I'm sorry. I don't."

I produce one of the photographs already in evidence. There is a clear shot of the handheld remote on a shelf against the wall, just off to the left side of the television.

"Yes, I see it," he says.

"So if the set was on at the time of the murder, and for some reason the killer wanted to turn it off, he would have to step over or around the body and either turn it off on the set itself or reach over and get the remote. In either case he'd have to

walk through the field of blood on the carpet to do it, is that correct? Or do you see
some other way?"

"Not unless he could fly," says Detrick.
"That's the only way."

"And in the photograph do you see any
indications or signs of bloody footprints directly in front of the television or the shelf
where the remote is located?" I show him
the photograph again. "Go ahead, take a
look."

He puts his glasses on again and looks
closely at the picture. "Not that I can see
in the photograph."

"So do you think it's possible that we
can safely conclude that the television was
off at the time of the murder?"

"Yeah. Probably."

"And if that was the condition of the
set at the time of the murder, that it was
turned off, a dark screen on that set would
have provided anyone sitting in the chair
where the victim was seated and who
looked at that screen with a pretty good
image by way of reflection of anything
moving around him or behind him, is that
not true?"

"If he was looking at the screen, yes."

"And if the television was off, it wasn't making any sound either, was it?"

"I assume not."

"Well, did you hear any music or television dialogue coming from that television when you arrived at the scene?"

"No."

"So it wasn't putting out any sound?"

"No."

"So in addition to providing a good visual cue, a warning by way of reflection in the screen, the fact that the television was off meant there was no noise to mask the sounds of any entry or footsteps approaching from behind, isn't that true?"

"That's true."

"Detective Detrick, in your capacity as an expert in crime-scene reconstruction, let me pose a hypothetical question. If the victim in this case, Professor Scarborough, was intensely focused, working on something, papers of some kind, and someone came to the door, someone he knew and trusted, is it not possible that he might get up, go to the door, open it, let that person in, and immediately return to the chair where he was working before this other person even entered the room?"

He thinks about this for a moment, all the little facets, and then tries to slip away. "I would expect that someone who opened the door and allowed a guest in would welcome that guest, show them in, and then close the door behind them."

"Yes, but remember, in my hypothetical the victim was very busy working, studying some papers. Assume he was pressed for time, in a hurry. And the person at the door was someone he was on a casual basis with, someone he trusted. . . ."

"It's possible, I suppose, although . . ." He thinks of something else. "In that case the victim would have seen the murder weapon, the hammer," he says. "I assume it would be in the assailant's hand when the victim opened the door."

"Let's assume that the hammer was concealed under a garment or in a bag or a briefcase. Now, isn't the situation that I posed a possibility?"

"It's possible," he says.

"If that were the situation in this case, that would leave the victim back seated in the chair, hard at work, and the perpetrator behind him, somewhere near the door in the entry hall, is that correct?"

"Um . . . yes."

"Now, if we can assume that the television is off, so that there is a reflection in the screen, and further that there's no sound coming from the set to mask footsteps approaching from behind—and we've already established that this was the case, right?"

"Right." The way he says it, it's almost a question. Detrick isn't sure where I'm going.

"But given those assumptions, does it really matter?"

"What do you mean? I don't understand the question," he says.

This is the best kind of response, one that allows me to testify.

"I mean if it's someone the victim knows and he knows they're already there in the room, why would he bother to pay any attention to reflections of movement on the screen or the sound of footsteps in the entry? He would expect these, wouldn't he?"

"Yes."

"Well, that would explain it, wouldn't it? Why the victim, Professor Scarborough, didn't react to any of the physical cues, the sounds or images, as the killer approached him? If it was someone he knew. He hears him coming from behind, so what? He's looking down, engrossed in his papers, maybe catches only a fleeting glimpse of motion on the screen. That would be a pretty good explanation, wouldn't it?"

This is important, because later testimony from the medical examiner will reveal that there were no defensive wounds on the victim's hand or arms. If he was surprised by a reflection in the screen or heard steps, why didn't he react, move, perhaps raise an arm to defend himself? But he didn't.

Detrick goes through a lot of shrugging here. You might think the collar on his shirt or his necktie is too tight. Then he says, "Possible. But the problem is there are other possibilities based on your own hypothetical."

"Like what, for example?"

"Well, using your own hypothetical," he says, "with only one simple variation, let's assume that someone did come to the door, but it was not someone the victim knew. Let's say it was someone he didn't know, but who he expected. Say, for example, the victim ordered a meal. . . ." As soon as he says the words, he begins to smile. He's wondering how I'm going to cut him off in front of the jury without leaving dangerous lingering questions. Something like, *I'll ask the questions, Detective.* But instead I let him go. He can't believe it.

"And the waiter with the tray arrives at the door." This is a hypothetical much more to Detrick's liking. I can tell, because if he had a mustache at this moment, he'd be twisting the ends. "The victim might open the door, let the waiter in, return to his chair, and find himself in the same situation as in your hypothetical," he says.

"And the hammer?" I ask. "Where was that, in your version?"

"Under a garment," he says, "same as yours. Or perhaps on the tray under a napkin."

"Ah, but then how do you explain the tray outside the door?" I ask. "From the blood spatter, we know the tray wasn't on the table at the time of the assault."

"Well, after the door was opened and the victim turned back to his chair, the perpetrator, a waiter in this case, would have had plenty of time. He could have put the tray down on the floor out in the hall, before he ever actually stepped into the room." He looks at me. Try that hypo on for size.

"So let me get this clear. The door is opened by the victim. Let's assume he looks through the peephole before he opens it."

"Sure, he would naturally do that." Detrick is being as helpful as possible now that he sees me headed down into a pit.

"The victim sees your hypothetical waiter standing just outside in the hall, holding the tray," I say.

Detrick's nodding, leaning forward in his chair, body language urging me on. I can tell he wants me to say it, to draw the mental image of how my client did the deed, right in front of the jury.

"Victim turns, goes back to his chair. By then the waiter has placed the tray with the food on the floor in the hall." I run through it.

"Exactly," he says.

"I take it your hypothetical waiter is by now holding the hammer, presumably in his right hand?" All the little details.

"I would assume so," says Detrick.

"Then he steps inside the room."

He's nodding.

"He closes the door."

"Yesss." He says it like a serpent hiss-ing.

"And so that I understand your version clearly, is it here, inside the entry with the door closed, the victim just a few feet away, that your hypothetical waiter stops, lays down the hammer, and puts on the rain-coat?"

This, the raincoat that no one has men-tioned since it was pulled from the evi-dence bag and identified for the jury, falls on Detrick like a lead anvil. A lesson in why you never want to wing it in front of a jury on a theory of how the deed went down. Unless it is carefully thought out and analyzed, more often than not, you will end up choking on the details.

Harry and I had spent four days going over every scenario of the murder that we could conceive. We made cardboard cut-outs, each one representing an item of evidence, and played them like game pieces, running them through a printed maze set out on separate pieces of large poster board. Each board represented one of the possible theories of how Scarborough was murdered, like prepping for a final in law school. The instant Detrick opted for the theory of the invited waiter, I knew he was dead. Harry and I had already done it and ended up holding the cardboard cutout that read "Plastic Raincoat."

The next time some wizened old judge tells you that trying any case is 5 percent theater and 95 percent preparation, you would be wise to believe him—or to find another line of work.

On the stand, Detrick hems and haws. He has stepped in it, but still, what happens next is something you don't usually expect from an experienced witness. He makes it worse.

I'm halfway back to the counsel table, getting ready to move on to another point, when he says, "It's entirely possible, in my scenario, that the hypothetical waiter could have been wearing the raincoat when he arrived at the hotel-room door."

This last desperate surmise allows me to wander through a field of dreams on horseback, dragging Detrick behind me over every sharp, jagged edge that it presents.

It's one thing to theorize that my client, Carl Arnsberg, wearing a raincoat, slipped into Scarborough's room in silence using a key when no one was looking. But the picture of a waiter in white livery carrying a tray, arriving at the door, knocking while he's all decked out in a clear, thin, plastic tarp with sleeves, something large enough to cover a pup tent, is quite another matter.

I make the point verbally in front of the jury. Then I ratchet up the notion of this house of horrors for Detrick by going visual. I have the clerk pull the raincoat and open it in front of the jury. It may say size small on the collar, but you wouldn't know it from the parachute of plastic now crinkling noisily in front of the jury box.

Even if Scarborough were in the middle of a mind meld, he would have to do a double take on any waiter showing up at his door wearing this, and he wouldn't have to look into a darkened television screen to see it, or for that matter hear it.

Harry, who is a cerebral vacuum cleaner when it comes to examining evidence, told me a month ago, right after he saw the plastic raincoat, that we could run riot through Tuchio's case, at least for a day or two. In Harry's words, "Anyone trying to slip up behind Scarborough wearing that may as well have on a cowbell."

Mercifully for Detrick, who would like to crawl under his chair, the judge allows only one more question before we break for the day.

"Let's get back to my original hypothetical," I tell him. "If the killer was someone Scarborough knew, presumably coming in from outside the hotel, wearing that same plastic raincoat in June in San Diego, where early-summer mornings are often shrouded in fog, sometimes light drizzle, isn't it probable, isn't it more likely, that that person wouldn't draw a second look from anyone, including the victim?"

Detrick has the look of a whipped dog. By now it doesn't matter what he says. The answer is so obvious that half the jurors probably don't even hear it. He shifts in his chair, his chin pressed down into his chest, and he mumbles: "I suppose it . . ."

The court reporter misses it. She makes him say it again.

"I said, I suppose it's possible."

FOURTEEN

The next morning on my way to court, I find Harry waiting for me out on the sidewalk a half block from where I park my car. He's all smiles. From the look on his face, I can tell he's not standing there waiting to talk about the weather.

"Figured you'd be coming this way," he says. "I've got some things here I think you're going to want to see."

He pulls several pages from his briefcase and hands them to me one at a time as we stand out on the street. "I found them about two o'clock this morning, going through the stacks on the conference table." They're computer printouts. Harry has been plumbing the depths of Scarborough's computer memoranda.

The first item is an e-mail, very brief, three quick sentences, no salutation. *"Regarding the item of which we spoke last week, I am informed that I will require access to the original. A copy will not do. Please reply."* It is signed T. Scarborough and dated eighteen months ago.

I look at the e-mail address in the "TO" box at the top. It is addressed to Aginnis@scotus.gov.

"What's this?" I point to the address.

"Supreme Court of the United States," says Harry. "It's Arthur Ginnis's e-mail address at the Court. Next," he says. Harry hands me another page.

It's another e-mail missive from Scarborough to Ginnis. *"Regarding my message of the 18th, I have received no reply. I assume it is possible to gain access to the original? As I stated previously, a copy does not satisfy the requirements of my third party. Please reply as soon as possible."*

"And it gets more interesting," says Harry. He hands me a third e-mail. This time it's a reply from the Court to Scarborough, with Scarborough's second message appearing below it. But the reply is not from Ginnis. The name on the bottom reads *"A. Aranda."*

"I write you on behalf of the Court. I have been asked to inform you that this site is for the conduct of official Court business only. If you have business of a personal nature, please direct it by way of ordinary mail to the following address." What follows is a street address in Washington, D.C., with a box number after the street name.

"So what do you make of it?" says Harry.

"Looks like Scarborough was trying to do business with Ginnis, used the wrong conveyance, and he got his hand slapped."

"Ginnis may have slapped his hand," says Harry, "but he didn't tell him to go away."

For a minute or more, Harry and I stand there on the street studying the brief lines on the paper like analysts trying to decipher language in a diplomatic code.

"The word 'original,'" says Harry. "I'll

give you ten to one that's Scarborough talk for the J thing, Mr. Jefferson's infamous letter. Remember what the gal in D.C. told you?"

"Trisha Scott."

"She said Scarborough only had a copy of the letter. That's why he needed the original, to authenticate it. It's dead-on," says Harry.

"She also said that Ginnis didn't know anything about the letter."

"Fortunately for you and me," says Harry, "we never believe people." We had already dropped both Trisha Scott's name as well as the name Arthur Ginnis into the middle of our witness list of possibles to be called, just in case. At the moment Scott's looking like an odds-on bet for a subpoena. Of course, there's always the risky unknown, what she might say if you put her on the stand.

"What do you make of this?" says Harry. He's pointing to language in one of the e-mails. "Scarborough's asking for the original, and then he says, 'As I stated previously, a copy does not satisfy the requirements of my third party.'"

Harry gives me a quizzical glance. "Is he trying to publish the letter, or is he trying to sell it?"

I shake my head. We need to move quickly.

"Tell Herman to hire a gumshoe in D.C.," I say, "somebody he knows or a good referral. Have them find out what's at this street address." I point to the D.C. address on the Court's e-mail reply. "And if it's a drop box, who rents it. Also ask them to check out the name A. Aranda on a directory of the Court's employees. I assume there must be one. If not, tell them to do whatever they have to, but find out. Tell them we need the information by tomorrow.

"This next item I don't want to job out. Ask Herman to get on his traveling clothes and catch the first flight back to D.C. If we end up having to drop a subpoena on Ginnis, first order of business, we're going to have to know where he is."

* * *

After Detrick was saved by the bell at yesterday evening's break, you can bet Tuchio spent much of the night with him in the woodshed doing a refresher course on their theory of the case. This morning the detective is looking a little worn and frazzled.

Between the saucer-size eyes and the razor-quick double take Detrick does when I say his name, you might think Tuchio has been feeding him Benzedrine all night.

I don't even ask Detrick about the detective's note from the interview in New York with Richard Bonguard, including the early reference to the "J letter" and why the police didn't follow up on this. This is another instance of their shoddy investigation, rush to judgment. But if asked, Detrick would no doubt simply say it was irrelevant. They already had their man and all the evidence that went with him.

This morning Detrick and I parry over one final point. We know that the killer tried to dispose of the raincoat by throwing it into a Dumpster. So if Carl killed Scarborough, why didn't he do the same thing with his pants and shoes instead of trying to clean them? After all, he had the better part of twenty-four hours to get rid of them.

Detrick and I go back and forth over this several times, tugging and pushing. At one point he tries to repeat the statement that Carl gave the cops during interrogation, that he kept them because he couldn't afford to replace them. I cut Detrick off before he can go there.

"Wouldn't you get rid of them," I ask him, "if you were the killer?"

"Oh, I would," he says. "But then in my experience as a homicide detective over the years, I've seen a lot of people do a lot of stupid things."

I could ask him whether in his long experience he has seen people burning their clothes or throwing them in Dumpsters when their only act was the misfortune of stumbling onto a crime scene where they'd picked up traces of blood. But that would be one question too many. Detrick would say, *No, of course not, but then those people would have gone to the authorities and reported the crime.*

"Thank you. That's all I have for this witness."

Tuchio spends twenty minutes on redirect trying to undo some of the damage from yesterday. He has Detrick repeat the state's theory of the key in the lock, a secretive entry into Scarborough's hotel room, and then emphasizes that in that case the killer would have been wearing the troublesome raincoat before he entered. It's this image that Tuchio wants to leave with the jury before we move on.

He excuses Detrick. I let him go, subject to recall in my case in chief.

Tuchio's next witness is Dewey Prichert, an employee of the police crime lab whose specialty is trace evidence.

Prichert has a kind of sad-sack look to him. If he were a dog, he'd be a basset hound. His sandy-colored hair is disappearing from his forehead faster than a glacier in global warming. The knot on his tie is a little crooked. He wears thick glasses and carries a small plastic pouch sprouting a couple of pens and a tiny metal ruler, all stuffed into the breast pocket of his sport coat. Professor Nerd, pass him on the street and you'd swear he spent his days in a physics lecture hall instead of squatting with tweezers plucking fibers and hair from around lakes of human blood.

The prosecutor moves quickly with Prichert as he has the witness identify specific photographs of blood spatter, close-ups of several small articles that were in the room. Prichert was the crime tech at the scene who lifted the two shoe impressions from the blood in the entry hall and gathered bits of fibers from the floor and multiple strands of human hair, none of which, it seems, matched the hair of the defendant and several of which appear to be idle strands belonging to no one in particular, at least that the police could identify.

"How do you explain that?" asks the prosecutor. "The unidentified strands of hair?"

"Any hotel room is going to be a transient scene," says Prichert. "We were able to account for several of the darker strands of hair that were found. They belonged to two of the maids who routinely cleaned that room. Others we assume at this point probably belong to previous occupants of the room."

"So what you're telling us," says Tuchio, "is that it's normal, that you might expect to find unidentified strands of hair in a place like a hotel room?"

"It's not as bad as an airport terminal, but basically, yes."

What Tuchio is trying to do here is to close the door on us, to diminish these loose strands of hair as SODDI evidence—"some other dude did it." He knows that I have an expert on my list of witnesses prepared to jump on the unanswered question of hairs found at the scene.

Tuchio has the witness specify the number and various colors of hairs he collected in the hotel room. You would think the hotel didn't own a vacuum. According to Prichert, he gathered eighty-seven separate strands, including fourteen hairs from three different animals. For a hotel with a "no pets" policy, if you could fork over the gold brick to pay the daily fare on the Presidential Suite, it seems the room came with a courtesy case of cataracts to blind hotel staff whenever Fifi or Fido emerged from the elevator.

Of the eighty-seven human strands, a good number, fifty-six, were multiple offenders. That is, they were classified as "questioned hair samples," meaning that their owners were unknown but that microscopic examination revealed they were duplicates and in some cases triplicates coming from the same unknown person.

According to Prichert, this would not be unusual for a hotel room where tenants might spend anywhere from one to several days in close living quarters. He tells the jury that most of the hair samples were collected using a special vacuum with a small micron filter to trap the hair and small fibers. In areas close to the victim's body where he did not want to disturb other potential evidence, he used tape to lift any hairs or fibers. He explained to the jury that in a suite that size, with deep plush carpets, heavy upholstered furniture, and heavy curtains that hung to the floor, you could easily find a good number of hair samples, most of which have probably been there for a long time.

Tuchio pays particular attention to the thirteen questioned samples of hair found on or near the back of the chair where Scarborough was murdered and six unidentified samples found in the bathroom on the tile floor either near or under the toe kick of the bathroom counter. There were several hair samples on the counter itself and in the sink in the bathroom, but all of these were identified as belonging to the victim. Of the thirteen in the living area, most belonged to the victim himself and were severed by the jagged edge of the hammer's claws as it punched holes in Scarborough's head. But five of them on or around the area of the chair where the body was located, one a kind of sandy brown color, three blond, and one that had been subjected to enough different dyes that Prichert could not determine its true color, are unidentified, so-called questioned samples and belonging to persons unknown.

In addition there were two blond hairs, one four inches long and the other much shorter—he can't remember the precise length—as well as several gray hairs and two brown samples, all of which were collected from the bathroom.

"Let's start with the five hair samples found closest to the body, the ones you couldn't identify. Can you tell the jury anything about these hairs?"

"Two of them I might classify as floaters, one blond sample of questioned hair about four inches in length and one shorter brown sample about an inch in length."

"What do you mean by 'floaters'?"

Prichert explains to the jury that if you're

looking for trace evidence deposited at the scene of a crime, you don't usually tear up the carpet and look underneath. In collecting fibers or hair, unless there is some other reason to probe deeper, technicians usually look for surface deposits likely to have occurred during or about the time that the crime was committed, what the witness calls floaters.

"These four strands, the brown and three blond, were not on the surface of the chair," says Prichert. "They were tucked into crevices formed by the back cushion at the level of the seat on either side at the back of the chair. They were sufficiently shallow that it was difficult to tell how long they might have been there."

"What about the other eight unidentified strands of hair found on or near the chair?"

"All of those were tucked deep enough into crevices in the upholstery of the chair that I was able to exclude them as not being part of the crime scene. Most of them were balled up and caught up in filaments of dust, indicating that they'd been there too long to be connected to the crime."

"Would you normally expect to find human hairs in that location, in the cracks of an upholstered chair?"

"It's very common."

"Why is that?"

"People sit, hair sheds, sometimes it gets caught in the tight spaces of the upholstery and is pulled out or more likely broken somewhere along the shaft. Repeated body movement in the chair and gravity can cause the loose strands of hair to migrate into crevices, usually between or at the edge of cushioned areas. In this case it was a leather chair. Loose hair would tend to slide easily, and unless it fell on the floor, it would slip into crevices almost immediately."

"Did you find any unidentified hairs on the body or the clothing of the victim?"

"I found several strands belonging to the victim himself, but no unidentified or questioned samples, no."

Tuchio turns his attention back to the club chair in which the cops theorize Scarborough was sitting at the time of the attack. He has the witness explain that the cushions on that particular chair were not loose. They could not be removed by a maid in order to dust and vacuum under and around them. Both seat and back cushions were stitched to the fixed upholstery of the chair.

"A maid would have to use a crevice tool to vacuum in the cracks," says Prichert. "And there was evidence that this had not occurred at any time in the recent past."

"And what evidence was that?" asks Tuchio.

"There were particles, small tufts of dust at or near the area in the crevices where both strands of hair, the one blond and the single brown hair, were found."

"And what if anything did you conclude from this?"

"That the area of the chair in question, the crevices along the back cushion at the level of the seat, had not been vacuumed recently."

I would give Prichert the Good Housekeeping Seal of Approval if he weren't doing such a good job undermining our evidence.

"So what you're saying is that those two strands of hair could have been there for some time?"

"Yes."

"In your opinion could they have been there as long as a week?"

"Yes."

"Could they have been there for several weeks?"

"It's a possibility. At some point you would expect them either to migrate deeper into the crevice of the upholstery or to fall victim to a cleaning, in which case they would be removed."

"If they were there for a long time, would they disintegrate?" asks Tuchio.

"The hair shaft itself will resist deterioration for years. In this case neither of the evidentiary strands of hair included a follicle or any tissue; they were broken at the shaft. So there is no way to determine when the hair shaft itself was parted from its owner. Determining how long they'd been there at that location would at best be a guess."

"Did you find any evidence of blood on either strand of hair?"

"Yes. Under microscopic examination both strands of hair revealed substantial evidence of dried blood."

"And what if anything did you conclude from this?"

"That based on the fact that the victim's blood had run into the crevices at the site where each of these hair strands was located, I concluded that it was not possible to determine whether either strand was deposited on the chair at the time of the commission of the crime or at some point much earlier and was therefore entirely unrelated to the crime."

"So is it your opinion that the questioned hair samples found on or in the crevices of the subject chair are inconclusive in terms of any evidentiary value?"

"That would be my opinion, yes."

"Let's turn to the unidentified hairs in the bathroom. Where did you find these?"

"Almost all of them were vacuumed from under the toe kick at the bottom of the built-in bathroom counter. There is a tight space there where the wood at the bottom of the counter meets the tile floor. Most of the questioned hair samples found in the bathroom were located there. There were, I think, two loose unidentified hair samples that were just under the toe kick. Both of these I collected with tape. The others I vacuumed.

"And what the colors of these samples?"

"Oh, it was the United Nations," says Prichert. "Bathrooms tend to be that way."

Everybody laughs.

Tuchio is trying to put as much distance as possible between any of the unidentified hair evidence and the victim or his blood. He doesn't want any ghost perpetrators popping up on our side of the case, a nameless, faceless killer with three hairs on his head.

"Let's take the two loose samples of hair that you found just under the toe kick in the bathroom. What color were they?"

"Blond."

"Anything else you can tell us about them?"

The witness goes back to his notes. "One of the samples was four inches, the other was just under two inches. They were broken at the hair shaft—that is, they were not pulled out of the scalp, and under microscopic examination they appeared to be of similar origin. In other words, under the microscope the characteristics of both samples were sufficiently similar that I concluded they were from the same person. In fact, this was the case with most of the hair samples I found in the bathroom."

Prichert explains that bathrooms are the place where people routinely comb and brush their hair, often causing breakage or shedding. So you would expect multiple hair samples from the same owner at that location. "I found the samples on the floor under the toe kick of the sink and counter area."

The prosecutor has the witness describe the area of the counter toe kick in the bathroom. Prichert explains that this is a recessed area running along the front of the bathroom counter at floor level, approximately three to four inches high and the same dimension deep. As the term implies, it is where your toes go when you belly up to the counter to brush your teeth.

"So," says Tuchio, "if you were standing—say, a maid with a mop—while the mop might fit under this area of the toe kick, would the maid be able to see back into this area to clean?"

Tuchio is trying to go to the same place he went with the chair in the living room, ancient hairs. "Objection. Calls for speculation," I say. "The witness is not an engineer or an optometrist."

"The observation is something within common knowledge," says Tuchio.

Quinn weighs the issue in his head. "The witness can answer."

"Probably not."

The inference here again is that the hairs in the bathroom could have been there for some time.

Tuchio knows that the road to reasonable doubt is paved with tiny bricks of imponderables, pesky items in the state's evidence raising questions for which there are no answers. He's done a good job diminishing the use of this evidence in our case, but he has missed one point, and I will catch it on cross.

Except for the shoe impressions, much of what follows is window dressing on the state's case. The heavy hitters will come later, the medical examiner who will testify that the killing was a crime of rage, fingerprint experts who'll tie Carl to the pinkie print on the hammer handle and the four fingerprints on the floor, and the capper— the two witnesses the cops have lined up, Carl's former friends who, if Tuchio is to be believed, will step forward with shovels to bury him.

Prichert tells the jury that in addition to the massive amounts of blood in the living room and entry he also found traces, in the form of minute streaks of human blood, on the tiles of the bathroom floor. According to the witness, these resembled similar striations of blood found on the exterior of the plastic raincoat. Prichert discovered that when they laid the raincoat on the tiles in the bathroom, the blood streaks on the floor and those on the raincoat lined up.

"Did you form any opinions or conclusions based on these findings?" asks Tuchio.

"Yes. It's my opinion that at some point after the victim was killed, the perpetrator entered the bathroom, where an attempt was made to remove blood from the exterior of the raincoat by laying it on the floor and wiping it, probably using a bath towel; that the raincoat was then wrapped in this towel; and that together the two items were then discarded where they were later found by police."

Prichert also notes that according to housekeeping, though they cannot be certain, it appears that two towels were missing from the hotel suite—a large bath towel, later found in the Dumpster with the raincoat, and another, smaller hand towel that police never found.

Next Tuchio pulls three evidence photos from the cart and has the witness identify them. Two of these are close-ups of items spattered with blood, the large sample case that was on the floor next to the chair where the victim was killed, and a legal-size, zippered, leather portfolio that was on a table near the television. The third shot is of the attaché case that was found open, lying on the couch in the living room out of the line of spatter. Prichert identifies the items in the photos. Then Tuchio brings him to the point.

He directs the witness's attention to one of the photos, a shot of the attaché case.

"Do you see that mark, that little smudge on the leather right next to the lock?"

"I do."

"Did you have occasion to examine that mark in your laboratory?"

"I did."

"Can you tell the jury what that mark is?"

"It's a bloodstain."

"Human blood?"

"Yes."

"Did it belong to the victim?"

"Yes."

"Can you tell the jury whether following your examination of that spot you formed any opinion as to how it got on the attaché case?"

"Looking at the stain under magnification, I observed minuscule, microscopic patterns not unlike brushstrokes in the dried blood at that spot. These strokes were made by the fibers from a fabric, probably cotton. Based on my examination, I concluded that the mark was a transfer stain imparted when a cloth fabric soaked in blood made contact with the leather, and that this contact was probably effected in an attempt to open the lock."

Tuchio is trying to deal with this, because he knows if he doesn't, it will fall into my lap. These little smudges of blood, some of them larger than others, were found on the attaché case, the top of the leather portfolio, and the sample case, though on the case they were difficult to make out because, since this was close to Scarborough's chair, large areas were saturated with blood.

"Let me ask you, with regard to the attaché case, did your examination reveal anything else?"

"Yes. There were similar patterns on the handle where it was touched, on the edge at the top where it was opened, as well as traces of dried blood, again showing evidence of fiber patterns, inside on the bottom of the case."

"And did you form any conclusions based on these findings?"

"Yes. It appears that someone, probably wearing gloves soaked with blood, opened the case and went through it."

"Do you know whether they took anything?"

"No."

Harry and I have had Prichert's forensics report for months, so I know what's coming next.

According to the witness, similar evidence of entry and pawing was found in the sample case, but not in the leather portfolio. Prichert says the portfolio was empty and that anyone attempting to open what was essentially a large zippered leather envelope with blood-soaked gloves would of necessity have left stains inside. There were none, either on the outside or the inside.

For Tuchio and the police, this is a puzzle. If anything was taken, it wasn't found in Carl's apartment when they turned it upside down during their search. They have also excluded robbery, either as the motive or as a passing frolic after the murder. Scarborough was wearing an expensive Rolex and a two-carat diamond ring, and he had more than three thousand dollars in cash in his wallet when they found his body.

Tuchio quickly passes over all this and gets to the point he wants to make: the gloves. If Carl was wearing gloves when he killed Scarborough, how did his pinkie print get on the hammer along with the other three prints on the floor?

According to the witness, the answer to this question is found back in the bathroom, on the tile floor. There, several fine cotton fiber transfer marks similar to those found on the attaché case were discovered on the bathroom floor. But these were not small dots the size of a fingertip. They were larger, one of them more than three inches in length.

"What, if anything, did you conclude from these transfer marks, the ones on the bathroom floor?" asks Tuchio.

"Based on the evidence, everything I examined, the entire pattern, it would be my opinion that at some point, probably at the same time that the raincoat was wiped down, the perpetrator removed the gloves from his hands, and at that point one or both of the gloves brushed the floor."

"Do you have any idea what might have happened to these gloves?"

"No."

The police have never found them.

Having disposed of all the nitty-gritty details they can't explain, Tuchio moves to the one they can: the shoe impressions left behind in the blood at the entry hall.

The prosecutor has Prichert identify the two dark running shoes already in evidence. These are the Nikes with traces of blood on the soles found in Carl's apartment the day they arrested him. The bailiff sets up the overhead projector, and within seconds the first transparency is shot up onto the screen. It shows a picture of the right shoe impression lifted from the tiles of the entry floor. Next to it is an impression lifted at the crime lab from the sole of the right shoe belonging to Carl, all the little swirls and marks, jurors leaning over the rail in the box to get a better look.

You don't need a microscope to see it. Right down to the tiny breaks in some of the ridges where the wear pattern on the sole has eroded them, like the whorls and ridges of a fingerprint, the two images are identical.

If it's possible, the transparency of the left shoe is even more dramatic. There is a small V-shaped cut near the heel, where Carl obviously ran over something sharp. It isn't large, but magnified as it is on the screen, all of the cut's peculiar and jagged edges stand out like a mirror image on the side-by-side impressions.

Two of the female jurors in the box are nodding their heads, another is standing bent over the rail looking closely. Almost all of them are making notes. That it proves a point not in dispute, the fact that Carl was there, can easily get lost in the clarity and definitive nature of the visual evidence. It makes you wonder, when the time comes for a verdict, will they ask themselves, *What do I believe—the picture I saw with my lying eyes or the spin of a hired lawyer in the courtroom telling me what it means?*

FIFTEEN

Why would the killer remove the gloves before he left the room?" This is my opening question to Prichert on cross-examination.

"The gloves had blood all over them. You're not going to leave the room and walk through a busy hotel with your hands dripping blood."

"Why didn't he leave the gloves in the room?"

"I don't know."

"How can you be so certain that he didn't take them off after he left the room?" This is the question. I can see Tuchio looking up at his witness, hoping he's caught the drift.

Implicit in my question, of course, is the fact that my client could not have been wearing gloves when he left the room. If so, how did his fingerprints get all over the entry floor and on the hammer?

"It doesn't fit the evidence," says Prichert. "Because it doesn't account for the smears, the transfer marks on the bathroom floor. Or any of the other evidence." He's sticking to his story. "For example—"

"I think you've answered the question."

"Let him complete his answer." Tuchio, slouched in his chair, directs this to me, but for the judge to rule on. "Your Honor, counsel asked a question, the witness should be allowed to complete his answer."

"Sustained. You can answer the question," says Quinn.

"For example, if he was wearing the gloves when he left the room, he would not have left fingerprints on the floor in the entry," says the witness.

Prichert turns it around on me in front of the jury and force-feeds me the theory of their case.

"Also, the blood smears on the handle of the door on the way out of the room. Gloves would be inconsistent with this evidence. Those smears were made by bare hands moving too quickly to leave clear latent prints."

Carl must have been flying at the speed of light on his way out of that room. From the smeared prints all over it, you might have thought he was frisking the door. Forensics couldn't get a single print that didn't resemble the inkblots on a Rorschach test, not that it matters given the bonanza of evidence they found on the entry floor.

"Of course, your answer assumes that the fingerprints on the floor and around the hammer belong to the killer and not someone else?" I say.

"Yes, but the issue is whether that assumption is reasonable," says Prichert, "and in this case I would say that it is eminently reasonable, considering the absence of physical evidence pointing to any other possible perpetrator." He sticks his sword in me one more time.

When I turn away from Prichert, I am greeted by Detective Detrick sitting at the prosecution table. If the toothy grin is any indication, he'll be organizing a human wave out in the audience any second.

"Let me ask you, if the killer took off the gloves in the bathroom, why were there no prints found at that location?"

"I would have to assume it was because he was very careful," says Prichert.

Of course this begs the question under their theory: Why was Carl so careful in the bathroom only to leave finger paintings all over the entry-hall floor? After being stabbed twice, I leave this as one of those rhetorical items you drop on the jury in closing argument, where Prichert won't be hiding behind a bush to give me an answer. If I were to pop the question to him here on the stand, he would no doubt say, *I don't know. You'd have to ask him.* The "him" in Prichert's answer naturally would refer to the killer, but you can bet that the glasses on the neon nerd would be flashing their beams at Carl. At the moment I have no need to be walking around with that particular pike sticking out of my chest.

I move on to the extraneous hairs.

"Mr. Prichert, can you tell the jury the purpose of gathering hair and fiber evidence at the scene of a crime?"

"To examine and preserve them," he says.

"Yes, but for what purpose? What do you use them for?"

"Well, in the case of hair, you would compare, say, a questioned hair sample found at the scene of a crime with a known hair sample taken from a suspect, or it might be a known hair sample, say, taken from a victim and transferred to an article of clothing belonging to a suspect."

"Is there some vast database of known hair samples maintained somewhere so that if you find an unidentified hair at a crime scene, you can go there and compare it in an effort to find a match?"

"Not in the way you describe it," he says. "There may be some small collections of known samples held by some law-enforcement agencies, but these would be specialized, confined to certain crimes. Repeat offenders, for example, in sexual-assault cases."

"But that wouldn't apply in a case like this?"

"No."

"So in this case you're left to compare the so-called questioned hair samples found at the scene with known hair samples that you find where?"

"On various parts of the body. It depends on the particular crime." Like a cab-driver, Prichert knows where I want to go, but he takes me on a ride through the park.

"But whose body?"

"Ah. I see what you mean. That would depend."

"On what?"

"Well, for example, you might want to take hair samples from known subjects who might have had occasion to contaminate the scene. First responders, for instance, police officers or emergency medical personnel who might have come on the scene."

"Was any of that done in this case?"

"Yes."

"And who did you take those samples from?"

"Maids at the hotel, the officers who first arrived at the scene. I think we may have even taken a few hairs from Detective Detrick over there."

"That's why some of us have flat feet and bald heads," says Detrick. Everybody laughs.

"I hope you used pliers to pull these

from the detective's head?" More laughter.

"Aw, that's mean." He's still laughing. Detrick may be the enemy, but as a person he is quite affable, the kind who might make a good neighbor if you didn't have to drill his teeth every other day in court.

Quinn taps his gavel and brings us back to the subject at hand.

"These people that you took hair samples from, were any of them considered suspects in this case?"

"No."

"Even the maids, the other hotel employees you might have taken samples from?"

"No. Certainly not at that point."

"So other than torturing Detective Detrick, what was the purpose of all this?" A little laughter in the audience.

"We were clearing the scene. One of the things you have to do before processing a crime scene is to identify all the people who may have been there for legitimate purposes and who may have contaminated it by inadvertently leaving trace evidence—"

"Or footprints?" I ask.

He nods. "Sometimes."

"But not this time, right?"

"I don't understand the question," he says.

"Then let me clarify it for you. You took samples of hair from officers at the scene, some hotel employees, and I emphasize the word 'some,' because in your mind, or perhaps at the direction of Detective Detrick, these persons were determined not to be suspects in this case, is that correct?"

"That's right."

"And this was done so that you could eliminate any trace evidence connected to them that you might find at the scene?"

"That's correct."

"But when you got to the defendant, you weren't treating him as just another hotel employee who left trace evidence at the scene, were you?"

"No."

"Why not? Was it simply because of the quantity of evidence, the footprints and fingerprints that belonged to him at the scene?"

"Objection," says Tuchio. "The question assumes facts not yet in evidence."

"Your Honor, the prosecutor in his opening statement has already told the jury that he intends to prove that the fingerprints and shoe impressions belong to my client. There is no dispute over that. The defense will stipulate to those facts," I tell him.

In fact, I have offered this stipulation to Tuchio, who has refused it, wanting instead to trot out all these details in front of the jury, with pictures they can remember.

"I renew my objection," says Tuchio.

He's trying to break my rhythm.

"Overruled. I'll allow the question," says the judge.

"Was the only reason that you refused to clear Carl Arnsberg from the scene as you did the other hotel employees based on the quantity of evidence, his fingerprints and shoe prints found at the scene?"

"I don't know. I didn't make that decision."

"Who did?"

For a second he looks like one of those dolls on the dash of your dad's car, head on a spring. "Detective Detrick," he says. "He was in charge of the case."

I turn and look at Detrick. He knows he

will be heading back to the woodshed when I get to my case in chief.

"Let me ask you." I'm back to the witness. "Did you take any samples of hair from my client, the defendant, Carl Arnsberg?"

"Yes."

"Did you take any samples of hair from any other suspects besides my client?"

"No."

"So to your knowledge there were no other suspects who were even considered with regard to the commission of this crime?"

"I don't know. All I know is that hair samples were not taken from any other suspect or person of interest."

"Mr. Prichert, let me ask you, did you find any questioned samples of hair at the scene that matched the samples you took from my client, Carl Arnsberg?"

"No."

"Then let me get this straight, so that I understand. According to the state's theory of the case, the position taken by Mr. Tuchio, my client entered the room, bludgeoned the victim to death with a hammer, went back out into the hall, retrieved a tray with food on it, and brought it into the room, putting it on a table. Then, according to this theory, my client searched the room looking for something, went into the bathroom, where he wiped down the raincoat, took off a pair of gloves, then proceeded to leave, and— let's not forget—then panicked or was startled by something and left shoe impressions in the entry, where he slipped and fell, leaving his fingerprints on the floor as well as on the murder weapon, and then finally left the room—and during all this he never dropped a single hair from his head or his body anywhere in that suite? Is that what you're saying?"

"No. I'm simply saying that we didn't find any questioned hairs that matched your client." The witness is good. He's only going to play in his ballpark. As far as Prichert is concerned, the re-creation of events at the scene of the crime is a boat that Detrick and Tuchio have built. Let them sail it out to sea.

What is becoming abundantly clear is that the cops jumped before they had all the pieces to the puzzle. If Carl hadn't run from the scene, we wouldn't be here today. If he had gone to his supervisor and reported what he found, the police would have questioned him, taken his prints—both shoes and hands—plucked a few hairs from his head, and cleared him, at least initially. That's what they did with the other hotel employees. No doubt they would have checked him out, found his friends, and probably even discovered that Carl had met in the bunker with his buddies and talked about doing evil things to Scarborough. But that would have taken time, and in that time the forensics experts from the crime lab would have been piecing together all the little details that would have told them that Carl didn't do it, at least not in the way that Tuchio and Detrick have described.

It may be a minor point, no doubt one that Tuchio will step around in his closing argument. But I take Prichert over the falls on it anyway.

"During your investigation at the scene, did you find any small bloody transfer marks on or under the tray with the food or on the tablecloth underneath it?"

He thinks about this for a moment. "No."

"How would that be possible if the perpetrator, immediately after killing the victim and still wearing these blood-soaked gloves, retrieved that tray and the tablecloth from the hall outside and then brought them in and placed them on that table?"

Prichert thinks about this in silence for a long moment. The tray, how did it fly into the room? "It's probably not possible in the scenario you present," he says.

"That's not my scenario. That's the scenario presented by Detective Detrick when he testified earlier."

"Whoever crafted the scenario, it's inconsequential," says Prichert. "Change the order in which the tray came into the room and it's entirely possible that there would be no blood on it."

"How, for example?"

He smiles at me. "I don't know. I'm not a crime-reconstruction expert."

"You mean like Detective Detrick?"

He looks at me but doesn't say anything. Unlike Detrick, Prichert is smart enough to avoid playing God, rearranging the cosmos of physical facts from the stand. He knows that somewhere, sometime, something will be punching a hole in the side of the universe when he's done.

I let it drop. Tuchio and I will argue over this in closing. He will try to finesse it, bury it like a bone, and I will try to dig it up. In the end it is probably one of the multitude of items the jury will sleep through— bloody little smudges that aren't there, unlike the fingerprints and shoe impressions that are.

I'm just about to move on to my centerpiece with Prichert when I remember the little item that Tuchio ignored in his direct questioning of the witness.

"One last question on hair," I tell him. "When you testified earlier, you stated that there were a number of questioned hair samples, those with unidentified owners you said were collected from the area around the toe kick under the counter in the bathroom."

"That's correct."

"And I think you testified that two of these—blond samples, I believe—were collected with tape from under the toe kick?"

"That's right."

"And that from your examination, both

of these appeared to be hair samples from the same unidentified person?"

"Yes, the characteristics of the hair were sufficiently similar in each case, and that's what I concluded. Yes."

"You also stated that you found a number of blond hair samples—unidentified, what you call questioned samples—out in the living room, some of them on or around the chair near the victim?"

"Ah, I know what you're getting at," he says.

"Let me ask the question," I tell him. "Did any of the blond hairs in the living room match the blond hairs found in the bath so as to cause you"—he's already nodding—"to conclude that they also came from this same unknown, unidentified person whose samples you found in the bathroom?"

This was in his forensics report.

"Yes. One of them," he says. "Do you mind if I consult my notes?"

"I have no objection." I turn and look at Tuchio.

He shrugs.

Prichert flips through his report. He finds the page. "Yes, it was the potential floater," he says. "I couldn't tell how long it had been in the crevice of the chair, but it did appear based on hair characteristics to match the questioned samples in the bath. But like I say, many of the samples we found in the suite turned out to be matches."

"Yes, but were any of those matches found in different rooms in that suite?"

"Absolutely. A number of them," says Prichert. "We found hair, questioned samples—that is, unidentified owners with hair samples—in the bedroom and out in the living room. There were matches between samples in the living room and the dining room. It's a problem," he says. "You have a lot of transient use, and it's all in a confined area."

I move to the last issue with Prichert. It was Harry who first noticed it, looking at photos of the scene sent to our office by the crime lab. Even after he pointed it out to me, I couldn't see it. The problem is, neither of the two photos catch it with any clarity. One of them is an oversize magnification concentrating on the zipper at the top of the leather portfolio, showing it in the open position. The other is a distance shot so far out that it's almost impossible to see. Harry admitted that he would never have caught it himself, except for the fact that the two photos were included in an envelope labeled "Blood-Spatter Tracks." Harry kept returning to the one close-up shot, searching for the blood, when he suddenly realized what he was looking at.

* * *

Three weeks ago, right as jury selection was ending and the trial was getting ready to start, Harry sauntered over to the police department's property and evidence room. In actuality, this is a good-size warehouse just out of the downtown area. He wanted to look at some of the items taken by the police and inventoried in our case. Most of these came from the crime scene, along with some items from Scarborough's apartment in Washington, boxes of files and his desktop computer. When Harry saw the number of boxes with files from the victim's D.C. apartment, he made a note to send one of the paralegals back to the evidence room to go through them just in case Tuchio hadn't sent us everything. To Harry it looked like there was a lot of boxed-up paper, more than the D.A. had sent us in discovery.

Of course a sergeant hovered over him in the caged locker as Harry surveyed what was there. Harry was not allowed to touch any of it, just look. It took him less than a minute, scanning down a printed inventory list, to find what he wanted. The box was pulled and put on a table outside the cage, where the same officer eyed Harry as my partner carefully went through the box wearing a pair of latex surgical gloves. When he got to the item, Harry barely slowed down. He knew that if he looked at it too long, the sergeant standing behind him would make a mental note and call Tuchio's office with a report as soon as he left. An hour later Harry was back at the office telling me that what he'd seen in the photograph was there in physical form. He also warned me that unless we moved quickly, because of the way things were stored, stacked in boxes in the caged locker, it might not survive for long.

* * *

Back at the counsel table, Harry hands me the photo. I ask Quinn if I may approach the witness. I set the eight-by-ten color glossy on the light table in front of Prichert. Instantly it is projected on the overhead, where the jury, the judge, and Tuchio can see it. The close-up shot catches just the faintest glimmer of what I'm interested in, an area just over two inches long on the photograph.

"Mr. Prichert, do you recognize this photograph?"

"Yes."

"Can you tell the jury what it is?"

"I believe it's been marked for identification. That's a partial shot of one of the leather cases. Unless I'm wrong, it's the zipper on the light leather portfolio."

"That's right."

Tuchio opened the door on this evidence in his own case when he got into the little blood spots, the transfer marks.

"Can you tell the jury what that is, right there?" I circle the area on the photo with the retracted point of my pen. Prichert looks at it, craning his neck. He removes his glasses for a second and polishes the lenses on the sleeve of his coat. He puts them back on and looks again.

"I'm sorry—but I don't think I see what it is you're referring to."

"Right there." I point to it again.

"It looks like maybe the shot is a little out of focus at that point. I'd say the focal point is farther out at the leather thong on the pull of the zipper."

"You're right, it is. It's very hard to see in this photograph."

In the picture it is nearly translucent, a thin, fine line that unless you studied it intently, you would never notice. Magnified nearly to a blur in the photo, it seems to disappear into the smooth, deep finish of the calfskin. It is why Harry, searching for evidence of blood, thought he was seeing a seam in the leather. Until he finally realized that it was a tiny section of a line straight as a ruler with a fine, dried mist of what looked like faded rust on one side and clear, smooth leather on the other.

"I think if we looked at the real item, you could see it more clearly," I tell Prichert.

"Your Honor, I'm going to object." Tuchio is out of his chair. "Whatever Mr. Madriani is doing, it is beyond the scope of direct. If he wants to do it, let him do it in his own case."

"What I am do—"

"No. No." Quinn cuts me off. "Bring it up here," he says. He flips the sound button, and we go at it along the far side of the bench, away from the jury.

Tuchio is arguing that he never touched the folio during direct and that I shouldn't be allowed to do it on cross.

"Your Honor, Mr. Tuchio went on at length regarding blood evidence, on the floor in the bathroom, blood on the victim's chair, and blood transfer marks on the briefcases. All I'm doing here is addressing blood evidence on one of the cases, the small portfolio."

"There were no transfer marks on the portfolio," says Tuchio.

"I beg to differ. There is blood on the portfolio, and it was delivered there by centrifugal force. I'd call that a transfer."

"Transfer involves touching," says Tuchio.

"Maybe I should ask your witness," I tell him.

The judge tells me to go ahead, and he flips the switch so everybody can hear again. Tuchio sits down, and I ask Prichert whether drops or particles of blood flung from an object such as the hammer, imparting themselves onto an object such as a briefcase, could be considered transfer evidence.

"Sure. You could look at it that way."

"I'm going to renew my objection," says Tuchio.

"Overruled," says Quinn.

I ask the judge to have the clerk retrieve the portfolio from one of the evidence carts.

To this point we have been using photographs to document much of the physical evidence for reasons of convenience—they're easier to handle—and because they provide a more permanent record. But the best evidence in this case will be the item itself.

Ruiz puts on gloves before he touches the leather portfolio, then brings it over and lays it on the rostrum just next to the witness stand. The portfolio had been on the table near the television in the hotel room, approximately twelve feet from where Scarborough sat on the morning he was murdered.

"This right here." I point with my pen, avoiding contact.

Prichert studies it, this time leaning back

in the chair. He can see it now. I'm guessing that he didn't notice it during the investigation that day because two crime-scene photographers were moving among the items in the hotel room taking pictures with macro lenses, close-ups of the gloved prints in blood on the other two briefcases.

The portfolio, the top opening of which was unzipped, bore no gloved print marks. Moreover, it was empty. When Prichert turned his attention to these items in the lab, the one he concentrated on was the clean attaché case, which was on the couch in the living room, out of the line of fire from the blood spatter.

"Do you see what looks like a kind of rectangular outline of clear leather, here in the center of the portfolio?" I point to the area with my pen.

He looks more closely. "The distinction is faint," he says. "Hard to see. But I think I see what you're referring to."

"And around the outside of that outline, do you see that?"

"Yes . . ."

I can tell by the look in Prichert's eyes that he already knows what's happened here.

"Can you tell the jury what that is, covering the surface on this side of the portfolio, almost all of it except the inside of the rectangular outline?"

He looks more closely. "I probably wouldn't be able to tell you, except that I know where that portfolio was located at the time of the murder. While it doesn't look normal, from the appearance I would say it's a very fine mist of blood spatter. Though it's much lighter in color than what you would usually associate with blood evidence."

"As a trace-evidence expert, you deal with minute amounts of blood fairly regularly, don't you?"

"I'm not a blood-spatter expert, if that's what you mean."

"No, but I assume you've attended crime scenes involving traumatic head wounds before?"

"I have."

"In your experience in dealing with those cases, is there anything unique about the blood in those cases, particularly the density and color of the blood?"

"You're talking about spinal fluid."

"That's what I'm talking about."

"I would say that's probably a good guess," he says. "Blood diluted with spinal fluid might very well account for the near transparency of the stains on that leather."

"So you've seen something like this before?"

"Not quite like that," he says. "No. Every case is different."

"Could the fine mist also be the result of the distance between the leather portfolio and the point where the hammer was swung?"

"It could."

The seminal rule in asking any question in court is to know the answer before you ask. Harry consulted two experts with regard to an explanation for the fine film of blood that landed on the portfolio. The first was a blood-evidence expert who told us that distance from the point of origin would be one contributing factor; the farther the distance, the finer the spray. The other expert, a medical pathologist, provided the missing element, cerebrospinal fluid. The human brain virtually floats in this. Puncture the skull and what you get is not only a vigorous flow of deep red blood, often surging with the force of a pump, but a

less-viscous, almost clear flow of spinal
fluid. It is the reason that blood from massive head wounds often appears to be diluted, almost watery.

"Let me draw your attention back to the
clear rectangular area in the leather on
that side of the portfolio. Can you tell the
jury what might have caused this outline
to be formed?"

"If I had to guess, I'd say that something was lying there covering that area
when the blood spatter hit the portfolio."
Prichert just says it right out, matter-of-fact,
no big point. He knows that to belabor
what is now obvious is to be pounded
with it.

"Do you have any idea what that item
might have been?"

"No."

"Then I assume you don't have it?"

"Of course not."

"Do you know whether the police have
it?"

Prichert looks over at Detrick, who is
now huddled with Tuchio at the counsel
table. The detective gives him a quick
shake of the head, then turns back to the
prosecutor.

"I think you can be fairly certain that they don't have it either."

It's the only available answer, because if the police have it, they haven't turned it over to us in discovery.

"So it appears that the item is missing?" I say.

"It would appear so."

"Earlier I believe you testified that from your examination of the attaché case, while there was evidence of the case having been opened and traces of blood inside, you couldn't be sure whether anything was taken. Let me ask you now: After looking at the leather on that portfolio, do you think there's a fairly good chance that whoever killed Terry Scarborough took something from that room?"

"In light of the physical evidence, I'd have to say yes, there's a pretty good chance that they did."

SIXTEEN

I am told that the phenomenon on the surface of the leather portfolio is sometimes called "a shadow." It is similar to what often happens in structural fires where a book, a sheaf of paper, or some other object covers the surface of, say, a wooden table. If the table isn't destroyed by the flames, its surface will be smoked or charred, except for areas covered by the object. There, the surface will present the precise outline of the item resting on it at the time of the fire.

The difference here is that we're dealing not with flames but rather with the fine mist of blood cast across the room by the repeated blows of the hammer as Scarborough was beaten to death.

Harry and I have measured the rectangular shadow on the leather portfolio. The only edges that are sharply defined are the bottom—the edge closest to Scarborough's chair, the edge that caught Harry's eye—and the shorter right edge of the rectangle. Because of the angled trajectory of the blood, the other two edges were provided a kind of small defilade by the object resting on top of the portfolio, so that the shadow in these areas is less sharply defined. Along the bottom, the sharper and more defined edge, if you look closely, you can see a slight smear of blood. This was probably made when the killer lifted the item from the leather.

Still, when we measure the rectangle, Harry and I come to the same conclusion. The shadow on the leather matches the size of an ordinary business envelope, or perhaps letter-size sheets of paper folded in thirds, in the manner of a letter, the contents you might stuff into a business envelope. To say that this has inspired us is an understatement.

From everything we know, the information from Richard Bonguard, Scarborough's literary agent, and Trisha Scott, the former Supreme Court clerk who lived with the victim, Scarborough possessed only a copy of the Jefferson Letter. While the original was probably larger, it is likely that a facsimile made on a modern photocopy machine might well have been reduced down to a more convenient size, eight and a half by eleven inches, modern letter-size paper, the size of the rectangle on Scarborough's leather portfolio.

* * *

We are done for the day, finished in court. Harry and I are milling around in the office after hours, collecting our messages and trying to get a grip on what may happen tomorrow. Harry comes into my office.

"News from Herman," he says. Herman is back in D.C. trying to chase down or get a lead on the whereabouts of Arthur Ginnis.

Harry is holding a telephone slip stapled to a page of typed notes, information I assume Herman dictated over the phone to one of the secretaries while we were in court.

"Has he found Ginnis?"

"No. Not yet." Harry is reading as he settles into one of the two client chairs on the other side of my desk. He looks at the telephone slip. "It came in just after noon," he says. "He has gotten the information from the investigators we hired back there, though.

"Interesting stuff," says Harry, "but no surprises. What I expected. Aranda, full name Alberto Aranda, age thirty-two, Yale Law grad. It doesn't say here, but I'm guessing Mr. Aranda would be at or near the top of his class," says Harry.

"Why?"

"Because he was selected last year to become a Supreme Court clerk by Associate Justice Arthur Ginnis." Harry looks up from the paper. "I told you so."

What Harry means is that the e-mail from the Court to Scarborough telling him to take his inquiries away from the Court's official e-mail domain to a numbered snail-mail box was not dealt out by some obscure tech guarding the Court's electronic access points.

"The mailbox, the box number sent to Scarborough in the e-mail for the pursuit of private business. What we thought," says

Harry. "An address of convenience. Says here it's one of those private parcel-and-post places that small businesses use. The box number is registered—oh, this is interesting," says Harry, "—to 'A. Aranda.'" He looks up again.

"So it's not registered in Ginnis's name?" I say.

Harry shakes his head. "Get the sense we're dealing with a very careful man here? Now here's something else."

"What's that?"

"One of the investigators Herman hired was able to glance into the postal box through the little glass window in the front. He told Herman it looked like there were a couple of items inside, but he could only read the one on top. It was addressed to Aranda."

"Well, he owns the box," I say. "I think we need to talk to Mr. Aranda."

"It had a funny stamp on it."

"What had a funny stamp on it?"

"The item in the postal box the investigator was reading," says Harry. "According to the note, the stamp was something foreign, overseas. He couldn't make out the entire return address, but he said the street name was very long and appeared to be more than one word. The investigator told Herman that it looked like the address was written in German."

We regard each other with quizzical expressions.

Harry reads on. "The street named ended in the word 'straat.' But the man did get the country—'Curaçao.' Where the hell is Curaçao?" says Harry.

As he's saying the word, I am already turning in my chair to the computer behind me. I do a Google search on the name. Harry spells it out. What pops up at the top of the screen are three small thumbnail photos, pictures of two small maps on the right and the left, what looks like the shape of the same island in each. In the center is a picture of a sugar-white sand beach lapped by azure waters, a woman in a bikini lying with her lover at the ocean's edge.

I can see enough on the site lines below the pictures to pick out the word "Caribbean." I tell Harry.

"Trisha Scott told me that according to the Court staff she talked to, Ginnis was down in the Caribbean."

By now Harry is out of the chair, leaning

over my shoulder looking at the center thumbnail photo, the picture of the beach and the bikini. "Yeah. Recovering from surgery, as I recall," he says.

I open the first site on the page and try to read. It's in Spanish. I try the second site, Wikipedia.

A few lines in, I have one answer. "That explains the street address," I say.

"What does?" asks Harry.

"It wasn't German. It was Dutch. It's part of the old Dutch West Indies, the ABC islands—Aruba, Bonaire, and Curaçao."

"I've heard of Aruba," says Harry. "Vacation island."

"Yeah, and a young American girl disappeared down there a while back. It was all over the news."

"That's right."

I have opened up a larger map. Harry is still looking over my shoulder.

"What the hell?" he says. "Is that it?"

I nod.

"That's as far away as you can get and still be on an island," says Harry.

He's right. Curaçao is just off the coast of Venezuela, the absolute tail end of the Antilles.

*   *   *

Next morning, early court call, neither Harry nor I have time to be looking at maps. Tuchio is beginning his run for the finish, bringing out the big guns.

He starts with his fingerprint expert. For the better part of a day, using charts, magnified photographs of the full set of Carl's fingerprints taken at the time he was booked after his arrest, and comparing them to the partial prints lifted from the entry-hall floor of Scarborough's hotel room, the witness explains the art of fingerprint identification to the jury.

He tells them that based on studies of the millions upon millions of fingerprints classified over the last nearly one hundred years, no two sets of prints from different individuals have ever been found to be identical. In addition to being unique, they are immutable. Except in the event of physical injury, fingerprint patterns do not change over a person's lifetime.

The witness explains that comparison between known fingerprints taken from a known individual and those found at a crime scene turn on the analysis of ridge characteristics, known as minutiae, as well as the location and proximity of these characteristics one to another.

The testimony, questions and answers, drones on for hours. Tuchio risks putting the jury to sleep with evidence of what everyone in the courtroom already knows to be fact: The fingerprints at the murder scene belong to Carl.

Asked how the small pinkie print landed on the handle of the hammer, the witness testifies that based upon photographs taken by police of the hammer's location on the floor, it appeared that the fingerprint in question was made at the same time as the other prints on the floor. According to the testimony, the defendant's contact with the handle caused it to move several inches away, accounting for the later gap between the print of the third finger of Carl's right hand on the floor and the fourth finger, the pinkie print on the handle. Nonetheless, the fingerprint in question, the one on the hammer's handle, is sufficiently clear to identify it conclusively as belonging to the defendant.

Tuchio turns the witness over to me. I pass on him without a single question. It is, after all, exactly what Carl told the police when they questioned him, the same story he told Harry and me the first time we met him.

The judge looks up at the clock on the wall. It's approaching four. Friday afternoon, and Quinn decides that's it for the week. He cuts some slack and allows the jury to go home early. Monday will be a big day, the intimate details of death. The state is scheduled to bring on its medical examiner.

* * *

On the way to the parking lot, Harry and I shake the last two reporters about two blocks out. By now they know we're not going to say anything, so they take a few file shots of our backsides and retreat toward the courthouse.

Harry is holding a note delivered to us in court by one of our secretaries. It's an e-mail from Herman back in D.C. While we don't have a street or an address, we are now pretty sure of the general whereabouts of Arthur Ginnis.

I have sent three successive letters and left numerous telephone messages for Ginnis during the time since my meeting with Trisha Scott in Washington. I offered to converse by phone, or if he wished I would travel once more to Washington at the justice's convenience. I told him that I was representing the defendant in the murder of Terry Scarborough and that I would appreciate it if I could speak to him just briefly. To date I have received no reply.

When Herman arrived in D.C., he made a polite phone call, got through to a clerk in Ginnis's office, told the woman what it was about—an ongoing criminal trial in California, a capital case, an urgent matter—and requested a brief meeting with the justice. After some confusion in which the clerk thought the request involved a case on appeal and nearly hung up, she finally got it straight. Not that it mattered. Herman was told that Ginnis was on medical leave from the Court and that if Herman had a request, he should reduce it to writing and mail it in. When Herman asked for the address, he was given not the mail drop rented by Aranda but the name and address of another clerk at the Court.

Herman's helpers, the PI's he hired in D.C., got the nugget. One of them was sent by Herman to check Ginnis's house in

Chevy Chase. He rang the doorbell. Nobody answered. He talked to a few of the neighbors. One of them, a woman, a neighbor next door, told him that Maggie and Art went where they always went when they needed a rest, down to the islands. She said she'd gotten a postcard from them and that Arthur was coming along well, recovering from his surgery, though they were not quite ready to return home yet.

The investigator thought about asking to see the postcard, but he figured the woman might feel that this was a little too intrusive. She might go back into her house and close the door. So he simply asked, "What island?"

Ask for the time and some people will tell you how to build a clock. She explained that their old house, the one the Ginnises owned on St. Croix, a really cute little place, stone and old timbers, right on the beach—she knew this because she and her husband had been there two years ago for a short visit—was damaged in a hurricane last year. Since their place was under repair, the neighbor told the investigator, Maggie and Art had rented a place, on the island of Curaçao.

* * *

Harry and I come to the corner where we part company. We stop for a moment to talk.

"Are you going back to the office?" I ask.

He nods grimly. Harry has yet to comb through all the items Tuchio dropped on us that first day of trial. The paralegals have prioritized them the best they can, and Harry is just now finally approaching the bottom of the pile.

It seems that lately Harry and I are doing an increasing amount of our conferencing out on the street, in the halls at the courthouse, on the run, or on the phone late at night. Harry is growing bags under his eyes. I'm afraid to look in a mirror.

The opening of our case in chief is still over the horizon. If I had to guess, I would say a week, maybe ten days off. The few witnesses we have lined up are no problem. They're either experts who are being paid or cooperative local witnesses who've agreed to testify and are already under subpoena.

But even with this, what we have lined up, the evidence at hand, our case in total would have to be drawn out to last much beyond two days. You can only go so many rounds beating up Detrick before the judge rings the bell. By the time we get started, Tuchio will have gathered with his forensics wizards so that he can skate on ice around the inconsistencies in his own case. The absence of little bloody prints on the tray and tablecloth will be tucked neatly into some variation on the theme of his theory, how Carl did the deed. This, along with what we already know based on discovery—that the state's most damaging evidence is yet to come—has me deeply concerned.

"If we're to have any kind of a case," I tell Harry, "we need a centerpiece."

Harry knows what I'm talking about. Some lawyers call it "the golden idol."

In every case you look for something to fix the attention of jurors. If they can't actually see it or touch it, they must, at a minimum, be able to hear about it. It can be virtually anything—another possible perpetrator, a business dealing that offers the prospect of an alternative motive to the one your client had, the hint of a love tryst out on the margins along with the rumor that it went bad. It helps if you can believe in this, though it is not entirely essential. Depending on the candlepower and its mesmerizing qualities, this, the golden idol, is used to dazzle the jury, while the defense flies figure eights over the box, dusting them with the magic powder of reasonable doubt.

Harry and I stand on the corner and talk, toting heavy briefcases that hit us about the knees every few seconds like the gongs in cathedral bells. We dance all around it without actually saying the words: "the letter."

Given what we know—the information from Bonguard and Trisha Scott, the e-mails from Scarborough to Ginnis requesting the "original," and the rectangular shadow in leather, the item missing from the scene—you might think that the gods had reached down to give us precisely what we needed, an idol of platinum with a nuclear-powered laser light. But there is a problem.

Without hard evidence, someone who actually saw the Jefferson Letter or the copy in Scarborough's possession and who can testify to its existence, or better yet its contents and potential value, we have nothing.

Everything—the conversations with Bonguard, the agent, and Trisha Scott, both of whom claim they never saw the letter, as well as the e-mail missives between Scarborough and Ginnis's office—it's all hearsay. In a word, all inadmissible. As far as the law is concerned, without a solid evidentiary foundation, the Jefferson Letter becomes the product of pure speculation. Bottom line, we cannot mention it in court, not in the presence of the jury.

"So what we do have," says Harry, "is a pregnant question. We have a shadow in blood on a leather portfolio and a concession from one of Tuchio's witnesses that something is missing from the crime scene. It's a start," says Harry. "At least we have their attention. You can bet that the jury is wondering what the item was."

"Yes, but without more we can't connect the dots for them, and if there's anything worse than no play at all, it's one that has no second act. If the jury goes in to deliberate and we haven't told them what that item was that's now missing, they're going to wonder why. Of course, *we* know the answer: because the court wouldn't allow us to tell them. But *they* don't know that."

"So other than sign language, how do we give them the answer?" says Harry.

"As far as we know, there are only four possible sources for information to lay a foundation for the letter."

"Ginnis, Bonguard, Scott . . . and who's the fourth?" says Harry.

"Scarborough's editor. I can't remember his name."

"James Aubrey." Harry's magnetic brain. "Herman talked to Aubrey and got the same business you did from Bonguard and Scott. He heard about the letter, but he never saw it. Strange how everybody went blind whenever the letter came out," says Harry.

"It's human nature," I tell him. "If one of the goals in life is to stay free of en-tanglements with the law, it is often best to be blind," I tell him.

"So you think they're lying?"

"I can tell you that Trisha Scott didn't want to testify."

"And she lied about Jefferson's letter," says Harry. "Remember? First she told you she knew nothing about it. Then she recanted over dinner later and told you another lie."

Harry's right. According to Scott, Ginnis couldn't be involved, because he hated Scarborough. Not enough to kill him, mind you, but on a professional level. The only problem is that all this ill will did not run deep enough to prevent the two men from exchanging e-mails, even if Ginnis refrained from pushing the "send" key on the computer with his own finger.

"Maybe it's not a question of who lied as much as who told the biggest lie. The whopper," I tell him.

Harry puts his briefcase down on the sidewalk and looks at me, a question mark.

"Bonguard."

You would have to be Snow White to buy into the fable that the agent had tried to run past Sarah and me in New York.

"Claimed he knew nothing about the particulars of a letter that according to his own words on Leno's show would have been the basis of another zillion-dollar book, if only the golden author hadn't been killed."

"I've been thinking about him since we saw the tape." Harry smiles.

"On top of that, Bonguard was super-glued to his client on a book tour that rivaled Sherman's March to the Sea. This included the burning of Atlanta in miniature, according to the newspapers," I tell him, "with torched cars, broken windows, and flaming trash cans through . . . what? Six states and thirteen cities? The fact that he knew about the letter, enough to attribute its origins to Jefferson, and given what he told Leno, has to make you wonder—if he didn't know what was in it, he must have been burning with curiosity."

"You know, the thought has crossed my mind," says Harry, "that Bonguard wouldn't look bad dressed up in killer clothes."

What Harry means is in a plastic raincoat and brandishing a hammer.

"If we can't find the letter or some way to talk about it, to get it into evidence," says Harry, "Bonguard gets my vote for runner-up in the 'golden idol' awards."

"Except why would Bonguard kill the client who was filling his coffers?"

"Maybe the letter was worth more than his fifteen percent on book sales," says Harry.

"Even if it was a copy?"

"Okay, I'm still working it out," says Harry, "but think about it. If the shadow on the leather portfolio means anything, it means that the Jefferson Letter was in Scarborough's possession at the same time Bonguard was bird-dogging him out on the tour. To believe that the agent never saw it when he must have been in the same room with it on countless occasions is to believe in the tooth fairy."

Harry has a point. Aside from Scarborough, Bonguard would have had the best access to the letter.

He reaches down, picks up his briefcase, and starts shuffling toward the garage. "What was it Scarborough called it? Then I gotta run," he says.

"What do you mean?"

"The letter. According to Scott, he had a name for it."

"You mean the 'infamous Jefferson Letter'?"

"Yeah. Damn," says Harry. He's smiling. "Forget Bonguard. Anything with a name like that, we gotta find a way to get it in. Almost begs you to fly it in front of the jury, just out of reach, keep 'em wondering what's in it," he says.

My partner is starting to believe in paper dragons.

"That's a dangerous trip," I tell him, "seeing as we don't know what's in it. It could be a story with no punch line."

"You gotta have faith." Harry is moving away from me toward the garage. "Trust me, we want to fly 'infamous Jefferson.' I'm betting one or more of them—Bonguard, Scott, or Aubrey—saw the copy and knows what's in it. There's our foundation. Of course, it's just a guess."

"Don't stay in the office too late," I tell him. "I'll call you in the morning."

Just when he gets to the door, he stops and turns.

"One thing is certain, though," he says. He's no longer smiling. The look on Harry's face is stone sober. "Scarborough's e-mails. If we're tracking, if those mean what we think they do, then Ginnis has the McCoy, the real item, the original letter."

SEVENTEEN

Eight o'clock Saturday morning, and I'm planted in my favorite chair in the large den of the bungalow I call home, tucked away on Coronado Island.

For the most part, my house is now a sanctuary, safe ground from the snarling media, though occasionally one of the satellite news vans will cruise by to take a look. It doesn't matter any longer whether your phone is unlisted or your mail is delivered to a post-office box—these people will find you. It's the one thing you learn about the media: They possess an olfactory nerve that would shame a bloodhound.

And as soon as one of them locates you, the rest of the pack is right behind.

I had to live with it for about two weeks just before the trial started. Three mobile video trucks blocking traffic on the narrow street in front of my house, my lawn littered with cigarette butts and decorated with discarded paper coffee cups. Each morning I had to wave, smile, and be polite, since they were filming as I tried to bulldoze my way out of the garage, heading for work.

This was before they met Suki. Suki Kenoko is my Japanese gardener. He drives a 1957 Dodge pickup that once belonged to the original owner, his father. This accounts for the sign on the truck's door: KENOKO AND SON, YARD SERVICE. Hitched to the truck, he tows a trailer with all his gardening equipment—mowers, rakes, you name it, Suki's got it. Behind the wheel he never drives faster than ten miles an hour. I can verify this, having been stuck more than once in the train of cars behind him. Regardless of speed, however, you never want to cross an intersection in front of him, because until Suki gets where he's going, he never stops. It doesn't matter if there is a stop sign or a traffic light or what the color is, Suki will drive right through it, and everybody on this end of the island knows it. To my knowledge, he has never been ticketed. None of the local traffic cops want the hassle. Suki owns one of the more stately houses on the island, and his brother, who is a lawyer, is on the city council.

Late one afternoon I thought I might inherit another case when Suki showed up to do the garden. He looked at the front lawn, strewn with coffee cups and crushed Coke cans, cigarette butts in the bushes. For a moment I thought there might be blood in the street. He just stood there like a stick in his tan long-sleeved shirt and pith helmet, shoulders hunched forward, and shook his head.

It's true that you would have to know the man in order to realize that for Suki this was a display of raw emotion; think rattlesnake with the rattles removed. Nonetheless, one of the sound guys was sitting in a folding chair not ten feet from Suki's trailer, and he was laughing—toying with death.

Suki dropped the ramp on the back of the trailer and was getting a rake and a bag to get all the trash off the lawn. That's when he saw it. One of the cameramen had migrated with some of his equipment— a camera, a tripod, and cables—into a corner of the front yard, probably angling for a picture through one of my windows. In doing so the guy had snapped a limb off a small tree, a miniature Japanese maple. God help him. Suki wanted him out. And the fool resisted. The next thing I knew, my gardener was going at one of the legs on the camera's tripod with a large, curved pruning saw, a thing about eighteen inches long, sprouting glinting teeth like Jaws.

Confronted by Asian fury, they not only moved the camera, they moved themselves across the street and behind one of the vans. The tripod, which like Captain Ahab was now missing the better part of one leg, Suki calmly tossed into the street. It was followed a second later by the missing appendage. Through all this the gardener never said a word.

What was more amazing was that after days resting on their haunches outside waiting for something to film, not one of the news guys got a picture, not a single frame of the helmeted, saw-wielding ninja as he drove them out of the yard. They stayed huddled behind the van while Suki picked up the trash, mowed the lawn, and pruned some bushes. They didn't come out until the truck with the trailer, and the crazy guy driving it, left.

The day the trial started, the gypsy caravan camped in front of my house pulled up stakes and disappeared. Having missed the only pictures worth taking, they motored their movable feast back across the bridge to catch the rock-throwing Renaissance faire taking shape out in front of the courthouse.

I drink tea, Earl Grey, and scan the coroner's report, prepping for Monday's testimony. Across the room I have the television on, but with the sound muted. It is a much more peaceful way to catch cable news, without all the frenetic screaming. If somebody blows up a city, I can turn up the sound. Otherwise I'm not missing a thing.

This morning the screen is filled with election news, the presidential primaries, flashes of smiling faces, handshaking, and toothy grins, the political postmortems. Two Republicans and one Democrat are down and out, folding up their tents and tossing in the towel. But the real day of reckoning is just around the bend. The final state primary elections or caucuses. When that party ends, you'll need a dump truck to pick up all the bunting, banners, buttons, and body parts left over from the fallen candidates. If it isn't decided by then, within weeks—at most a month—the two principal party candidates, the nominees, will be the only ones left standing.

Then hostilities will begin in earnest, partisan warfare, politics as blood sport, all that matters is that our side wins, at every level, all the marbles—executive, legislative, and judicial.

When it's over, all the eminent talking heads will wax eloquent, telling us that now, with a new president elected, America and Americans, Democrat and Republican, will once again return to the great tradition of unity, binding up their differences to work together for the common good.

It might have sounded comforting coming from a network anchor a quarter of a century ago or more, but to hear it today is to wonder what weed the speaker is smoking and where he got it. In case you haven't noticed, the toxin of partisan politics that was once trapped inside the asylum on the Potomac and bottled up in a few other political hot spots around the country has suddenly been pumped, undiluted, into the national vein.

Cable news, much of it political and almost all of that partisan; talk radio, some of it virulent; the graceless decline of network news, until it stood undisguised, naked and seemingly unashamed in its ideological partiality; and major metropolitan newspapers, too many of which have given up the ghost of objectivity in their reporting to become obvious and open house organs for political parties—these were the forces that pushed the plunger on the syringe.

Having been flushed from our lives of political indolence, we suddenly discover that it is no longer possible to cast a vote and run for the sidelines. So we choose up sides, pin on labels—conservative or liberal, Democrat or Republican—and become emotionally invested in the only thing that is important: winning.

And of course the contest, as always, is all or nothing, a tug-of-war to see if we can rip the nation down the middle.

I watch the silent happy-warrior faces on the screen and wonder. In the age of e-mail and the Internet blogger, how long can we survive before those at the polar lunatic edges drag us all to a future where differences in politics and social ideology are settled Beirut style?

The phone rings. I reach over on the side table and answer it. It's Harry.

"I didn't call," I say. "I didn't think you'd be up yet."

"Houston, we've got a problem," says Harry. "Don't go anywhere. I'll be there in ten minutes." The line goes dead. Harry must be calling from his cell phone in the car.

* * *

We huddle over my kitchen table, and Harry tells me about the state's two witnesses, Carl's friends from skinhead heaven, Charlie Gross and Walter Henoch. Actually, the problem pertains to only one of them, but it's big enough to go nuclear if we play it wrong.

The bad news came in a sealed envelope from the prosecutor that was delivered to our office yesterday afternoon. If Harry hadn't gone back there, we wouldn't have seen it until Monday morning.

Gross and Henoch were the two confidants that Carl decided to go backslapping with at a bar where the three of them entertained each other with funny stories of how they might drag Scarborough from his hotel room out to a shooting range in the desert and pin him to a target. They also discussed the ease with which they could kidnap Scarborough. All these alcohol-fueled plots and plans were of course facilitated by the fact that Carl worked at the hotel and presumably had access to the victim. The author had been kicking up dust his whole way across the country, and because racial discord was his theme, he'd drawn the attention of groups that Gross and Henoch ran with, in particular the Aryan Posse.

Ordinarily Harry would be digging for dirt on the two witnesses, Henoch and Gross, looking to see if they have criminal records or charges pending that the cops might have traded away to get their cooperation, their statements against our client.

Charlie Gross has a rap sheet showing three felony convictions in the last ten years. That's the good news.

The bad news is that Walter Henoch has another first name. It is "Agent," as in FBI. Henoch was in fact wired, and unless we can catch his secretary making typographical errors in the transcription of the tape, every word emanating from our client's mouth during his meetings with Henoch is, as they say, gospel.

Harry and I both knew as soon as we saw the typed witness statements that it was highly likely that one of the two witnesses was wired for sound. We figured it was Henoch, because his signed statement reads like a screenplay, with everything but stage direction. We were hoping that at worst we might be dealing with a snitch, a member in good standing with the local Nazi club who was rolled by authorities and agreed to wear a wire. An FBI agent is another matter.

"It's bad," says Harry, "but there may still be some wiggle room."

"What do you mean?"

"Well, I've been thinking about it all night. I almost called you last evening, but I figured I would let you sleep."

"Thanks."

"Don't mention it," he says.

"So what's your point?"

"The disclosure by Tuchio in the sealed envelope delivered late yesterday. Why do you think he waited so long?"

"I don't know. Tell me."

"Tuchio has to know we're going to raise hell with the judge," says Harry.

"You bet. First thing Monday morning," I tell him.

"So why didn't he lay it on us earlier?" says Harry. "We guessed there was a wire. He had to know there was an agent."

"What are you getting at?"

"I don't think Tuchio knew until very late in the game, maybe as late as yesterday, whether the FBI would cooperate."

These are the kinds of tea leaves most people might try to read. Harry, it seems, can smell them.

"Think about it," he says. "You're the FBI. You got your man burrowed deep in the bowels of some hate group. He's taken a lot of risks, and you've taken a lot of time and effort to get him there. Suddenly a local prosecutor, with a dead body in a hotel room, discovers some of the affiliations of his principal suspect."

"Carl and the Aryan Posse," I say.

Harry nods. "It wouldn't be hard for a diligent prosecutor to find out that, say, a local state-federal task force had penetrated the group."

"Go on."

"Tuchio was throwing the dice. Can you imagine the smile on his face when he found out how lucky he was, that of all the people in the local chapter of the Third Reich, Walter Henoch had selected our boy Carl to take under his wing in the bar that day?"

"True enough," I say.

If Tuchio was having any second thoughts about his rush to judgment in charging Arnsberg, Carl's chat with Henoch and his enthusiasm for kidnapping and target-shooting at the victim would have eased his conscience.

"Hell," says Harry, "I'm surprised after reading Henoch's statement that Tuchio didn't file a motion to skip the trial, go right to execution, and ask for an order shortening time."

"But you're thinking the FBI was not hot to trot?"

He's shaking his head. "Murder isn't a federal rap," says Harry, "even if it takes place in the Presidential Suite of a five-star hotel. Their job is protecting their agent and making sure their investigation stays on track. So here they sit, the FBI and Tuchio, eyeball to eyeball. The feds have a tape and a transcript of three men talking, two possible witnesses. You can be sure they tried to feed Charlie Gross to Tuchio. They would have offered him the transcript of the tape and Gross's testimony."

"But the transcript wouldn't come in," I say.

"Right," says Harry. "Because Gross couldn't lay a foundation for it. He couldn't testify as to the wire, because he wasn't wearing it and he didn't know about it. So if that became the deal, the best Tuchio could do was try to have Gross memorize what was in the transcript, vomit it up in court, and hope we didn't find out about it. Or he could rely on Gross's memory of the conversation in the bar. Of course, Gross was probably drunk that night, and being a three-time loser, you have to figure he's likely to have the IQ of a paper clip."

"Plus the felony convictions. We could impeach him," I say.

"So from every angle you have to admit that this would not be a good deal for Tuchio. He would have gone from the elation of an FBI agent in his hand, the knowledge that he could break our back, to the realization that he was going to have to sit through two months of memory courses with Quasimodo and then pray that Gross could get through it all without having to untie strings from each of his toes while he was on the stand. Bust his balloon," says Harry. "But let's not feel too sorry for him. After all, somewhere along the way he managed to pull the chestnut out of the fire. He's back up to an FBI agent. That's why we got the disclosure so late, yesterday afternoon," he says.

I look at Harry. "It would take a while to get through all the little rabbit warrens back at Justice in D.C. Of course, when you have a few thousand people jumping up and down out in front of the courthouse, it doesn't take a lot to imagine them lighting torches to burn a city or two if the jury were to deliver a result they don't like."

"Yeah, I'd bet that's the kind of optimistic thinking Tuchio would have laid on them," says Harry. "With that thought you're bound to be able to stick your foghorn in somebody's ear in Washington."

"The question is, what exactly did the Justice Department tell Tuchio? How much rope did they give him? How firmly does he have Henoch in hand?"

EIGHTEEN

Monday morning Harry and I hook up at the same corner where we'd parted company Friday afternoon, two blocks from the courthouse. We may be dressed in Armani and wearing cordovan loafers, but inside is that age-old feeling you had in the fifth grade on the way to school when you knew your homework wasn't done. We are no closer to spinning a defense than we were a month ago.

Outside on the street in front of the courthouse, the crescendo has quieted considerably. The helmeted riot squad is now down to a handful, bracing themselves against their scuffed acrylic shields like farmers leaning on hoes while they talk.

The mob carnival, what's left of it, is not even a shadow of the beast from the first day. There are a few signs, one small group, maybe twelve or fifteen, walking in a circle chanting some mumbled mantra— St. Apathy's Order of Indifferent Monks. A few teenagers in baggy pants, their belts down at knee level, are laughing and cavorting, gangsta wannabes, jumping from the steps trying to get on camera. In front of them with their backs to the kids, a line of reporters like victims at a firing squad stand erect, talking into an opposing line of cameras.

It is difficult to sustain the fighting morale of a fevered following when the bone over which you're snarling turns into cerebral, scientific evidence. Still, Harry and I know that the armies of Hannibal and the Carthaginians will be back, and in full war paint, just as soon as they hear that a jury is about to boot the ball through somebody's goalpost.

* * *

Tuchio brings on the medical examiner, Dr. Dwight James. The courtroom is filled to overflowing. Judge Quinn warns family members and friends of the victim that they may wish to leave the room, for there will be lurid descriptions and graphic images.

Here things get much worse, for the reason that the M.E. brings along his own set of photos, pictures from the autopsy he performed on Scarborough at the morgue.

While Harry and I fought tooth and nail to keep most of these out, at some point the judge threw up his hands and admonished us once more that after all there was a crime and it involved a dead body.

The problem with many autopsy pictures is that, depending on the case, they can be much more graphic than shots taken at the scene. As they look at the photos on the overhead, I can tell that some of the jurors are having a hard time reconciling these with the person they saw beaming at them from the back of Scarborough's book during Tuchio's opening statement.

In the first shot, Scarborough is lying on the slab faceup. The blood from the wounds has been washed away, so that the lifeless complexion of his face is the white pallor of bleached paper. His mouth yawns, dragged open by the dropped chin that seems to hang slack as if it were not attached to the upper part of his head. All resemblance to the living form is gone.

The photos go downhill from there, shots of the scalp severed from the rear of the head and dropped like a flap over the victim's face so that the M.E. can better examine the wounds.

The pictures are hideous enough that many of the jurors avert their eyes, so that when I look over again, they are staring at Carl. Arnsberg has not been able, since Dr. James began, to even look at the screen. Instead his gaze is fixed on his hands, clasped and resting on the table in front of him. His head and upper body are swaying back and forth as if he were in a rocking chair. Were he the subject of a van Gogh painting, you might title the image *Man Teetering on the Edge*.

According to Dr. James's testimony, his examination revealed seventeen separate stab wounds to the back of the head, neck, and top of the cranial area of the victim. Each of these involved a double set of puncture wounds, one from each of the two claws of the hammer head.

The medical examiner testifies that Scarborough was rendered unconscious by the first blow, the only merciful thing, it seems, the witness has to say.

There are sounds of sobbing coming from out in the audience. Quinn raises his gavel, about to silence it, when he realizes it is coming from Scarborough's sister, seated in the second row. Instead the judge motions with the gavel to one of the deputies. A moment later she is ushered to the door, the deputy with one hand on her arm, the other over her shoulder to steady her.

Dr. James picks up where he left off. Based on the autopsy, the witness believes that the first blow was administered to the right side of the victim's head just below the temporal lobe and below and behind the right ear. Here the hammer's claws penetrated both bone and tissue to a depth of more than three inches. It may not sound like much, but according to the witness the angle of entry and the location allowed the sharp metal claws to reach the victim's brain stem, the medulla oblongata, where the spinal column joins the base of the brain.

"From that instant," says James, "the victim was unconscious and his body was paralyzed." He asserts that this and the element of total surprise account for the complete absence of any defensive wounds on the hands or arms of the victim. He simply never had a chance to turn and defend himself.

"Was this a mortal wound?" asks Tuchio.

"For all intents and purposes, it was. Within minutes a victim suffering this type of wound would die, since the medulla, the brain stem, controls vital functions such as respiration and heart rate."

Tuchio then has the witness take the jury on a tour of the rest of the wounds, almost every one of which would have been fatal, as all but two of these punctured the skull and entered the brain at various locations.

According to the wound patterns, it is Dr. James's opinion that the assailant, who approached the victim from behind, was right-handed and that he used two hands to wield the hammer for maximum force. This latter conclusion is based upon the torque, or twisting action, evident in the claw wounds as they penetrated the skull. As the doctor puts it, "This was the kind of torque you might see on the head of a golf club from the over-and-under grip on the club's handle as it turned through the arc of a swing."

"Could you tell," asks Tuchio, "whether these separate blows—I think you said seventeen in all—"

"That's correct."

"Were they administered slowly over a period of, say, many seconds or minutes, or were they done quickly, in rapid succession?"

"No. No. In my opinion they were administered in rapid succession, in the time it would take to remove the claws from the previous wound, extend the arms fully for the next blow, and swing. The only thing that might slow the assailant down was if the claws got hung up or if the assailant was forced to stop from sheer physical fatigue."

According to the witness, it was the latter, fatigue, that finally ended the attack. The killer simply became too exhausted to continue.

"Dr. James, can you tell the jury, is there a word or a term for this kind of attack?"

"There is."

"And what is that word?"

"It's called 'rage.' Sometimes the term 'rage killing' is applied."

"Why is that?"

"Because of the frenzied nature of the attack and the fact that the evident emotional and physical energy expended is far more than anything reasonably necessary to deliver a mortal wound or to achieve the objective of simply killing the victim. The attack in a case of rage reveals a desire on the part of the assailant to destroy the victim, to erase him from existence, not simply kill him."

As the witness says this, Tuchio is looking at Carl, as if to focus the jury's attention on the defendant. I can tell by the satisfied expression on his face that the prosecutor has already measured how he can use all this in his closing argument.

"Doctor, is it safe to assume that there could be any number of emotional triggers that might bring on a rage killing?"

"There are."

"Can you give us some examples?"

"A frustrated romantic liaison, a jealous lover. It could be based on a long-standing feud between the assailant and the victim, something that may have gone on for years seething under the surface."

"In your experience, in the cases that you've seen or studied, would a rage killing require that the victim know his assailant?"

"No."

"So as far as the victim is concerned, the killer could be a complete stranger, somebody that he or she doesn't even know?"

"Yes. I've seen cases."

"Could such a rage killing be predicated on or brought on by perceived differences in social or political views between the as-sailant—"

"Objection, Your Honor." I'm up out of my chair.

"—and the victim?" Tuchio finishes the question.

"May we approach?" I ask the judge.

Tuchio and I are at the bench off to the side, the court reporter huddling right next to us with the stenograph machine, taking it all down.

"This is beyond the scope of the witness's expertise," I argue. "He is not a psychiatrist or a clinical psychologist. And besides lacking the expertise, he has never examined or even talked to my client."

"Jeez, Your Honor, I've not mentioned the defendant's name," says Tuchio. "It's a simple hypothetical question, put to an expert. The witness should be allowed to testify as to whether he has seen or observed such cases, within his own experience or from scientific journals in his field: Can a rage killing be triggered by political or social disagreement? Simple question," says Tuchio.

Quinn thinks about it for a second or two. "Reframe the question," he says.

I start to argue.

The judge puts his hand up and sends us back.

Tuchio restates the question and mentions the words "scientific journals" in the field of pathology, the ticket to passage for an inferred head job by the county coroner on Carl and his presumed motive for murder.

The question isn't even finished, and James is leaning so far forward in his chair he nearly falls out of it before he can answer. "Yes, there are documented cases involving political and social triggers for rage killings. I have personally been involved in cases involving homophobia and racial hatred. Based on studies in pathology journals, acts of genocide—often in times of war, but not always—have been documented to involve rage killings almost by definition. Any form of deep-seated emotional and oftentimes utterly irrational hostility can form the basis for such a killing."

"Thank you."

For a second I think Tuchio is done with the witness. Then he stops. "There's one more issue I'd like to cover."

Quinn wants to know how long this is going to take. The judge is looking at his watch, wondering if we should break for lunch.

"Five minutes," says Tuchio.

"Keep it short," says Quinn.

"Dr. James, when you arrived at the scene, the hotel room, I assume that you attended the body at the scene?"

"I did."

"When you arrived there, where was the victim's body situated?"

"On the floor in the living room," says James.

"On the floor, not in the chair?"

"That's correct."

"Could you tell how long the body had been there, in that position, on the floor?"

"No."

"But you testified earlier that the initial attack on the victim had taken place when the victim was seated in the chair, is that correct?"

"That's right, judging from the position of the body on the floor at the base of the chair, the location of wounds, and the blood evidence at the scene."

"So based on your testimony, can we assume that at some point after the initial attack the victim was either pushed or fell from the chair onto the floor?"

"I doubt if he was pushed from the chair. Or if he was, it was with a minimal amount of force."

"Why do you say that?"

"Because of the position in which the victim came to rest on the floor. The upper part of his legs and the anterior midsection of his body, the area at his midsection in the front, were actually elevated just off the floor, and the body was twisted. That was because the lower part of his body, his feet and lower legs, were wedged against the front of the heavy chair when his head, shoulders, and upper body hit the floor. If someone had pushed him forcefully out of the chair, it's my opinion that he would have landed clear of the chair in a prone or more-prone position on the floor."

"So is it more likely, in your opinion, that the victim wasn't pushed but that he fell from the chair onto the floor?"

"Probably. I would say so. At some point, from whatever force, I believe that he tilted forward and fell."

"And would this necessarily have occurred—the victim falling from the chair, I mean—either during or immediately following the assault?"

"Not necessarily."

"But you said earlier, did you not, that the victim was unconscious, paralyzed, and that he died almost instantly or within a very short period of time following the initial blow from the hammer?"

"That's correct."

"So how is it possible that he could have fallen from the chair later?" says Tuchio.

"Lividity," says the witness.

James explains that after death unclotted blood in the upper extremities of the body begins to move, due to gravitational forces, toward the lower portions of the body. For example, a body that is leaning at the edge of a bed at death can actually be tumbled or rolled by the gradual force of lividity so that it ends up on the floor.

"Just as the victim here ended up on the floor?" Tuchio's leaning toward the witness, urging him on.

"It's possible. If the victim here were leaning slightly forward and his weight were stabilized at the time of death, held up or balanced by, say, the arm or the side of the chair. In this case the right side of the chair, since he fell to that side. Then lividity as the blood settled—in this case toward the anterior or front of the chest and stomach, since he would be leaning slightly forward— might very easily cause the body to topple forward out of the chair."

"Would this explain the awkward position on the floor in which the body was found?" asks Tuchio.

"It could."

"Could this happen as soon as, say, four or five minutes following death?"

The science may be garbage, but I can see where Tuchio is going with this, back-filling one of the holes in his case.

"Ordinarily I would say that it would take longer," says James, "but it's possible, depending on how precariously balanced the body was at death. It might not take much of a change in body mass, the weight of the blood moving, to disturb the balance point if the body were in a position at death that was already close to falling."

"Thank you, Doctor. Your witness."

Tuchio is happy with this, smiling toward the jury as he heads for the counsel table.

He should be pleased. Thin as it may be, Dr. James has just supplied the answer to the question that has been causing Tuchio's case to sag in the middle: What was it that made Carl panic and run, slipping in the blood and leaving his prints all over the floor at the scene? What else but the seeming apparition of a moving dead body suddenly toppling from the chair onto the floor as the defendant was getting ready to exit the room?

We take the noon break and come back. I grill James on the issue of lividity. I ask him whether it isn't true that all the professional literature, studies on the subject, agree that it takes anywhere from a half hour at a minimum to two hours after death before lividity, the gravitational force on blood in the body, takes effect.

He concedes the point.

"So if that's true, how could lividity move the body in this case from the chair to the floor in the period of four or five minutes following death?"

The cops and the prosecutor know that Carl, and no one else for that matter, after having murdered Scarborough in the way he did, would have stuck around more than four or five minutes. From all the evidence, the killer would have stayed just long enough to leave the gloved prints on the attaché case while searching for whatever it was and to clean the raincoat, God knows why, and then he would have jetted out of there like the Road Runner. My guess would be two or three minutes, not four or five.

James refuses to back off. "It's possible," he says, "that the body, if it were just at the tilting point in the chair at the time of death, could have been affected by the very earliest stages of lividity."

"Or I suppose it could have been an earth tremor, or a puff of wind, or maybe a séance going on across town—"

"Objection." Tuchio's out of his chair.

Quinn slaps the gavel. "The jury will disregard counsel's last comment," says the judge. "Any more questions?"

"None, Your Honor."

"Good. Next witness."

* * *

Tuchio takes up the remainder of the afternoon with Carl's former supervisor, the head of catering and the manager of the hotel dining room at the Presidential Regis. The witness testifies that Carl was not the best employee. He was often late for work, argued with other employees often over issues of politics, and was twice caught stealing items of food from the kitchen.

When asked why the defendant wasn't fired, the supervisor explained that in the last year, following two raids by ICE,

Immigration and Customs Enforcement, it had become very difficult to get good help, or to keep it. In other words, Carl only had the job because he didn't need a green card to work.

Notwithstanding Carl's shaky record as an employee, the witness told the jury that Carl Arnsberg, like most employees at the hotel, either possessed or had access to a master card key, which would have given him access not only to the victim's hotel room but to the maintenance closet where the murder weapon, the hammer, was stored.

According to the witness, on the morning of the murder, the defendant left the hotel, disappeared without telling anyone, and failed to clock out with his time card.

* * *

End of the day, and Harry and I hoof it back to the rendezvous point.

"I know what I'd like to do. But given the fact that we live in a civilized society, Quinn would probably say no to waterboarding," says Harry. "We may just have to settle for a few early subpoenas. Turn the screws and hope," he says. "Let 'em cool their ass on a hard bench in the courthouse, wondering when and whether they'll be called."

On Harry's short list of recipients for witness subpoenas is the literary agent, Richard Bonguard; the Washington lawyer, Trisha Scott; and Scarborough's editor, Jim Aubrey.

"We bring them out early and sweat 'em," says Harry. "How much time do you think we have before Tuchio wraps his case?"

"I don't know. Two weeks at the outside. No more," I tell him.

Harry and I have gone over the state's witness list. Besides Carl's tavern buddies, Tuchio has several witnesses he will no doubt call, one of them a psychiatrist prepared to talk about hate crimes and how political hostility can fit the mold. He will no doubt get the shrink talking about the contents of Scarborough's book as well as taped videos of some of the author's more provocative interviews on television and how these might trigger hostility. There are also two hotel employees who argued with Carl about politics and who presumably will testify as to the level of anger he displayed. One of Carl's neighbors also has a tale along these lines and is on Tuchio's list. If he wants to put a few flourishes on his case, there are two or three members of the Aryan Posse he could drop on us. Though according to investigative reports, most of these had only a passing acquaintance with Carl. They told the cops that Carl was so far out on the fringes of the group that they didn't know who he was, and when they were invited to classify Carl as a wannabe with the group, they said they didn't know. Show the jury pictures of these guys, chopper gauchos with tattoos from here to hell, and the fact that they didn't know him becomes Carl's most positive character reference.

"So let's play it safe and say we have a week," says Harry. "We serve Bonguard, Scott, and Aubrey ASAP—tomorrow if we can do it—and bring 'em out now."

We suspect that at least one of them, maybe all, has seen the Jefferson Letter and certainly knows more about it than he or she has revealed to us. If we're right and we can squeeze it out of one or all of them, we could build a legal bridge, permitting us to talk about the letter in front of the jury. This, plus the shadow in blood on the leather—the inference, because we may not be able to say it overtly, that this silhouette represents the missing letter—gives us at least the bones of a case. Dress it up in a few of the inconsistencies from Tuchio's own presentation and the skeleton might dance long enough in front of the jury to inflict two or three of them with a terminal case of reasonable doubt.

A hung jury. It may be like kissing your sister, but it's better than a lethal injection. And who knows? If the gods of reason are asleep over the jury room and somebody switches off the lights, we could even get an acquittal.

"What makes you think they'll be more cooperative once they come west?" I ask Harry. I'm talking about Bonguard, Scott, and the editor.

"We get them thinking about that hot ball of sun," says Harry, "the media spotlight over a witness stand in a trial with charged racial overtones.

"Take them out to dinner, separately," he says, "and talk about the book."

By the look I give him, he knows I'm not following him.

Perpetual Slaves," he says. "That book

is positively full of all kinds of hideous history. Tuchio is going to use it to brain our client. So over salad we ask Bonguard his thoughts on the intimate details in the book and its effect on race relations in modern America. Now, that's some touchy stuff," says Harry. He stops walking and looks at me.

What Harry has in mind is the modern equivalent of a Renaissance Florentine inquisition—everything but the stake, the pyre, and the burning bodies. If the restaurant would let him in, he would dress in a robe with a hood, holding a staff with a skeletonized hand nailed to the end of it.

"I wouldn't want to have to talk about that stuff in open court, under oath, on the stand, with reporters in the front row working their pencils to a nub taking notes," says Harry. "Hell, a single word, an unintended inference, or maybe just the wrong inflection in your voice—on a sensitive subject like that, you could fall on your own sword, kill a career in full bloom right there in front of the world.

"And we haven't even gotten to the bad

stuff yet," says Harry, "whether Bonguard and Scarborough ever had conversations about all the violence that seemed to be following them around on tour. You know, I'll bet if we subpoenaed the publisher's sales records on that book and plotted them against newspapers in the cities where the fire tour visited, you would see a direct correlation between the flames on the front page and the spikes in sales. Scarborough wasn't an author, he was a firebug."

To listen to my partner, you'd think that whoever murdered the man didn't commit a crime, just simply killed a pyromaniac before he could burn another city. If we can't spring something loose on the letter, this may become our best defense.

"Give me an hour with Bonguard," he says. "No. No. Forty minutes," says Harry, "tops. Before we get to dessert, he'll tell me everything he knows about that letter, whether he saw it, and how many times. Believe me, he'll be anxious to get on the stand as long as he can talk about anything except that book and how they marketed it."

"And even if he didn't see the letter, he'll swear he did. Right?"

Harry starts walking again, trudging with his head down, hauling his heavy briefcase. "Hey, if he doesn't tell me he's lying, how am I supposed to know?"

NINETEEN

The subpoenas, all three of them, went out this morning, for Richard Bonguard, Trisha Scott, and Jim Aubrey.

By 9:00 A.M. the subpoenas aren't even on our radar screen any longer. Harry and I have moved on to trying to put out the next fire. We are back in court, but not in front of the jury.

The judge has given them the morning off. Instead we are gathered in Quinn's chambers, where Tuchio is scrambling to account for the late disclosure of an FBI agent on his witness list.

He tells the judge there was nothing he

could do. According to Tuchio, he disclosed the existence of his witness and the entirety of the man's statement given to police the moment the D.A.'s office received the information. All this was turned over to the defense as required by discovery.

"The fact that this witness was an agent of the FBI, working undercover, I did not know until later," says Tuchio.

"How much later?" Quinn wants to know.

This morning his office is crowded. Besides Tuchio and his assistant, Janice Harmen, and Harry and I, there are two other men present, sitting on the couch against the wall behind us. One of them is the agent in charge of the FBI's San Diego office. The other gentleman is a deputy United States Attorney from the Justice Department in Washington. Apparently the matter is of sufficient importance that Justice sent its own man out from D.C. instead of simply handing it off to the United States Attorney in San Diego.

Trying to answer the judge's question, fixing the precise date when everything was known, Tuchio looks like a one-man band, juggling his notes, riffling files in his briefcase, and whispering out of the side of his mouth to his assistant. Then they both huddle with the FBI agent. When the prosecutor finally turns back to the judge, he says, "About ninety days, Your Honor. We knew with certainty about ninety days ago."

"Three months!" says Quinn.

"Yes. About ninety days." For some reason this seems to sound better to Tuchio.

"And you disclosed the existence of the agent when?" says the judge.

Tuchio coughs a little, covers it with the back of his hand, and says, "Friday, Your Honor."

"Last Friday?"

Tuchio nods.

Quinn nearly blows a fuse. "There are cases on point," says the judge.

"Not with regard to collateral crimes, Your Honor. We've checked the cases." Tuchio wants to split legal hairs with the judge, who looks as if he'd like to lean across the desk and smack him.

"I see," says Quinn. "So you want to make a new law and have me reversed on appeal in order to do it, is that it?"

"No, Your Honor. That's not what I'm saying."

"Lemme get this straight," says Quinn. "You have a law-enforcement officer, part of the government—albeit the federal government, not somebody playing under your own tent—and he's in the middle of your case."

"By sheer circumstance, Your Honor. The D.A.'s office had no idea." Janice Harmen tries to draw some of the heat off of Tuchio.

"I appreciate that," says the judge. "But just so I understand, you have statements made by the defendant, statements against penal interest made in the presence of this agent. You want to bring those statements before the jury to show the defendant's state of mind prior to the commission of the crime."

Tuchio is nodding.

"And you failed to disclose the fact that the witness is a federal agent until three days ago?" says the judge.

"That's it," says Tuchio.

"Not in my courtroom," says Quinn. "What do you have to say to this, Mr. Madriani?"

Why should I interrupt Tuchio's train wreck? I'm about to tell Quinn that I second his motion, that he shouldn't sully his courtroom, but Tuchio cuts in before I can say anything.

"First of all, Your Honor, all the defendant's statements were made prior to the commission of the crime. There is no question of Miranda here, no need to caution the defendant, because there was no focus of suspicion. The crime had not yet been committed."

Quinn looks at him, that death stare again. "Tell me something I don't know," he says. "What I'm concerned about, Mr. Tuchio, is the fact that the witness carries the mantle of government on his shoulders, a material fact withheld from the defense in the preparation of their case."

Tuchio finally tells the judge that while the witness Walter Henoch's name appeared on the prosecution witness list, and while his statement was disclosed, the consent of the federal government for the witness to actually testify, to appear at trial, had been granted only four days earlier, on Thursday afternoon, the day before the prosecutors delivered the disclosure to our office.

Both Justice and the FBI, seated on the

couch, confirm this. They tell the judge that the witness was part of an active, ongoing undercover investigation and that disclosure was hampered by serious concerns for the personal safety of their agent.

Harry was right. It's an eleventh-hour deal.

This takes some of the edge off the judge. Though Quinn is still not completely mollified, his sense of indignation goes back in the box.

"I can appreciate that," says the judge. "Still, there are questions of fundamental fairness that have to be discussed." He turns to me. "Did you have any idea that you were dealing with an agent of the government?"

"We had no formal notice of any kind until Friday," I tell him. This is not exactly responsive to the question he asked. Harry and I had guessed that there was too much polish to Henoch's typed statement, so that there was little doubt that somebody was wearing a wire, but as to the FBI we were blind.

"Well then, I guess we're down to the question, what do you want to do about it?" He puts this to me.

"I would move to suppress the witness's statement, Your Honor, and request an opportunity to prepare points and authorities."

Out of the corner of my eye, I can see that Tuchio is jumping up and down arguing that suppression is an overkill, given that the witness and his statement were disclosed.

As Tuchio argues, my gaze wanders the room. It doesn't require clairvoyance to pick out the man in the middle, the one with the occasional pained expression like a sudden attack of gas whenever the prosecutor turns a new argument, the guy with his head in a vise.

Welcome to the wonderful world of bureaucracy. You can bet that the FBI agent seated on the couch has never found himself in this position before—locked up in chambers in some judge's courtroom, pulling for the defense in a criminal case.

He sits there quietly watching as his superiors in Washington, who want to make sure they aren't caught off base, without political cover in the event of a riot following the trial, flush his investigation by outing his undercover agent. And that's if the

Aryan Posse doesn't kill Henoch before he can testify.

"Your Honor, I have an alternative." Tuchio finally gets to his punch line. He wants to confer with the FBI and the Justice Department for a moment. They huddle at the couch, murmuring. I can see the agent's face. At first he seems not to understand what Tuchio is proposing. When he finally gets it, he has another attack, only this one is major, and overt. The agent is sitting there shaking his head, trying to argue with the attorney sitting next to him. It takes a few seconds, but the lawyer from Washington has the final word. He silences him.

Tuchio turns back to the judge. "Your Honor, I would propose that the witness be allowed to testify but that there be no statement or disclosure to the jury that the witness is an agent of the government or involved in any way with law enforcement. It makes perfect sense," says Tuchio. "It conforms to our earliest disclosure of the witness and his statement." Then he gets piggy. "In return," he says, "we would ask that the defense refrain from mentioning or disclosing to the jury the prior convictions of our other witness, Charles Gross." He sort of slips this in sideways, as if his proffered concession on the agent weren't being forced.

"That's not going to happen," I tell the judge. "Unless—"

"I don't think so, either," says Quinn.

"Fine," says Tuchio, "forget the second part. Gross's prior record can come in."

"Unless what?" The judge is looking at me.

The prosecutor's offer is a bad deal for us any way you cut it. Under Tuchio's proposal the state has two corroborating witnesses. With Henoch's testimony, every *t* crossed and *i* dotted, and with Gross on the stand later to confirm as much of it as he can remember, it won't matter that Henoch's badge is covered up and that Gross's prior record is out on the table in front of the jury. The details of Henoch's testimony and the confidence with which he delivers it will kill us. Jurors can smell credibility, and Henoch—or whatever his real name is—will reek of it.

"I have a different proposal, Your Honor. The prosecution presents their testimony through a single witness, Mr. Gross. In

return, the defense would refrain from disclosing the witness's prior convictions."
Then I add the sweetener. "The undercover agent, Walter Henoch—who I assume is already under subpoena?" I look
to Tuchio.

"He is."

"Mr. Henoch will refuse to testify and
accordingly will be jailed for contempt."

At first Tuchio shakes his head and
laughs. It takes a second or two before he
turns and looks at the FBI agent, a sim-
pering expression on his face like, *Why in
the hell would we jail one of our own?*

But by then the FBI agent is already
burrowed deep in the ear of his compatriot
from Washington, talking fast enough that
you might swear he was going to chew
right through to the ear on the other side.

When Tuchio turns to face the judge
again, his head all the way to the back of
his neck is the color of a ripe radish. He
calls it a fraud. "The court in good conscience cannot go along with such a proposal," he says. "It would be a sham on
the judicial process."

I ask the judge what his powers are if a
witness under subpoena refuses to testify.

"Contempt," says Quinn. "The witness is in the bucket."

And if there's one thing that will put your man in tight with his friends in crime, it's telling a court to go screw itself and doing time at the county lockup, all for the purpose of protecting his buds.

It is exactly the point that the FBI agent has now drilled into the head of the lawyer sitting next to him on the couch. The feds, having been given a glimpse of the nirvana that a little jail time could do to boost their program with the Posse, are having second thoughts.

When Tuchio tries to get them back on board, the lawyer from Justice tells him that the risks involved for their agent are suddenly looking much worse.

Listening to the two feds as they talk on the couch, I can see it's obvious they think that telling the D.A. and the court to go to hell sounds like a much better idea.

Tuchio stands there burning. It's the best deal he's going to get. If he pushes back, I withdraw the offer on Gross's rap sheet. The look on his face says it all, every four-letter word you can imagine except the one that he actually speaks.

"Fine. I'll drop Mr. Henoch from my witness list, on the condition that it is part of a deal on the record so that it's clear I'm not volunteering this." This he directs to the two feds sitting on the couch. "That Henoch and his statement are unavailable to either side and that Gross's prior criminal record is off-limits."

It's good by me, but I'm not so sure everybody else is happy.

To get out of the judge's office, Tuchio has to squeeze through the door glued to the two feds, one talking in each of his ears. By now they have come to appreciate fully the unbridled benefits that could be afforded to a scofflaw witness followed quickly by the judge's hammer.

*   *   *

The day Harry found Scarborough's shadowed leather portfolio in the police evidence locker, he also noticed a number of boxes, files, and other materials belonging to the victim that authorities had gathered from Scarborough's apartment in Washington.

Harry looked at the number of boxes and realized that if they were full, and most of them looked as if they were, the volume

of materials had to exceed by a considerable amount the documents given to us
during discovery by the D.A.'s office. Later,
of course, Tuchio dropped the mountain of
paper on us right at the start of trial, Scarborough's computer printouts, and for a
few days we thought this might account
for the difference.

In the interim, however, Harry had sent
one of our paralegals back to the evidence
locker to check out the boxes. Jennifer
Sanchez is young, pretty, and relentless,
not necessarily in that order. Ask her to
pick up a piece of lint from your carpet and
she'll vacuum your entire house.

What she found was not paper files but
rather DVDs, and some older VCR tapes,
hundreds of them dumped into twenty-three
cardboard boxes and stacked against the
partitions of the evidence locker.

Scarborough apparently had a fetish for
making and collecting copies of his appearances on television. From some of the
labels, it was clear that at some point he'd
hired a company that provided this service, taping his appearances and providing copies. The numbering scheme on the
labels, a kind of Dewey decimal system,

makes us think that Scarborough, or someone he hired, had probably organized
these on shelves or in cabinets in his apartment. But when the authorities grabbed
them during their search, they indiscrimi-
nately dumped them into boxes. Jennifer
found scores of blank tapes and DVD
disks, brand-new, still in their original cel-
lophane wrappers mixed in with the copies in the evidence boxes.

Tuchio had in fact disclosed to us the
existence of these materials on his police
property's list, in a single line: "Boxes of
tapes and digital videos (various)." What
this meant was that we were free to look
at them whenever we wanted. The D.A.'s
office didn't copy them, and the police
probably never looked at them. It would
take two lifetimes to view them all.

Whether they even bothered to go
through them as Jennifer did, just checking out the labels, we may never know.
But this morning, as I was dueling with Tuchio over the FBI, Jennifer hit pay dirt.

It wasn't a label but rather a yellow
Post-it, a two-inch-square note, stuck under the clear plastic cover of the DVD's
jewel case. The Post-it had two names

penned on it in blue ink: "Arthur Ginnis" and "Edgar Zobel." Jennifer did the only thing she could. She had the DVD copied by one of the evidence and property clerks, along with making a photocopy of the jewel case's cover, showing the Post-it note.

Harry has been fielding text messages from her since two-thirty this afternoon, three of them, telling us there was something urgent waiting for us back at the office.

By the time we get there, it is almost seven. Jennifer is waiting at the office door, her forehead furrowed and her dark, oval eyes the size of teacups.

"You're gonna wanna see this," she says. She is so excited she's almost crying.

We dump our briefcases on the floor just inside the door and follow her to the conference room, where the lights are on and there are voices. One of the secretaries and another paralegal are seated at the conference table hunched over legal pads and holding pencils. As soon as they see us, one of them says, "Start it over," and the secretary punches a button on the remote.

A second later, just before the screen flickers to blue, I see the image and recognize the face.

I look at Jennifer. "Arthur Ginnis."

She nods. "But there's more," she says. And now she does cry.

"What?"

Both of the paralegals and the secretary know that Harry, Herman, and I have been on a hunt for the Jefferson Letter for more than eight months, since before the trial started, wondering if it existed and, if it did, who had it and where it was.

She wipes away the tears and teeters on her tiptoes, wringing her hands in front of her like she's going to break her knuckles. "We think it's there, on the video," she says.

"Punch it up," says Harry.

For the next twenty-six minutes, the five of us sit around the table, our eyes glued to the television screen, watching the image of Arthur Ginnis talking to someone across a table in what appears to be a crowded restaurant—white linen tablecloth and crystal glassware, the clink of dishes and the cluttered sounds of conversation and laughter drowning out almost everything Ginnis says on the video. You can make out maybe every sixth or seventh word.

This is what they've been working on since midafternoon, the three women with pencils and pads, listening to the video over and over again, trying to write down words, partial sentences, trying to work out a rough transcript of what is being said on the video.

The curved end of Ginnis's cane can be seen hooked over the edge of the table.

Every once in a while, he will laugh, and the intelligible few words that follow can be heard, but it's just idle chatter. At one point he's buttered a piece of bread when he laughs, throws his head back, and says, "I know. It was hilarious. I saw that on CNN." Then his voice drops again, and his words are swallowed up in the surrounding noise.

Several times he leans with his elbows against the table and talks fervently to whoever it is on the other side. We can't see the face of this person, just his right hand, the sleeve of his suit coat, and the starched cuff of his shirt where it sticks out.

Each time Ginnis leans against the table, the camera shakes. From this, and from the slight fish-eye wide angle of the video and the fact that he never once looks at the camera, it's obvious: Ginnis doesn't know he's being filmed. I'm guessing that the lens on the camera was probably not much larger in circumference than the eraser on the end of a pencil. It was probably concealed in a small binder, a day planner, or the hollow case of a cell phone, good enough to capture thirty minutes, maybe an hour, of low-quality video and sound. You can buy one in any spy shop.

We are just over nine minutes into the tape when the camera shakes a little and the hand on this side of the table disappears from view. When it reappears a second or so later, it is holding a sheaf of paper, folded in thirds.

"There it is." Jennifer's pointing at the screen.

The hand comes back into view, and the papers are unfolded. They are stapled together at the top left-hand corner, what appears to be four pages. This is obvious because the forefinger of the other hand idly fans them at the bottom as if to show the camera the individual sheets.

"What do you think it's worth?" The man holding the letter is speaking, and with the elevated volume of his voice you can hear it clearly. "The original, I mean." This is even more audible.

Harry looks at me and mouths the words, *The firebug.*

We have both heard Scarborough's voice enough times from videos of appearances on his final book tour to recognize it.

The look from Ginnis is dour. You can't hear his words, but you can read his lips: "Put it away."

For almost fifteen seconds, you can see the reduced image of elegant handwritten script, something from another age, on the open page in front of the camera. If you froze the picture with the proper equipment, you could read it. Just on the inside margins of the page, you can see the shadowed line from the edge of the original document that was copied.

He tries to hand the letter to Ginnis, but the old man occupies himself with a piece of bread in one hand and the knife going for the butter in the other. He mumbles something.

"We think he said, 'I don't want to talk about it,'" says Jennifer. "We've listened to it a dozen times, but he's leaning forward, his head is down, and we can't make it out."

There is some wobble with the camera, and when Ginnis settles back against his chair again, the letter is open, faceup, in the middle of the table. Scarborough's empty right hand now lifts the crystal wineglass in front of him. The hand and the wine both disappear. A few seconds later and the glass is back on the table.

"When can I have the original? I need it before I can deliver." Over the din of laughter and the clatter of dishes, you can hear this clearly. It is obvious now that not only is the volume of Scarborough's voice elevated but that he is much closer to the concealed microphone.

Across the table Ginnis's thin face shows the taut strings of flesh from his jawline down his neck. His face may wear the stress of recent illness, but his expression is the classic portrait of the furtive look—Gollum from *Lord of the Rings.* He is holding the buttered bread, but he is not eating. Swallowing nothing, yet his Adam's apple is bobbing.

"Have you finished it?" Ginnis says. You can't hear his words, but you can once more read his lips. The women all agreed. That's what he said.

We cannot hear anything from Scarborough. He may have said something and we didn't hear it, or he may have gestured, but it appears that he communicated something to Ginnis, because the old man smiles and says, "Good."

Just like that, he is affable once more. He wipes the butter off both edges of his knife. Then he reaches out with the knife and lifts the letter just enough so that it slides back across the table toward Scarborough. He smiles. Nods a few times and says, "Put it away. You'll have what . . ."

"'Put it away. You'll have' what?" says Harry.

"What you need," says Jennifer. "It took us three or four times, but we finally got it."

Both hands come out once more, and the letter is folded. Within seconds it disappears, back where it came from, probably into the inside breast pocket of Scarborough's coat.

Ginnis and Scarborough talk quickly now. One of the women flips her pencil into the air, and it lands on the pad in front of her. "We tried to get some of this, but his face is in his plate most of the time. At one point he says 'good work,' but that's all we could make out."

The video ends, and we turn off the set.

"It's yeoman service," I tell them. "Bonuses all around." Even if I have to pay them out of my own pocket. "And you." I look at Jennifer. "Don't let anybody ever tell you that you're not tenacious," I tell her.

The party goes on for a while as they debrief and unwind all the details of the morning and afternoon since Jennifer returned with the disk and they first punched it up. Twenty minutes later Jennifer is the last of our staff out the door, walking on air, headed for home.

Harry watches her from the open door as she disappears under the arch and out to the street, and then closes it. "You know, it's only a guess, but I would bet she'll never forget this day."

"No. I doubt that she will."

"Not to diminish what any of them did. Hell, this morning we weren't even sure that the letter existed. Now we have a picture of it," says Harry. "For all the good it will do us."

"I know," I say. "There's no foundation to get any of it in, unless we can produce the person who made the video, and he's dead."

"Did you see the look on Ginnis's face when Scarborough dropped that letter on the table?" says Harry. "That old man is up to his teeth in this thing. There's a lot of fear in that video."

"That wasn't fear you saw. That was anger."

Harry shoots me a questioning look.

"Ginnis's face on that video brought back something that Trisha Scott told me months ago, when I met with her in Washington. She said Ginnis despised Scarborough and that he wouldn't have anything to do with him. It was her way of trying to get me to leave Ginnis alone."

"Yeah, and as I recall, she lied to you about other things, too," says Harry.

"I'm not so sure."

"Well, you just saw them sitting there on that video, or are my eyes deceiving me?" says Harry. "I grant you they may not have been all warm and fuzzy over each other. But apparently there's enough commercial avarice between them to bridge any troubled waters."

"I also read the book," I tell him.

"What book?"

"The one Scarborough wrote about the Supreme Court, *Case of the Century,* about the presidential election and the razor's-edge balloting decided by the Court."

"How can anyone forget?" says Harry.

The election was nearly twelve years ago, the administration long gone.

"I ordered the book from Amazon. It's been on my nightstand for four months."

"Not a lot of leisure for nighttime reading, is what you're telling me," says Harry.

"I finally got around to it last weekend. It's a real page-turner."

"Don't keep me in suspense," he says.

"In it Scarborough does for the Court what Martin Luther did for the Catholic Church. He excoriated the nine of them. But he saved the bitterest bile for Ginnis, *the swing vote* in the big case. According to Scarborough, Ginnis handpicked his own president."

"Lucky man! Still, somebody had to do it," says Harry. "As I recall, after all the lawyers showed up, the two candidates were no longer willing to pitch pennies for the post."

"Scarborough called Ginnis a party hack, and that was among the more gracious things he had to say."

"Sour grapes," says Harry.

"No, not sour. Poisonous," I tell him.

Harry looks at me.

"The real cross Scarborough left Ginnis to carry was the charge that the justice had committed ethical violations. Scarborough claimed that Ginnis engaged in private, out-of-court communications, ex parte, during the case with some of the lofty lawyers representing the soon-to-be-anointed president. And Scarborough said there was a point to all this talking. Ginnis was lobbying for another judicial post, and he was doing it from a point of leverage."

"Something higher than the Supreme Court?" says Harry.

"Chief justice!"

This draws a pair of arched eyebrows from Harry.

"According to Scarborough, Ginnis wanted to head up the Court."

"I don't remember that. I remember when the position came open, chief justice," says Harry. "That was a few years ago. But I don't remember Ginnis being mentioned as a candidate."

"That's the point. He wasn't. Trisha Scott told me the charges were a lie. She may have been right. I don't know. But it didn't matter. When the position of chief justice fell vacant two years after the razor-sharp election, Ginnis didn't even make the short list."

"Maybe he was too old," says Harry.

"No. That wasn't it. It wasn't in Scarborough's book either, but it did make *Newsweek,* a tiny one-column article at the time. A source in the White House—unnamed, of course—said Ginnis was the president's first pick for chief justice. The problem was, they couldn't put him on the list because of Scarborough's book and the charges he'd made. To nominate Ginnis would lend credence to the charges, and the administration, Ginnis's handpicked president, didn't want the heat. How's that for having your career capped?"

"The top of the pyramid is always slippery," says Harry.

"And I've been told that time heals all wounds. But you do have to wonder," I say. "The two of them sitting there breaking bread."

"So where does that leave us?"

"Without the Jefferson Letter, the only evidence we have is that video. That means we don't have a choice," I tell him. "We've got to find Ginnis, track him down and serve him. Shackle and drag him if we have to, but get him here, and get him into court."

TWENTY

Harry called Herman in Washington at the crack of dawn this morning and asked him if he had his passport with him. It seems Herman never leaves home without it. The man has been chasing leads on cases long enough to know he can never be sure where the next one will have him stepping off.

As I'm heading downtown, to Quinn's ten o'clock court call, Herman is winging his way to Miami for a connecting flight south to Curaçao.

Tuchio spends the next couple of days combing his list for witnesses to fill in some of the cracks. He calls his psychiatric witness and lays out in more detail the elements and driving mental characteristics that can detonate rage in the commission of a homicide. Among the inventory of motives the psychiatrist cites is social and political animosity, particularly the kind grounded in racial hostility. Since we haven't put Carl's mental state in issue, via a plea of insanity or diminished capacity, the state's witness was not able to interview, test, or examine Carl. This is no doubt a plus for our side. There has never been a realistic hope of mounting a defense on these grounds, so exposing him to examination by a state's expert would most likely result in a finding that Carl meets all the criteria for the commission of this kind of crime. It's the problem with putting Carl on the stand. Tuchio would eat him for lunch, pepper him with questions about Scarborough and his book. He would turn down the lights and show Carl videos of the author in provocative interviews, and when the lights came back up, there's no telling what might be the first words out of Carl's mouth.

*   *   *

On Wednesday morning I'm climbing the courthouse steps and see a small convention of bikers, lots of leather and denim across the street. People riding Harleys today could be a clan of executives from IBM, but not these guys. I count maybe twenty of the outriders from the fabled Aryan Posse, badasses all of them.

Associates and members are estimated at close to seventy-five on the street and roughly twice that number in prisons around the country. It's not the size of the organization but its deep roots within the Aryan prison community, where the racial divide is deep, sharp, and violent, that have the attention of authorities.

The reason they're here this morning is Tuchio's main attraction, his witness of the day, Charles Gross. He is one of their own. I'm guessing that the state is bringing Gross on now in order to sandwich him between other witnesses so that the rough edges don't look so bad.

As I clear security on the courthouse main floor, I can see fifteen, maybe more, uniformed officers moving quickly toward the stairs at the back of the building.

Something is happening, but I can't tell what.

When the elevator door opens onto the corridor upstairs and I step out, I notice four of the Posse members down the hall, at the door to Quinn's courtroom, each trying to get a ticket of admission.

After leaving thirty pounds of chain, dangling Nazi Iron Crosses, metal skulls, and other symbols of evil in a box downstairs at the security check, they still can't get inside.

As I draw closer, I can hear why.

"Court dress code," says the deputy. "No messages. No signs."

They are all wearing leather vests, the uniform of the day, no shirts underneath, enough hair on their chests and in their armpits to build an entire condo complex of nests for a flock of crows. In an arc across their backs in leather, in various colors and assorted fonts are the words ARYAN POSSE.

"I been in court before. I wore this." The one talking is six feet and well muscled, with frazzled blond hair to his shoulders, frayed and brittle enough to have been

STEVE MARTINI

fried in a Chinese wok. He could make a good living as an extra doing Conan the Barbarian movies.

"That was then, this is now," says the officer. "You can't get in wearing that, not here, not today. Take it outside," he says.

"Fuck that shit!" This comes from the Norse god who's in the deputy's face, in a voice loud enough so that everyone in the corridor has stopped moving, including me.

The deputies are standing in the airlock between the two sets of double doors leading to the courtroom, the outer doors are open. The inner doors look like they're closed.

"You're just doin' this because of who we are. You know it, and I know it."

His three buddies in biker boots and frayed jeans are bunched up behind him, all nodding, discrimination being a terrible thing.

"You can't even see it if we're sittin' down. Hell, it'll be up against the back of the chair."

"Hey, I told you. I'm not gonna tell you again. No exceptions. No signs, no messages," says the deputy. He and another officer are wedged in the door like a stone wall.

What I saw downstairs now becomes clear. By now the small army of uniforms is probably standing just on the other side of the closed door in the stairwell about ten feet behind Conan and his buddies—no doubt getting ready to play jack-in-the-box with cans of pepper spray and nightsticks if things get pushy.

The bikers move a step or so away to confer, then Odin is back in the deputy's face. "Fine, we'll take 'em off."

"Excuse me?"

"Our jackets. You don't like 'em, we'll take 'em off."

"Fine, take 'em off, take 'em outside, get a shirt, and come back," says the cop.

"Where the hell are we gonna get shirts? By then all the seats'll be taken."

"That's your problem. But you can't enter the courtroom without a shirt."

The blond one says, "Shiiit." His arms are flexed, he's leaning in like maybe they can just blow past the two cops, into the room, and grab seats. This has all the dynamics of a budding brawl. The guy's ego is way out to there; he's wearing it on his chin. A hundred people in the corridor watching it. You can feel it in the air. He's not going to back off.

It is at this instant that a small patch of gray sticks her head out from behind and under the flexed elbow of one of the deputies in the door. Before he can move, she slips past him. She must be eighty-five and can't weigh much more than that in pounds. She's holding a small water cup in her hand. One of the courthouse regulars, she has picked this moment to go take her meds. Standing in no-man's-land, she is stopped in her tracks, her eyes just at the level of the blond guy's belt. She looks up at him and smiles.

His fighting gaze locked, he's staring at the deputy, snorting bull breath.

She tries to squeeze through between the open door and Armageddon, but he has her blocked.

The deputy leans faintly forward as if he wants to reach out and pull her back. But he knows if he moves, it's going to trigger a brawl, and the old lady, frail as a bird would be crushed in the middle.

She looks up one more time and says—and you can hear it clear as a bell in the silent corridor—"Excuse me." This tiny little voice.

Like "open sesame," something from a Stooges movie. The four bikers, their heavy boots taking baby steps in unison as if they were all connected at the hip, give her just enough room to get by. As she squeezes through, the four of them are left standing there, watching as she trundles past. Just like that, an instant of diversion and the moment passes, the time for action melts.

You can almost hear the cops in the stairwell bouncing cans of pepper spray off the walls and jumping on their hats.

The old woman heads for the water fountain, looking around in wonder at all the people standing in the hallway staring at her like statues.

As she gets up on tiptoe at the fountain with her cup, I'm thinking we need to clone this, package up all the parts, and ship boxes to the Gaza Strip, Beirut, and downtown Baghdad.

Then, like stop motion, people start moving again. The Posse passes me going the other way, toward the elevator. I can hear a few "goddamn"s and "kick his ass"es as they go by. They'd better watch it or the Gray Missile may get into the elevator with them.

Whether they're here in support or measuring their friend Mr. Gross for a box after he talks, one thing is certain. Unless they have a supply of long-sleeved dress shirts in the saddlebag of one of their choppers—or they can sprint down to Nordstrom at the speed of light—they won't be getting into Judge Quinn's theater of thrills this morning.

* * *

Inside the courtroom I pass through the gate at the railing. Tuchio is standing at his table talking with his assistant, Harmen. She glances up and sees me.

"Good morning," I say.

She smiles and returns the greeting.

Tuchio looks at me, a near-death stare. He doesn't say a word. His head goes back down, and he's talking to Harmen again. He is still stinging from the meeting in chambers and the loss of his federal agent.

As I slip into my chair at our table, Harry has already caught this.

"Man's positively furious." Harry is busy

lining up his three pencils and a pen along one side of his legal pad. Then he reverses them and puts them on the other side. "Which looks better to you?" he says.

I smile and ignore him.

"Good news," he says, "from the East. One of our process servers tagged Scarborough's editor, Jim Aubrey, with the subpoena just before noon, New York time. One down, two to go," he says.

There is still no word on Bonguard or Trisha Scott.

"In case you're feeling bad, he treated me the same way," says Harry.

"Who?" I'm busy looking at notes, a summary of Charlie Gross's statement to the cops.

"Tuchio. When I showed up this morning, I said hello. He was like dry ice, frozen solid and still smoking." Harry abandons his Monopoly game with the writing implements just long enough to bring his closed fist gently up to his chest in the region of his heart. "And I have to tell you, it hurts."

"So you want to send him a sympathy card?"

"You joke, but I haven't felt this bad since my dog died of rabies," says Harry.

"You don't have a dog."

"I know, but if I had one and he died of rabies, I can imagine that he might look a lot like Tuchio does right now. I've been thinking. The next time we screw him over, maybe we should try to be a little more polite. When a prosecutor starts foaming at the mouth, you have to begin to wonder what he might do if he really got mad."

When I glance over at Harry, I get the sense that perhaps he's only half joking.

* * *

Tuchio brings on his witness of the day, Charles "Charlie" Gross.

When the jury is in the box and Carl is planted in his chair between Harry and me, Arnsberg gives me a strange look when he sees the witness, as if to say, *Who's that?*

Gross, if he is to be believed, is one of the charter members and the chief financial officer for the Aryan Posse.

According to an investigative report, Gross keeps track of the group's beer and booty fund as well as the accounts receivable from meth and other pharmaceuticals they sell, often jotting down numbers in ink on the palm of his hand. That way he figures if he gets busted, sweat will dissolve all the evidence. I guess if the IRS wants to see the Posse's books, they're just going to have to cut off his hand. It's thinking like this that got Gross right to the top in the organization.

If you saw any of his mug shots, you'd have to admit that Tuchio has done a crackerjack job of cleaning the witness up for today's appearance. Gross looks like they've put him through a car wash and had him detailed.

Gone are the long, sparse, stringy strands of dirty blond hair that hung down below his shoulders from the craggy, bald summit of Half Dome. The state probably spent forty bucks having the hundred or so hairs on the top of his head styled and clipped. The back and sides of his head are as neatly trimmed as if Suki ran his mower over them.

This morning Gross is wearing a pair of dark blue cuffed slacks with a sharp crease to them, a maroon polo shirt, and a watch that looks like a Rolex, probably a knock-off from Taiwan out of the police property room. The tasseled loafers are a nice touch. No doubt Gross's feet haven't seen the inside of anything that wasn't steel-toed, flapped, and hooked for lacing and that weighed less than ten pounds since he came out of the womb.

Looking at him on the stand, you might swear that you saw him playing the back nine at the village country club yesterday afternoon.

When the feds spring their trap and his pals go looking for Gross to shoot him because he was the idiot who recruited and sponsored the FBI agent, there will be no need to put him in witness protection. Tuchio's transformation of the man is so complete the Posse will never recognize him. I'm almost wishing that Conan and his friends had gotten in. By now they'd be sitting out in the audience and asking, "Where the hell is Charlie, and who the fuck is that?"

Since he looks like your average accountant on his day off, when they asked him to raise his right hand to be sworn and Gross lifted the left by mistake and then the right, I took a good look at both palms. I wanted to see if he was still keeping books. Unfortunately, it appears as if the scrubbing must have started with the hands.

Unless I can get Gross to take off his shirt, raise his arms, and turn a pirouette, displaying the story of his life ingrained in the graffiti on his body, it's hard to imagine how the jury is going to get the full flavor of the man.

Tuchio uses a good deal of finesse here. He moves carefully through the witness's background, covering everything except his three felony convictions and the fact that he has spent almost thirteen years of his life in prison. This is out of bounds under the deal we cut in chambers. Tuchio knows I can't get at it on cross-examination, so he's free to ignore it.

But he does not try to hide the fact of Gross's long association with the Aryan Posse. He explores this in detail, because he knows if he doesn't, I will expose it on cross, making it look as if they were hiding it.

He takes more than twenty minutes, hitting all the possible low points in Gross's life, including two divorces, problems with drugs, and the fact that he's had difficulty holding jobs.

Then Tuchio makes clear his tactic with the witness: The world loves a reformed sinner.

"Let me ask you," says Tuchio, "are you still a member of the Aryan Posse?"

"No. I'm no longer involved with that group. I want nothing to do with them."

"Can you tell the jury when you quit this organization?"

"It was after I saw the news," he says.

"What news?"

"The news. The man killed here," he says.

"You mean the victim in this case, Terrance Scarborough?"

"Yeah. That's the one."

"Why did that make you quit your membership in the Aryan Posse?"

"Because of things I saw and heard. I was ashamed," he says. Gross looks right at the jury as he says this. "The people in that group did some bad things," he says, "and I wanted to change my life. I didn't want to be involved anymore."

If you listen closelys, you can hear the violin music in the background. This is not something Tuchio pulled out of the bag yesterday or the day he lost the agent's testimony in chambers. This has all the signs of careful stage direction and chore-ography.

"And why were you ashamed?"

"Because it was a bad life," he says. "All that hate against other people because of the color of their skin. It was wrong, and I didn't want to be part of it anymore."

One woman, an African American in the jury box, is nodding as she hears this. Tu-chio will be handing out prayer books and hymnals any minute.

"Was there anything in particular that brought you to this decision, to change your life?"

"Yeah, it was a conversation with him." Gross sticks his arm out and points. The "him" he's talking about is Carl.

"Let the record reflect," says the judge, "that the witness has identified the defen-dant."

If I could cut off the prosecutor right here, at this moment, I could pick up the theme and explain how my client led this man from a life of sin to redemption, and we could all march out to the strains of "The Old Rug-ged Cross." But somehow I'm guessing that this is not where Tuchio is going.

"And can you tell the jury, what was it in particular that the defendant said that brought you to this point, to take your life in another direction?"

"I was drunk," says Gross. "And he said some things . . . terrible things, some awful things about this man who was murdered, this Mr. Scarborough, and I was ashamed. Not right then," he says, "but later, after he was murdered, because I had laughed when Mr. Arnsberg said this stuff. That memory stayed with me for a long time."

"I see." Tuchio makes all this sound as if he's hearing it for the first time. Gross's delivery is fervent. There's just enough scent of the old malefactor lingering about him so that even a cynic like me—on a bad day, if someone blinded me, jammed cotton in my ears, and stuck garlic up my nose—might find myself believing him.

Tuchio carefully takes the witness through his association with Carl, the fact that the two of them had met only a total of eight or ten times, and often in bars. Gross admits that he had a problem with alcohol, but, like everything else that was bad in his life, this, too, is now behind him.

Then Tuchio draws him up and gets specific. He gives the witness the date and then asks him whether he remembers meeting with Carl at a bar off Interstate 8 out near El Centro.

"Yes, I remember that meeting. It was at the Del Rio Tavern," says Gross.

"Can you tell the jury why you happened to meet at that particular location?"

"Because we were goin' to a meeting at a range," he says.

"What kind of range?"

"It was a shooting range. They called it 'the reserve.'"

"Who called it . . . ?"

"The Aryan Posse." Gross makes it sound as if the term, the very name of the organization of which he was a charter member, is alien to him.

"But before you went to this shooting range, you and Mr. Arnsberg were together at the Del Rio Tavern, is that right?"

"That's right."

"How long were you there, at the tavern?"

"Oh, I don't know. Maybe an hour. Maybe a little more."

"Now, when you were at the tavern, was

the defendant drinking, having any alco-
holic beverages at the time?"

"Not much," he says. "He mighta had a
beer or two, but that's all."

"Did it appear to you that he was drunk
or under the influence of alcohol or drugs
at that time?"

"No. He was sober," says Gross.

"And during this time, at the tavern, how
many beers did you have?"

"Oh, I don't know. Maybe four or five."

"Were you drunk at the time?"

"Well, a little," he says. "I mighta had a
little buzz on. But I remember very clearly
what was said."

This, of course, is the whole point.

"Let's get to that, what it was exactly
that was said. At some time during your
meeting with the defendant at the Del Rio
Tavern, did the subject of Terry Scarborough come up?"

"Yeah, it did."

"And how did the subject come up, do
you remember?"

"As I remember, this guy's picture, Scarborough, came up on the television behind
the bar, on the news when we were sittin'
there. And Carl there got real upset. He

was talkin' out loud about how the guy was causing all kinds of problems. That he saw him on the news and how Scarborough wanted whites to pay money to the blacks because of slavery. He was sayin' how this guy, Scarborough, wanted to turn the country over to 'em."

"Over to whom?" asks Tuchio.

"You know. African Americans," he says.

I'm wondering how long it took Tuchio to get Gross to drop the N-word and say the two he just said in their proper order.

"What else did Mr. Arnsberg say?"

"He was braggin' about the fact that he worked at the hotel where this man, this Mr. Scarborough, used to stay in San Diego and probably would again. There was a lotta talk. And he said it would be easy to kidnap him."

"Kidnap him?" Tuchio's voice goes up two octaves.

"That's what he said."

I glance at the jury box at this moment. They are rapt, not even taking notes. They're listening, which is worse.

"Did he say why he might want to do this, to kidnap Mr. Scarborough?"

"Well, it was pretty clear he didn't like the man."

"Scarborough?"

"Yeah. He kept callin' him an agitator. Said he was causing all kinds of problems."

"What kind of problems?" says Tuchio.

"Racial problems," says Gross.

Tuchio gives it a good, long pause, so that the words settle all the way down to the floor in the jury box.

"From what the defendant said to you, then, did it appear that he had disagreements with Mr. Scarborough's beliefs and values with regard to issues of race?"

Ask an obvious question and you get an obvious answer.

"Yeah, I would say so."

"When he talked about this, did he appear to be angry?"

"Oh, yeah. He'd talk your arm off."

People in the audience laugh.

"Was he agitated, excited?"

"He wasn't happy, if that's what you mean."

More laughter.

Gross is starting to enjoy this.

"Was he mad?"

"Oh, yeah, mad as hell," he says, and then he looks up at the judge with a nervous smile.

Quinn ignores him.

"I see," says Tuchio. "Did the defendant say anything about how he might carry out this kidnapping?"

"Yeah. He said it would be no problem to hit him on the head and dump his body into a laundry cart and take it down a service elevator."

"He said 'hit him on the head,' and he was talking about Mr. Scarborough?"

"Yeah, that's what he said."

Now the jury is taking notes.

"Let me ask you, at the time the defendant said this, that it would be easy to hit Mr. Scarborough on the head"—Tuchio wants to repeat this, a good sound bite and right on message—"did you think he was serious?"

"At that time, no," he says. "But later—"

"Objection," I say.

"Sustained," says Quinn. "The jury will disregard the last part of the witness's statement. Just answer the questions that are asked. Don't volunteer anything," the judge tells him.

"Yes, sir."

Tuchio has an embarrassment of riches here. He's not sure which one to pick next, so he goes back to the same fruit.

"Besides hitting Mr. Scarborough on the head"—he can't say this one enough—"and dumping his body into a laundry cart and taking it down the elevator, did the defendant say anything else?"

"Yeah. He said we could take him out into the desert and shoot him." This, coming from Gross, is worse than what is actually on the transcript from Henoch's wire, because it sounds real. It is cast in the language of a credible threat.

To read the words in the transcript, it's clear that Carl was bragging, turning macho phrases. "Hell, we could have his ass out in the desert tied to a post in front of a firing squad before he knew what hit him. Skin his ass before we shoot him." I know this because the passage from the transcript is in my notes right in front of me on the table. But I can't use it to cross-examine Gross, because neither the agent nor the transcript is in evidence. We made sure of that.

Around the edges of this testimony, it

begins to settle on me that Tuchio isn't angry at all. And he isn't stupid. He has outfoxed us. If Gross was properly schooled, closeted for weeks and tutored, and it appears that he has been, he could in fact be more valuable than the transcript. Reading it, Tuchio must have realized that some of the verbatim language could actually become a burden. He also knew he couldn't play games with the words if he had a government agent on the stand.

But with Gross he can paraphrase his way around the rough spots in order to smooth out his case.

As I sit here listening to him work us over with this witness, it suddenly dawns on me. Tuchio never wanted to call the agent in the first place. What he wanted was for us to take Henoch and his statement off the table, so that we couldn't use him in our own case to prove discrepancies in Gross's testimony. Now he is free to soar. Gross can say anything he wants, and unless we can shake him on cross, Tuchio is home free.

As the blood in my veins begins to chill, Tuchio and the witness take the jury for a verbal ride out into the desert, to the place the Posse called "the reserve"—the shooting range.

Gross tells the jury that somebody, he doesn't know who, obtained large, poster-size photographs of Terry Scarborough and stapled them to targets, so that by the time he and Carl got to the range, some of the Posse members were already shooting at these with pistols and rifles.

Tuchio retrieves a copy of *Perpetual Slaves,* Scarborough's book, from the evidence cart and shows the witness the picture of the author on the back cover.

Before he can even ask the question, Gross says, "That's the one. That's the picture they used."

Now the jury has an image to go along with the words.

"Did you shoot at any of these targets, the ones with the victim's picture on them?"

"No." Gross is shaking his head earnestly. "I didn't want to do that."

"Why not?"

"I just didn't want to do it. I didn't think it was good. That's all."

Of course not, God forbid. Harry leans forward, looks past Carl to me, and rolls his eyes.

"Did Mr. Arnsberg shoot at any of the targets with the victim's picture on—"

"Objection, Your Honor." I am up out of my chair. "May we approach?"

Quinn waves us forward, off to the side of the bench.

"Your Honor, I'm going to object on the grounds of relevance. The victim wasn't shot. This is being used for one purpose and one purpose only—to prejudice my client." I cite 352 of the Evidence Code and tell Quinn that whether Carl shot at these targets or not, the issue has no probative value. It proves nothing. At the same time, the prejudicial effect on the jury is overwhelming.

Before I can even finish, Tuchio is over my shoulder. "Your Honor, it goes directly to the defendant's state of mind. It's in close proximity in point of time to the murder. It supports the theory of rage, and there has already been testimony on that."

Quinn puts up a hand. He's heard enough. "Gentlemen, we could split fine hairs on this one. And I could allow it to come in. It's the kind of thing that reasonable minds can disagree on." He's whispering over the edge of the bench at the side away from the jury. "But I have to worry what the three figures in black who sit above me might do with it when and if they see it." He's talking about the appellate court. He looks at Tuchio. "You don't want to have your case reversed on this, and neither do I."

It's one thing to have the feeling yourself, but when the judge says this, it becomes clear: Quinn senses that my client is going down.

"The wisest and safest course at this point is not to allow it. I'm going to sustain the objection. I think you should move on to another subject, Mr. Tuchio." He sends us back out.

Gross is looking around as if he's not sure whether to answer the question. Even though Tuchio never got a chance to finish it, the witness knows what it is. No doubt they have practiced it enough times.

As soon as I sit down, Carl is in my ear. "What happened?"

"Don't worry about it. It's okay," I lie.

Tuchio is back, centered in front of the witness again. "Let's leave the shooting range for the moment. Let's go back to the tavern. To the Del Rio," he says. "You testified earlier that the defendant talked to you and made statements regarding a possible kidnapping of the victim, Terry Scarborough, is that correct?"

"That's right."

"That he said he could hit the victim over the head and dump him into a laundry cart."

"Yes."

Tuchio thinks for a moment.

"During your meeting with him that day at the tavern," he says, "back at the Del Rio, besides kidnapping, did the defendant ever say anything else to you, anything that you thought that was in any way . . . Let me rephrase this."

Tuchio seems to be having trouble here, trying to change gears in a ham-handed way, and I'm wondering why, if he's back at the Del Rio, he didn't remember to bring whatever it is up earlier.

"When you were there at the tavern, at the Del Rio, did the defendant, Mr. Arnsberg, ever tell you how he might gain access to Mr. Scarborough if in fact Mr. Scarborough was in his room at the hotel behind a locked door?"

"Yes, he did."

"And what was that?"

"At one point he was talking about how he had access. How he could get into rooms at the hotel real easy because he could get a master key."

Carl's sitting next to me, shaking his head, whispering, "I never said that."

"And then he said, because he could get right up to him real easy, he said it would be real easy to hammer 'im."

Out in the audience there is murmuring. *What did he say?*

"Were those his exact words?" asks Tuchio. "That he could hammer him?"

"That's what he said."

"That's a lie!" Carl says it out loud now, and there is an eruption of voices in the audience. Two of the reporters in the front row break for the door at the back of the room.

Quinn slaps his gavel. "Keep your client quiet," he tells me. Carl is pulling on my arm. He wants to tell me it's a lie. But I already know it.

"Officer, stop those people right now," says the judge. The two reporters stop dead in their tracks halfway up the main aisle. "Sit down," says the judge. "You can file your stories during the break."

Before Quinn can even put down his gavel, Tuchio turns to me and says, "Your witness."

TWENTY-ONE

Quinn takes the noon break. I ask for a meeting in chambers, and all of us, the lawyers and the judge, end up hovering over his desk in the back.

"The man's lying." Harry's had a bellyful of this. He's leaning with both hands against the edge of the judge's desk, bearing down on Quinn, who is seated in his padded black leather chair. "Look at the transcript of the wire," says Harry. "There's not a word in there about any of this, a master key or anything about hammering the victim."

"You've got a good point, except for one

thing," says Quinn. "The wire transcript and the witness who was attached to them are not in evidence. As I recall, that was based on an agreement made right here in chambers by your partner, Mr. Madriani."

"It's one thing to keep evidence out," says Harry. "It's another to suborn perjury."

"I resent that," says Tuchio.

"Resent it all you want," says Harry. "How do you explain the fact that these inventions by your witness don't appear on the wire transcript?"

"Very easily," says Tuchio. "The agent, aka Mr. Henoch, who was wearing the wire, was not with Gross and your client during the entire time of their conversation at the bar. It seems he stepped out twice—once to go to the john and again to make a telephone call from his cell phone outside, because he couldn't get reception in the bar. At least that's what he told us."

"And unfortunately, we can't put him on the stand to ask him," says Harry.

"That's not my fault," says Tuchio. He smiles.

Harry glances at the judge, who gives him a shrug.

"And I should remind you," says Tuchio, looking at me now, "that I never asked the witness whether anybody else was present during the conversation at the Del Rio, and you better not either. If the wire transcript and the agent are off-limits, that means as far as the jury is concerned he doesn't exist. Am I right, Your Honor?"

Quinn nods. "That's correct."

* * *

My turn in the tumbler with Gross on cross-examination reveals just how well Tuchio has trained him. I ask him how many times he has met with the prosecutor, his assistants, or the police to discuss his testimony before appearing here today.

"Quite a few times," he says.

"How many is quite a few?"

"A lot," he says. He can't remember the number of times or the precise duration or location of all these meetings, but they were held at various places, including a hotel downtown where he admits that the state picked up the tab for four nights immediately preceding his testimony here.

I ask him why they put him up in the hotel.

"It was for security." He smiles and just lays it out there like a land mine waiting for me to step on it.

If I probe further, what he'll say is that he's putting his life on the line and that he's in danger from his former friends in the Posse because of his testimony today, the inference being, why would a man put his life in jeopardy just to come here and lie?

I ask him if he has any criminal charges pending against him in this state or any other state at the federal level or anywhere in the universe, now or at any time since the police started talking to him.

He says, "No."

I ask him whether the police or the prosecutor have offered him anything in return for his testimony.

Again, his answer is no. To listen to him, Gross is just your average, ordinary citizen willing to take a bullet in order to tell the truth.

"Have they offered to put you in any witness-protection program following your testimony here?"

"You mean the police? No," he says.

"Or any other level of government, including the federal government?" I ask.

He doesn't answer. Instead his eyes make a beeline for Tuchio's table.

"Bench conference," says Tuchio.

Before we even get to the side of the bench, it's clear what has happened. The feds have rolled Gross up in their investigation and eaten him like an enchilada. They won't need any pending criminal charges to cut a deal and gain cooperation. And because there were no charges pending, Gross wouldn't even have a lawyer. For the man who extended a friendly hand and invited the feds to join the Posse party, a few months in the club for Agent Henoch and a peek at his badge would turn Gross into jelly.

As soon as the rest of the Aryan world found out, they would chain Gross, tasseled loafers and all, to the back of one of their choppers and drag him between here and Alamogordo a few hundred times, just to make sure he had no additional handwritten notes on other body parts.

At the side of the bench, a smiling Tuchio explains to the judge that while the federal government has not in fact made any formal offer of protection to Gross, they have discussed the possibility of such an offer in the future.

Of course they have, just as soon as they squeeze every seed and all the pulp out of him. In the meantime they'll have him tucked into a cave complex somewhere on the other side of the moon, reminding him every few seconds of just how dangerous the world is. No wonder he's dried out and off drugs. In such an environment, there would be no need for a prosecutor or the cops to suggest anything by way of invention regarding Gross's testimony. The thought of being turned into an asphalt sled tends to make the mind not only cooperative but highly creative. A few newspaper clippings about the case, the evidence at hand, and rumors of what's to come and Gross could fill in the blanks. After all, you always want to keep the people who are keeping you alive happy.

Tuchio tells the court that any additional questioning along this line will compel the witness to disclose the existence of Agent Henoch and the government's undercover investigation. Quinn agrees. This is out of bounds, and I find myself back in front of the witness exploring other areas of discussion.

These quickly dry up. Under questioning, Gross admits that he is one of the founding members of the Posse, but as he said earlier, this is all behind him.

He concedes that Carl was not formally a member of the Aryan Posse. But then, as if to take this back with the other hand, he adds that the defendant was called on several occasions and invited to attend Posse events.

"Whenever he was invited, he always seemed to show up at these events. And he enjoyed himself," says Gross.

If I go any further along this line, I will invite Tuchio on redirect to get into these outings and to explore whether perhaps the Posse was into late-night cross burnings and hooded gatherings. Tuchio would then tell the jury that this would explain the nature of the rage visited on Scarborough's body.

So I turn to the only thing left that is available, Gross's invention on the stand.

"Mr. Gross, let me ask you a question. Haven't you ever heard people use the phrase 'I'll hammer him' or 'I'll hammer them' as a figure of speech, something someone might say in a kind of macho way?"

"No."

"Seriously? You've never heard it used like that?"

He shakes his head.

"You have to answer out loud," says the judge.

"No. I already told him."

"Come on, Mr. Gross, surely you've been around enough bars that you've heard people use that term before?"

"I don't think so," he says. "Not till I heard your client say it."

"Have you ever watched a baseball game, Mr. Gross?"

"Yeah."

"Have you ever heard an announcer say after a home run, 'He really hammered that ball'?"

"I don't know. If I heard it, I don't re-member it," he says. Gross isn't going to give an inch on this.

"Well, let me ask you then, have you ever heard anyone say, 'I'm gonna nail him'?"

"Oh, I've heard that," he says.

"Well then, let me ask you, when you heard that 'I'm gonna nail him,' did you really think that the person who said it was actually going to go out and get a nail and nail it or drive it into the person he was talking about?"

"Probably not," he says. "But I never heard anybody say 'I'm gonna hammer 'im' before I heard him say it."

"Your Honor, may the record reflect that the witness is referring to the defendant?" says Tuchio.

"So ordered," says the judge.

"Since you watch baseball— You do, don't you?"

"Sometimes," he says. "Not very often."

"I suppose it is pretty hard to balance that forty-inch screen on your motorcycle when you're out there riding with the Aryan Posse, isn't it?"

"Objection," says Tuchio.

"It's a fair question, Your Honor."

Quinn smiles. "Overruled. You can answer the question."

"I've never done that," says Gross.

"When you were a kid, when you were

growing up, I assume you watched base-ball then, maybe even played it a little?"

"Then I did, yeah."

"Good. Then you must remember a player—because he was big-time, very fa-mous, well known, a major home-run hit-ter. In fact, he held the record for most career home runs for many years. A player named Hank Aaron?"

"Yeah."

"Well then, you must remember his nick-name?"

"No."

"You don't remember Hammerin' Hank Aaron?"

He looks at me. "Yeah, but he was hittin' baseballs, not heads," he says.

"Move to strike, Your Honor."

"Strike the witness's last statement," says Quinn. "The jury will disregard it."

"Your Honor, we have no further use for this witness." I turn and start back toward my chair.

"Mr. Tuchio, any redirect?" says the judge.

"No, Your Honor."

"The witness is excused," says Quinn.

"Then we can either think about a break, or perhaps if it's short, you can call your next witness."

"Your Honor, the people have no further witnesses. The state rests its case."

With Tuchio's words my knees nearly buckle under me as I'm heading toward the table. The look on Harry's face matches my own—thinly veiled terror. Wednesday, not even the end of the day, a week early, and Tuchio wraps his case. Quinn will expect my opening statement to the jury in the morning, outlining our evidence, our theory, and what we intend to prove. Without some way to talk about the shadowed leather and the missing letter, we have no case.

* * *

In the judge's chambers, we argue tooth and nail, asking Quinn, begging him for time.

"Mr. Madriani." Quinn is holding up both hands, palms out. "I warned everyone at the beginning of trial, no delays, no continuances."

We make an offer of proof, I tell him about the letter and what we know, the information from Trisha Scott and Bonguard, Scarborough's agent.

Quinn remembers seeing the videotape of Bonguard's appearance on Leno. He has vague recollections regarding the mention of some historic letter, but nothing more.

Tuchio is sitting on the couch against the wall, relaxed, taking the whole thing in, watching Harry and me bleed all over the judge's desk. If he is surprised by any of the information regarding the missing Jefferson Letter, you wouldn't know it by looking at him. He doesn't even look up when I mention the name Arthur Ginnis, though Quinn does a double take.

"You're talking about *the* Justice Ginnis?" he says.

"Your Honor," Harry wades in, "if you would just . . . if you would take just a couple of minutes to look at something." Harry is feeling around in his briefcase.

"I have no time for this," says Quinn.

Harry dances around the desk toward the judge's desktop computer behind his chair.

Quinn is waving him off. "It's not going to do you any good."

I hand him a stapled sheaf of papers a quarter inch thick.

"What's this?"

"That's a transcript," I tell him.

While he is talking to me, Harry is loading the DVD into the judge's computer.

"A transcript of what?" Quinn looks at the pages now stuck in his hand.

"It's a transcript, Your Honor, verbatim. The audio on what you're about to see is not very good. But that"—Harry points to the stapled pages—"is word for word."

"Word for word of what?" asks the judge again.

"This." As Harry says it, the judge swings around in his chair to face the computer monitor.

"Where did you get that?" This is the first comment from Tuchio since we've entered the judge's chambers.

That Tuchio by now would have seen the video of Ginnis and Scarborough played out over the table in the restaurant comes as no surprise. The evidence clerk would have made sure that a copy of the DVD was sent to his office the moment Jennifer left the property room. Unless I miss my bet, it is the reason that Tuchio wrapped his case and dropped the ball into our court so early. He knows there is something out there. He is gambling that we haven't had time to find it. And as bets go, this is not a long shot. What surprises Tuchio is the transcript. There's no way we could have sent the disk out to a lab and gotten a transcript back in the few days since Jennifer found it. For the moment I ignore his question.

For all of his hesitancy, Quinn is now turned in his chair with his back to us and seems riveted by the video the instant the familiar face appears on the screen. At first he tries to listen, and then he starts reading, turning pages.

"Your Honor, I've seen the video. It's meaningless." Tuchio is trying to draw Quinn's attention away from the screen. "You can't even understand what they're saying. Some pieces of paper," he says. "For all we know, it could be a grocery list."

"Be quiet," says Quinn.

If there is any group in society that is stratified, rigid, and tight, it is the American judiciary. Judges are ever conscious of those above and below them. The pecking order comes with the robe. If you want to catch a judge's attention, show him someone higher on the food chain, in what appears to be, what may be, a compromising situation. It is human nature. He may not act, he may never say a word, but you can bet he'll look.

Twenty-six minutes later, the computer monitor flickers. The video ends. When the judge finally swings around in his chair, it is not with the kind of vigor and dispatch you might expect if he were going to dismiss us outright. The chair turns slowly, like the grinding wheels of the master it serves. I get the first glimmer that maybe we've bought some time.

For a while he is silent, leaning forward, elbows on his desk, steepled fingers to his chin. "I take it it's Scarborough on this side of the table?"

"Without question," I tell him.

"You can't see him," says Tuchio.

"No, but you can hear his voice," says Quinn. "This, ah . . . this item on the table," he says. "It's only a copy."

"As far as we know, but that may not matter," I tell him. "The words on the page, what it says, may have intrinsic value, not necessarily in dollars but to the person who took it."

"You mean whoever killed Scarborough."

"We know who killed Scarborough," says Tuchio. "He's in the lockup downstairs, on his way back to the jail as we speak. He—"

"Humor me, Mr. Tuchio." The judge cuts him off.

"It may not be the letter itself," I tell Quinn. "The original, I mean, but the message it delivers—or doesn't deliver, if it's destroyed or disappears."

"What are you saying?" says Quinn.

"Scarborough ignited considerable racial unrest with the current book. According to Bonguard, he was planning on going nuclear in the next book with whatever was in that letter."

"And you think a two-hundred-year-old letter could cause that kind of an uproar?" says Quinn.

"I don't know. But we do know a few things. Scarborough had it in his possession when he met with Ginnis over the table in that restaurant. And you saw all the furtive expressions on the justice's face and read the transcript."

"I'd like to see that transcript," says Tuchio.

"And the letter wasn't found in the hotel room after Scarborough was killed, or in his Georgetown apartment. So where did it go?"

"The item on the leather portfolio," says Quinn.

I give him a look like, *Bingo.* "You saw it come out of Scarborough's pocket. Letter paper, folded in thirds. It matches the size of the shadow," I tell him.

"Any piece of business correspondence folded for an envelope would fit the size and shape of that shadow," says Tuchio. "Your Honor, we've been all over that video. The police have seen it and listened to it. I've seen it and listened to it."

"I'm surprised you had the time," says Harry. "Since the property room delivered it to you only two days ago, after we discovered it in the police evidence locker."

Tuchio shakes this off. He doesn't respond.

"Is that true?" says Quinn. "The police never saw this?" He waves the transcript at him. "You never saw this or the video before charging Arnsberg?"

"I still haven't seen that, Your Honor." Tuchio means the transcript. "I'd like to know where they got it, and for that matter whether it's even reliable, because you can't hear a damn thing on the video."

"Where did you get it?" Quinn looks at me.

"We have a certified declaration," says Harry.

As Harry is fishing this from his brief-case, I tell Quinn, "We got it from a man named Theodore Nons, Your Honor."

"Teddy Nons." Quinn looks at me with arched eyebrows. "I haven't had Teddy Nons in my court since analog tapes went out."

"Who is Teddy Nons?" says Tuchio. The judge hands him the transcript, and Tuchio starts scanning it, flipping pages.

"He's a blind man, sightless since birth," says the judge. "But he has an extraordi-narily acute sense of hearing. He's a qualified audio expert."

"They say he can hear some things that dogs can't even pick up." Harry hands the declaration to the judge, who glances at it and sets it aside.

"Sounds like an urban legend." Tuchio is still riffling through the transcript.

"No, you can take it to the bank," says

Quinn. "Teddy used to make the claim in newspaper ads in the local legal sheet advertising his services. Some lawyer challenged him in my courtroom, a demonstration on that very point. And Teddy beat the dog."

Quinn is looking at the calendar on the blotter of his desk. He bites his upper lip, sucks some air through his teeth, as he dances a pencil over the blotter. "Ordinarily I wouldn't do this, but it looks like you caught a little luck, Mr. Madriani."

"How is that, Your Honor?"

"Monday is a holiday. Memorial Day."

"Judge. Your Honor!"

"Relax, Mr. Tuchio. I know it gets confusing, but it's not just about winning and losing. The world won't come to an end if we give the defendant two more days. Today is Wednesday. The court will go dark Thursday and Friday," says Quinn. "With the weekend and Monday, that gives you five days. Make good use of them. Come Tuesday morning you will be in my courtroom with your opening statement, ready to go. Is that understood?"

"Yes, Your Honor." Harry and I say it in

unison as he is popping the disk out of the judge's computer.

"I wonder, could I keep the disk and the transcript over the weekend?" says Quinn. "I'll make a copy of the transcript for Mr. Tuchio."

Harry looks at me.

"Sure." Something tells me there will be a lot of black robes huddled around Quinn's computer between now and the weekend.

He smiles. "Then I wouldn't waste any more of your precious time here," he says.

Harry and I are out the door.

TWENTY-TWO

They say bad news comes in threes. I believe it. When Tuchio rested his case, we didn't know it, but messages were waiting for us at the office. The process servers in New York and Washington both missed their last two marks. The only one they've managed to serve is Scarborough's editor, James Aubrey.

According to her office, Trisha Scott left on a sudden vacation that afternoon, off to Europe for the next three weeks, and Bonguard just as quickly disappeared somewhere out on the road with a client. His secretary wasn't sure when he would be back. She asked our man if he wanted to leave a message. First rule of process serving: When you're trying to tag somebody with a subpoena, you don't leave voice mail.

*   *   *

Ten o'clock Wednesday night, Harry and I are trying to catch some Z's crushed into coach seats like steerage on a packed flight somewhere over the Southwest. I'm learning more than I ever wanted to know about the island of Curaçao. For one thing, if you want to get there, you have to slingshot across the country to Miami before you can even start to head south—almost fourteen hours in transit, and this is one of the quicker flights. I'm beginning to think that this island is a remote dark hole in the earth, off the beaten path, a place where a person might go if he wanted to hide out for a while, perhaps dodge the scent of scandal.

In the office, going out the door, Harry fielded a phone call from Harv Smidt, the crusty newspaper reporter. He has been dogging the trial from behind the scenes since it started. Harv only occasionally graces the courtroom with his presence.

He has brought in two younger reporters from the L.A. newsroom of his paper. While they are in court, Smidt is humping up and down the back corridors talking to people in offices—judges, bailiffs, clerks, anybody with a little excess dirt to share. He wanted a quote from Harry about some historic mystery letter that was supposed to be on Scarborough when he was killed.

When Harry swallowed his tongue and went mum, Smidt told him to get on his computer and go online. Harv's story was already running on the national AP wire, setting forth every little detail we had mentioned in chambers, starting with rumors about Ginnis and including the backgrounders on the J letter from Trisha Scott and Bonguard.

This would explain why they both disappeared. You would, too, if your phone started lighting up with calls from every reporter in the Western Hemisphere. This is what happens when you start sharing videos and transcripts with the curious in the courthouse.

If we're lucky, we might be twenty-four hours ahead of the press and media mob when they parachute onto the island. People in the marble temple, the Supreme Court and its staff, will no doubt close around Ginnis like the Praetorian Guard to seal off his whereabouts. Unfortunately, we can't count on the same kind of discretion from "Art and Maggie's" neighbor out in Chevy Chase. As soon as the media dig her out of her garden, they'll be flogging jets southward. Harry suggested that we stop off on the way and bag the lady so she could join us on a quick trip to the islands. But the law being what it is, people tend to frown on kidnapping.

*　*　*

Just before eleven the next morning—and we're only half awake—Harry is squinting in the bright sunshine as I drive and he navigates the rental car from the airport toward Willemstad. It's the only sizable town on the island and the seat of government for the five islands that make up the Dutch Antilles.

Curaçao was once a Dutch colony and today is a dependency of the Netherlands. The island has its own parliament, prime minister, and council of ministers, along with a governor-general appointed by the queen of the Netherlands.

Harry and I are trying to find our way to

the Kura Hulanda, the hotel in town where Herman is staying. Strangely enough, Harry tried his cell phone, Verizon, and it worked. Roaming charges from the States are probably a million dollars a minute, but he hooked up with Herman, who is now headed into town from another direction.

Herman has been combing the island for the better part of two days, trying to hunt down the location of Ginnis and his wife. It may not be a huge island, but apparently it's big enough that Herman is still searching, with no luck.

The island is arid, desertlike, a lot of rock and dry scrub, with patches of large cactus. Occasional glimpses of the ocean in the distance from the highway reveal azure waters, translucent to the white sand bottom. The sea is tinged green in places by shallow coral reefs. From what I can see, it is the image that might pop into your mind when you hear the words "tropical beach." Unfortunately, Harry and I aren't here to swim, though we may drown in Quinn's courtroom if we don't find Ginnis.

"Living history," says Harry.

"What?"

Harry is looking at some literature he

grabbed at the airport while I was getting the rental car.

"Says here 'Living History, Museum Kura Hulanda.' Apparently it's by the hotel," says Harry.

"Does it tell us how to get there?"

"No. But it does say, 'See how the slave trade was done.'" Harry is reading again.

I glance over. Harry is holding a small printed flyer on card stock, what appears to be a pencil or ink drawing on one side. He flips it over. "'We will take you back in time to the selling of newly arrived slaves from the west coast of Africa, around the 1700s.'" Harry looks up at me. "Interesting."

* * *

The Hotel Kura Hulanda is situated on the main waterway, the channel that leads from the Caribbean to a generous harbor that spreads out in the center of the island. The harbor includes an oil refinery that was built in the early part of the last century. Today it provides revenue and good jobs for islanders. This, along with tourism and the export of Curaçao liqueur made from the peels of an orange native to the southern Antilles, keeps the island going.

The town of Willemstad itself is split by the channel, maybe three hundred yards wide, enough to admit oceangoing vessels, tankers, and midsize cruise liners.

On the north side, where our hotel is situated, are a number of restaurants, a few offices, taverns, and a small plaza with some shops.

Across the inlet on the other side are buildings three to four stories high, many of them with quaint Dutch façades, painted in bright colors, yellow and aqua, pink and maroon. These stretch for several blocks until they reach an old stone fortress that guards the mouth of the inlet at the sea.

The only way across the channel that divides the town is either to drive on the main highway over a high arch that spans the inlet at the point where it widens toward the refinery or to walk across a broad pontoon bridge. The floating footbridge, situated a few blocks to the west of our hotel, swings open for ships to pass and then closes again like a gate to connect with the other side.

The bridge is hinged on our side. At the far end, on the bridge at the other side, is a small hut. Every once in a while, you can see the belching exhaust from the roof of the hut and hear the diesel engine as the operator engages the prop that drives the gatelike bridge to open and close.

The hotel, the Hulanda, is actually a series of low-lying buildings situated around a large, meandering courtyard set into the hillside on the north edge of the inlet. It is separated from the waterway by a street with paved sidewalks on each side. A few shops and a restaurant—the Gouverneur de Rouville, a three-story red and white Dutch Colonial building with louver-shuttered windows and a veranda overlooking the water—complete the complex.

Harry and I dump our luggage in our rooms and join Herman at a table on the restaurant's veranda to compare notes and find out what progress he has made. Given the lack of sleep, Harry has iced tea. I have soda water, and Herman hunches his broad shoulders over a beer.

"So far I've tried every real-estate office I can find that handles seasonal rentals," says Herman. "None of 'em, at least the ones who would talk to me, recognize the name Ginnis."

Herman has been telling the rental

agents that there is an emergency back home and that friends and relatives have been unable to contact the vacationers with the news. So he is trying to locate them.

"I figure it's a waste of time to check the hotels and resorts, since the neighbor in Chevy Chase told us Ginnis's wife rented them a house," says Herman.

"Is there any way to check passport control or immigration?" asks Harry. "They gave us a form on the plane coming in. One of the questions was where we were staying."

"I thought about it," says Herman. "The fort over there—" He points toward the old stone fortress at the ocean end of the inlet on the other side. "Inside is government square. The problem is, we go in there askin' questions about passports and who's landed on the island in the last year and they're gonna wanna know why."

"We could just cut to the chase and ask them where Ginnis is," says Harry. "They have to know. Hell, with all the security, U.S. Marshals service, he probably came in on a government jet. You would think they'd know."

"If they do, they're not going to tell us," I say. "And they'd probably call the marshals and warn them that somebody is nosing around. Once Ginnis finds out, he'll be off the island in a heartbeat."

"But there may be a way," says Herman. "I gotta find the right person to do it."

"I don't know what you're thinking, but I'd rather not do jail time down here," says Harry.

"No," says Herman. If he can do it, Herman will try to find a local PI, someone with connections, maybe former police. "They'd be more willing to let their guard down and tell somebody like that where he'd be—Ginnis, I mean." So far Herman hasn't been able to find anyone who fits the bill. "How much time have we got?"

It is now midday Thursday. "Three days. Come Monday morning Harry and I have to be on a plane headed back," I tell him. "By Tuesday morning, if we haven't found Ginnis and served him with a subpoena, my opening statement to the jury is going to be a very brief and sad story."

"That's not much time," says Herman.

"Tuchio did a number on us," says Harry.

"And that's *if* we can serve him," I tell Herman. "What I'm hoping is that maybe Ginnis will sit down and talk to us. Tell us about the letter and what was going on with Scarborough. So if you tag him, try to be as friendly as possible. See if you can stay with him until we can get there."

"With thoughts like that, you must still believe in the Easter bunny," says Harry. "What if Ginnis killed him? You saw the look on his face when Scarborough laid the letter on the table in the video. For a second I thought he was gonna reach out and cut his throat with the butter knife. In which case," says Harry, "I don't think Ginnis is going to wanna talk to us or anybody else. And if he appears in court, which I doubt, he'll spin some yarn and say he doesn't know anything about the letter."

"In which case we can treat him as a hostile witness and impeach him with the video," I tell him. "Because then we have a legal basis to bring it in, along with a witness who can tell us when and where it was taken, since his face is all over it."

"True," says Harry. "But what if he doesn't appear, subpoena or no subpoena? What do you tell the jury in your opening then?"

"I've thought about that. If we can serve him, I'm prepared to wing it on opening. I'll tell the jury what we know, based on the conversations with Scott and Bonguard and what's in the video. We'll have to do the best we can to fill in the blanks."

"Like who gave the letter to Scarborough," says Harry, "and what's in it."

"I'm prepared to tell the jury that Ginnis gave Scarborough the copy and that Ginnis has the original. I think that's pretty clear from the video and the transcript. The contents of the letter are another matter."

"And what if Ginnis doesn't show and you have no witness?" says Harry.

"Then at least we have an argument for more time," I tell him. "Our entire defense in a death-penalty case hinges on one witness, a justice of the United States Supreme Court who has been duly served with process and who refuses or has failed to appear."

Harry mulls this in silence for a moment.

"You would have to think that every

judge up the chain," I tell him, "from Quinn to the top, would have to ponder that and pause at least for a second or two, before they vote to slip the needle into Carl's arm."

Harry thinks about this for only a second or so. Then he slaps the surface of the table. "Let's go find the bastard and serve him," he says.

The only real downside to any of this is if we can't find Ginnis.

Herman gives us his notes including the real-estate and rental offices he hasn't had time to check yet, along with a few private parties who have listed homes on the island for rent on the Internet. A few of these we can check by phone; the rest we're going to have to visit. We all have cell phones, and they work. We all agree that the minute any one of us finds Ginnis, before we even move on him, the call goes out. The three of us will try to gather and get in close before one of us tries to pounce and we lose him.

Harry and I split up. He takes Herman's rental car along with a map and heads north.

Herman gets on the phone. His task is

local. If he needs wheels, he'll use a cab. His task is to find an investigator or some-body else who can get to passport control or riffle the forms for inbound visitors.

I take the rest of the rental list, get into the car from the airport with the map from the rental company, and head south. The problem is that some of the real-estate and rental agencies that Herman called didn't answer their phones. They were probably closed or out showing houses or property. We may have to rattle a few doors or ask around to find the agents.

I drive the island, getting lost three times on winding back roads and find four rental agents, two of them with distinct British accents, Dutch who learned their English in the U.K. I use the same story that Her-man used: an emergency in the States, and I'm trying to notify the vacationers. They are all friendly and helpful, but none of them have ever heard the name Ginnis, except as an ale in a pub, and then it was spelled differently.

I drive until after dusk, checking with Harry and Herman every few hours. They are having the same success I am— none.

By nine that night, we are back in the hotel. Harry and I are dead on our feet, jet-lagged and suffering from lack of sleep. We each grab a light meal in our rooms and collapse.

We do it again the next day, Friday, early morning until dark, and come up with nothing. We are beginning to wonder if Ginnis's wife may have rented the house under a different name, either because she knew he was in trouble or to keep the press away while he was recovering from surgery.

Saturday morning we pick up again where we left off. The morning passes with nothing. And then about one o'clock, the cell phone on my belt vibrates. It's Herman.

"Where are you?" He's excited.

I look at my map. "A wide spot on the road called Salina."

"The south end of the island?" he asks. "Good. Look at your map."

"I am."

"See a place called Jan Thiel? It's on the ocean, southwest edge of the island. I found Salina on my map. It's just south of where you are."

I search the map with my finger and find it. "I see it."

"Head there," he says. "What time have you got?"

I look at my watch. "A few minutes past one. What's happening?"

"All hell's breaking loose here," he says. "Government square inside the fort. Media, American news crews with cameras. They're all over the place, asking questions about Ginnis. Why the local government on the island doesn't know there's a justice of the U.S. Supreme Court vacationing here."

"They didn't know?"

"No," says Herman. "According to what they told the press, not a clue."

I knew the cameras would all show up, but I was hoping they would give us one more day.

"How do you know he's at this place, Jan Thiel?"

"I don't," says Herman. "But his clerk, Alberto Aranda, swims there every day about noon."

"How do you know that?"

"Because his girlfriend back in the States told one of the reporters. I heard the newsies talking about it. He calls her every day about noon from the beach. She says he swims somewhere near a sunken tug. Get your ass down there. You don't have much time."

"Harry is at the north end of the island," I tell him. "He'll never make it in time."

"I know that." I can hear him breathing heavily, running. "I'm catching a cab. Be there as fast as I can," he says.

*   *   *

Even though I'm only a short distance away, it takes me more than twenty minutes to find the brackish backwater of the inlet and the dirt road that leads to the beach at the place on the map called Jan Thiel. The road forks at a steep hill. I take the left fork and go up and around. On my right as I skirt the hill, I can see a circular, fortresslike tower, old stone, probably planted on the top of the hill three or four centuries ago and now abandoned.

As the wheels of my car hit pavement again and I get past the brush blocking my view, I see the small harbor. There is a cargo ship of some kind tied up at one dock and a large four-masted schooner—

more than a hundred feet in length, I would guess—tied off at another. There are several other, smaller sailing vessels moored in the harbor, one of them a party boat. Passengers in swimsuits are swinging from ropes out over the bow, doing dives and belly flops into the water.

I keep driving maybe a quarter of a mile, until the road I'm on dead-ends in a parking lot. Directly in front of me, tied up at the dock, broadside, is the large schooner. I turn right, into one of the open parking spaces. That's when I see the beach, a broad shelf running down to the water maybe two hundred yards long. There is a line of shacks and huts behind it, bamboo and palm leaves for shelter, what looks like a take-out counter for food, and an outdoor tavern for drinks.

Midday Saturday, and there must be more than two hundred chairs and lounges spread out along the arc of the beach, and every one of them is occupied. Kids playing in the water, couples holding hands, bodies slick with tanning oil. Finding Aranda here is not going to be easy.

I turn off the engine and step out of the

car. I see a couple of divers with tanks and wet suits heading the other way, out toward the dock and the schooner.

"Excuse me."

One of them turns to look at me.

"Either of you know anything about a sunken tugboat around here?"

They keep walking, hauling their heavy gear, but the guy looking at me waves his left arm as if to point, in the general direction they're going. So I follow.

We walk through the lot, past parked cars toward the schooner. Just off to the left, toward the bow of the vessel, is a small building with a white metal roof and a sign over the door that says DIVE SHOP. I follow the two guys toward it, and just before I get there, I see a large boulder, a jagged piece of gray basalt the size and shape of a headstone. It is painted red with a white diagonal strip running across it from top left to bottom right, the international symbol for a dive site. Across the stone at the top right is the word TUGBOAT painted in black letters.

As I look off to the left past the stone, I see a small cove, no sand beach but a shelf against the cliff, covered by broken pieces of gray coral. There are maybe eight or ten plastic chaise lounges set out on top of the coral, a few with towels on them. Two at this end, closest to me, are occupied by a couple readying their masks and fins for a snorkel adventure. Farther back in the cove, perhaps forty yards away, is a solitary figure, a guy sitting sideways on the lounge, facing me. He is talking on a cell phone.

* * *

I've never seen a picture of Aranda, but the man's appearance fits the bill. He looks to be in his early thirties, short-cropped dark hair, well built, broad shoulders and narrow waist. With him seated, I can't tell how tall he is, but he is lean and appears very fit.

I keep checking my watch every few minutes, hoping that Herman will get here.

If the man sitting on the chaise lounge is Aranda, I know that he is not going to talk on the phone for long, not with roaming charges just off the coast of Venezuela. And when he hangs up, he's going to either hit the water or head back to wherever it is he came from. I could approach him and try to talk to him, but I'm afraid he would simply get up and run, in which case I would have to track him in the car on winding dirt roads through clouds of dust. And you could be sure that he would not go anywhere near Ginnis until he was certain he'd lost me.

Once Herman gets here, we can take our chances. Herman can block him with his girth while I talk. Herman always packs a folding knife. If we have to, he can punch one of the tires on Aranda's car and we can trap him in the lot until we talk his ear off. Give him a ride and let him show us where Ginnis is.

I check my watch again. Herman should be here any second. Then I see it, a cloud of dust, a fast-moving vehicle coming this way from the land side of the hill with the towered fortress. Herman to the rescue. When the large, dark SUV comes out of a line of brush and turns this way, it's moving so fast that the rear end fishtails on the sand and loose gravel.

As soon as they stop and two of them get out, one of them with a good-size camera, I know I'm in trouble. Part of the media mob has found its way to Jan Thiel, and they're ahead of Herman.

*   *   *

Now there's no time to waste. I head directly toward the man on the phone, long strides, my shoes digging into the broken pieces of coral. As I walk right up to him his head is down, he's smiling, talking on the phone. When he sees my feet stop a yard or so in front of him, he finally looks up.

"Are you Alberto Aranda?"

The expression in his eyes is one I have seen before, whenever I am forced to surrender a client to be taken into custody by police in my office.

"Sweetie, I gotta go. I'll call you later." He snaps the clamshell phone closed. "Who are you?"

"My name is Paul Madriani. I'm a lawyer from San Diego—"

Before I can even finish the sentence, he slips rubber thongs on his feet, grabs his snorkel gear, gets off the chaise lounge, and brushes right past me.

"You better not go that way. The media is waiting for you with cameras in the parking lot."

This stops him like a bullet.

He turns and looks at me. "What do you want?"

"I want to know where Arthur Ginnis is."

At this moment his expression is a mask of anxiety. He thinks for a second, then looks toward the parking lot again. "Are you with them?"

"No. I just want to talk to you. All I want to know is where Justice Ginnis is."

"Get me out of here," he says, "and I'll take you to him."

A towel over his head for shade, carrying his gear, and me walking beside him, we draw little or no attention. We head back through the parking lot. By now the cameras have swelled to two crews, who are gathering their equipment. One of the reporters is scanning the forest of chaise lounges and oiled bodies on the beach at the other side of the parking area. Their vehicles, two full-size SUVs, motors still running with drivers behind the wheels, are parked not in spaces but behind other cars, blocking them. One of these is mine.

I'm a step or so ahead of Aranda, wondering how we're going to do this, finesse our way past them. I'm hoping that they don't have a picture of him, when suddenly I realize he is no longer behind me.

By the time I turn and look, Aranda is ten feet away. He has the door open, and before I can take two steps, he slides into the car, a compact rental, slams the door, and locks it. As I reach the car and grab the handle on the outside, he already has the engine started and he's rolling, shooting gravel at me from under the rear wheels as he pulls out. I have to throw my body onto the hood of the vehicle behind me to keep from being crushed as he does the turn, pulling out.

I'm up on the hood of the vehicle on my back watching as he jams the car into first and guns it straight ahead through the parking lot. Of course, the screeching tires and the sound of flying gravel draw the attention of the cameras like bees to honey.

By the time he tears past them and I'm back on my feet running toward my car, the obstacles blocking my vehicle are gone. The two camera cars with lenses protruding from the rear passenger windows pull U-turns, and within seconds they're in hot pursuit.

As I get in and start the car, I'm guessing that I'm already a quarter of a mile behind Aranda. Turning to exit the parking lot, I see their dust ahead of me as Aranda goes straight, taking the road I came in on. One of the camera vehicles follows him. The other cuts off to the left on another road. I don't follow it. I stay with Aranda.

A few hundred feet up, there is a bend in the road, and I see a large cloud of dust. As I enter it, I'm forced to slow down. When the dust begins to settle, I see the car with the cameras off in a ditch on the right and what appears to be a taxi with its nose stuck into the side of the hill on my left. I know it's a taxi because Herman is standing just next to it talking with both hands, Italian style, to guys crawling out of the SUV.

I slow down and get a mouthful of dust as I open the window and wave him toward me. The instant he sees me, Herman stops talking and sprints to the passenger side of my car and gets in. Before his feet even hit the floorboards, we're moving again.

"It's Aranda up in front of us," I tell him.

"Damn near killed us," says Herman. "I thought we were clear till the other car nailed us. Couldn't even see 'em in the dust."

"I had him in the parking lot. He got away. The press showed up."

"As soon as I saw the cameras in the car, I figured," he says.

We are racing, bouncing along in ruts on the unpaved road. Herman hits his head on the roof of the car and finally gets himself strapped in.

Heading down the grade on the other side of the hill, I can see Aranda's car moving at speed now, on pavement. The other SUV is behind him, less than fifty yards back, with a camera all the way out the window, trying to get film of the chase. There must be another way around the hill on the other side. Their vehicle has now closed the distance. The clerk in his small rental car is not going to be able to stay ahead of them for long, not on pavement.

Herman and I struggle to catch up. When we reach the pavement, I put the pedal all the way to the floor. Down on the flatlands, we can no longer see them.

The two cars have disappeared. For a while, more than a mile, there are no intersecting roads, so I race at full speed, taking some dogleg turns and fishtailing.

As I negotiate one of these, I see the SUV. It's turned around, facing the other direction on the wrong side of the road. Its rear end is up against a metal light standard, with a good wrinkle in the bumper and the rear hatchback. All four of the occupants are out, stretching their legs and checking their body parts to see if they're still working.

Up ahead I can see a traffic light where the road dumps into the main highway. The light is red in our direction. There's no sign of Aranda's small car. He has made it to the main highway and merged with traffic. With dozens of roads to turn off onto and probably more than a mile ahead of us, there's no way we're going to catch him now.

Herman and I cruise the back roads along the coast on this end of the island for the balance of the afternoon and into the early evening, looking for any sign of Aranda or the small car he was driving.

Herman calls Harry and tells him what has happened.

Just before dark we arrive back at the hotel and end up out back on the veranda of the Gouverneur de Rouville.

By now Ginnis will know that the world has found him. He and his entourage will be making plans for a quick exit off the island.

Harry suggests that we stake out the airport. It's a thought, but the chances are slim. You can be sure that a member of the Supreme Court—and there are only nine of them in the world—can call in one of the sleek white government passenger jets anytime he needs it, so that even if he leaves from the main airport, he won't be going through the terminal. They would take him out through one of the private hangars, guarded and behind locked security gates. We wouldn't even be able to get within two hundred yards of him.

We've lost him, and we know it.

The three of us sit there having drinks. We order dinner, and Harry and I begin discussing plans for an early return to San Diego. Herman makes a call to his process server in Washington and warns him that Ginnis may be on his way home shortly, so to watch his house and to try to serve him with a subpoena there.

We are talking over our meals. I'm seated with my back to the bar, looking out over the narrow inlet, the bright lights and neon from the buildings on the other side dancing off the water as Harry talks.

"We use the witnesses we have, draw out their testimony, and stall for time," says Harry. "Sooner or later Ginnis has to pop up. The other members of the Court will be putting fire to his feet to make him show up at work once they realize he's not in recovery mode, he's hiding."

As Harry is talking, I'm so exhausted that my mind dances with the neon across the way. People walking, a small boutique hotel, next to it a bar all lit up. Jazz music floating across the water. People coming and going, tourists arriving, a few more leaving.

"We have to get out of here. We have to get home." It doesn't click in my mind until the figure hauling luggage is joined by the other two. Then I see the large, dark Town

Car pull up in front of the steps under the bright orange neon.

"What's wrong?" Harry is looking at me. His back is to the water. He turns around.

"It's Ginnis. . . ." I'm out of my chair before the words are out of my mouth. "Do you have the subpoena?"

Herman has it in his pocket. He's still looking, but he doesn't quite see what I'm looking at.

"There, under the hotel sign on the stairs. Aranda with the luggage, the man with the cane," I say.

Then they see him. In a shot, Herman is through the restaurant and out the door. Harry and I empty our wallets onto the table. We don't even have a bill.

We are fifty yards behind Herman on the sidewalk running along the waterway toward the floating bridge. A few seconds later, Herman is on it, clambering across. You can hear his heavy footsteps. None of us are up for this. Harry is falling behind. "Go on," he says. "Don't wait for me."

As I look across the water, the tall, willowy figure is still at the top of the stairs. When you are tired, your mind plays funny tricks, but I swear that the other person hauling the luggage down to the car is Aranda.

Ginnis is wearing white slacks, a dark sport coat, and a panama hat drawn low over his face. In the distance I can see the head turning as he checks out the street in both directions, no doubt making sure that the media crews chasing him are not in sight. He isn't even leaning on the cane. When he comes down the stairs, he has only the arm of the stout woman standing next to him for support. This would have to be Margaret.

Herman is nearly across, thirty yards from the quay on the other side, when the diesel engine starts. The bridge begins to rattle, and within seconds it swings free from the concrete dock and begins the long arc back across the water to where we started. Herman stops, puts his hands on his knees to catch his breath. Then he runs to the hut and the operator inside and pleads with him to close the bridge just for a second, long enough for him to jump onto the sidewalk on the other side.

"No, mon, there's a freighter coming."

We stand there and watch in total frustration as the arc of the bridge brings us within fifty yards of the dark Town Car, before the pontoons slide us away and across the water. By this time Ginnis and his wife are already in the backseat.

I cannot tell if he sees me or, if he does, whether he recognizes me, but when he looks this way, over the roof of the car, just before he slides behind the wheel and they pull away, there is no question that the driver is Alberto Aranda.

TWENTY-THREE

Monday morning, and Harry and I are back in the office, still jet-lagged from the long flight home.

Saturday night after watching the Town Car disappear around the corner as we watched helplessly from the moving bridge, Harry, Herman, and I raced to the airport in Curaçao in hopes that maybe we would see the sleek, dark vehicle somewhere near the terminal. But if it was there, it was already secluded behind locked gates in a secure area. There was no sign of the car or any of its occupants. The three of us scoured the terminal, which isn't that big.

Harry thinks Ginnis probably gave up the rental house the moment he discovered that the world was looking for him. They would have moved to the hotel in town for a day or two, just after Herman hit the island. They could have stayed in rooms rented probably in another name, killing time until they could coordinate their move off the island out of the sight of the press.

"God knows where they went," says Harry, "because they didn't go home." Harry knows this because our processor server, who has been camped in his car outside Ginnis's house in Chevy Chase, hasn't seen hide nor hair of the justice or his wife.

And there's more bad news.

Wednesday evening, about the time Harry and I were taking off for Curaçao, Judge Quinn, on his own motion, decided to sequester the jury. After winning points with jurors, giving them what looked like a long weekend off, the judge was suddenly overwhelmed by second thoughts thanks to the budding news reports that Harv Smidt had filed on the AP wire.

Smidt no doubt had called the judge for

a comment. The wire-service story about Scarborough's having an important and perhaps historic letter in his possession when he was murdered, and mentioning in the same paragraph the name Arthur Ginnis, apparently sent shivers up Quinn's spine. The fact that this story was obviously inspired by Quinn's sharing clips from the restaurant video with some of his buds in black didn't diminish the judge's fear level.

How do you complain to a judge about his own violation of his own gag order?

Understandably, Quinn wanted to corral the jury before they piled up at the newsstands to buy Harv's story. The judge dispatched half the county sheriff's office and part of the highway patrol to round up all the jurors and have them get their toothbrushes and pajamas. He now has them all incarcerated in a hotel downtown, where they get to read censored newspapers with rectangles cut out of them and play around-the-clock Parcheesi with seven armed bailiffs.

Sequester a jury and the rule of probability is they will take it out on one person— the defendant.

* * *

Harry is seated across the table from me in my office as I paw through a stack of papers and envelopes in the middle of my desk, mail that showed up Thursday and Friday when we were gone.

I flip Harry a couple of catalogs—he likes to shop but never buys—and scan through the correspondence, which is already opened by my secretary, with the envelopes stapled to the backs of the letters in case we ever need proof of a postal date on anything.

I work my way to the bottom of the stack, and there is a large manila envelope with my name and office address printed neatly on a label. Just below this, in bold caps across the bottom of the label, are the words PERSONAL & CONFIDENTIAL, the reason the secretary didn't open it. There is no return address. No stamp or postage-meter tape.

Herman has just arrived in the outer office. I can hear him chatting with Jennifer, the paralegal. The rest of the staff is off. It's a holiday. All the government offices, including the courts, are closed. Jennifer should be home as well, but by now she is attached to Arnsberg's case in the way a magnet attaches to metal.

"Where did this come from?" I look at Harry, who is still paging through one of the catalogs.

"What is it?"

"I don't know."

"Jennifer, you out there?" says Harry. "Come in here for a second."

A second later she slips her head around the corner of the door.

"Any idea where this came from?" I hold up the envelope.

She looks at it, then comes in and takes a closer look.

"How you guys feeling?" Herman comes in and leans up against the book cabinet inside my office.

"I could use a few more hours' sleep, but other than that, a signed declaration showing proof of service for a subpoena on Arthur Ginnis and everything is chipper," says Harry.

"Oh, that," says Jennifer. "It was under the door when I got to work Thursday morning."

Whatever is inside, I'm guessing a business envelope containing more than one page, based on the heft and the fact that it's sliding around, too small for the larger manila outer envelope.

* * *

I can feel it in my bones. Tuchio is laying something on us at the last minute. I've been expecting it for days, the midnight motion. I talk with Harry as I slit the top of the manila envelope with my letter opener. I peer inside for the business envelope, looking for the district attorney's printed address in the corner.

My fingers are halfway into the manila opening when I see what's inside. Instantly I stop what I'm doing and withdraw my hand.

Harry reads my face and looks at the envelope as if maybe there's a snake inside. "What's the matter?"

Carefully I lay the envelope back down on the desk.

Harry and Herman are both looking at me, like maybe they should run.

"Do we still have those tweezers, the big forceps we use on the printer?"

"I think so. What is it?"

"Just get them, and a towel, something clean."

In seconds Harry is back. He hands me the forceps, large tweezers about seven inches long. Harry bought these a few years ago in a hardware store. We use them for plucking small pieces of torn paper from the printer when it jams. I check them to make sure there is no ink or toner powder on the metal. He hands me a small, square cotton dust cloth from the cleaning closet, where the janitor keeps a supply in a bag.

"You're sure it's clean?"

"Got it out of the bag," says Harry.

With the cloth I gently hold the manila envelope to the top of the desk and slip the forceps inside. I snag the folded pages and slide them from the envelope. With the folded letter now exposed on my desk, you can see it clearly: a fine, rust-colored filigree, oblong ringlets of blood where kinetic energy had stretched them as they collided with the paper and later dried.

This delicate, lacelike pattern is interrupted by four bloody dots, spaced in a slight arc in the middle of the folded page. I lift the pages with the forceps and check the other side: a single rust-colored dot near the bottom edge, where the killer's thumb gripped the envelope on this side as he used the blood-soaked gloves to snatch it from the leather portfolio. The existence of this thumb mark on the letter explains the slight smear of blood at the lower boundary of the rectangle on the portfolio, made when the killer grabbed the letter.

"See if you can find something for that." Using the cloth, I slide the envelope across the surface of my desk toward Harry. "Maybe a legal-size folder. Or something bigger."

Jennifer's fingerprints and my own are already on it, along with how many others, we don't know.

I lay the folded pages, four of them from what I can see, on the blotter in the center of the desk.

The side of the paper facing up is covered by countless tiny, hollow, oblong ringlets in rust where it was spattered by Scarborough's blood as it lay on top of the portfolio by the television in his hotel room.

Harry gets two more cloth dust towels and hands the rest of the bag to Herman in case we need more. Instead of a legal-size folder, which would be too small to encase and protect the entire manila envelope, Harry has an empty transfer box with the lid already off. Using two of the cloth towels, he picks up the manila envelope by the edges, carefully compressing the two edges between his hands to lift it, and when he does, an item I had missed inside slides out and falls onto my desk.

It is a tiny Ziploc bag, maybe two by three inches in size. I don't touch it, but I look closely as it lies on the surface of my desk. Inside are what appear to be several short strands of blond hair.

"All of you saw it," I say. "Where it came from?"

There are nodding heads all around, Herman, Harry, and Jennifer.

Twenty minutes later I'm on the phone. Judge Quinn is calling from his house. We have had to go through the bailiff's office at the courthouse, staffed by only a skeleton crew on a holiday, to have them call Quinn at home and have him call me at my office, an emergency.

Before I can say a word: "Mr. Madriani, if you're looking for more time, the answer is no."

When I tell him what has happened, there is a moment of stone silence from the other end of the line. "Have you told Mr. Tuchio about this?"

"I don't know how to get ahold of him on a holiday," I say.

"Leave that to me," he says. "He'll have to have somebody from his office or forensics pick it up."

"Good."

"Stay there until they come. Be in chambers before court tomorrow morning. Let's make it seven A.M.," he says. "In the meantime don't touch the damn thing. Leave it for forensics."

We hang up. There's little sense in telling him, since I already have touched it, at least with the tweezers.

Before I talked to Quinn on the phone, I dispatched Herman to call our forensics expert, to track him down at home so that he can be here when Tuchio's people show up to take the letter and the hairs back to the police crime lab. I don't want the letter or the little bag of hairs going anywhere unless our own expert is glued to them.

Then I spend ten minutes with Harry hovering over the desk as I pry open the folded pages using the forceps and the rag. It is ordinary twenty-pound copy paper, the kind you can buy in any Office-Max. As soon as I got it open, I knew. Whoever made it used a color copier. The elegant hand-scripted letters bore the tobacco-colored hue of the original ink. The script had obviously been reduced in size, though it was still quite readable. The four pages are stapled at the top left-hand corner. It is identical to the image I recall from the video over the restaurant table, the letter laid open as Scarborough and Ginnis talked.

On the copy you could see the outline of the outside edges of the original, larger page on which the script was written, freehand with no lines. I tried to remember. On a trip to Williamsburg with Sarah several years ago, hearing a name for the page size commonly used in Jefferson's day—a quarto or a folio, something like that. I wondered if this was it.

I had Harry clean the glass surface on the copy machine, no chemicals just a damp cloth and elbow grease. Then he dried it thoroughly.

We both checked to make sure there were no fibers from the cloth left behind on the glass that might stick to a page and send the crime lab on a wild-goose chase. Then I took the pages.

Harry and I agreed that we could not remove the staple. The holes and the missing staple are something forensics would pick up on immediately. Also, if the dinner video of Scarborough and Ginnis comes into evidence, the missing staple becomes a problem in terms of comparison. And we wouldn't dare try to replace it. You could never get it precisely in the same place, not so that a forensics expert wouldn't know, and there is no doubt evidence of blood on the original staple.

Consequently we were left to ham-hand the copying process. With Harry helping me, four ham hands being better than two, I held each scripted page down on the screen of the copier as Harry supported the other pages, trying not to bend or tear them from the stapled corner. Each page was copied with the copier cover up and out of the way. Doing this, holding the pages between pieces of cotton cloth took more than five minutes. Harry was sweating so profusely that he was afraid he might drip on one of the pages.

We took particular care with the last page, the one with the filigree of blood on the center fold on the back. I knew that this would be critical, that the pattern of these little spots was now most likely the key item of evidence in our entire case. I tried to copy the scripted side as best I could without entirely flattening the paper.

I also copied the front of the large envelope with the label, not that it was going to tell us much without a return address or postmark.

Then I took a long, deep breath. I wasn't sure this was a good thing to do, but I was going to do it anyhow. The way you might gingerly handle a touchy detonator on a bomb, I carefully laid the back of the last page on the glass surface of the copier. This was the side with the filigree of blood across the center. I left the other two folds, the top and bottom third of the page, sticking straight up, and with the cover of the copier lifted, I pushed the "copy" button again. As the heat of the light element from the copier warmed my face, I prayed that it would do nothing to impair or destroy the spiderwebs of dried blood touching the glass.

After taking photos of the pages, including the blood on the back of the last page, I placed the call and waited for Quinn to call back.

Ninety minutes later, with our forensics expert already at the office, a uniformed officer and a plainclothes investigator from the D.A.'s office arrived to collect the transfer box with the Jefferson Letter, the envelope, and the small Ziploc bag containing the strands of hair. Together with our forensics expert, the whole caboodle headed for the crime lab.

TWENTY-FOUR

As we head off to court Tuesday morning, Harry and I are plagued by the thought that some sick mind reading of the details of the trial in the newspapers or online may have put together its own package of manufactured evidence and slid it under our door.

The world is full of such sickness, armies of miscreants giving birth to computer viruses and laying waste to other people's lives for their own amusement. If they have, the crime lab and our own expert will know, before the morning is out.

* * *

Seven A.M., and we are with Quinn in chambers, behind closed doors.

Tuchio is already wading in. Having been briefed by his forensics people, who are still laboring over the bloodied Jefferson Letter and the blond hairs in the bag, the prosecutor is busy working up options, trying to stretch the sidelines for some open-field running, if it turns out that the evidence is real.

New evidence, so he demands the right to reopen his case. Quinn assures him that if the evidence is verified, he will entertain the motion. Fairness requires this.

"It could be nothing, a sham, but if it turns out to be the item that was taken from the scene, it doesn't change a thing," says Tuchio. "The defendant himself could have taken it at the time of the murder." He pauses to look at Harry and me, just for a second. "Of course, this could explain how it showed up so conveniently in his lawyer's office at the last minute."

"In case you forgot, our client is in jail," says Harry. "He would need long arms to slip it under our door."

"Use your imagination," says Tuchio. "A confederate, a friend, a family member—or maybe it was already there."

What he means is, in our office. He is suggesting that Harry and I have had this, the bloodied Jefferson Letter, for some time, presumably given to us by Carl, or one of his friends or a family member, and held it for just such an occasion, so that it could be mysteriously delivered to ourselves and used in just this way.

This is the fanatic divide between prosecutors and the criminal defense bar. So ingrained is it that I am barely annoyed by the innuendo. Any prosecutor in the same situation who didn't at least make the suggestion, you would have to assume had the flu and a sufficiently high fever to affect his normal instincts.

"And what about the blond hairs in the little Ziploc bag?" I ask him.

"They may be nothing," says Tuchio.

"But what if they are?"

Tuchio is biting his lip on this one. We are both thinking the same thing, that the loose blond hairs that arrived with the letter may match the ones found by police forensics techs on the bathroom floor of

Scarborough's hotel room. If not, and unless there is some sick brain teaser out there, why were they included with the letter?

"If there's one thing we know with certainty, it's that Arnsberg isn't blond," says Harry.

Tuchio knows that if the hairs turn out to be a match, the prosecution will find itself waving off ghosts in its closing argument. The specter that some other dude did it will not only be walking in front of the jury, this phantom may be doing the jig.

Tuchio turns to Judge Quinn. The judge thus far has been leaning back in his chair, counting ceiling tiles, taking in all the various arguments and innuendos.

"It could be," says Tuchio, "if those hairs, the ones in the plastic bag, prove a match, then it's possible there could have been two assailants in the hotel room that day."

I was wondering how long it would take him to arrive at this.

The prosecutor pushes this thought out in front of the judge to see if he might start a test drive for a new theory—that is, if the wheels don't fall off—one that might carry him to the end of his case.

"The only problem, Mr. Tuchio, is that I don't remember you talking about any assailants other than the defendant in your opening statement, or for that matter presenting any evidence in that direction," says Quinn.

Tuchio could reopen his case and try to bring some in, but the fact that this evidence would be at such stark odds with what he has already presented does not allow this as a real and viable option.

"That's not entirely true, Your Honor." He argues that there's evidence of possible conspiracy in the state's case, or at least that efforts were made by the defendant to enlist the assistance of others in the commission of violence against Scarborough.

Tuchio reminds the judge of the testimony from Charlie Gross, about the bravado by Carl in the bar about kidnapping Scarborough from the hotel, and the fact that Carl's words, according to the witness, were all cast in the plural—that "we" could kidnap the victim, that "we" could haul him out of the hotel, that "we" could take him out into the desert and shoot him.

Quinn is suddenly sitting forward in his

chair. "I hope you're not suggesting to this court that your own witness is a co-conspirator to the crime?"

Tuchio had better hope not, because if he is, he has just rung the bell for a mistrial, in which case we can all go home, including Carl, at least until Tuchio charges him again.

"No, no, not at all." Tuchio's hand is up like a traffic cop's. "Not at all. I'm not saying that. What I am saying is that there *is* evidence already in the state's case that the defendant himself spoke in ways that might lead a reasonable person to conclude that others may have joined him in the commission of the crime. That's all I'm saying."

This is the seam, as narrow as it is, that Tuchio wants to crawl through.

You can bet that this sudden parsing of the language off the tripping tongue of Charlie Gross is not something that has sprung from the cortex of Tuchio's nimble mind as we sit here. He has probably been up all night praying that the letter and the hairs in the envelope are a hoax, while periodically measuring the depth of the crater he's in if they're not. He is testing the judge to see if Quinn will go for it, if the court will allow him to argue on close, despite the state's earlier theory that Carl acted alone, that there may have been two perpetrators, Carl and a blond person whom apparently they have not been able to identify.

He explains to the judge that this could make sense—that is, if he can just pound all the little parts that are sticking out into place, so that they fit into his own case, the goal being the continued march toward the death house for Carl.

"Don't you see, Your Honor? The defendant's blond confederate was probably the one who slipped the envelope under their office door," he says.

This is, of course, more polite than suggesting that we opened the door and that Blondie handed it to us, along with a lengthy explanation of what it was.

But as Quinn says, "All this"—Tuchio's sudden sighting of a second killer—"is strangely missing not only from your opening statement before the jury but from most of the evidence so far presented by any of your witnesses."

The prosecutor pounces on a word. "I

would agree that it is missing from *most* of our evidence," says Tuchio. "But not from all of it."

What he wants to know is whether the judge will allow him to venture into the realm of multiple killers before the jury in his closing argument.

Harry and I are looking at each other wondering if Tuchio has been smoking something. But given the ways in which he has burned us so far, I'm not willing to take any more bets.

"Fine, you want to argue on that narrow basis, be my guest," says Quinn.

Tuchio has his answer.

*   *   *

Just before noon, with the jury in a holding pattern, we get the answer regarding the Jefferson Letter. Forensics experts, employees of the police crime lab, together with our own expert, agree. There is no question that this letter, the four pages from the manila envelope, is the item that was resting on the shadowed leather portfolio at the moment Scarborough was killed.

We end up in Quinn's chambers again. He wants to know if, based on this information, Tuchio wants to reopen his case for the prosecution.

All morning the prosecutor has been closeted with his assistant, Janice Harmen, and Detrick, the lead homicide detective.

The judge seems surprised when Tuchio says no, they're prepared to go on as is.

Quinn asks me if I'm ready to present my opening statement. I tell him that I'm not prepared to give the jury the full outline of our case until the results from the comparison of hair samples comes back from the lab. This is not expected until later in the afternoon.

The judge excuses the jury and tells me to be ready with my opening statement first thing in the morning.

*   *   *

Just after four o'clock in the afternoon, Harry and I are secluded in the conference room at the office going over notes to make sure that I hit all the high points in my opening, when the news arrives by telephone.

It is Robert Stepro, our expert on hair and blood-spatter evidence. Harry puts him on the speakerphone.

Stepro tells us that when Dewey Prichert, the state's expert on hair and fiber, opened the tiny plastic bag from the manila envelope at the police crime lab, he extracted and counted five blond hairs. Microscopic examination revealed that all five had been cleanly clipped from their owner's head, probably with a pair of scissors. All five samples from the baggie belong to the same person.

And then the clincher, based on examination and findings, by both Prichert and Stepro: The characteristics of the five blond hair samples from the baggie are a positive match to the two blond hairs found lying free, under the toe kick in the bathroom of Scarborough's hotel room. In addition, they match the one bloodstained blond strand of hair lifted from the crevice between the cushions in the chair where Scarborough was murdered.

* * *

It is just shy of 9:20 Wednesday morning when I find myself standing in front of the jury box in Plato Quinn's crowded courtroom. Every seat is filled, and there is a line outside in the hallway that stretches beyond the elevator at the far end of the corridor.

"Ladies and gentlemen of the jury. My name is Paul Madriani. As you already know, my partner, Harry Hinds, and I represent the defendant, Carl Arnsberg." I point to Harry, who nods and smiles, and then to Carl, who nods and waves one hand.

"You have heard and seen a good deal of evidence to this point in the trial. But you have not heard or seen all the evidence in this case. When all the evidence is before you, you will be instructed by the judge regarding the law that you must apply in evaluating that evidence.

"Among the items of instruction that you will be given by the judge are two fundamental and important rules. First is that the defendant is to be presumed innocent until and unless his guilt is established by the prosecution, by Mr. Tuchio, based on proof beyond a reasonable doubt.

"The second fundamental rule is that the defendant in this case bears no burden of proof. He is not required by law to offer or to produce a single item of evidence establishing his own innocence. To the contrary, his innocence is fixed by law, established by law unless and until the state, the prosecutor"—I point at Tuchio with my arm fully extended—"can overturn the presumption of innocence by carrying his burden, proof beyond a reasonable doubt.

"I could, if I wished, sit down at this moment and rest our case. And I could argue that my client should be freed, acquitted, found not guilty. But I am not going to do that, because we have evidence, considerable evidence—some of you might call it abundant evidence—evidence that you have not seen, that will not only establish reasonable doubt in your minds as to the defendant's guilt, but evidence that will allow you to see the shadowed hand of the true perpetrator of this crime."

I move laterally in front of the jury box now, the six alternates seated outside and just in front of it.

"So what is the defendant's case, his case in his own defense?"

I begin to outline it for them.

I start with the rush to judgment, the fact that there has already been considerable evidence and that there will be more evidence that the police conducted a shoddy investigation. I remind them that they have already heard evidence from Detective Detrick, the lead homicide detective, that from the start the police pursued no suspects other than the defendant. I remind them that the police fell on Carl the moment they found his fingerprints and shoe impressions at the scene, this despite the fact that the defendant, along with other hotel employees, had a business reason for being in or near the vicinity of the victim's room.

"Objection, that last is argument," says Tuchio.

"Overruled," says the judge. "The jury can decide."

I turn back to the jury. Now I must tread carefully. You would think, with the Jefferson Letter and the samples of hair contained in the manila envelope, that this would be a slam dunk. But it is not. Unless this is carefully presented, gingerly handled, the outlining of this evidence, the convenient fashion in which it landed in our office may produce the very result hoped for by Tuchio—skepticism and the feeling among jurors that they are being manipulated, that Carl or someone he knew delivered this to our office.

So I back into it and tread lightly.

"You have already seen and heard evidence by the state's expert, Mr. Prichert, that investigators and police crime-lab technicians failed to discover that something was missing, taken from the victim's hotel room in the minutes following Mr. Scarborough's murder."

I remind them of the shadowed leather portfolio, shaded in the victim's blood, and the item missing from the top of it, and I tell them that this is further evidence of a shoddy investigation.

"Moreover," I tell them, "we will produce evidence explaining to you, showing you, what that mysterious missing item was. Additionally, we will produce evidence that the item in question was not found by police in the possession of the defendant following his arrest, but that it was found elsewhere, during the time that this trial has been ongoing. And, ladies and gentlemen, I will warn you that the contents of this item will shock you."

Now I have their attention, which for the moment is all I want.

As I turn, Tuchio is smiling at me. He senses the problem we are having with this evidence, and he is enjoying it. As the saying goes, "Beware of Greeks bearing gifts."

"In addition to the mysterious missing item, you have seen and heard evidence from Mr. Prichert regarding samples of hair found at the murder scene, in the bathroom and between the cushions of the chair in which the victim was seated when he was murdered.

"According to the testimony produced by the state, by the prosecutor, these hair samples, none of which match the defendant's hair, are simply random strands of hair deposited by former hotel guests or employees.

"But we will produce evidence that this is not so. We will present evidence here in this courtroom, conclusive evidence that at least three of these strands of unidentified human hair found by police evidence experts at the scene, hairs none of which match the defendant's, that these hairs are directly and conclusively linked to the mysterious missing item taken from the victim's hotel room in the minutes after he was murdered."

Harry and I decided last night, near midnight, in the conference room that we had no other choice during our opening statement but to build our case around the Jefferson Letter, to keep veiled its contents, to hang everything from this enigma like a Christmas tree, and to ignore for the moment the manner in which the letter came into our possession.

To tell a jury in so many words in our opening statement that it was slipped under our door in the middle of the night by an unknown messenger is to invite disbelief on a nuclear scale.

We are banking on two things. If we are careful, we can control the order of evidence and testimony as it comes in. We can lay groundwork with the credibility of our witnesses to dull, to an extent, the natural suspicion of how this evidence was acquired.

The second thing we are counting on is the shock effect of the Jefferson Letter itself. While you always want to keep a jury in suspense, the stunning contents of the

Jefferson Letter—what it says and what it means—are a dynamic unto themselves. That, and the timing with which this is delivered, is critical.

"Finally," I tell them, "you will see evidence in the form of a videotape that will explain to you the importance, the significance, of the mysterious item taken from the victim's room in the moments after he was murdered."

This is vague, and left vague for a reason.

"When you have heard all the testimony, and seen all the evidence, I believe you will finally understand why Terry Scarborough was killed and that the defendant Carl Arnsberg had nothing to do with this crime. I believe that the evidence will show and that you will come to understand that the murder was committed for other reasons, by another perpetrator, and that the motive for this murder was connected to the mysterious missing item—the item that you will see and hear about, here in this courtroom, because we, the defense, will present it to you in evidence."

I look them in the eye, slowly, from one end of the jury box to the other, in silence.

I am six or seven feet back, just in front of the six alternates seated outside in front of the jury railing.

"I ask you to watch and wait, to keep an open mind, to listen to the testimony, and to look at the evidence. Because I believe that the evidence will show that the killer of Terry Scarborough is not in this room today. He is elsewhere. I ask you to look carefully, because if you do, the evidence will reveal the shadowed figure of this killer as he moved through the hotel room that morning, around the body of Terry Scarborough, to reach out and to snatch the missing item from the top of that leather portfolio. Look carefully, ladies and gentlemen, look very carefully, because if you do, you will see . . . the shadowed hand of a murderer at work. Thank you."

TWENTY-FIVE

The problem we are having is with the video, the reason for the fuzzy reference in my opening.

Early in the morning, before our opening statement, the judge entertained argument in chambers as to whether he might allow the restaurant video showing Ginnis and Scarborough huddled over the table talking, along with Teddy Nons's transcript of their conversation.

Tuchio argued that nothing has changed, that there was no foundation for the video, since we still cannot prove when it was made or who made it.

Harry and I argued that the video should come in for the limited purpose of further verifying that the letter spattered with blood is in fact the same item that Scarborough unfolded on the table as the two men were talking. We now have a video expert prepared to testify that freeze-frames of this video, processed by computer and magnified, show that the letter laid out on the dining table at the restaurant is identical to the first of the four pages in the Jefferson Letter delivered to our office. The comparison is exact, right down to ink smears in the writing and shadows in the margins showing the edges of the original letter where it was copied. Audio comparison of Scarborough's voice patterns from the restaurant video have also been matched with known videotaped interviews of the author, so that there is now no question that it is in fact Scarborough who is seated across from Ginnis on the video.

Once the video is in, even for this narrow purpose, Tuchio knows that the game is up. With images of the letter open on the table, and all the furtive looks and glances from Ginnis, even if the jury doesn't know who he is and can't hear his words, they can fill in the blanks, ghost killer on the half shell.

Quinn has reserved judgment on whether the video can come into evidence for the limited purpose of further verifying that the copy of the letter was in Scarborough's possession. It's a long shot, but he wants to think about it. And Harry and I certainly want to give him the time.

What we did convince the judge to do was to allow us to use the video of the Leno show, the interview with Richard Bonguard, Scarborough's literary agent, talking about the letter and its presumed importance, even though Bonguard claimed never to have seen the letter himself. Bonguard still has not returned to his office. He is obviously hiding out, waiting until the smoke clears. The foundation for this video can be laid by a production coordinator for the show who will testify as to when and where the video was made and who the participants were.

The fact that everything on the program video is hearsay, since none of the participants are here to be cross-examined, doesn't seem to bother Quinn. For the moment it allows me to make my opening statement, including vague allusions to a video while at the same time permitting the judge more time to consider whether he will allow us to use the real video, the one with Ginnis in the hot seat.

Thursday morning, nine o'clock, and our first witness hits the stand. When you're cruising through a magnetic minefield, it's best to do so in a slow boat made of wood. So you might say that our opening witness is a bit dull—except for one thing: He can explain to the jury how the murder weapon, the hammer, found its way into the hands of the killer.

From the inception Tuchio and the cops have been welded to the theory that Carl possessed special access both to the victim in his hotel room and to the murder weapon, the hammer, because Carl had access to master card keys due to his job in the hotel. All their evidence has confirmed this—from Carl's supervisor, who verified this fact and testified to it on the stand, to Carl's own boasting and bravado at the Del Rio Tavern, where he bragged about having access to Scarborough because of master keys. It is one of the linchpins of their case, that only someone with access to the locked maintenance closet could have gotten the hammer. That pin is about to be pulled.

Wally Hettinger has worked for the Presidential Regis Hotel for almost eight years. He is a maintenance man, one of eleven people working around the clock to keep the hotel running smoothly and to repair any problems that may crop up twenty-four hours a day.

After he's given his name and background and told the jury where he works, the first thing out of Hettinger's mouth in response to a question is that the lock on the maintenance closet on the top floor of the Presidential Regis was broken. This is the place where the state claims the hammer was stored.

This is one item of evidence that catches Tuchio by surprise. Herman found the witness in the way Herman finds everything, by hanging around and talking to people, often people on the bottom corporate rungs.

"If you tried to turn the knob on the door, it would feel like it was locked," says Hettinger. "But if you pulled on it, the door would open. It had been that way for a while." He shrugs a shoulder. "The latch bolt on the lock didn't quite meet the opening on the metal striker bar that fits in the doorframe. It's a common problem on doors. It was a big problem at the hotel. You ask me, I think it's a problem with the way they were manufactured—I mean the doors at the Regis."

This draws an objection from Tuchio. "The witness is not an engineer or an expert on door manufacture."

Quinn strikes the witness's comment and tells the jury to disregard the bit about manufacturing problems.

"Were you required to repair hotel doors often?" I ask.

"All the time." The witness tells the jury the doors were heavy, solid-core metal. "So over time gravity gets a hold, and they sag," he says. "Either the screws in the hinges work loose and the door slides down a little—doesn't take much, eighth of an inch sometimes is all—or else sometimes just the screws in the top hinges come loose and the door will lean a bit in the frame. Either way," says Hettinger, "the bolt from the lock won't hit the opening in the striker right, and the lock won't catch. In which case the door may look closed, but it's not locked."

"Why didn't you fix it? The maintenance closet door, I mean?"

I can see Tuchio and Detrick at their table poring over my witness list trying to find Hettinger's name buried in all the chaff. Six hundred names in all. We stuck him somewhere in the middle, so that if they started checking them out, working from either end, Hettinger might be the last they would get to.

"I had that door on a list for repair," he says, "but it wasn't priority. Guest rooms are priority."

"Did you tell the police that the lock on the maintenance-closet door was broken?"

"No. Nobody ever talked to me. When it happened—the murder, I mean—I was on vacation. Visiting my brother up in Idaho."

Of course the cops talked to the hotel maintenance manager, who didn't know anything about it, since no one had ever told him.

"I mean, he knew about the problem with the doors," says Hettinger. "A major headache," he says. "But he didn't know about that particular door. If we told him about every door every time it happened, none of us would ever get anything done."

According to Hettinger, he had become a kind of specialist at fixing the doors, he and one other maintenance man. If there was a problem with a door lock anywhere in the hotel, they got the call.

Whether the cops knew that the lock on the maintenance-closet door was broken and chose to keep it out of their notes, or whether they simply tried turning the handle, assumed it was locked, and had one of the hotel employees use a card key before they actually pulled the handle, opened the door, and checked out the closet, we will never know. But if I had to guess, I would say it's the latter. They simply didn't know.

No doubt Tuchio will try to play with this on cross. That if the police couldn't figure out that the maintenance-closet door wasn't bolted and locked, how could a random phantom killer be lucky enough to figure it out? The problem for Tuchio is that he can't know what's coming next.

I ask Hettinger if this problem—the bolt on the door locks hanging up—to his knowledge had ever occurred on the doors to the Presidential Suite, the room Scarborough was staying in the morning he was killed.

He says, "Yes." He remembers fixing them a couple of times. According to the witness, they were a particular problem because they were double doors, a six-foot span instead of just three, with one of the doors bolted to the floor and the doorframe above and fixed in place, while the other door swung open and closed.

I then put on a pair of latex surgical gloves and have the clerk retrieve the hammer, the murder weapon, from the evidence cart. I show this to the witness.

"Have you ever seen this hammer before?"

He looks at it closely, puts on a pair of glasses. "Is that it?" He seems surprised. "Is that the hammer that was used to kill the man?"

I assure him that this is the murder weapon and ask him again if he has ever seen it before."

"Well, yeah," he says. "The paint marks there on the handle and the number stamped into the top. That was one of the hammers I used all the time to fix the doors. I just thought somebody stole it when I came back from vacation. I didn't even put in a claim, 'cuz I knew the hotel wouldn't pay for it. So I just bought another one. Replaced it," he says.

"We'll get to that in a moment," I tell him. "For now, let me ask you a question. If this hammer was inside the maintenance closet on the top floor of the Regis, and the lock on the door to that closet was broken so that it didn't catch, is it not a fact that anyone could have pulled on that door, opened it, and taken the hammer?"

"I suppose so."

"Would they have needed a key to open the maintenance-closet door?"

"Not if the lock wasn't working," says Hettinger. "But it really wouldn't have mattered," he says.

"Why not?"

"Because that hammer, the one you got there, it wasn't in the maintenance closet."

This sets off a stir out in the audience. Tuchio, who has been making notes, points of attack to use in coming at the witness on cross-examination, puts down his pen.

"If it wasn't in the maintenance closet, where was it?"

"Oh, we kept a couple of hammers in that closet, but that one, because of the straight claws on it"—he points with his finger—"that one I kept on an open shelf in the main staircase on the eighth floor."

"Why would you do that?"

"Because we only had two good ones, tempered-steel hammers with straight claws, I mean. All the rest were round, curved claws," he says. "The straight claws we kept in the staircase, along with a screwdriver and a couple of wooden wedges. They were a special set of tools," he says. "To fix the doors."

I have him explain to the jury how this worked. That he would loosen the screws on the door hinges with the screwdriver, then use the straight claws on the hammer to lever the door from the bottom, by slipping the claws in the crack between the floor and the bottom of the door. Using the leverage of the hammer handle, he would jimmy the door in place until it was square and then slip a wooden wedge into the space beneath the door to hold it in place while he tightened the hinge screws

again. To listen to Hettinger, it was an endless job.

"We kept one set of tools—the
straight-claw hammer, the screwdriver,
and the wedges—on a shelf on the eighth
floor and the other one four stories down,
in the same staircase.

"Why not in one of the maintenance
closets on those floors?"

"We did that for a while. But on the day
shift there's eight of us working maintenance, three at night. Seemed like every
time I got a call to fix a door, I'd go to get
the hammer, and somebody else had it.
All that was left was the curved claws, and
they were useless. Because of the way
the claws are rounded," he says. "You
couldn't get the claws under the door because the hammer handle would jam
against the side of the door. I'd have to run
all over the hotel and find who had straight
claws and get 'em back. So I figured it was
easier to take 'em out of the closet and
store 'em someplace else."

The witness tells the jury that the stairwell where the hammers were stored was
open to the public. It had to be. It was the
main fire escape. Anyone wanting to use it

could simply walk in and climb the stairs. But according to Hettinger, almost no one ever did.

"Would you climb fourteen stories if you had an elevator?" He looks to the jury as he asks the rhetorical question. "That's why I figured, a couple of tools on a shelf in a corner, down low where it was hard to see, who's gonna mess with them?"

We now know one other thing. Whoever killed Scarborough didn't use the elevator.

* * *

Quinn calls the midmorning break, and as soon as we are back in court, Tuchio tries his best to shake Hettinger's testimony concerning the hammer and where it was stored in the days just before the murder.

First he browbeats Hettinger to soften him up, demanding to know why the witness did not come forward to report these facts—the location of the hammer, the broken lock—to police, after he realized that this was the murder weapon.

"I never knew it was the murder weapon till today," he says.

This is true. When Herman was talking to Hettinger, while springing for sandwiches and a beer in a bar during Hettinger's lunch hour, Herman managed to gather up all the interesting little tidbits about dysfunctional doors and locks in the hotel. He was busy scribbling notes as to how the doors had to be jimmied up in order to repair them.

When Hettinger started complaining that his hammer was gone when he came back from vacation, and that he had to buy a new one out of his own pocket because he knew the hotel wouldn't pay for it, since he didn't store the missing hammer in the "locked" maintenance closet, Herman almost dropped his pencil. It wasn't hard to figure what had happened, especially after Hettinger described the straight claws and the reason he hid the hammer in the stairwell in the first place.

Herman never told the witness that the hammer he had stored there was the murder weapon, and from reading the newspapers how was Hettinger to guess? According to the cops, the hammer was taken from the maintenance closet, where the witness hadn't gone looking for a hammer in months. He had to assume that the police knew what they were talking about.

Tuchio now stands in front of the witness, incredulous, disbelieving that Hettinger didn't realize. "Didn't Mr. Madriani tell you?"

"Who's Mr. Madriani?" says Hettinger.

"The lawyer who just questioned you!" says Tuchio.

"I never saw him before today, just now," he says.

"Then who did you talk to? Somebody from his office?" he asks.

"I don't know. I didn't get the man's name," he says. "I just had lunch with him. Big guy, black fellow," he says. "Nice guy. He bought me lunch."

Tuchio wants a conference at the side of the bench. By the time I get there, he is hopping mad, and this time you can tell he's not acting. "We had no disclosure as to this witness," he tells Quinn.

"The man was on our list," I tell Quinn.

"You know damn well what I mean."

"Your language, Mr. Tuchio, for the record." Quinn gestures with his head toward the court reporter standing behind the prosecutor with her stenograph machine, taking it all down.

"This is trial by ambush," says Tuchio.

"Your Honor, we're not responsible for the state's investigation—or lack of it, for that matter. Mr. Hettinger has been going to work every day for months since Mr. Scarborough was murdered. The police had every opportunity to go out and talk to him."

"Did you have a signed written statement from the witness?" Quinn directs this to me.

"No, Your Honor, we did not."

"Then without a written statement, there was nothing to disclose except the witness's name," says the judge, "and from what I understand, you received that, Mr. Tuchio."

Having gotten no sympathy from the court, Tuchio marches back out and locks horns with Hettinger.

Under questioning, the maintenance man admits that he was out of town for almost a week just before Scarborough was murdered and that he didn't return to work until almost two weeks after the crime.

"So if you weren't there, in the building, in the hotel on the day in question, the morning that the victim was murdered, you really can't tell this jury whether that hammer"—Tuchio points toward the evidence cart—"was in the stairwell or in the maintenance closet or anywhere else, can you? Yes or no?" he says.

"All I know is that the hammer—"

"Yes or no!" says Tuchio.

"Objection, Your Honor. The witness should be allowed to answer the question in his own way."

"Sustained," says the judge. "You can answer the question any way you want."

"Why are you being so nasty?" Hettinger directs this at Tuchio.

"Except that way," says the judge. "Just answer the question—if you can. Do you remember the question?"

"Yes, I remember," says Hettinger. "What I was about to say is that all I know was that the hammer was in the stairwell where I kept it when I left on vacation and that when I got back, it was *gone*." He says this with such venom that Tuchio takes a half step back and a quick glance toward the jury.

This is not the verbal image the prosecutor wanted. It cuts too close to the bone of the shadowed hand in my opening statement.

Tuchio pauses, steps back and thinks for a moment.

"Perhaps we got off on the wrong foot," he says. "Mr. Hettinger, let me ask you a question." Tuchio takes a different approach now. The volume of his voice drops, his demeanor becomes friendlier, less imposing. "I understand that you were brought here today not fully understanding what was happening."

"Objection, Your Honor. Is that a question? Because it sounds to me like Mr. Tuchio is testifying," I say.

Tuchio turns it around and makes a question out of it, asking Hettinger if anyone from our side assisted him in the preparation of his testimony.

"No. Just lunch with the man, like I said."

"And this man you had lunch with, did he make suggestions regarding your testimony here today? Did he tell you anything to say?"

"No. He just took notes."

Dead end. Tuchio still searching.

Now with a more sociable style, he goes back to the point he wanted to make earlier. "You were gone for how long on vacation, around the time of the murder?"

"Three weeks."

"So during that three-week period, you really couldn't know whether that hammer was still in the stairwell where you left it, could you?"

"No."

"You couldn't be sure, for example, whether perhaps one of your colleagues might have picked it up and used it and perhaps put it back in one of the maintenance closets, could you?"

"How could I? I wasn't there," says Hettinger.

"Exactly," says Tuchio. "So for all you know, as you sit here today, that hammer could have been anywhere on the morning of the murder, or for that matter during the week before the murder, because you don't know where it was during the time that you were on vacation?"

"That's true."

"For all you know, the murderer could have found that hammer the day after you left for vacation and had it in his possession for days before the murder was committed?"

"Objection, leading, calls for speculation."

"Sustained," says Quinn.

"But since you couldn't see that hammer from all the way up there in Idaho, there are a lot of possibilities as to where that hammer might have been, right?"

"I suppose anything's possible," says the witness.

This looks like the best Tuchio can do. Then he pauses for a moment and tries to reach further.

"I think you testified that the lock, the one that didn't work on the maintenance closet upstairs, was on a list for repairs. Isn't that what you said?"

"That's right."

"Isn't it possible that the lock on that maintenance closet might have been repaired while you were gone on vacation, so that on the day that the victim was murdered, if that hammer was in that closet, it would have been locked behind closed doors. Is that not a possibility?"

Tuchio is leaning forward, waiting for the words "Anything's possible," but instead the witness says, "I doubt it."

"That's all I have for this witness, Your Honor." Tuchio tries to turn and get away.

"'Cuz the lock was still broken when I got back from vacation."

Why you never want to ask a question unless you already know the answer.

TWENTY-SIX

Quinn calls the lunch break, and Harry and I meet with Jennifer Sanchez, our paralegal, at a small bistro two blocks from the dwindling army of demonstrators in front of the courthouse.

Jennifer is decked out in her best going-to-court suit, slacks and a jacket with a white blouse and ruffled collar. She's nervous, and you can see it. I tell her that I'll be with her the entire time, that if Tuchio tries to get rough, I'll be all over him.

She nods and smiles, but in her eyes I can see the anxiety.

"Just think before you answer any

questions. If you don't know the answer, say you don't know."

Harry says, "Listen, you won't have any problems on direct. Paul will lay it all out for you. But when Tuchio gets up on cross-examination," he says, "he is going to try and pick up speed, get a quick rhythm going so that you can't think between questions. Don't let him do it," says Harry. "Pause between answers. He can't ask another question till you've answered the one before it, and if he tries, we'll object. All you have to do is stay calm. Just tell the jury what you saw, what happened."

Jennifer doesn't want any lunch. She's afraid she may not be able to keep it down. Harry and I go light, and less than an hour later we're back in the courtroom.

Jennifer is on the stand, sworn and seated, her back straight as a board, hands in her lap. She takes a deep breath, and I take her carefully through the preliminaries—the fact that she has spent her whole life in San Diego and attended local schools, her training as a paralegal, her employment with our office, the fact that she loves her work, any piece of information that might endear her to the jury.

Our entire case now hinges on whether they believe her.

"I think it was exactly a week ago, Thursday morning, can you tell the jury what time you arrived at work?"

"It was about seven A.M.," she says. "I had a lot of work to do, and I wanted to get an early start."

"And when you arrived, was there anyone else in the office?"

"No. I was the first one there."

"Please tell the jury what you found when you opened the door to the office that morning?" I try to make this sound as matter-of-fact as I can.

"When I unlocked the door and opened it, there were a couple of items on the floor. There was an envelope and a flyer, I think an advertisement, and the flyer was from a new restaurant that was opening down the street."

"And the envelope, did you know who that was from?"

"No."

"Did it have a return address on it?"

"No."

"Did it have any postage on it? Stamps or a tape from a postage machine?"

"No. Just a label addressed to you and a typed notation under the office address saying 'Personal and Confidential.'"

"Was it unusual to find letters or other pieces of literature slipped under the door in the morning when you arrived at work?"

"No. Happens all the time," she says. "Clients sometimes slip envelopes with checks for payment of bills, advertisements, sometimes even reports from expert witnesses if they're small enough."

"So finding this envelope on the floor didn't surprise you?"

"No. Not at all."

"Can you tell the jury what you did with this envelope after you found it?"

"I picked it up, and I put it on your desk."

"In my office?"

"Yes."

"You didn't open it?"

"No."

"Can you tell the jury why you didn't open it?"

"It's firm policy," she says, "that items coming in marked personal or confidential are to be delivered unopened to the person they're addressed to in the office."

"What about other mail, not marked personal or confidential? Can you tell the jury what happens with that?"

"It's opened by one of the secretaries. If it's business or legal, the correspondence is normally removed from the envelope, and then the envelope is stapled to the letter or whatever it is, so that if there's a postmark or a cancellation on the envelope, we have it."

"But this didn't happen with the envelope you found on the floor?"

"No."

"Because it was sent to me, and marked personal and confidential?"

"That's correct."

We talk about the size of the envelope, large enough to hold letter-size paper laid flat, unfolded. I ask her if she touched the envelope again at any time after she set it on my desk, and she says no.

I ask her if anyone else touched it, and she says she doesn't think so.

I ask her if she knows when the envelope was finally opened, and she tells the jury that this happened the following Monday morning when I returned to the office.

"And were you present when this was done?"

"I was in your office," she says.

"So between Thursday morning when you discovered the envelope on the floor inside the door to our office and Monday morning when I returned to the office, as far as you know the envelope in question remained on my desk, unopened?"

"That's correct."

Now I have her tell the jury where Harry and I were during all this time, from the moment she discovered the letter on the floor until I returned on Monday morning to open it.

"You were out of the country on business," she says.

"And how do you know that?"

"Because I helped make the travel arrangements, one of the secretaries and myself," she says, "and because in preparation for my appearance here today, both you and Mr. Hinds showed me your passports with both entry and exit stamps for the dates in question from the island of Curaçao in the Caribbean."

We have had certified copies of the passport pages prepared. I show them to Jennifer, we have them marked for identification, and we enter them in evidence.

"Do you know the date and time that we departed the airport en route to Curaçao?"

"It was just before eight last Wednesday night," she says. "I think seven-fifty or seven fifty-five."

"And can you tell the jury where you were at that time, on Wednesday night— this would be the night before you discovered the envelope on the floor?"

"I was having dinner with a friend at a restaurant on Coronado Island."

"And what did you do after dinner?"

"I went back to the office for about an hour."

"And what time did you arrive at the office?"

"A little after ten," she says.

"And how long did you remain at the office that evening?"

"I had some work to finish. I left the

office to go home. I think it was a few minutes after eleven."

"When you left, was there anyone else in the office?"

"No."

"And I assume that the envelope you discovered the next morning was not on the floor in the office when you left the office Wednesday evening?"

"That's correct. It was not there."

"Now let me change gears here. Do you know why Mr. Hinds and I traveled to the island of Curaçao?"

"Objection, hearsay," says Tuchio. "All she can know is what they told her."

"Sustained."

I stop and think. At this moment we are winging it. Tuchio's objection suddenly has me reaching for something I hadn't planned on, something I've never discussed with Jennifer in our preparations.

"Apart from anything I may have told you, or that Mr. Hinds may have told you, put that out of your mind," I tell her. "Apart from any of that, do you have any independent knowledge of your own, based on your own observations, your own work in the office, things you have personally observed or witnessed that give you any independent knowledge as to what Mr. Hinds and I were doing on the island of Curaçao during the period in question?"

"Objection, Your Honor." Tuchio is on his feet, leaning over the table, both hands extended. He can't get around the corner of the table fast enough. He wants a conference at the side of the bench.

By the time we get there, Quinn is already leaning over.

"Your Honor, they're trying to come in through the back door on the restaurant video," says Tuchio. "We know that this witness discovered the DVD in the evidence locker. We have to assume that she's seen it. Madriani is trying to use the video to leverage her into saying Ginnis's name, because as soon as she does, he'll have the jury distracted, looking in all the wrong places for the killer. There is still no foundation for that video"—Tuchio pounds the words home—"and no basis in evidence to mention Arthur Ginnis's name."

I go back to my argument that the Jefferson Letter, Scarborough's copy, which we now have, and its appearance in the restaurant video link these two items inextricably. To allow the letter into evidence without the video of Scarborough and Ginnis is to leave the jury half blind.

"Apart from that," I tell Quinn, "Ms. Sanchez knows, based on her own independent observations and her own work product, that Mr. Hinds and I were searching for a witness on that island, and she knows who that witness is. She knows what we were doing in Curaçao. Mr. Tuchio would have the jury believe that we took a vacation in the middle of the trial."

"Sounds about right to me," says Tuchio.

Quinn is nodding. "I'm not going to allow you to talk about the video, Mr. Madriani. So stay away from that line of questioning," he says. "However, I think it is fair to inform the jury that you were in Curaçao on legitimate business. The witness can confirm that you were on the island searching for a witness. But that is all. There is to be no disclosure as to the identity of that witness. Do you understand?" He looks at me.

I nod.

"No, better yet," he says, "I'll take care of this myself, from the bench."

The judge waves us away. What Quinn is worried about is that Jennifer and I will get our signals mixed and that before anyone can stop her, she'll blurt out the name Arthur Ginnis.

Quinn wheels around and sits upright in his chair.

By the time I get back to the witness stand, Jennifer is sitting there on needles. I can tell she knows where I'm trying to go, and she's itching to answer the question.

The judge clears his throat and intones, "The jury may take notice of the fact that Mr. Madriani and Mr. Hinds were on legitimate business and that during the period in question they were searching for a witness on the island of Kureasaw." He murders the name. "The record will so reflect."

He looks down at me. "Now move on, Mr. Madriani."

Jennifer gives me a slight shrug and an innocent smile as if to say, *All we can do is try.*

I draw her attention to Monday morning and the envelope on my desk.

For the next forty minutes, through questions and answers, she describes to the jury what she saw when I opened the envelope in my office that morning—the folded pages with the spots of blood—and then later when Harry picked up the envelope and the tiny plastic bag with the strands of hair fell out. We include testimony describing the awkward copying of the Jefferson Letter that went on in the office and the photographs that were taken.

The state will waste no time stirring the toxin of cynicism with innuendos and inferences, if not outright assertions that we planted the letter in our own office and that we choreographed all this for the benefit of the jury.

When Jennifer is finished describing what happened in the office, I retreat to the evidence cart.

First I show her the outer envelope with my name and the words "Personal & Confidential" typed on the address label. This is now encased in a clear plastic evidence bag from the police crime lab.

She identifies it as the envelope found on the office floor Thursday morning.

Next is Scarborough's copy of the Jefferson Letter, the folded document with the rust-colored blood on one side. For the moment the letter is sealed in a clear plastic bag, though this will be removed later to better preserve the blood evidence on the paper.

Jennifer identifies this as one of the items extracted from the envelope that morning. She still does not know the contents of the letter, nor do any of the other members of our office staff or expert witnesses, who have been instructed not to read it. The reason for this is the need to carefully control the timing of this evidence before the jury. If we slip up and open the door for Tuchio to get into this in his cross-examination of one of our witnesses, it could destroy the entire strategy of our defense.

*   *   *

She then identifies the other item, the small plastic bag, though the hairs that it once contained have now been removed for preservation.

"Now let me ask you, do you have any idea, any information at all, as to who might have placed this envelope under the door to our law office on Coronado?"

"No. I have no idea at all."

"So the only thing you can tell the jury is

that the envelope was not there Wednesday night when you left the office at approximately eleven o'clock and that it was there at approximately seven the following morning when you arrived for work?"

"That's correct."

I turn to Tuchio. "Your witness."

* * *

He wastes no time. He goes right for the jugular.

"Lemme get this straight, Ms. Sanchez. You expect this jury to believe that you never saw those items, the bloody letter," he calls it, "and the little baggie of hair before they magically appeared on your office floor last Thursday morning, is that right?"

"I don't know what the jury wants to believe. All I can do is tell them the truth."

Good girl.

"Come. Come now," he says. "Are you telling us that Mr. Madriani didn't instruct you on what to say here this morning, that he didn't dictate it to you line by line so that you would get it *straight*?"

To Jennifer these are fighting words. "That's exactly what I'm telling you." She looks at the jury now and ignores him. "What I am telling you is what I saw, everyth—"

"You're telling us you never saw those items—"

"Your Honor, he's cutting the witness off. If he wants to ask a question, he should allow the witness to answer."

Tuchio turns to look at me. "I thought she was finished."

"She wasn't," I tell him.

"Gentlemen, direct your comments here, to me, not to one another," says Quinn. "The witness will be allowed to complete her answers." The judge gives Jennifer a courtly smile and tells her to go ahead and finish.

She looks directly at the jury once more. "What I'm telling you is what I saw, all of it, everything, nothing added and nothing taken away. It is the truth." She says this with an earnestness and a fire in her eyes.

When she turns back to him, Tuchio just stands there. For at least six or seven seconds, there is nothing but silence. Then he asks, "Are you finished?"

"Yes." She looks at him, one of those drop-dead expressions that only a woman can give you.

"I wasn't sure," he says. "Let me ask you another question," he says. "Did Mr. Madriani prepare you for your testimony here today? Did you spend any time talking with him about it, discussing it?"

"We did."

"How much time?" he says.

"An hour, maybe a little more."

"And Mr. Hinds, let's not leave out Mr. Hinds. Did you spend any time with him preparing for your appearance here in court?"

"Some," she says.

"How much?"

"About two hours."

"Was that together with Mr. Madriani or separate?" he says.

"Part of it was together with both of them. Part of it was separate."

"And where and when did this take place, this preparation?" Tuchio makes it sound like a four-letter word.

"In the office, last night and the night before."

"So it was all very recent?" he says.

"Yes."

"Well, I guess that makes sense," he says. "After all, there wasn't much time to prepare this whole thing, the mystery missive, and the little hairs being dropped on everyone so late and so suddenly," he says.

"Is there a question in any of that?" says Quinn.

"I was about to frame one, Your Honor."

"Then get on with it."

"When this envelope was opened by Mr. Madriani in his office that day, Monday, I believe you testified that there were four people present in the room, is that correct?"

"Yes."

"Mr. Madriani, Mr. Hinds, yourself, and Mr. Diggs, is that right?"

"That's right."

"Now, I can understand why Mr. Madriani can't take the stand to testify. He is counsel in the case, as well as is Mr. Hinds. But did they tell you why you were selected to come here and tell us this *story*?" Tuchio would use the word "fable," but the judge would jump on him.

"First of all, they didn't tell me to do it. They asked me, and I said yes."

"So you were anxious to come here today and testify?"

"No. I can't say I'm enjoying the experience," she says.

Some of the members of the jury laugh.

"But if that's the case, why are you here instead of Mr. Diggs? He saw the same things you did, didn't he?"

"Not exactly," she says. "Mr. Diggs didn't find the envelope on the floor. I'm not a lawyer," she says, "but I didn't think he could testify to that. Could he?"

Quinn's chuckling up on the bench, and then he whispers, "You may not be a lawyer, but you're doing fine." He looks at the court reporter and wags a finger. He doesn't want the comment on the record.

"Well, other than the economy of witnesses," says Tuchio, "was there any other reason Mr. Diggs couldn't testify here today? I mean, you certainly could have taken the stand and told the jury how you found the envelope, but the rest of it, why not use Mr. Diggs?"

"Why bother, since I'm here already?" she says.

"Mr. Diggs is the African American investigator in your office, isn't he?"

"That's correct."

"Well, wouldn't it be more natural for an investigator—who sees things, investigates matters, and I assume who testifies regularly in court—to appear here today to tell us what he saw rather than a paralegal? And believe me," he adds, "I'm not trying to denigrate what you do for a living. We have paralegals in our office, and without them we couldn't survive. But why you and not the investigator, that's what I want to know."

"I don't know," she says. "Maybe he was busy."

"Ah," he says. "Too busy to testify in the biggest case in their office?" He looks over at our table, then back to the jury box.

"I don't know," she says. "All I know is that they asked me if I was willing to do it, and I said yes."

"Is it possible that they—by 'they' I mean Mr. Madriani and Mr. Hinds—may have asked Mr. Diggs to testify here today and that Mr. Diggs declined?"

"What would make you think that?" she says.

"I get to ask the questions. You get to answer them," says Tuchio. "Is it possible that Mr. Diggs declined to testify?"

"No," she says.

"Do you know that to be a fact?" he asks.

"Well, no, I don't know it, but I know Herman—"

"So you haven't discussed this with Mr. Diggs, whether they asked him to testify here today and what he may have said?"

"No. We've been busy," she says.

Tuchio can be sure that this was a tactical decision made by Harry and me. He could also be certain that we wouldn't share the rationale for this decision with Jennifer, for the very reason that if he asked her on the stand as he has, she would be able to say truthfully that she didn't know why she was here instead of Herman. Why force your witness to tell jurors to their face that you're trying to manipulate them?

Besides the fact that she discovered the envelope on the floor, something Herman couldn't testify to, is the simple fact that with a majority of women on the jury, she is the sympathetic witness, a woman on the stand testifying before women on the jury. Tuchio would have to use more restraint in the manner in which he attacked her on cross.

So now he feels free to damage us in other ways, planting the false seed, the innuendo, that perhaps Herman knew something, maybe about the way in which the letter and the hairs arrived at our office, and that therefore he either declined or was not permitted by Harry and me to testify.

When I look over, Harry is already working his cell phone under the table, sending a text message to Herman, telling him to come on over and join the party.

"Since you're not sure about the answer to that one, let me ask another question," says Tuchio. "When Mr. Madriani opened the envelope on his desk that morning—Monday, I believe—I think you testified that he pulled the bloody letter out of the envelope with a large pair of tweezers, not his hand, is that correct?"

"That's right."

"Why did he do this?"

Jennifer gives him a quizzical look. "I don't understand the question."

"What I mean is, when you open an envelope, don't you usually just reach in and take out whatever's inside? I mean, unless you think there's a bomb, or a snake, or a bloody letter in there, why would you go and get a pair of forceps before you even reached inside with your hand?"

"I think I testified that he did reach inside," she says.

"But he didn't take it out, not with his hand, did he?"

Jennifer hesitates.

"Did he?" he says. Tuchio knows I didn't, because my prints were not on the letter when the crime lab examined it.

"No. I think he may—"

"You've answered the question," he says. "The answer is no. So let me ask you a different question." He's starting to get into a rhythm. "I know you're not a lawyer," he says. "But you have worked on this case, right?"

"To some extent."

"You know what it's about, most of the evidence, right?"

"Some of it."

"Well, you know about the mysterious

missing item?" As he says this, Tuchio turns and looks back at me.

When she doesn't answer, he looks back to her. "The bloody letter?" he clarifies it for her.

"Yes."

"And the hair evidence, the strands of hair in the bathroom and on the chair at the scene."

"I know what I've read in the papers," she says. Jennifer's getting cautious now.

"That would be enough," he says. "If someone wanted to plant evidence—say, slip it under a lawyer's door, an item that was taken from the scene of a murder in order to show that the person who was charged didn't do the crime, and let's say there was evidence, clear, conclusive evidence that the defendant had in fact been at the scene of the crime—wouldn't that present a problem?"

"I guess I'm not following," says Jennifer.

"What I mean is, if we know that the defendant was at the scene and that the item was taken from the scene, doesn't it stand to reason that the defendant could have taken it in the first place, and if so, how does that clear him?"

"I'm going to object, Your Honor. Hypothetical questions. Counsel is asking the witness to speculate. She's not a lawyer. She's not a crime-scene-reconstruction expert."

"No, but she is here testifying as to how the envelope arrived at their office. The question doesn't go to her expertise, it goes to credibility. If she doesn't understand what may be happening here, then maybe she's in the clear."

What Tuchio is saying is maybe Jennifer thinks she is telling the truth and that she's being used, on the stand, for this reason.

"Overruled," says Quinn. "I'll allow it."

Tuchio restates the question without mentioning names. How could Carl be exonerated, cleared by the sudden and mysterious appearance of an item that was at the scene, when we know that Carl was at the scene?

"Well, if he didn't have the item when he was arrested and he's been in jail, how could he—"

"Deliver the item to your office?" Tuchio finishes the question for her. "Easy. He could have handed it off to someone else.

A friend, a family member, a *lawyer*," he says.

Jennifer shakes her head. "No. No . . . no."

"How would you know?" he says. "Are you familiar with every item, every scrap of paper, every scintilla and wisp of evidence in the files at your office? Do you know what's in everybody's desk drawers or for that matter what they might have in their possession outside of the office?"

"How could I?" she says. "That's not possible."

Harry is leaning back in his chair, running his hands through his hair, trying to catch her attention, get her to take a deep breath and to stop.

"My point exactly. All you actually know is what you've seen. Isn't that so?"

"That's all anybody knows," she says.

"Precisely."

"No," she says. "That can't . . . no. And what about the hair?" she says.

I glance over, and Harry rolls his eyes.

"Ah, now we get to the nub," he says. "The hair, isn't that convenient?"

She looks at him but doesn't answer.

"I mean, once you realize that simply

producing the item taken from the scene isn't going to do the trick, that you need something more, isn't it convenient that this something more, whatever it is, just happens to be in the same envelope?"

She doesn't answer.

"Well, isn't it? Convenient, I mean?"

"I don't know," she says.

"Well then, let me ask you one final question. Who stands to benefit the most from the items in the envelope that were slipped under your office door in the middle of the night? That should be an easy one," he says.

She looks at him.

"Come on now, isn't the answer obvious? Who else could possibly benefit? It's the defendant, Carl Arnsberg, Mr. Madriani's client, isn't it?"

"I don't know."

"You don't know?" His voice goes up a full octave from the first word to the last.

"I suppose," she says.

"You suppose?"

"Yes."

TWENTY-SEVEN

The next day, to avoid the media crush downstairs, Quinn allows Harry and me to slip out for lunch using the elevator reserved for judges and high court personnel, located in a back corridor behind chambers.

Jennifer's testimony regarding the package slipped under our door has resparked the electronic media's attention gap. Secrecy, "the bloody letter" wrapped in a possible scandal, how it turned up in our office—it now has them salivating.

By the time Harry, Herman, and I meet up at the pub downtown for lunch, news updates from the trial are going head-to-head with primary election returns.

We are seated at a table scarfing sandwiches, watching election numbers on Fox News on the television over the bar. We are eating fast, trying to clue Herman in on Jennifer's testimony and Tuchio's insinuation that for some reason we were keeping Herman out of court because he knew something about the envelope under the door.

"They're saying I did it. Put it under the door?"

"They can't be that stupid," says Harry. "By now the cops have to know that you were in Curaçao with us."

"Tuchio's trying to throw up smoke," I tell him.

"There is breaking news. . . . A report from San Diego and the Scarborough murder trial in just a moment. Are . . . are we ready? Okay, Howard, are you there?"

I ask the bartender to turn up the sound so we can hear it.

"I am here."

"Can you tell us what's happening?"

"All we know at this point is that Jennifer Sanchez, a twenty-two-year-old, alluring, dark-haired paralegal, took the stand this morning. She told the jury how she found a mysterious envelope on the floor in the law office where she works last Thursday morning."

"This is the defense lawyer, the man representing Carl Arnsberg, the defendant?"

"That's right."

"So I imagine the prosecution and the police are pretty suspicious at this point?"

"Suspicious is an understatement. According to sources close to the investigation, the police are so angry that there is talk that the D.A.'s office may ask for an investigation by the state bar. According to Ms. Sanchez, the envelope with whatever was inside of it was shoved under the office door sometime after eleven o'clock last Wednesday night."

"Do we know what's in the envelope?"

"So far there's no solid word from investigators on any of that. But according to the testimony, and what was shown in court today, apart from the envelope itself, the one that supposedly came under the door, there was a folded piece of paper, maybe several pages—we couldn't tell, because our producers weren't that close. The prosecutor kept referring to this as the 'bloody letter.'"

"The bloody letter!"

"That's what he said. Now, this could be important, because if you remember, two weeks ago this same defense lawyer, Paul Madriani, was able to get one of the prosecution's main witnesses, a forensics expert, to admit that there was evidence of something missing from the crime scene."

"I remember that, a leather briefcase or a binder. Something like that."

"No, actually, it was what the lawyer called a shadow left on the surface of a light leather portfolio by blood, what they call spatter evidence. It's a long, complicated story, but the bottom line is that the expert witness from the police crime lab was forced to admit that this blood shadow on the leather surface of the case meant that something was taken from the scene before the police got there. Then you have to step back about a week—"

"Make it quick, 'cuz we're comin' up on a hard break."

"As fast as I can. You remember the stories last week on the AP wire reporting that Scarborough was supposed to have had an important letter or some historic correspondence with him at the time he was murdered, and there was talk of a Supreme Court justice, Arthur Ginnis, being the possible source for this item?"

"And you think that's what this is all about?"

"We don't know, but it's certainly a possibility. We're checking it out."

"Listen, I gotta go."

"Catch you later."

"Keep us posted."

Harry gives me a sideways glance. "If we could just take out the part about the state bar investigation, maybe we get a copy of that and see if Quinn will let us put it in front of the jury. I mean, it doesn't have Ginnis's face in it, and it only mentions his name once."

Considering that the jurors are corralled in the courtroom in the daytime and locked up in a hotel all night with the television unplugged, the cable disconnected, and an armed guard outside their door, I'd take bets they aren't watching cable news.

It's the problem we're having. Before we're finished, everybody in the world is going to know about the Jefferson Letter and the Ginnis connection, except for the people who count—Carl's jury.

*   *   *

In the afternoon Harry and I bring Herman to the stand.

In rapid order I have Herman verify and corroborate Jennifer's earlier recollections, her testimony regarding the opening of the manila envelope in my office, and the processing of its contents.

Because we have not prepared Herman, there are a few discrepancies based on his memory of events. His testimony is a little ragged around the edges. But if anything this seems to work to our advantage. It sounds believable, unrehearsed, because it is. Herman uses different words than Jennifer did to describe things. He talks about "forceps" instead of "large tweezers."

Best of all, Herman does not try to fill in what he doesn't know: how it came to pass that I saw the letter inside the envelope and therefore avoided touching it with my hand. When I ask him this, he says he doesn't remember.

But he does remember seeing the look on my face. "At that moment," says Herman, "I thought there might be something dangerous in the envelope, because of the way you looked at it and the way you moved."

"So what were you thinking at that moment?"

"If you wanna know the truth, I was thinking it might be a letter bomb," says Herman. "It does happen. Happened to a lawyer in Atlanta last year," he tells the jury.

If we had warned Herman about Tuchio's pitch to the jury, that I avoided touching the letter because I already knew it was there, you get into problems. You could end up inspiring a witness to "remember" trivial details of things that never happened. Some people just want to help. But when it comes to details and the magnetic ability of the human mind to remember, there are limits to what a jury will believe. Anxiety over a possible bomb in a letter is not a problem.

Then I take him to the point, the reason he's here. "Before this morning did I or Mr. Hinds or anyone else in our office ever ask you to testify in these regards?"

"No. Not until Mr. Hinds contacted me this morning."

"Is there any reason why you might not want to testify regarding the manila envelope and the contents and how it was opened in my office?"

"No."

"So if someone were to tell the jury that you had been asked previously by Mr. Hinds or myself to testify in these regards, and they told the jury that you declined to do so, for some secret or unstated reason or for any reason, what would you say to that?"

"I would say they either didn't know what they were talking about or they were lying," says Herman. He looks at the jury. "It's not true."

Then I nail the lid on this coffin, asking Herman if he has any information or knowledge as to who might have slipped the evidence, the manila envelope, under our office door.

He shakes his head. "Not a clue," he says.

"Do you have any knowledge as to why they might have done it?"

"No."

I move to the evidence cart and lift the plastic sealed envelope, the folded letter, and the small bag so that Herman and the jury can see them. Quinn has them identified for the record.

"And to make clear to the jury, have you ever seen any of these items, or any of the evidence contained in them, before last Monday morning when I opened the contents of this envelope on the desk in my office?"

"No, sir. First time I saw any of that was after you opened that envelope."

"Your witness."

* * *

Tuchio tries to take Herman for the ride he took with Jennifer earlier in the day, over the same falls. That Herman knows only what he has seen and heard from Harry and me, and then the question: How can he be sure that he is not being badly used here in court today?

Herman looks the prosecutor in the eye. "I don't understand the question," says Herman. "So why don't you just say what you mean? Get it on the table," says Herman.

"Fine," says Tuchio. "How do you know that the evidence in that envelope wasn't put there by one of the lawyers in your own office, or by someone associated with or related to the defendant, Mr. Arnsberg?"

"Because I have known Mr. Madriani and Mr. Hinds for years, and I know that neither of them would ever do such a thing, that's how I know."

"But what you're saying is based on faith," says Tuchio, "not fact. You believe they wouldn't do it, but you don't know that?"

"Are you asking me?"

"Yes."

"*I* know it. Maybe *you* don't," says Herman.

The jury laughs.

"I'll have to ask you to forgive my natural cynicism," says Tuchio. "It comes from years of prosecuting cases."

"That's all right, I forgive you," says Herman.

A little laughter from the audience and more from the jury box.

Tuchio steps away from the witness. He ponders for a moment, and when he stops, he ends up at the evidence cart. He returns to the witness. He is now holding the clear plastic bag containing the Jefferson Letter. He holds it up, and he asks Herman, "Do you know what this is?"

Herman nods. "Yeah. It's the pages that Mr. Madriani took out of that envelope on Monday morning."

"That's not my question. My question is, do you know what the document is?"

"I know what it's called," says Herman.

"Objection, Your Honor."

"I haven't asked a question yet," says Tuchio.

"Ask your question," says the judge.

"If you know, can you please tell the jury what this document is called?"

"Objection. Exceeds the scope of direct, Your Honor."

"Sustained," says Quinn.

One of the rules of the road on cross-examination, a lawyer cannot ask questions that go beyond the bounds of the subject matter raised by his opponent during direct examination of the witness. Since I have not asked Herman or any other witness to tell the jury what the letter is called or to disclose any of its contents, Tuchio cannot simply pull this question out of his hand and play it like a trump card on cross.

He puts the bag with the letter down on a table near the witness. Herman glances at it, the item for which we have laid a quest for months, and Herman still doesn't know what it says. He has hinted a few times that his curiosity is burning. But Herman says he understands. He is confident there must be good reasons Harry and I are keeping the contents of the letter to ourselves. Still, it would take the spirit of a saint not to feel like the odd man out after all we've been through.

Then Tuchio edges into whether Herman feels awkward testifying on behalf of a defendant, a client with the kinds of associations of Carl Arnsberg, "the Aryan Posse," he says.

"I do my job," says Herman. "That's what it means to be professional."

"But it doesn't bother you? You never think about that."

"No."

This doesn't work, so Tuchio goes back to basics.

"You say Mr. Madriani and Mr. Hinds wouldn't be responsible for putting that envelope under the door, but what about Mr. Arnsberg? What about the defendant?"

Herman looks at Carl. "You're asking me my opinion?"

"Sure."

"I don't think he would do it either."

What else can Herman say?

"To save his life, you don't think Mr. Arnsberg would have a friend or a relative—let's leave Mr. Madriani and Mr. Hinds out of it—"

"Thanks for the courtesy," says Harry.

The jury laughs.

"Not at all," says Tuchio.

He turns back to the witness. "You don't think that to save his own life, Mr. Arnsberg would have a friend, someone he knows, slide that envelope and the contents under his lawyers' door? Is that what you're telling this jury?"

"If you're asking me my opinion, my answer is no, I don't."

Whether the jury will believe this, who knows? But the fact that Herman would say it, knowing Carl's native inclinations and his prior associations . . . And then suddenly, with this thought halfway through the cortex of my brain, I realize where Tuchio is going.

"Would you tell the jury what that opinion is based on? Your considerable opinion of Mr. Arnsberg?"

"Your Honor, I'm going to object. This exceeds the scope of direct. The witness is not here as a character witness. He's here solely for the purpose of refuting the false implication raised by Mr. Tuchio that the witness refused or declined to testify because he was supposed to have some secret knowledge about that envelope, which he does not."

"Nah, nah, nah. Bring it up here," says Quinn.

We end up at the side of the bench.

"Your Honor, this witness was brought in here for a very narrow purpose, and Mr. Tuchio knows it. If he wants to cross-examine the witness as to what he saw in the office that day, the day the envelope was opened, fine, but getting into the defendant's character is way off base."

"The witness is on the stand," says Tuchio. "He's testified as to what he says he saw when the envelope was opened. He claims he never saw any of it before. Now he says he doesn't believe that Mr. Arnsberg would have anything to do with slipping it under the door or having friends do it. That's all fair game," he says. "And I have the right to test the witness's credibility, Your Honor."

"Objection overruled," says Quinn.

Just like that, we're back out. Tuchio is one of the craftiest lawyers I've ever met. We didn't deliver the right witness to him this morning, so he baited us, laid inferences that we were compelled to refute so that he could get Herman in here on the stand. I know where he's going, and there's nothing I can do about it.

"Where was I? Oh, yes. You stated that you don't believe that Mr. Arnsberg would have anything to do with putting that envelope under your office door. Is that correct?"

"That's right."

"What is that opinion based on? Your considerable opinion of Mr. Arnsberg?"

"You get to know someone. You talk to them. You generally get a feel for them."

"Intuition?" says Tuchio.

"If you want to call it that."

"Let me ask you, how well do you know Carl Arnsberg?"

"I don't know. I've known him for some months now."

"Have you ever gone to his house for dinner?"

Herman looks at him and smiles. "He's been in jail since I met him. You know that."

"Of course. Have you ever been to his parents' house for dinner?"

Tuchio plays the racial divide.

"Can't say as I have."

"Have you met his parents?"

"I've talked to Carl's father. I don't think I've ever met his mother."

"Have you ever met any of Carl's friends, his associates?" Tuchio smiles as he says this.

You can see where he is taking it, and there are a dozen intersecting avenues once he gets there. Set Herman up and ask him about the Posse, Carl's buddies. Oh, and by the way, what do you think they might do to you if they got you out on the reserve alone? If that doesn't get the witness's juices flowing, Tuchio will trout out the "traitor to your race" theme.

"I don't think I ever met any of his friends," says Herman.

"So, during the course of your investigation, your work on this case— You have done work on this case?"

"Some," says Herman.

"During the course of that work, you never had occasion to interview any of the friends or associates of the defendant?"

By now Herman has seen it and scoped out the terrain.

"You're talking about the Aryan Posse?" He deals with it in the way Herman deals with everything, directly. "And you want to know why the firm didn't send an African American investigator out to interview the members of the organization?"

"It was on my mind," says Tuchio. But this is not exactly the way he would have approached it.

"Well, first off, your question assumes that these are Carl's friends, and to be honest, I don't know that."

"We'll get to that later," says Tuchio. "For the moment let's just stick to the question of why your firm didn't send you out to the reserve, to interview members of the Aryan Posse? If they weren't his friends, they certainly *knew* your client."

This is what Tuchio has wanted to get at all day.

"Well, it ain't rocket science," says Herman. "Some people might think that if I went out there, I might not come back."

Full-out laughter from the jury box. Belly laughs from two of the bailiffs.

"So the thought was that if you went out there, harm might come to you."

"No, you got it wrong," says Herman. "Harm never comes to you unless you go looking for it."

This of course is the answer to the

prosecutor's question, but Tuchio doesn't like it.

"Still, you just said that if you went out there, there was a chance you might not come back?"

"There's always the chance, but there's one thing you can be sure of."

"What's that?" says Tuchio.

"If I didn't come back, it wasn't 'cuz I joined up," says Herman.

More laughter from the box. Some of the deputies are turning toward the walls they're laughing so hard.

Tuchio is getting tired of Herman's one-liners.

So he tries to go frontal with him.

"Let's cut to the chase. Let's make it clear for the jury," he says. "The reason your firm didn't want to send you, an African American, out to the reserve to talk with the Aryan Posse was that they knew it wasn't safe. Isn't that a fact?"

"I thought that's what I just said."

"So those are dangerous people as far as you're concerned? The Aryan Posse?"

"Let me put it this way—"

"No. No. Just answer the question. Yes or no," says Tuchio.

"That kind of rigid attitude will give you ulcers," says Herman.

"Don't worry about my ulcers, just answer the question," says Tuchio.

"But I do worry," says Herman. "People like you get ulcers and screw up, and then people like me get sent out to the Aryan reserve undercover."

More laughter. Two of the deputies out in the audience, faces red as beets, are laughing their way toward a coronary.

"That doesn't answer my question," says Tuchio.

No, but the jurors are rolling around like bowling balls in the box. There's nothing that can kill a serious prosecution faster than laughter. Herman is loose on the stand, and Tuchio is starting to feel like he's center stage at Comedy Club Central.

"The Aryan Posse, are they dangerous people? Yes or no?"

"I can't answer that question."

"Yes or no?" says Tuchio.

"I'm not gonna answer the question yes or no." Herman sits in the chair, dwarfing it, his arms folded, and his lips clenched like those of a third-grader refusing to eat his carrots, all 285 pounds of him.

"Answer the question," says Tuchio.

"You want an answer, I'll give you an answer. I just can't answer it yes or no. You don't want an answer, I'll go home. Either way is fine by me," says Herman.

"Your Honor, I'd ask that the court direct the witness to answer the question," says Tuchio.

"He's offering to answer the question, Your Honor. Counsel won't let him," I say.

"Let the witness answer the question," says Quinn.

"Answer it!" says Tuchio.

"I don't know whether the Aryan Posse is dangerous or not. How can I say that everybody, just because they belong to a group, is dangerous or not dangerous? The reason I wasn't sent out there wasn't necessarily that they were dangerous— though they might be, I don't know—but the reason was because the purpose of an investigation is to get information. What do you think those people are gonna tell me when I get out there on the white man's reservation? You think they're gonna open their souls and tell me their secrets? You believe that, then you're no cynic," says Herman. "You gotta either be terminally stupid or the reincarnation of Mahatma Gandhi."

This brings the roof down around Tuchio's ears. Even the judge is laughing.

Tuchio clears his throat, looks around a little, and waits for the laughter to die, but it doesn't. He looks at Herman and considers whether there might be another tack to take. Finally he just shakes his head.

"No further questions." You can barely hear it as he walks back to the counsel table.

TWENTY-EIGHT

When Harry and I arrived at the court-house just after eight in the morning, groups were already starting to form out-side. The carnival atmosphere was gone, driven off by tension in the air, like an ap-proaching army, a sense of siege, a feel-ing that the moment had arrived.

Even with the secrecy imposed by the judge's guillotine, Plato Quinn's gag order looming over all our heads, the press has now punctured the seal. Fragments of in-formation concerning the infamous letter are beginning to surface, stories running on cable news and the networks.

By the time we get to the courtroom, Ruiz, the clerk, is busy waving all the lawyers down the hall toward the judge's chambers. When we get there, Quinn is standing in the middle of the room leaning against the front edge of his desk, watching the television. He puts a finger to his lips to keep us quiet as we file in.

". . . news that a copy of the letter was found, what undisclosed sources are now referring to as the 'Jefferson Letter.' It is being described by unnamed sources as a document of 'immense historic importance.'"

It is one of the cable channels. The reporter holding the microphone is staring intently into the camera as he stands in front of the Capitol building in Washington.

"The trial of Carl Arnsberg, a reputed neo-Nazi, for the murder of author Terry Scarborough has been ongoing now for nearly five months. The trial has been hotly covered by the media both here and abroad. Scarborough's best-selling book Perpetual Slaves, *based on the historic lan-*

guage of slavery in the Constitution and dealing with modern race relations, has been an international bestseller for nearly a year. The book sparked racial violence in at least five cities during the forty-seven days that Scarborough was on tour, before he was murdered.

"It was reported last week, and confirmed by court testimony yesterday, that an item of evidence missing from the scene of Scarborough's murder, and presumably taken by the killer, has surfaced and had somehow been delivered to the law offices of Madriani and Hinds in Southern California. Madriani and Hinds are the lawyers representing the defendant, Carl Arnsberg.

"However, the information disclosed late last night that the item of evidence in question may be the reputed Jefferson Letter places a whole new dimension on the trial.

"Members of Congress are now weighing in. With reports that the letter may contain damaging information regarding African slavery at the time of the American Revolution, information never previously revealed, there are deep concerns in Congress and in the White House that disclosure of this information could spark renewed and broader racial violence.

"This is Howard Chamrow reporting from Washington."

They cut back to the studio.

"Tom, do we have anything more on this?"

"This story seems to be growing by the minute. According to wire-service stories, the Congressional Black Caucus is now demanding immediate federal action to investigate whether or not the reports are accurate and, if in fact there is a Jefferson Letter, that it be secured by the FBI to make sure that it doesn't get lost or destroyed.

"And there were also reports, though these are older, that there may be some connection, though it's very vague, between some kind of a letter, though it's not clear that it's the Jefferson Letter, and a member of the United States Supreme Court, Arthur Ginnis. But as I say, those reports were filed last week.

They're very sketchy, and we haven't heard anything more about this since, so it may have just been rumor. I'm hearing, according to one source, that Justice Ginnis, who is off the Court on sick leave right now, is a history buff and is considered something of a scholar on Jefferson's papers, so it may be that someone simply contacted him at some point to check this out and that may be his only connection. We're just not sure."

With this last little bit, Quinn looks over at me, a mass of wrinkled eyebrows.

I'm having the same thought, wondering if perhaps the video of Scarborough and Ginnis over the table and Teddy Nons's transcript of their conversation are all just part of a bad dream.

They switch to another story, and Quinn turns off the set.

"Close the door," he says.

Five of us are in the room. Tuchio and Harmen, his assistant. Harry, myself, and Quinn.

"First question," says Quinn, "is who leaked the information? Unless somebody raises a hand in the next second or so, I am going to assume that it was nobody in this room." He waits for a few beats, looks at each of us and says, "At least *that's* good news.

"Next order of business, I want to secure the letter, have it locked up in a safe place. Since it's already been examined by forensics, is there any objection to working with a copy off the evidence cart from now on?"

I look at Harry. He shrugs. We all agree.

"Good. Then I'm gonna lock it up. I'll have the county treasurer put it in their vault in a locked box."

"As long as the evidence is preserved," I tell him. "In the event of an appeal or retrial."

"I'll make sure of that," says the judge. "Next," he says. "How many of you have copies of the letter?"

I raise my hand. Tuchio raises his.

"You each have one?"

"As far as I know," says Tuchio. "Nobody else in my office has one. I don't know about the crime lab."

"Find out," says the judge. "You, Mr.

Madriani. Do your forensics people have one?"

"I don't know."

"Find out," he says.

"I want every copy that was made of that letter secured by you, Mr. Tuchio, and you, Mr. Madriani. I want them locked up in a safe. I don't want your staff reading it, and if they already have read it, I don't want them talking to anyone about it. Find out," he says. "Do I make myself clear?"

Nothing but nodding heads in the room.

"When you leave here, call your offices immediately. Have them locate every copy that was made. Then I want to know, by three o'clock this afternoon, how many there are. And make sure you get them all.

"And I'm holding you responsible. If the crime lab has copies, if your forensics experts have copies, get 'em back. I don't want to see anything more regarding the contents of that letter on television, and I don't want to read about it in the newspapers, not until I decide whether what's written on those pages is gonna come into evidence or whether it's not." He looks at his watch.

"Is there some question about that?" I ask.

"About what?" he says.

"About the contents of the letter coming into evidence?" I say.

"It's something we're going to have to talk about," says Quinn. "I think it's pretty clear to all of us at this point that we don't have much time. Pretty soon I have a feeling that I'm going to be up to my hips in federal agents, U.S. Attorneys, and federal court orders, so the sooner we can wrap this trial the better.

"Are you ready with your witnesses?" He looks at me.

I nod.

"Good, then let's get movin'," he says.

Tuchio and Harmen are out of their chairs, moving toward the door. Quinn is wrestling with his robe, struggling to get it on, running over me, as I try to get in his way.

"Your Honor, before we leave, I have to know whether I'm going to be allowed to introduce the contents of that letter into evidence and, if not, what your legal basis is for denying admission."

He looks at his watch as he's trying to

move around me. "Not now," he says. "This afternoon we'll talk about it."

"You got that, Mr. Tuchio?"

"Got it, Your Honor."

"I'll be prepared by then to entertain all arguments. If we need time for points and authorities"—he's already heading down the hall toward the bench—"it can be arranged. Otherwise I'll be prepared to enter a ruling on the restaurant video and the contents of the letter at that time. Now, let's go."

* * *

By ten o'clock, before the midmorning break, you can hear the drumbeat, the resonant pounding like that of Zulu warriors striking spears against their shields on the street outside. Periodically there is the electronic bleep and blare of an emergency vehicle.

Through all this we work with our witness. Fortunately, he is solid.

Robert Stepro is our resident forensics expert, the man who accompanied the envelope and its contents to the crime lab and watched as they processed and examined the bloodied side of the letter and the samples of hair.

This morning Stepro is equipped with enlarged photographs, taken with a macro lens and mounted on poster board, so that minute specks of blood appear the size of a nickel.

I sense that Tuchio has the feeling of a big-league baseball manager, ahead on the scoreboard but with the game about to be called on account of rain.

With the commotion growing outside and the risk that we may have to evacuate the courthouse, Tuchio tells the judge that he's prepared to stipulate that the bloodied surface of the letter matches the shadow on the leather portfolio and that the letter is in fact the item taken from Scarborough's hotel room that morning.

I insist on presenting at least the principal evidence, a prima facie case, so that there is no doubt in the minds of jurors when they go in to deliberate.

It's clear that Tuchio does not intend to contest either this or the hair evidence contained in the envelope. His forensics experts have told him that any dispute over these items is a nonstarter.

It's also clear that Tuchio has already settled on a changed theory: two killers

working in tandem, Carl and a blond compatriot who slipped the envelope under our
office door in the middle of the night. He
will no doubt embellish this with hints of
complicity by our office in order to tip the
scales enough that jurors will excuse the
inconsistencies in his own case.

* * *

In a period of less than two hours, Stepro,
using his poster-board photographs on an
easel in front of the jury, nails down the
comparison evidence of the shadowed
leather portfolio and the bloodied letter.
The pattern of blood on the back of the
letter at the edges where paper meets
leather matches perfectly with spots of
blood on the portfolio.

You would not have to be a scientist to
see that, magnified many times, traces
of blood—numerous, minute, oblong
ringlets—had been severed by the covering edge of the paper. When the letter was
placed back in the shadowed rectangle on
the portfolio, these detached ovals were
once again complete.

When asked for his opinion, Stepro
states, "Better than any fingerprint, the
complexity of the pattern and the countless

intersecting matches between paper and leather put the issue beyond any possible doubt. The four folded pieces of paper were without question the object that created the shadow on leather."

Stepro also testifies that examination of the paper reveals that the documents, the four pages, were stapled only one time. Further microscopic inspection of the staple at the folds in the metal where it was bent and closed to bind the pages indicates that it was probably driven in by an electric stapling machine and that, because of the tight closure, it is his opinion that no pages were removed or appear to be missing.

Finally I ask him about fingerprints on the pages and whether any were found.

"We found several fingerprints. I believe there were at least thirty-two full or partial prints on the four pages."

"Were you able to lift these, and were you able to identify whom they belonged to?"

"We lifted all of them, and they all belonged to the same person, the victim, Terrance Scarborough."

Ginnis knew exactly what he was doing

in the video when he refused to touch the letter over the dinner table in the restaurant. When he finally reached out to dispose of the letter, to get it off the table, he did it with the butter knife, flipping the pages back to Scarborough.

According to Stepro, and included in the police crime lab's report, is the finding that four small bloody spots on the folded surface of the letter, the spattered side, as well as a single blood spot on the reverse side, show traces of fiber transfer, similar to the spots found on and inside Scarborough's attaché case, evidence of the blood-soaked cotton gloves of the killer.

When I finish with the witness, Tuchio gets up and asks a single question: whether the witness, during the course of his examination of the four pages, examined the writing or read the contents of the communication written on them.

The judge nearly swallows his tongue.

Before I can even object, the witness responds and says, "No. I was instructed by my client not to read the contents of the correspondence for the reason that it was confidential."

"No further questions." Tuchio takes his seat.

That he would pop this question in this way tells me two things. One is that Tuchio is as convinced as I am, despite what Quinn may be saying, that the contents of the Jefferson Letter will at some point be admitted into evidence and read to the jury. Second is that if it must come in, Tuchio would prefer that it come in now, before the defense has completed presenting its case. He's hoping that this might dissipate its effect. Or at least remove it as far as possible from the point of deliberations so that its impact on the jury will be lessened, once they're sedated a bit by the passage of time, closing arguments, and other evidence.

* * *

For the first time I can recall, ever in a trial, the judge has lunch brought in for the lawyers. With the pressure on, he's not letting any of us out of the courthouse. He tells court staff to stay close, to eat in the cafeteria. The race to a restaurant is not worth the risk of the melee outside, and Quinn wants everybody back in court by one o'clock.

* * *

A little past noon, and the rhythmic pounding of demonstrators, the ceaseless chants and yelling, against the pitched wail of electronic sirens outside, has the constancy and power of roiling surf.

It seems to overwhelm, until I realize that there are at least six solid walls of reinforced concrete between those of us in the building and the hell that is happening out on the street. I cannot fathom what the bedlam must sound like there.

Every few minutes Quinn takes reports from one of the senior bailiffs, updating him on the situation on the street in the event that it becomes necessary to evacuate the building. So far there have been no shots fired and no fatalities, but eight officers have been hospitalized and an untold number of civilians have been caught up in the burgeoning battle and injured.

According to the bailiff, a delegation from the local chapter of the NAACP and the National Lawyers Guild have appealed for calm, while another group has appeared at the courthouse's main entrance and demanded a copy of the Jefferson Letter. One of the deputies, a lieutenant, told them that he would relay their request to the judge, who would take it under advisement.

*   *   *

By one o'clock we're back in the courtroom. Quinn is running a taut ship at this point, hustling to get the case to the jury before the folks outside can burn the building down. His biggest fear is more revelations regarding the letter. But sooner or later it has to come out.

*   *   *

Our last two witnesses are both educators, one more surprise for Tuchio and, if the letter comes in, what may prove to be a hideous shocker for the nation.

Kathy Lafair is a teacher who also holds a joint degree in clinical and educational psychology and has been tucked into our witness list for months. She has given us nothing in writing that we would have to turn over to the prosecution, though Harry and I know what she will say.

Lafair teaches classes in the evenings at a school in the eastern area of the county. It is part of an extension program for special education, serving adults who dropped out of school when they were kids due to learning disabilities and who now find themselves locked out of the system because they lack basic skills.

Under oath and on the stand, she tells the jury that with counseling, encouragement, and sometimes one-on-one tutoring, some of these adults can find their way back to the dreams they once had as children, to learn and to enjoy more productive lives.

Sadly, however, this was not the case for Carl Arnsberg.

Harry was the one who discovered the problem, and he felt bad about it. He'd made a wisecrack about Carl early in the case, just after the three of us had met for the first time at the jail.

Harry and I were talking, and the issue was whether Scarborough's book might have set Carl off, especially if he were a nutcase. Harry brushed it aside with one of his glib comments.

The comment came back to haunt him two weeks later in a meeting with Carl to go over some items of evidence delivered to us by the D.A.'s office. By that time Harry had some suspicions, but he wasn't sure. He handed Carl a slip of paper and told him to take a look at it. Harry was busy hunting for other documents in his briefcase.

Carl picked up the slip of paper, studied it for a few seconds, and then put it down.

Harry regarded Carl and said, "What do you think?"

"Oh, it's fine. Looks good."

The half slip of paper was a form with some printing on it and some boxes to be checked. Two of the boxes had X's typed in them. It was the charging document for "special circumstances"—the legal justification, and the basis if he is convicted, for the State of California to execute Carl Everett Arnsberg.

Carl is illiterate. It's not that he has difficulty reading. He can't read a word. He never told us, didn't say anything. Carl has been hiding this from people all his life. We didn't know the full story until he gave us the name of Kathy Lafair.

This morning she sits on the stand and smiles at him.

Carl's head is down. He glances up at her every once in a while, but he won't

look her in the eye. Kathy Lafair is just another reminder of failure in Carl's life, one
of many.

"Can you tell the jury how you came to
know the defendant, Carl Arnsberg?" I ask
her.

"He was one of my students," she says.
"For about six weeks. Three times a week
at night, he would come to classes."

"And what did you teach?"

"Basic reading comprehension."

"Can you tell the jury what that is?"

"It's what you call beginner's reading.
What you would normally teach to children
in kindergarten and first grade."

"Was Carl able to read at all?"

"No." She looks over at him. "Carl, you
shouldn't be ashamed. It's not your fault."

"Your Honor, I'm going to object to this."
Tuchio is up out of his chair. "If she wants
to testify, that's fine. But to be having conversations with the defendant . . ."

"Mr. Tuchio, relax," says the judge. "Sit
down." He looks at the witness. "Go ahead,
Mr. Madriani."

"When you say he couldn't read, did he
have the ability to comprehend any words

typed or written on a page? For example, could he recognize his own name if it were printed or typed?"

"No."

"And you know this for a fact?"

"I do."

"Before we go any further, can you tell the court what degrees or special training you have?"

"I hold a bachelor's degree in education from the University of California at Berkeley and a master's degree in clinical and educational psychology from UCLA."

"As a clinical and educational psychologist, can you tell the jury what you do?"

"I do a good deal of testing. I administer standardized tests and conduct evaluations."

"To what purpose do you do this?"

"To determine whether students suffer from any recognized learning disabilities. It's diagnostic. There's a wide range of learning disabilities, from hyperactivity and attention deficit disorder to autism and dyslexia and more," she says.

"And how long have you been doing this?"

"Twenty-two years."

"Did you have occasion to conduct any tests on the defendant, Carl Arnsberg?"

"I did."

"When?"

"Let's see. That would have been about two years ago."

"So the tests were not performed in connection with this case?"

"No. They were related to his schooling."

This is important, to avoid a claim by the prosecution that we had tests conducted and failed to disclose the results in discovery.

"And as a result of these tests, were you able to determine whether Carl suffered from any known or recognized learning disability?"

"Yes. He suffers from dyslexia."

"Can you tell the jury what that is?"

"Dyslexia manifests itself in an inability to process certain visual signals, usually symbols, letters, and written words. It can affect verbal abilities as well, but that's not as common."

"Is it curable? Can it be treated?"

"Not in the ordinary sense. You can't prescribe medication for it. There's no pill you can take. It can be overcome in some cases, but depending on the severity it can be very difficult, very frustrating, and in some cases it can take years. Basically what you're doing is therapy, educational intervention, but it's usually more effective in early childhood. The older the person is, the more difficult it may be to treat."

"What about in Carl's case?"

"Carl had a problem," she says. "Because no one knew he suffered from dyslexia. He managed to hide it very well. His parents didn't know. He didn't know himself until he was tested and diagnosed in our office."

"And how old was he then?"

"I think he was twenty or twenty-one years old."

"So he went all the way through school with dyslexia, and he never knew it."

"Unfortunately, that's not uncommon, especially years ago. It went undiagnosed in many cases."

"Can you explain to the jury what it's like to suffer from dyslexia?"

"The best example I can give," she says, "is a ciphering machine. It would be as if every written message that you received was enciphered in a code and everyone else in the world was given a decoding machine, except you. They would be getting and sending messages constantly. You would be getting messages, but you wouldn't be able to understand any of them. And you wouldn't be able to send any either, because you didn't understand how to encode them."

"So I imagine that would be very frustrating."

"That's the problem," she says. "It's the frustration and constant anxiety that generally overwhelms the person. But it's a very slow, agonizing process."

"How do you mean?"

She explains that it generally starts in childhood when the sufferer is just beginning to socialize with other children. As they all begin school, the other children progress, because the learning process is so heavily dependent upon reading skills. This leaves the person suffering from dyslexia looking at those around him and wondering why they're progressing and he's not. This results in a multitude of other problems—acting out in an effort to compensate for the inability to learn, aggression, feelings of inadequacy, depression, a whole range of psychological problems. "Depending on the child, many of these attendant problems become worse as the child gets older with major problems in adolescence, in the teenage years."

"Can the frustration result in violence?"

"It can, and there are many documented cases of this. Studies show that a considerable number of inmates incarcerated in correctional facilities suffer from dyslexia. Of course, it's not possible to know how their lives might have changed had this been diagnosed in early childhood and the disorder remedied."

"Does dyslexia have anything to do with intelligence, how smart or how bright a person may be?"

"Albert Einstein suffered from dyslexia. Does that answer your question? There is absolutely no correlation at all between intelligence and dyslexia. Go online sometime and check the lists of names—celebrities, inventors, writers. Agatha Christie, if you can imagine. Alexander Graham Bell and Thomas Edison were both dyslexic."

"How do you account for the fact that some people are able to cope with and overcome the disorder and others aren't?"

"That's impossible to say. In some cases it may have to do with the severity of the disorder. In others it may have more to do with the fact that they had someone around them in their early developmental years who was willing and able to spend the enormous amount of time that is required to overcome dyslexia."

"With regard to Carl, based on your testing and evaluation, can you tell the jury how severe the dyslexia was in his case?"

"Severe. On a scale of one to ten, with ten being the most severe, I would rate Carl at nine."

I walk to the evidence cart and collect Scarborough's book, *Perpetual Slaves*. I show the witness the cover. I call her attention to the bold lettering, the title. In your opinion, if I were to show this to Carl, the title of this book, would he be able to read it?"

She shakes her head. "I don't mean this in a bad way, Carl." Then she looks back at me. "There isn't a chance."

"And if there was some correspondence—say, a letter, a handwritten
letter—and I told Carl to go and find that
letter, would he have the ability to distinguish that letter based on the writing from
other letters and correspondence that
might be at that location?"

"No."

"Thank you. Your witness."

Tuchio gets up, looks at the witness.
"Ms. Lafair, is it?"

"Yes."

"Would the defendant's condition, dyslexia, interfere with his ability to watch television or process visual images such as
video, news programs, things like that?"

"Generally, no. But if there was any writing on the screen, he wouldn't be able to
read it."

"But he could understand the sounds
coming from the television, the spoken
words and the pictorial images?"

"Generally, yes."

"Let me ask you about the hypothetical
situation that Mr. Madriani raised, the
handwritten letter in the room and the defendant's ability to distinguish it from other
correspondence. Let me give you a little

variation on the theme. If there was a handwritten letter in that room and the letter in question was written in a unique color of ink, say, a tobacco color, brown as opposed to blue or black. If I told Carl to go and get the letter written in the brown ink and there was no other letter written in that color ink, would he be able to distinguish that letter from other letters?"

"Dyslexia generally doesn't affect the ability to distinguish colors."

"So he would be able to distinguish in that case?"

"In the circumstances that you outlined, yes."

"I have no further questions, Your Honor."

Tuchio has taken half of the loaf away from me. He will argue that it didn't matter that Carl couldn't read Scarborough's book, because what fired him up and sent him over the edge were the television interviews with the victim. And as for the letter, if he knew the color of the ink, he would be able to find the Jefferson Letter. Of course, this begs the question: Why would someone suffering from severe dyslexia *want* a handwritten letter, especially if it had no intrinsic value because it was a copy, not the original?

* * *

The end of the day, and we do battle in chambers over Quinn's desk. There are two issues, the restaurant videotape showing Ginnis and Scarborough quibbling over the letter spread out on the middle of the table and the Jefferson Letter itself.

To be honest, it's a hard call. The video, if Quinn would let me have it, shows the victim with Ginnis across the table, as well as the letter in the middle between them. With a little maneuvering room, Teddy Nons's transcript, and a few carefully timed winks and twitches as the jury watches the video, it wouldn't be difficult to get them leaning in the right direction, into Ginnis's lap over dinner.

The only problem is, I promised them a shocker in my opening statement, and moving pictures of Ginnis, even with a scowl, isn't going to cut it. And there's no group on earth less forgiving than twelve angry people sleeping in hotel rooms who have been promised a punch line that isn't delivered.

Right out of the box, Quinn is worried

that disclosure regarding the contents of the letter is the equivalent of tossing jet fuel on a fire.

"Can you guarantee that there won't be violence if that letter is read?" Quinn is looking at me.

But Tuchio pipes up first. "Besides, there is no way to know whether the letter is authentic."

"Let me suggest that we put the letter aside for the moment and take up the question of the video," I tell them.

"Well, there's no basis for that to come in at all," says Tuchio. "It's hearsay, and there's still no foundation. Good luck," he says.

I go back to my original argument that it's all one big package; pictures of the letter in the video serve to verify that the two documents, the one in the video and the item taken from the murder scene, are the same thing. Since the video shows the interested players huddled over the item, why not let the jury in on the secret so that everybody knows?

There's not the slightest chance in the world that Quinn is going to go for this, and before I can lean back in my chair, he says so. "The video's off the table. It's not coming in."

Precisely, and since every judge wants to play Solomon, we're down to the basic questions: What part of the baby is he willing to give me, and how do we sever it?

"We could stay here and argue all night," I say. "But Mr. Tuchio made a point, and I think it's a good one."

"You agree with something Tuchio said?" Quinn stares at me.

"At this particular moment, I'm tired, Your Honor. Forgive me."

"No, that's all right. What were these words of wisdom?"

"The question of authenticity. We will stipulate to the fact that there's no way we can prove that the letter is authentic, but that's not really at issue here."

"It sure is," says Tuchio.

"No, the letter is physical evidence taken from the scene of a murder. The presumption, and it's a reasonable one, is that the killer took it. The unanswered question is why. Now, if the pages on that paper were blank, there wouldn't be an issue. We would have to tell the jury that the idiot took blank paper. Except they aren't blank.

There are words on them. But here's the kicker. We're not offering those words to prove the truth of what is stated in the letter, so there's no issue of hearsay. The question goes to motive. Why did the killer take the letter in the first place, and that's a question of fact for the jury."

Quinn is following all this. "He's right."

"No," says Tuchio. "He's not. There's still a question of authenticity. Is the letter real?"

"No," I say. "In this setting, as a matter of law, it doesn't matter whether it's real. The killer took it because he had a reason to take it. That reason is an issue for the jury."

"Well, why do you think he took it?" says Tuchio.

"That's for me to know and you to find out. There is a question of authenticity, but it doesn't have anything to do with the law," I say. "Or this case. It has to do with public safety."

And here comes the hook for Quinn. "There are probably a few thousand people out there who'd like to set fire to this building right now, and God knows how many other buildings around the county.

And when they find out what's in that letter, they're going to want to redouble their efforts. Those are the people who should be concerned about the authenticity of the letter.

"So let me make a suggestion. Tomorrow you turn off the lights in the courtroom and we go dark. The eyes of the world are on this place right now. The federal government is threatening to come and take the letter away. The court sends out a press release tonight, to every media outlet it can find. In the press release, you tell the world that there is a letter. It purports to be in the hand of Jefferson, but the court cannot verify whether the letter is real or not. Furthermore we may never be able to answer the question of whether it's real, because we don't have the original; we don't know where it is or whether it even exists. That should pour cold water on hot heads. When they realize that the party favor may not pop, that there's no *there* there, we can hope their feet will get sore from standing around and they'll go home. If we're lucky."

"Or," says Tuchio, "the court could order

that the letter not be read in court. Much simpler," he says.

"But to draw the jury right to the edge of the railing," I tell Quinn, "to produce evidence of blood-spattered paper and to argue in closing that this paper is the reason the victim was murdered without telling them what was written on it is to invite them to take out their disappointment on the defendant."

"No, I like Mr. Madriani's idea," says Quinn. "Besides, his analysis on the law is right. There's no legal basis to keep the letter out. If I let you convince me to do that, and you convict his client, it's just going to get overturned on appeal. Waste of time and money. On top of that, whether the letter gets read here or someplace else, the problem is the same—fires all over. So as long as I still have the letter, why don't we do something judicious with it?"

There's a knock on the door. It opens, and the bailiff sticks his head in. "Your Honor, the governor's on the phone."

"The governor?"

"Yeah, they got a *big* problem up in

South Central L.A. He wants to talk to you."

"Man has a problem. And I have a solution. Good timing!" says Quinn. "Is my secretary out there?"

"No." The bailiff is halfway down the hall. "She went home."

He looks at me. "You any good at writing press releases? I have to take a phone call."

TWENTY-NINE

We have rested our case. The trial of Carl Arnsberg is over, and so we await the verdict.

I'm home watching television. It's nighttime, the courthouse is closed, but the sky is lit up. Two of the buses used to barricade the front of the building are burning, black smoke spiraling into the sky. People have been gathering since after the revelations of the letter, and now thousands of demonstrators have converged on the courthouse. They have smashed windows on storefronts and set fire to vehicles. There is talk of calling out the National

Guard. Riots have broken out in Detroit and Chicago, and so far three people are dead.

There is now concern that when the rest of the world wakens to news of the Jefferson Letter and the pictures of violence in America, mayhem may spread and go international. There are preparations being made in some of the nations of Africa and on the island of Haiti, where martial law has already been declared.

All the best-laid plans went forth, Quinn's press release went out to the world. The problem was, the world wasn't listening, or at least the media world wasn't. The release was nothing negative, nothing terrible. They treated it like a footnote to a nonstory. The impending reading of the Jefferson Letter was much more exciting, promising better ratings and better revenue. The governor went on the air and emphasized the points in the release. They ran fifteen-second clips between weather and sports. By then the rioters weren't home watching television—they were out on the street burning cars.

Having Quinn's courtroom go dark for twenty-four hours only served to delay the inevitable. Angry minds were already on the streets. The delay in releasing the letter, rather than quell the mob, seemed to fire their passions. When the letter was finally released, the revelations surpassed even their wildest suspicions.

*   *   *

To read the letter to the jury, Harry and I employed the talents of an antiquarian and historian, a professor from Stanford who was an expert on the colonial period. Rather than lending credence to the letter, the witness testified that he could not verify the authenticity of the writing based on the copy. He stated that while the handwriting certainly appeared genuine, he was guarded, in that certain stylistic features in the letter and word usage left him harboring doubt. At one point he went so far as to say he was dubious. Then he read and explained the contents of the letter to the jury.

*   *   *

First was the revelation that some of the Founding Fathers, most notably John Adams and Benjamin Franklin, while publicly excoriating the practice of slavery and rebuking the slave trade, were in fact profiting from it through secret investments with northern shipowners whose vessels regularly carried slaves. Together with Jefferson, who owned slaves all his life, the three men carefully choreographed a political theater for the public and for posterity that allowed them to posture during debates over independence. This dance included a vigorous fight to retain language in the Declaration of Independence that would have ended slavery in the new nation—a fight that of course the three revered founders lost.

But the worst part was reserved for the last three pages of the letter.

If true, this revelation so tarnishes the experiment in American liberty as to unmask it as a virtual fraud.

Based on its contents, the letter was written by Jefferson in 1787, in Paris, where he was serving as ambassador to France. Under instructions contained in the letter itself, it was carried by a private courier and personally delivered to Adams and Franklin, who at the time were heavily involved in the framing of the Constitution. Also according to instructions in the letter, neither Adams nor Franklin was allowed to retain the letter, only to read it. The original and only copy was then returned by the courier to Jefferson in Paris, where presumably it remained with his papers in his private library until he returned home to Virginia.

The letter was intended to press Adams and Franklin on the issue of slavery and to ensure that the practice would not be abolished in the Constitution. Jefferson reminded the two men of their earlier performance in Philadelphia in 1776 and the fact that Jefferson retained evidence of their former *"investments* in shipping enterprises" in New England.

But what makes the letter truly infamous is the revelation that the founders, including the three icons—Adams, Franklin, and Jefferson—had at the time of the debate on independence in 1776 entered into secret negotiations with powerful slaving interests in Britain to enlist their political support in convincing the Crown and the British government to let the American colonies go. The British slaving interests included shipowners and tycoons with highly profitable plantation holdings and investments in the West Indies. According

to the letter, the secret deal that was offered to the British slaving interests was
that if they could assist the colonies in se-
curing their independence through political negotiations rather than war, the new
government that was formed from the old
colonies would agree to provide by treaty
and by its "organic law"—what would first
become the Articles of Confederation and
later the Constitution—a perpetual safe
haven for slave traffic and for the institution of slavery itself in every part of the
new nation, even if Great Britain were to
eventually abolish slavery in the British
Empire.

* * *

When news of this last item in the letter hit
the airwaves, it was as if someone had
pushed a red button in Alamogordo. The
nation erupted.

I look at the flickering images on my
set.

Riots on the half screen, the news anchor in the foreground, talking over the
swirling firestorm in Detroit, flipping to
Chicago and then L.A., indistinguishable
flames as the voice of the anchor intones:

"The ancient rust-colored ink, presumably in Jefferson's own hand, revealing that the cornerstone of liberty, before it was pried from Britain with blood, had first been laid on the auction block in an attempted deal with the devil, is threatening to fracture the country's confidence in its own national identity."

I flip the channel and see another talking head.

"While the court tried to put distance between itself and the letter, it appears that the terrible proof may in fact be there, in God's own hand, Jefferson's words.

"The social experiment conceived in the Age of Reason by intellectual giants, men who labored against a flawed world, who struggled against all odds, and who in the end were forced by terrible circumstance to make an agonizing compromise that left slavery alive and crawling on American soil at its birth, may in fact be a myth."

THIRTY

Because of the riots, Quinn has had to move the jury across town to a hotel where they deliberate in a conference room for two days while the police battle with rioters in the streets downtown.

Three days later they finally return to the courthouse where burned-out vehicles along Broadway are still smoldering. And they continue to deliberate.

*   *   *

It was that morning that Harry came into my office and reminded me that in our rush to the island, our search for Ginnis, and the forty-eight-hour forensic mayhem after the delivery of the Jefferson Letter, we had forgotten to follow up on one item. He had it in his hand.

It was a copy of the Post-it note on the inside of the jewel-case cover holding the DVD found by Jennifer in the police evidence locker, now nearly two months ago, the one with Ginnis's name on it.

But it was the other name on the slip that Harry was talking about, the name Edgar Zobel. He hands me a stapled stack of pages, maybe twenty in all.

Edgar Zobel, a French émigré to the United States, came to Virginia with his parents as a young boy. Zobel had always had an interest in writing, not so much with an eye toward content as style. In his youth he had mastered the art of calligraphy. He actually held two U.S. copyrights for scripts that were later developed into type fonts first used on old Selectric typewriters and later incorporated in digitized type fonts for computers, but that would be later in life.

Growing up in Virginia, he was immersed in the Colonial history of the area. Museums in and around Washington often exhibited the private and public letters of historic figures. As a child Zobel marveled at the different colors of ink and the elegant flourishes of script, on paper yellowed by age, the edges of which were often frayed. He practiced the fine styles of penmanship employed by those composing letters that now rested under glass in the display cases of museums. By the time he was fifteen, he possessed his own collection of these in replica form. Several of them were mounted, framed, and hung on the walls of his room.

In an age before computers, when other kids were out playing baseball or swimming, Edgar was busy indulging his fetish, replicating more items for his collection of historic documents. He became adroit in the use of sealing wax and collected old metal stamps created to impress an image in the hot wax that sealed folded letters in the time before envelopes were invented.

* * *

By the time he was thirty, Zobel could copy the elegant freestyle script of more than eighteen of the early U.S. presidents so closely that even experienced handwriting experts would have difficulty identifying the replica from the real. Without a thorough analysis of the paper and ink, it would have been impossible to tell.

It was about that time that Zobel was approached by two men who owned a small shop in the historic district of Fredericksburg, Virginia. The shop dealt in antiquities, mostly Civil War memorabilia with an occasional item dating back to the Revolution. The men wanted Zobel to craft some elegant replicas of historic correspondence that they could sell to customers who either couldn't afford to or didn't want to pay the high prices of historic originals. To make a few bucks, Zobel was happy to do it.

The copied documents always carried a printed disclaimer, "Hand-Reproduced Replica," on the back. Almost all of Zobel's early copies were of well-known historic letters or documents, but they were different from the usual lithograph copy you might find in typical curio shops, much more authentic to the eye in terms of paper texture and ink. They had a kind of three-dimensional quality, including the folds in the paper and its frayed edges, that made them look astonishingly real. Each document was scripted on unique paper. For Colonial documents Zobel would use custom-made paper, large sheets similar to those used in the Colonial period, which were then either cut or torn into quarters to make traditional "quartos," the quarter pages often used for writing. Sometimes he would employ a smaller "folio" size.

In time the owners of the shop where Zobel's work was displayed came to realize that collectors of rare documents were traveling long distances, some from as far away as New York, Boston, and Chicago, to buy up everything that Zobel created, as fast as he could produce it. When the shop raised its prices for Zobel's works, while the profits rose, the result was the same. Their inventory of his work was gone almost before it could be hung. Tony decorating salons in Georgetown and Manhattan began to call, asking if they could commission specific items. If the shop could have cloned Zobel, they would have made a fortune.

The problem was, there was a built-in economic ceiling for his work. The moment the prices started approaching the cost of an original, demand disappeared. It didn't take long before it dawned on them that if people with money in New York and Boston were decorating the walls of their studies and libraries with Zobel's elegant copies, how much more would they pay if they thought the article was real?

They didn't have to argue long to convince Zobel. He had been working up calluses on his fingers, was running out of turkey quills, and had less than twelve hundred dollars to show for eighteen documents, all of which were sold nearly before they were written. Zobel was having visions of dying like van Gogh, broke, only to have collectors trading his works for millions years later, as pieces of art.

The first item they crafted was an original letter from Washington to one of his aides, an obscure two paragraphs about military stores for his troops. For provenance the shop owners claimed that the item was found pasted to the back of a drawer in an eighteenth-century dining set that came into their shop. The piece sold at auction in New York for eighteen thousand dollars. They did it again, a different letter, a different author, and this time they used a party not connected with the shop who said she found the item behind an old photo, a family heirloom. They netted twenty-three thousand dollars at auction.

Now they were in business. They kept the documents sufficiently obscure, with only one notable signature, so the price would stay in the realm of reason and the buyer would not be induced to have experts examine the paper and ink. In fourteen months they'd sold seventeen pieces, netting nearly half a million dollars. It was that last piece, the seventeenth item that brought the roof down. It seems they'd gone to the well once too often. One of the auction houses in New York got suspicious. Unless someone had found a chest of forgotten letters, a mother lode of historic grocery lists penned by the pantheon of American founders, there were simply too many new finds coming from one region all at one time. A quick check of the ink and paper and it didn't take long for the FBI to trace everything back to the little shop in Fredericksburg.

* * *

It is from the statement of facts in the circuit court's opinion that Harry gleaned all these details of Zobel's early life.

* * *

Edgar Zobel did six and a half years in the federal penitentiary in Atlanta for interstate fraud, wire and mail fraud, and lost his house, paying a fine of a quarter of a million dollars. He sat in prison while his lawyers filed an appeal that was ultimately denied by the federal Fourth Circuit Court of Appeals in Virginia, an opinion written by the Honorable John R. Logan, circuit judge. It took Harry a few minutes longer to find the names of the other two judges on the three-judge panel: the Honorable Rufus James and Arthur J. Ginnis, both concurring. That was twenty-six years ago.

* * *

Immediately I called Quinn and told him. I gave him the citation so he could find the case.

He told me that it was interesting, he would look at it, but that it was outside the record of the trial and could not be given to the jury.

I told him I knew that, but that it was the first solid piece of evidence we had that the Jefferson Letter, more than likely, was a fraud.

* * *

It took Herman a little longer than Harry—and some shoe leather—to discover that Zobel was still alive and to find him. In nearly a quarter of a century, he hadn't ventured far. Zobel was living in a small house that unless you looked closely you might swear was a barn, along a dried-up creek among scrub oaks twelve miles outside Charlottesville, Virginia. The inside walls of his house were literally pasted with historic documents, some of them framed, some not.

Since getting out of prison twenty years earlier, Zobel had gone back to his roots. For a price he would sell you a replicated piece of history, anything you wanted, signed by a historic figure. Most of his business was done over the Internet and via e-mail.

Replicated documents or whimsical originals were sent out by UPS ground shipment, unless the buyer wanted to spring for overnight delivery.

According to what Zobel told Herman, he almost never saw the people who commissioned his work. He imposed only two requirements on his customers. First, they were required to sign and mail in a disclaimer, the form that was on Zobel's Web site, verifying that they were commissioning the work and that there was no intent on

their part to use the document for any fraud-
ulent or unlawful purpose. Second, they had
to agree that the document, when completed, would bear a discreet notation in in-
delible ink printed on the reverse side that
the item was "a hand-replicated copy, and
not an original." That and payment, either by
credit card to his site on the Internet or by
check with return of the disclaimer, was all
Zobel required.

When Herman showed Zobel a copy of
the Jefferson Letter, the man nearly col-
lapsed behind the counter. He had been
waiting for the FBI to arrive for three weeks.
When he saw the copy, he assumed that
Herman was there to arrest him. Herman
assured him that what he wanted was information and nothing more.

Zobel told him that from the start it was
an unusual transaction, but that he'd
done everything by the book. It had been
ordered not over the Internet, but by
phone. A price had been quoted, and a
few days later an envelope arrived with
typed memoranda of the contents to be
penned in the letter, along with the signed
disclaimer form, apparently printed off
Zobel's Web site. There were also fifteen

crisp one-hundred-dollar bills, the price quoted.

All this made Zobel nervous. He was no longer on parole, but he didn't want to go back to prison, so he did the right thing. He called his lawyer.

The lawyer assured him that as long as he had the signed disclaimer and he printed the notation on the back of the replicated document, he was in the clear. So he did it. According to Zobel's records, the "original" of the J letter, written on four custom-made quarto-size sheets, was picked up by a private courier service two weeks later. Zobel didn't note or write down the name of the courier service. When he pulled the disclaimer form from the file that included a copy of his work and the original envelope containing the money, the return address on the envelope read "T. Scarborough," with Scarborough's Georgetown address. And the disclaimer form bore the signature "T. Scarborough." Herman used a subpoena to get the envelope and the original of the disclaimer form, leaving the subpoena and a copy of the form in Zobel's files.

* * *

Back in the office, Harry, Herman, and I labor over the signature. While none of us are handwriting experts, Scarborough's signature was somewhat unique. It would be difficult to copy. The signature at the bottom of Zobel's disclaimer form appeared to be an original in blue ink, and from everything we can see—all the little nooks and crannies, right down to the tailored wisps of ink from his favored fountain pen—it appeared to be authentic.

So if someone else had commissioned the letter, how did they get Scarborough's signature on the form?

*   *   *

Closeted with Quinn and Tuchio in chambers, we find this even more mystifying. The judge has been playing racquetball with the jury for more than ten days now, what with their constant requests for clarification on bits of evidence, some granted, some denied. They have returned three times to ask that Carl's signed statement to the police following his arrest be read to them once more or, in the alternative, that they be given a copy.

Quinn has said no to a copy, from which they might end up parsing the words, but he has sent his clerk, Ruiz, in twice to read it to them.

If it's possible to interpret their questions, with all the evidence that's been presented to the jury, the stunning revelations of the Jefferson Letter and the matching evidence of hair samples from the envelope to those found at the scene, the jury seems hung up on a single point: how Carl could have gotten the tray with food to the table in Scarborough's room without first seeing his body.

Guess what a jury will do with the evidence and you'll be wrong a dozen times out of a dozen.

* * *

Quinn is now mired in another trial in a courtroom down the hall, so he has little time for us this morning.

"What the hell is going on?" says Quinn. "From the videotape and the transcript, the two of them having dinner, Teddy's transcript, Ginnis gave Scarborough the copy of the letter. Now you bring me this," he says.

The judge is holding the disclaimer form signed by Scarborough. "Why is Scarborough asking Ginnis for the original if he already had it?"

"It's a good thing that video didn't come in," says Tuchio.

"I'm beginning to think that that video is the only thing that is real," I tell him.

The judge has to get back to court. He is ushering us out just as Ruiz, his clerk, is coming the other way.

"You guys better stick around," says Ruiz. "Your Honor, the jury is back," he says.

"A verdict?"

Ruiz shrugs and shakes his head. He's not sure, but they've notified the bailiff that they're ready to come out of the jury room.

*   *   *

Twenty minutes later the courtroom is packed, Harry and Carl seated at the counsel table with me.

"What do you think?" says Carl.

"I don't know. They've been out a long time."

The general rule is that a quick verdict is a guilty verdict. The longer the jury is out, the greater the possibility that Carl will be acquitted. At least that's the rule of thumb. I've told him this, but I haven't dwelled on it. There's the risk of rising expectations and the shattering shock if I'm wrong.

We wait for another eighteen minutes before the jury files in. When a jury comes in, it is always the same, the rush of emotions, the anxiety. My stomach produces enough acid to etch the concrete on my driveway. You find yourself leaping at every little sign, looking for signals. The sure and certain giveaway is when one or more of the jurors smiles at the defendant.

None of them do this today. The fact is that not a single one of them makes eye contact with Carl, or anyone else at our table. This is not good.

Quinn allows them to settle into their chairs. "The court will come to order."

He waits for things to settle down out in the audience, until all you can hear is a couple of coughs and some throat clearing. "Mr. Foreman."

The jury foreman rises.

"Has the jury arrived at a verdict?"

"It has not, Your Honor. We are deadlocked."

A hung jury. There is commotion in the audience behind us, people up out of their chairs.

The judge hammers his gavel. "The court will come to order. You people out in the audience, take your seats and be quiet."

When I turn, I see the expression of concern on Sam Arnsberg's face, Carl's dad, seated in the front row directly behind us. He's not sure what this means, nor is Carl.

"What's happening?"

"Just sit tight. Don't talk to anybody, don't say anything."

Two of the deputies move up and stand just behind the bar railing at our backs. They are both facing out to the audience.

Everything now rests in Quinn's hands, and I can tell by his expression that he is not happy.

He clears his throat. Quinn is considering his options as he sits up there on the bench. "Mr. Foreman."

"Yes, Your Honor."

"Now, I don't want you to tell me what the vote is or which way the jury is leaning, but if I were to send you all back into the jury room to deliberate a little longer, do you think it's likely that you would be able to arrive at a verdict?"

"I doubt it, Your Honor."

This is not what Quinn wanted to hear.

"I'm going to ask the jurors to return to the jury room and just sit tight for a few more minutes. You're not to deliberate, just sit there and relax."

"What's going on?" says Carl. "Does that mean I'm free?"

"Not yet," I tell him.

The jury files out.

"I'll see counsel in chambers. The defendant can go back in the lockup, just for a few minutes."

The lawyers follow Quinn back to his office, but before he gets there, he stops for a second, tells us to go into the office while he talks with his clerk, Ruiz, just outside the door.

When he finally comes in, he doesn't take off his robe but flops into his chair.

"Any motions?" he says.

Quinn is inviting Tuchio to make a motion for the dynamite charge.

"We would move that the court issue the modified Allen instruction to the jury, Your Honor."

This is the polite name, the formal name. Many defense lawyers call it the "dynamite instruction," because to them that's what it is—a means to blast recalcitrant jurors, holdouts, into knuckling under and voting for conviction. The instruction in modified forms and variations has been around since the late 1800s and derives its name from the case that coined it, *Allen v. United States*.

It is generally brief, no more than a page when printed out on paper. In short, what it allows the judge to do is to instruct the jury that the state and the taxpayers have spent a great deal of money and the lawyers and the court have spent a great deal of time and energy to try the case. It also reminds them that if they fail to arrive at a verdict, the case may have to be retried. In effect it's a mistrial, and that if this happens, it will cost more money and time. After some soothing words assuring the jurors that no one is trying to jimmy them into giving up an honestly held conviction, it ends with the bold statement that it is their duty to arrive at a verdict if they can do so.

Of course, by now all they remember is the last line, the "duty to arrive at a verdict" part delivered to them by God, who has just scowled at them from the bench. Some defense lawyers will tell you of cases in which the jury didn't even get out of the box and back to the jury room before they voted to convict.

"Your Honor, you heard the jury foreman when you asked him if they could arrive at a verdict," I say.

"He said he doubted it," says Tuchio. "He didn't say they were irreconcilably deadlocked."

"Yeah, well, that's a mouthful for anybody," says Harry.

Quinn reaches into his drawer and pulls out the binder with jury instruction, looking for the page with the dynamite charge.

His clerk comes into chambers behind us and closes the door.

"Your Honor, can I ask you that before you read the charge to the jury—" I begin.

"Just a minute," says the judge.

Ruiz cups a hand and whispers into the judge's ear. Quinn swivels around in his chair so that they are both sheltered by the high back of the chair between us.

When the judge finally wheels around ten seconds later or so, he looks at me. "You were saying something, Mr. Madriani."

"I wanted to ask you that before you read the charge to the jury, if you could one more time talk to the jury foreman to gain some kind of sense as to the real feasibility of a verdict?"

"That's a fair request," says Quinn. "Let's head on back out."

*   *   *

Eight minutes later the jury is back in the box. Carl is seated between Harry and me.

"The court will come to order," says Quinn. "Mr. Foreman," he says.

The jury foreman is back on his feet.

"Let me ask you one more time. If I were to send the jurors back into the jury room for further deliberations do you think they would be able to arrive at a verdict?"

"It's not likely, Your Honor." He says essentially the same thing a second time.

Quinn looks out from the bench. "At this time the court is going to declare a mistrial. The defendant is discharged. Mr. Tuchio, you're free to file new charges."

"Your Honor! Your Honor!" Tuchio is on his feet, one hand waving behind him at the audience, trying to get them back into their seats. This is like putting the genie back in the bottle. "May I request that the jury be polled?"

"That's a fair request," says the judge. "Everybody take your seats. Sit down, please. We'll be through in just a minute."

"Am I free?" says Carl.

"You are for now."

He smiles at me, then turns and looks at his dad, a broad grin.

One by one they stand in the jury box and announce their verdict. Harry is taking notes on the jury sheets, the pages from jury selection, so we will know how they voted.

When they're finished, Harry doesn't have to tell us the tally. It is eleven to one for acquittal. The lone holdout, the woman in the jangling jewelry.

You can almost see the relief on Tuchio's face. He has dodged a bullet by half an inch.

"The defendant is discharged," says Quinn. "Free to go," he says.

At least for now, unless Tuchio decides to recharge him. There is no double jeopardy in the case of a hung jury. The prosecution can do it all over again to the same defendant, with the same charges.

"Court is adjourned," says the judge.

There is pandemonium in the court-room, reporters leaning over the railing. They want to talk to Carl.

I tell him not to say a word, to keep his mouth shut. Harry takes him by the arm and goes with him back to the lockup and the jail to get his personal items and keep him away from the media.

One wrong word and Tuchio will jump on his back and use it against him in an-other trial.

At least in terms of a jury, the shock of the Jefferson Letter is past. It is not likely to have the same numbing effect if Tuchio does it over again. He also knows, as I do, that the Jefferson Letter is, without ques-tion, a tin-plated phony.

THIRTY-ONE

Over the phone that night, Harry and I put our heads together and came to the same conclusion, that the magic pill that caused the judge to declare a mistrial was not the declaration of the jury foreman but the whispered message of R2-D2, his clerk, as they huddled behind the judge's chair in chambers seconds before we came back out.

Quinn had said something to Ruiz as we were first going into chambers to argue over the dynamite instruction. Harry and I will never know, but if we had to guess, the judge had dispatched his clerk to talk to one of the bailiffs who normally usher the jury around. Dirt travels, and people talk. It is not unusual for deputies and bailiffs to pick up smoke signals and drums telling them with some certitude what's going on behind closed doors.

This is what Ruiz was telling the judge behind the chair. That they were deadlocked eleven to one and that the single holdout had her heels dug in and her position had become a question of pride.

The blond hairs in the envelope presented me with a process of elimination, a question between the two of them, Trisha Scott and Richard Bonguard. If you didn't think long and hard, you might flip a coin trying to come up with the answer.

I made the long-distance call and left a message with the secretary. Less than an hour later, the secretary called back, a meeting was set. The next day I flew east.

Harry had asked me once what possible reason Bonguard might have to kill the golden goose, his megabucks client Terry Scarborough. Among the theories is that it's possible he had no choice. He knew Margaret Ginnis. They met at a political function. He thought that Antonin Scalia, the leading edge of the right wing on the Court, was the wit, but he didn't like his politics. Ginnis held the balance of power on the Court. So when things happened in the islands, who was Margaret to call but her friend, her former agent, her political ally, Richard Bonguard? It was possible that working together, in secret, they could change history. It was possible, but not likely.

The reason, unless I miss my bet, is that there's no way Bonguard could have known at the time of the murder that the Jefferson Letter was a fraud. And it was this fact that propelled the murder. Unless I'm wrong, Ginnis would never have told his wife what he was doing. The risks were too great. He would not want to put her in jeopardy if things went wrong, risked having her accused of collusion and conspiracy. But there was one person, sufficiently in the shadows and therefore safe, with whom he might share the secret: his trusted former clerk.

That night, as Harry and I flew east toward Miami and south to Curaçao, we must have passed Trisha Scott in the air, jetting the other way. She was in a frantic dash to reach our office, racing to slip the envelope with the Jefferson Letter and a few of her own clipped hairs under our office door. Scott saw what was happening. Reading news reports of the trial, watching the revelations minute by minute on television, she knew that the only way to stop us from looking further, to prevent us from stumbling over what was really happening, was to deliver the evidence and hope that this would draw the attention of the world back to the trial. But she was already too late.

When I called to make the arrangements, I insisted that we meet in a public place. I no longer know who it is I'm dealing with. Here in a crowded room, I feel safer. It is the same Washington restaurant where we first met for dinner.

We spend a couple of minutes in false pleasantries—the weather, politics. I'm not entirely certain if she realizes why I'm here. She is animated, sitting erect in the chair, actually laughing once at something she heard in one of the campaigns. She is also very nervous.

Then I broach the subject. "I take it you do understand that it's over now?"

She gives me a quizzical expression, then leans in toward the table. "Excuse me?"

"It's over. All of it," I tell her.

She makes a perfect oval with her mouth as if she wants to say, *What's over?* But as she studies my face, she stops herself. She closes her mouth and doesn't say a word.

In this instant, Trisha Scott looks as if she's aged ten years in the seven months that have passed since our last meeting.

"I am not a cop. I'm not a reporter. Under other circumstances I wouldn't even be here tonight. But I have a client, and he's still hanging out there on the line, in jeopardy. Do you understand?"

"I read that in the newspapers. I'm sorry to hear it," she says. "But I'm not sure what that has to do with me."

"Then let's cut to the chase," I tell her. "I left a memorandum on my desk with an e-mail to my partner as well as to the district attorney with your name, phone number, and address on it, just in case something bad were to happen to me during my trip here tonight. I told them to find you and to pluck a few hairs and that all their questions would be answered."

This seems to freeze her in place.

Trisha Scott could feel safe sending off bits of her hair in an envelope under our office door because she knew there was no national database for hair samples as there is for fingerprints. Unless there was someone to point the way, to connect her to the crime, the hair evidence might serve to exonerate Carl without implicating her. I wanted this on the table early, so that if she had plans to send me to join Scarborough, she would know from the get-go that they are fruitless.

"It's over. Do you understand?"

It takes a few seconds, and then she seems to wither in the chair. Whatever will or determination was left evaporates almost in the blink of an eye. I find myself suddenly looking at a different person across the table, at what I can only characterize as a catatonic mask.

For a long time, she says nothing. She takes a drink of water, her eyes suddenly scanning the restaurant. She sets the glass back down and seems to look right through me as she gathers her thoughts.

"I want you to understand . . . I wonder . . . I wonder if I could go to the ladies' room?"

"I don't think that's a good idea," I say.

"Police?"

I nod. They're not here yet. They are on their way, but she doesn't have to know this.

"Oh, God! I want you to understand how it was. It's important that you understand."

"We don't have much time," I tell her.

"There was no other choice," she says. "All the way out on the plane, I got more and more angry. Terry Scarborough was the kind of person who left a trail of ravaged souls as he cruised through life. By the time I got to that hotel, I was seething."

"You don't have to say anything. You've probably already said too much."

"No," she says. "I've been holding it in so long. Nobody I could talk to. I have to . . . I was thinking as far ahead as my brain would allow. I had the cab let me out two blocks from the hotel so there'd be no record of a taxi having dropped me. For a time I actually thought that—given how I felt, the anger—that I could kill him with my bare hands. But he was bigger than I was, stronger. I didn't have a gun. Even if I did, I wouldn't know how to use it. I thought about a knife. Maybe I could buy one. But I'd read enough briefs on appeal in criminal cases. I knew if I did that, even if I got rid of the knife, there'd be a trail. Wounds in the body would tell them the length of the blade, whether it was serrated, probably right down to the make and model. I'd read enough about it. I knew they could do it. They'd start checking all the shops, recent sales, anybody buying a single hunting or butcher knife. And even if I used cash, the salesclerk would remember this woman, because her eyes were all red from crying. I decided I couldn't buy a weapon. I'd have to improvise, use whatever I found in the room—a lamp, a heavy knickknack off one of the shelves."

"But then you didn't have to go looking for a weapon, did you?"

"No. But you already know about that, the hammer in the stairwell. I didn't want to get into the elevator. Too many people would see me."

"How did you know what room he was in?"

"I called Dick Bonguard on his cell the night before. I had Dick's number in Outlook on my computer. I knew that Dick would be trailing along with Terry on the book tour. I told Dick I had something I needed to fax to Terry. He gave me the hotel and the suite number.

"I climbed fourteen floors, all the way to the top. Every three or four flights, I'd stop to catch my breath. That's when I saw it."

"The hammer?"

"It was as if God had reached down and put it there and I was his avenging angel. I took it, put it in my purse. I had a good-size bag I always used for travel. I carried it over my shoulder, and I climbed to the top."

"And the raincoat, the gloves?"

"The raincoat was in a little pouch, in the bottom of my purse with the gloves. I knew if I hit him with the hammer, there would be blood. It would get all over me and I'd be trapped there. From everything I read in the papers—and believe me, I kept up with the progress of your case every day," she says, "the police never found the gloves?"

I shake my head.

"I dropped them in a trash can someplace. I don't even remember where."

"The police wouldn't have looked very hard," I tell her. "It didn't fit the facts of their case. They had a fingerprint on the murder weapon. But it wasn't yours."

"I know," she says. This seems to bother her more than the actual killing itself, the fact that Carl and his parents have been dragged through hell. "I would never have let him go to prison or die," she says. "You have to believe that. I was buying time. That's all I was doing. I knew that sooner or later I would have to do something to put an end to it. When the news of the Jefferson Letter broke, it was almost a relief. The very thing I'd been hiding so long was now out in the open. There was no need to hide it any longer."

"So you fed it to us, hoping that it would be enough?"

She nods nervously several times. "Why didn't it work?"

"One obstinate juror," I tell her. "The way it goes sometimes."

"Then if he'd been acquitted, you wouldn't be here tonight."

I shrug. She's right. If Carl were on the street, free, out from under, this wouldn't be my job. And given the theory of the prosecution, if Carl were acquitted, they would never be able to convict Scott—that is, if they even found her, which is unlikely.

"So you went up the stairs, put on the raincoat and the gloves. You had the hammer in your purse."

She nods.

"How did you get into the room?"

"I knocked on the door. How stupid is that? I wasn't sure if he was in or, if he was, whether he was alone. I knew when he opened the door he'd be surprised to see me. And standing there in a raincoat. I had a story ready. I was going to tell him that I was in town on business and there was something I needed to talk to him about if he could spare two minutes—anything to get inside the room."

"Because you knew you were running out of time," I say.

"Yes."

"So what happened when he opened the door?"

"Strange thing was, he never even looked at me. He was busy reading something, a piece of paper in his hand. Before I knew it, he was walking away. He said, 'Put it on the table'—something about a check. Then I realized he thought I was room service. Suddenly there he was, sitting in the chair, his back to me, reading some papers, making notes, completely oblivious to the fact that I was even standing there. At that moment I think I just exploded. What he had put me through, and he didn't even know it. Not that Terry would have cared.

"You want to know the truth?" She looks me straight in the eye now. "It was easier than I ever thought it could be. I closed the door and walked up to the back of the chair, and I swung that hammer, over and over and over again, until the muscles in my arms burned." She breathes heavily, takes the napkin and wipes her eyes.

"At some point I must have closed my eyes, because when I opened them again, there was blood everywhere—on the ceiling, on the walls, soaking into the gloves I was wearing, spotting and running down the raincoat. I didn't realize it at first, but the reason I stopped swinging was that the hammer was stuck. The claws were lodged in the top of his head. I couldn't look at it. For some stupid reason, I had to pull it out. I pulled and twisted. The hammer came loose, and his body fell on the floor. I dropped the hammer.

"It's amazing. I . . . You'd think you would go into shock after something like that, but I didn't. I was overwhelmed with this incredible urge to run, to get out of there. I knew that any minute somebody with a tray was probably going to be at the door. But I wasn't finished."

"You had to find the video of Ginnis and Scarborough at the restaurant."

"How did you know?"

"It never came into evidence, but we have a copy," I tell her, "from Scarborough's apartment."

"The police had it?" she says.

"Yes, but they didn't know what it was."

"I assumed that Terry had copies, but I didn't think anyone would pay any attention to it. Terry had tons of tapes and DVDs all over the place. What was one more or less?"

"That was the reason you were running out of time?" I say. "You couldn't be sure how long you had before Scarborough went public about the Jefferson Letter, the fact that Ginnis, a member of the Supreme Court, had manufactured it."

"Arthur didn't know he was being taped. I had to find the tape and the letter itself, Terry's copy, the one Arthur had given him. I knew Terry well enough to know that he would have both of these with him. If he was getting ready to out Arthur in the media over the letter, he would never leave these behind in his apartment or trust them to a safe-deposit box. Terry was paranoid. Put something in a vault and people with power, especially people in government, can always find a way to get at it. The only safe place was in his pocket or the briefcase he was carrying. So I looked."

"And of course you were still wearing the gloves."

She nods.

This accounts for all the little smudges of blood on Scarborough's attaché case, the large sample case by the side of his chair, and the leather portfolio by the television, where she found the letter folded neatly, lying on top.

"Where did you find the videotape?" I ask.

"It was in his attaché case. Along with two DVDs. I had to worry about that," she says. "I didn't know a lot about the technology, but I knew if he had time to make copies of the tape and transfer them to DVD, there could be more copies someplace else. I had to assume that the video was also downloaded onto a computer somewhere. But Terry wouldn't have copied the tape himself. He wouldn't know how. He was always too busy to do anything like that, or learn how. He would have taken it somewhere and had it done. Why not? Raw footage of an old man talking about the value of some obscure letter over a meal in a restaurant wouldn't mean a thing without Terry to explain what was happening and how all the little pieces fit together. I could only hope that if anybody stumbled on copies or found the video computer file, it would have that same meaningless sense to them."

"And since they didn't find it at the scene of a murder, why would they try to connect any dots?"

"That's what I thought," she says, "until you showed up at my office that day. But at that moment in the hotel room, I had bigger problems. I tried to wipe as much of the blood off of the raincoat as I could, using a wet towel that was already on the bathroom floor. Terry must have taken a shower. I had to make sure there were no fingerprints on the plastic of the coat. I was racing. I wrapped the coat with the same towel and threw it in my bag. I took off the gloves, wrapped them in a small hand towel, and dropped them in the bag. As fast as I was moving, I was careful not to touch anything with my hands. I used wet toilet paper to wipe spots of blood off my face and off the top of one of my shoes and then flushed the paper down the toilet. I used a clean face towel to touch any surfaces in the bathroom, including the handle on the toilet. I checked myself in the mirror and then started for the door. By now the carpet was soaked, and there was blood on the floor in the entry leading to the door. I had to step around it, stay to the left in the entry. I used the sleeve of my coat to open the door, and I ran. I ran down I don't know how many flights of stairs before I got onto the elevator. When I got outside, I must have run for a mile. I threw the towel with the raincoat into the Dumpster in the parking lot. I got rid of the other towel with the gloves somewhere else. I can't remember."

"And of course you kept Scarborough's copy of the letter."

"You know, I've thought about that so many times. I don't know why I kept it. It had Terry's blood on it. It was the only thing left connecting me to that room, but for some reason I put it in a drawer when I got home. The DVDs and the videotape of Arthur talking with Terry in the restaurant, those I destroyed, but not before I watched one of the copies on my television. It was shot in early spring. Arthur was still recovering from his hip surgery. You could see his cane hooked on the edge of the table in the restaurant. This frail old man sitting there breaking bread with someone he despised, smiling, his eyes twinkling, thinking all the while that he was about to stick his fork in the devil."

"And then Scarborough opened the letter and laid it on the table. You saw the look on Ginnis's face," I say. "He wasn't smiling then."

"No."

"So that was the plan, to get Scarborough hooked on the Jefferson Letter, to get him to publish a book based on it, then reveal it as a fraud and leave him twisting?"

She nods. "Arthur had it all set up. He wrote the letter himself. You know, when you're dealing with Arthur Ginnis, you're dealing with a first-rate mind. He knew that the old code words for slavery in the Constitution, the fact that the framers had tried so hard to dodge the issue by avoiding the use of the word itself, made the substance of the Jefferson Letter completely plausible. Terry would buy into it in a heartbeat. Evidence of an offer to the slaving interests of Great Britain as the price to secure liberty for the American colonies and avoid a war—for Terry that was the stuff of dreams. Shatter the American myth. It was what he lived for. Terry hated the power structure. He hated authority, unless he was the one wielding it. He saw conspiracies everywhere."

She seems more comfortable now, out from under the dark cloud of the murder, the details of the Jefferson Letter almost seeming to amuse her.

"First Arthur tried to get Terry to include the Jefferson Letter as part of *Perpetual Slaves,* a kind of one-two punch—slavery in the Constitution and history's ultimate dirty deal in the letter. Arthur knew that Terry couldn't resist. The letter confirmed every evil thought Terry ever had about the white ruling class, rotten to the core from the instant they entered the promised land.

"If that wasn't enough, Terry was always the insecure author. Nibbling at the edges of his mind was the ever-present thought, 'What if I trot out the old language of slavery and all they do is yawn?' He could never be sure that the language was enough to ignite the firestorm he needed for success. But toss in Jefferson's letter and Terry had an instant flamethrower. When Arthur dangled it, Terry did a swan dive, chasing the copy."

"But of course you were there to stop it,"

I tell her. "You convinced Scarborough he needed to authenticate the letter."

"You bet I did. Arthur was angry. He could never forgive Terry for what he'd done to him. There's no question he would have been chief justice but for Terry Scarborough's lies. He's one of the most intelligent human beings I've ever known. Do you think he would have even considered doing something like this five years ago, even three years ago? Never! Here's a man with a lifelong reputation to protect, a judicial philosophy etched in law for a quarter of a century. And here he was taking a risk of immense proportions. He hated Scarborough. If you want to know what I thought, I thought Arthur was losing it. The reckless thing he was doing had all the signs of senility, and yet he seemed not to have dropped a single stitch. You bet I tried to stop it.

"Even after I convinced Terry to hold the letter and told him that he couldn't use it without authentication, Arthur wouldn't quit. God, that old man," she says. "Terry wanted the original, and Arthur wouldn't give it to him. Terry said he couldn't convince the publisher to go forward with another book unless he produced the original of the Jefferson Letter and allowed them to authenticate it. Arthur didn't buy it.

"He told Terry to call the publisher's bluff. If they wouldn't go forward based on the copy and a promise to deliver the original later, Terry should tell them he would take the project to another publisher. Given the sales of *Perpetual Slaves,* there'd be a bidding war for rights to the next book. When Terry thought about that, he stopped arguing. I think for a moment he might have even considered hiring Arthur to represent him.

"When Terry threatened, the publisher caved. They gave him a contract, told him where to sign, handed him a seven-figure advance, and promised to wait for the original of the Jefferson Letter that would have to be produced and authenticated before publication. They weren't happy, but they did it. Terry was throwing parties—not that he needed the money, but the advance was twice what he thought he would get."

"But if Ginnis knew he had to cough up the original of the letter before the book went into print, where was the downside for Scarborough? The publisher would know that the letter was a fraud before the book ever went to press," I say.

"That's what I'm saying. Arthur's smart. He had already burned the original of the letter. He knew he couldn't show it to anybody, not without revealing it as a fraud. The plan was to leak another copy of the letter to the media, with an anonymous note that Terry was doing a book and the name of the publisher—all this just about the time Terry was finishing the manuscript.

"The media would be all over the publisher, and they'd already have the contents of the letter, all the dirty little details, the bombshell of a letter, the offered deal on slavery. With all of this in the press, who needs a book?

"When the time came to produce the original, as far as Arthur was concerned, he was the original man from Mars. He knew nothing. He'd never heard of the Jefferson Letter. He didn't know what Terry was talking about. By then the publisher—caught between the press, their inability to publish, and the suspicion that Terry had turned the media loose on

them in an effort to force publication without the original letter—would have to go
into court against Terry even if he was a
hot property. When they found the paper
trail leading back to Scarborough . . ."

"Zobel's files with Scarborough's signature on the disclaimer form."

"You found that, too?" she says.

"Uh-huh."

"When they found that, the U.S. Attorney would be joining the party, and Terry
would be looking at both the civil and criminal sides of the same coin."

"How did Ginnis manage to get Scarborough's signature on that form?"

She laughs. "He not only had Terry's
signature, he also had his fingerprints all
over that form. As a lawyer, Terry didn't
even belong in Arthur's universe. But he
was an author, and he had a large ego.
He was used to autographing hundreds,
even thousands, of books every year. It
wasn't unusual to have someone come up
to him in a line during an autograph party
and tell the author that he'd left his book
at home. The person might have a paper
bookplate to be signed that he could

paste in the book later, or just a piece of paper that he could glue in. It happens often enough that writers don't even think about it.

"Arthur waited for an autographing appearance at a bookshop in Washington. That was for the book just before *Perpetual Slaves*. Arthur sent over a clerk with a sheet of paper that had a penciled line where Terry was to sign. The clerk was told not to say anything about Arthur or where the request was coming from. It was some kind of a surprise. The story was simple: She owned a book and had forgotten it at home.

"The night before the autographing, Arthur printed Zobel's disclaimer form on his home computer. All he had to do was put a copy of the form under a blank sheet of paper with a little light behind the two, and you could see where the signature went on the disclaimer form. That's where Arthur drew the penciled line. When he got the sheet back with the signature, he pulled up the form, ran the signed sheet through the printer, and there it was, the form with the signature, all in the right place. He used gloves so his prints wouldn't be on the form, only Scarborough's and the clerk's, who Arthur knew they'd never look for.

"I know what you're thinking. How can a man who's senile think that far ahead? What was happening in his head were all the details—the judgment needed to weigh the totality of what he was doing was gone. It's why in the video, when Terry tried to hand him the copy of the letter, Arthur went for the bread instead. He refused to touch the paper. He didn't want his prints on it. What he didn't know was that Scarborough had already discovered that the letter was a fraud and that Arthur was being taped and recorded as they talked about it over the table. I don't know how Terry found out. However he did it, the devil was getting ready to roast Arthur."

She picks up her glass and takes a drink.

"Which brings us to the point," I say. "When did Arthur Ginnis die?"

She looks at me over the curved edge of the glass. It's the first hint of surprise I have seen in her eyes, as a tear forms and runs down her cheek. "You knew?"

"Process of elimination," I tell her.

There is a long pause here as she catches her breath, a weight lifted from her shoulders. It was not Ginnis that Herman, Harry, and I saw on the steps of the hotel in Curaçao that night. It was Scott dressed in his clothes and playing the part from a distance. We never got close enough to see the face. But because Aranda was there, we made the natural assumption. Our eyes saw what we wanted to see.

Without realizing that Harry and I were already in the air headed for the island, Scott, after slipping the envelope under our office door, headed for Curaçao as well. She would have landed on the island the day after us, about the same time the media showed up. Scott, Aranda, and Ginnis's wife, Margaret, must have been in a panic by then. When I cornered Aranda at the beach and he slipped away, Scott was already there, coming up with the next plan to bail them out. It would not have been hard with a few phone calls to find out where we were staying, to watch the restaurant veranda with field glasses, and to stage the performance for our benefit across the water. Even if the floating bridge hadn't moved, Herman would never have gotten there in time. Ginnis-cum-Scott would have hopscotched down the steps, into the car, and away before Herman could have drawn within a block. It was all designed to convince us he was still alive and to discourage us from looking further, because he had escaped.

"So when *did* he die?" I ask.

"It was six weeks, almost to the day, before I visited Terry in that San Diego hotel room," says Scott. "Margaret, Arthur's wife, had called me from the islands down in Curaçao. Arthur had gone swimming in the ocean. He'd had a problem. He came out of the water all right, but he didn't feel good. There was something wrong. The clerk who was with him wanted to take him to a hospital, but Arthur refused. Margaret told me that they got him home, put him on the bed, and he lay there rambling on, mumbling that now everything he'd done was for nothing. Within minutes he was gone."

She stops, takes a drink of water, and wipes her eyes with the cloth napkin.

"Margaret told me that nobody else

knew except Aranda, his clerk. We talked about Arthur for a while. We cried. She talked about the things that were important to him in his life and the result, the effect this would have on the Court. We both knew what Arthur meant when he said it was all for nothing. He was desperate to stay on the Court until after the next election. He had talked to me about it before the surgery on his hip. It was ingrained in him, so many years and so many battles—then one appointment and it could all slip away. If he had died in a hospital or dropped dead on a crowded street, that would have been it, but instead here we were the only three people on the planet who knew he was gone.

"I don't remember how it started, whether it was a joke or if we were serious. But that's when we decided," she says. "It was right there, that day on the phone. We knew that it wouldn't be easy. We convinced ourselves that all we were doing was buying some time. I flew down to Curaçao the next day. We had the body cremated. Being on the islands turned out to be an advantage. Arthur and his wife had never been to Curaçao before. She had rented the house because their own place on St. Croix was being repaired. Nobody on Curaçao knew who he was. I won't tell you how we did it, but we were able to secure a death certificate with the date left open.

"I think we knew from the beginning that we couldn't make it all the way through to the next election. That was seventeen months away. We talked all night. Aranda, the clerk, was getting scared. I think he thought we were out of our minds. He was right. But that was the thing about Arthur—once you knew him, you couldn't help but fall under his spell, and Aranda was already there. He just needed a little convincing. We found a calendar and started looking at it. The more we looked, the more we realized we only had to keep the secret for nine months, from October until the following June—a single term. As we sat there in the islands, the Court was in recess. They wouldn't start their next term until October. If we could keep the world at bay from then until the following June, the Court would start its next summer recess. Any correspondence coming in would be easy. Margaret had signed Arthur's name on checks and other documents for years. We were far enough away that we didn't have to worry about visitors dropping in. The problem was the phone.

"Still, the longer we looked at the calendar, the more plausible it sounded. The media back home was already fixated on the presidential primaries. Members of the House and Senate were in election mode. By the following June, with a presidential election five months away and the Court in recess, nobody would be looking for Arthur or wondering where he was. By the time the Court reconvened, the election would be a month away. No sitting president was going to nominate a candidate to the Supreme Court and secure Senate confirmation when he's a lame duck and the election to replace him is a month out. Not in the climate of today's politics." As she says this, her eyes seem to sparkle. Trisha Scott is a true believer.

"You had it all worked out."

"I know that looking back at it, you must think we were crazy, except for one thing. We had a trump card. Without it we would never have given the idea a second thought. We told ourselves that anytime things got too hot, we could simply fill in the date on the death certificate, call the Court to send out a press release, pack up the ashes, and fly home. Who would ever know? At least that's what we thought."

"That's when Scarborough and his videotape caught up with you."

"Yes. For six weeks everything went like clockwork. If court staff called, Aranda took care of it, supposedly shuttling answers, as the justice was too tired to talk. It even worked with two members of the Court. You'd be surprised how few phone calls you get when everybody thinks you're sick and you need your rest.

"And then it happened. Out of the blue, from a direction I never even looked. It was the morning before Terry was scheduled to appear on Leno. He had been all over the airwaves for days. It was hard to turn on the television and not see his face. I got a call from a woman I knew. She wasn't really a friend. I would bump into her once in a while downtown shopping or jogging out on the Mall. You might say we once ran in the same circles. She was just coming to the end of a relationship with

Terry, and she was angry. Terry's liaisons always ended the same way. At first I thought she only wanted somebody to talk to. She knew that I'd been through the same wringer two years earlier. And so we talked.

"But partway through the conversation she said, 'You're a friend of Arthur Ginnis, aren't you?' I said yes. Then she told me that Terry had some video of the justice in a restaurant. He was looking at it on the television a few days earlier when she went to his apartment to pick up the last of her things. He didn't turn it off, but she didn't know what it was, only that Terry seemed to be gloating. This was something you would always recognize if you were around him regularly. Then she told me he laughed and said something weird, something she didn't understand. He said, 'That old man's about to find out what it's like to be the author of the Hitler Diaries.'" She asked if I had any idea what he meant. I told her no. By then the blood in my veins had turned to ice.

"With everything that had happened, with Arthur dead, I'd forgotten entirely about the letter. Margaret never knew about it, nor did Aranda. I hadn't thought about Terry in months. Suddenly I realized that Terry knew the letter was a hoax and that he was getting ready to go public. What seemed so easy in the islands six weeks earlier was now a nightmare, and there was no one I could share it with."

The reason she now unburdens herself becomes clear. Trisha Scott has been trapped in a psychic isolation cell of horrors for almost a year, without a soul to share her tortured thoughts with.

"I couldn't go to Terry and tell him that Arthur was dead. He wouldn't care. Terry would simply have a second scandal to take to the bank. If I did nothing and he went public with the letter and what he knew about it, every reporter in the Western Hemisphere would be looking for Arthur. He'd be at the top of every headline in the States. And then I thought if I tried to put a date on the death certificate and Arthur turned up dead just as Terry was breaking the story on the letter, you'd have to hunt with dogs to find anybody in the country who didn't believe that Arthur Ginnis had gotten caught in a scandal and committed suicide.

"What made it worse were Margaret and Aranda. They were innocents," she says. "They followed my lead. They knew nothing about Scarborough or the letter or how Terry had died. All they were doing was buying time, doing what they thought Arthur would want them to do. If we couldn't use Arthur's death certificate to bail out, they would be caught in the middle of investigations and risk possible jail time for their part in concealing Arthur's death. I had to stop Terry. I had no choice. What would you have done?" she says. "Tell me."

"So what you're saying is that Arthur Ginnis had to stay alive and Terry Scarborough had to die."

There is a long pause as she stares at me across the table. Her eyes seem like empty spheres, and she looks dazed, as if she's just caught a glimmer of the lights outside.

"I don't know how else to say it, how to make such an utterly insane act sound rational," she says, "but for me there really was no other way out."

I finish my drink, and I get up from the table. I don't say good-bye. I don't say a word. I just walk toward the door. Outside, the light bars are flashing on three D.C. Metropolitan Police cars. Two uniformed cops and a plainclothes detective are walking this way. Trisha Scott will have a long night of questions ahead of her, and a great many days to think about what she has done.

AFTERWORD

In 1772 a black slave named James Somersett escaped from his owner in London. The owner wanted to send Somersett to Jamaica to work on a sugar plantation, what was in effect a death sentence. These events forced a decision by Lord Mansfield recorded in *Somersett's Case,* in which it was determined that "slavery" did not exist and was not recognized under English common law. Mansfield came to this conclusion despite the fact that British ships had been hauling slaves for nearly two hundred years and many of its colonies in the British Empire could not survive without them. James Somersett was set free. This and a later decision in Scotland effectively abolished slavery in the British Isles. Though the institution of slavery continued to survive in the British colonies, including North America and the West Indies, the slaving interests of Britain were on notice by 1772 that an end to this "peculiar institution" was coming.

This is the historic backdrop for the "Jefferson Letter" and the deal that it portends, which is at the heart of the action in *Shadow of Power.*

When the Declaration of Independence was signed in 1776, there were more than half a million African slaves in the original thirteen British colonies of North America, constituting approximately 20 percent of the total population. In the southern colonies, African slaves made up 40 percent of the total population. At the time of the Declaration of Independence, its author, Thomas Jefferson of Virginia, owned more than a hundred slaves, a number that rose to more than two hundred during the course of his life.

Benjamin Franklin also owned African slaves, though not on the same order as

Jefferson. It is known that Franklin owned at least two slaves, "King" and "George," and held them in bondage for personal services and to work at his newspaper, the *Pennsylvania Gazette*. According to all known accounts, John Adams did not own slaves at any point in his life, even during his early presidency in Washington, when slave ownership among chief executives was common.

Jefferson made numerous statements, both verbal and in writing, evidencing his opposition to and abhorrence of the institution of slavery, and more than once he vowed to free his slaves. However, during the period between the adoption of the Declaration of Independence on July 4, 1776, and his death precisely fifty years later to the day, on July 4, 1826, other than a few individual cases of emancipation—two during his lifetime and five in his will—Jefferson continued to own, sell, and purchase slaves for his own personal use. There is evidence that he took pains to instruct his property managers and overseers to exercise care that his name not be associated with these transactions when they were recorded in the local press. He died bankrupt, never freeing his slaves.

The Articles of Confederation, the first organic law of the new nation following the American Revolution, were silent on the question of slavery, leaving to the individual states the option of whether to allow slavery, as well as the power to regulate and enforce it. However, with no ability to collect taxes or to enforce national laws the confederation was a failure. Within six years of its adoption, it was clear that something more was needed if the new nation was to survive.

In May 1787 delegates from twelve of the original thirteen states convened in Philadelphia; Rhode Island absented itself. The initial goal was to revise the Articles of Confederation, but this goal was rapidly abandoned. Meeting in secret sessions, the group was determined to write a new constitution. Delegates quickly coalesced around the concept of three branches for the new government—executive, legislative, and judicial—but just as quickly divided over the issue of how to apportion representation within the legislative branch. This resulted in the "Great

Compromise," by which large states would be assured of representation based on population in the House of Representatives and small states were assured of equal representation in the Senate, where each state would have two senators regardless of population.

Bound up in all this was the question of African slavery. The principal issue was whether slaves were to be characterized as property or as persons. Northern states, which generally opposed the institution of slavery as much for its effect on economics as a cheap source of labor as for reasons of ethics, wanted the slaves to be characterized as persons. Southern states became ambivalent until they realized that if the slaves were described as persons, this could enhance southern representation in the House of Representatives. Almost all the southern states were large in terms of geography but small in population as compared to those in the North.

In the negotiations that swirled around the language of the original Constitution, the issue of a state's populace was critical. Population would determine not only the number of representatives in Congress for each state but the number of electoral votes to be awarded to the various states in electing the president. Therefore, control over two of the three branches of government was directly determined by population, and the third branch, the judiciary, was indirectly controlled through presidential nomination.

For southern states, where 40 percent of the residents of the various states were owned by the other 60 percent, the importance of counting African slaves in the population and their characterization as such were vital. If the South was to survive, its slaves under terms of the Constitution had to be *called* persons, even though these particular individuals were to be *treated* as property. The disadvantage to the South was that state taxes paid to the federal government were also based on a state's population. This, however, was a blow the South was willing to suffer. Yet still there was no agreement. Southern states wanted all the slaves counted as persons. Northern states objected.

Lost in the mysteries of time, because much of what occurred was done in secret, is the question of how delegates arrived at the three-fifths compromise, by which black slaves would be counted as three-fifths of a person. Some believe that a trade-off was made by the southern states, giving to the North the so-called Northwest Ordinance, in which slavery was banned in the Old Northwest Territory (today the states of Ohio, Illinois, Indiana, Michigan, and parts of Wisconsin). The deals on slavery were endless.

Two other issues remained to be dealt with by compromise: the question of the slave trade (whether and for how long states could continue to import slaves from Africa) and the fugitive-slave clause that allowed bounty hunters to track down escaped slaves and return them to their owners. Georgia and both Carolinas threatened to walk out of the convention if continued importation of slaves from Africa were banned under the Constitution. In a deal with these states, and to keep them in the fold of the new nation, the North agreed to extend the slave trade to the year 1808.

In addition, and in part because a fugitive-slave provision had been included in the Northwest Ordinance, allowing slave owners to recapture slaves who escaped to the Northwest Territory, a similar clause was placed in the new Constitution. This provision resulted not only in the recapture of escaped slaves but in the enslavement of hundreds and perhaps thousands of free black citizens in northern states who had been freed by their owners.

In return for the Constitution's fugitive-slave clause, northern states received concessions from the South regarding shipping and trade. Some historians justify the northern founders in their dealings with the South, arguing that in 1787 the North viewed slavery as a dying institution. After all, how could anyone foresee that technology, in the form of Eli Whitney's cotton gin, would revitalize the economics of slavery a mere five years after the Constitution was written?

Still the question lingers. Would these men of reason and realism, merchants and lawyers, tread on the issue of slavery differently *had* they been able to foresee the future? The fundamental fact remains that they wanted a new nation. The price of holding on to the original thirteen colonies was slavery. It was a price that history records they were willing for others to pay.

ACKNOWLEDGMENTS

In the writing of this book, special thanks are due to Nils and Carolyn Schoultz for constant support and encouragement. Without them and others like them who showered their love on me during difficult times, this book would not have been possible.

I wish to thank my editor, David Highfill, for his careful attention to detail, his encouragement, and most of all his patience in my delivery of the manuscript.

And finally to my literary agent, Esther

Newberg of ICM, I owe thanks for placing this book with a caring publisher and for exercising sound business judgment, which she always does.